PRAISE FOR THE NOVEL THAT TELLS IT AS IT IS

"Gritty, intelligent...
reflects all the confusing complexities
of the region
with chilling accuracy."
San Francisco Chronicle

"Bold...Exciting...An insider's look!"
Kirkus

"One of the very few to rank
with Graham Greene's *The Quiet American*.
David Ignatius seems to have
perfect pitch."
Thomas Powers,
author of *The Man Who Kept Secrets*

"Thrilling and plausible,
the novel has the grit of real life."
Publishers Weekly

DAVID IGNATIUS

AVON BOOKS ⬥ NEW YORK

AVON BOOKS
A division of
The Hearst Corporation
105 Madison Avenue
New York, New York 10016

Copyright © 1987 by David Ignatius
Published by arrangement with W.W. Norton & Company,
Inc.
Library of Congress Catalog Card Number: 87-18583
ISBN: 0-380-70593-1

First Avon Books Printing: October 1988

AVON TRADEMARK REG. U.S. PAT. OFF. AND IN OTHER
COUNTRIES, MARCA REGISTRADA, HECHO EN U.S.A.

Printed in the U.S.A.

K–R   10   9   8   7   6   5   4   3   2   1

For Eve and Elisa,

and the nameless friends who shared
their knowledge of the Middle East
in the hope that it would do some good.

AUTHOR'S NOTE

I am grateful to the friends who read and commented on drafts of this novel: my editor, Linda Healey; my agent, Raphael Sagalyn; my wife and first reader, Eve Ignatius; my parents, Paul and Nancy Ignatius; Lincoln Caplan; Mark Lynch; and especially my friend of nearly twenty years, Garrett Epps, who encouraged this project from the beginning.

The story that follows is a work of fiction. Though it is drawn against the background of the Middle East, the characters, scenes, conversations, and events are the product of the author's imagination. The action takes place in the Lebanon of the mind, not in any real place.

Terror, and the pit, and the snare
   are upon you, O inhabitant of the earth!
He who flees at the sound of the terror
   shall fall into the pit;
and he who climbs out of the pit
   shall be caught in the snare.
For the windows of heaven are
   opened,
and the foundations of the earth
   tremble.

ISAIAH, 24:17–18

PART I

Prologue
Beirut; April 1983

Beirut; April 1983

Fuad heard the bomb twice. What stayed in his mind long afterward was the reverberation of the explosion, sounding in real life a fraction of a second after he heard it on the telephone. In that moment, which contained at once the past and the future, Fuad thought of Rogers and said a prayer.

Fuad was at a restaurant called Au Vieux Quartier in East Beirut, calling his hotel in West Beirut to check for a message, when he heard it through the earpiece. The roar of an explosion—loud even for Beirut—travelling through the telephone wires at near the speed of light. A millisecond later, in the time it took the sound waves to travel from West to East, he heard the roar in his other ear.

"A bomb!" shouted the frightened desk clerk into the phone.

"Can you see where the smoke is coming from?" asked Fuad. There was a pause as the clerk ran into the street to check.

"From the Corniche," said the clerk breathlessly when he returned. "Near the American Embassy."

"What color is the smoke?"

"White," said the clerk.

"Ya'Allah!" said Fuad with a cry of supplication. My God!

White smoke meant a very large explosion. A bomb that detonated so powerfully and quickly that it sucked the oxygen out of the air, leaving a white plume of smoke.

Fuad's first impulse was to bolt the restaurant and find

3

Rogers, dead or alive. But discipline took over. He had a meeting at one-thirty with a courier who was bringing an important piece of intelligence. For a brief moment, he imagined what Rogers would say when they met that night at the Ararat Restaurant and Fuad told him that, even on this chaotic day, he had managed to obtain the document that Rogers had requested.

Fuad took a seat at the bar, waiting for his contact to arrive. Everyone was talking about the explosion. Did you hear it? It was very loud! The bartender remarked that the bomb must have been in West Beirut and everyone nodded and relaxed slightly. West Beirut was on the other side. It was in another universe. Fuad said nothing. He ordered a glass of mineral water and sipped it quietly.

The bartender and his friends continued their conversation. Fuad listened unobtrusively. He seemed almost to blend into the surroundings. Though he was a Sunni Moslem, he looked like any of the rich Christian businessmen sitting at the bar. Like them, he wore a silk suit and lit his cigarettes with a gold lighter. The Arabs have a word for this sort of camouflage. They call it *taqiyya*. It means that deception and concealment are permissible, when they are necessary. If a Moslem finds himself in the midst of a group of Christians, he should say that he is a Christian. What does it matter? The truth is elastic.

A Lebanese man stuck his head in the door and shouted to the bartender: "L'Ambassade Américaine!" The buzz of conversation about the bomb grew louder. The American Embassy had been hit! Fuad felt his stomach tighten. He tried to think of something else, but every thought led back to the embassy and Rogers. He tried saying the names of Allah silently to calm himself. The compassionate. The merciful . . .

"The Marines will know what to do!" said the bartender knowingly. Several customers agreed.

No, they won't, thought Fuad. That was the problem. There were 2,000 Marines at the airport and no one could explain why. When Fuad had asked a member of the CIA station six months ago what the Marines were going to accomplish in Lebanon, the young CIA officer had explained that it was "a presence mission." "A presence mission," Fuad had repeated thoughtfully, nodding his head, not wanting to offend the young CIA man. "Of course." Perhaps Rogers would know what to do.

Fuad chain-smoked cigarettes and stared out the window. At precisely one-thirty, his contact, a dignified little man named Mr. Khoury, arrived to find Fuad lying in wait outside the restaurant. Fuad steered the man into a back alley, took the document from him and bid a hasty goodbye. Then he raced toward West Beirut and the wreckage of the embassy.

Bombs bring out the crowds in Beirut, and Fuad found throngs of people still surging along the Corniche toward the embassy when he arrived at 2:30 P.M. The area had been cordoned off and he had to show his American passport to a Lebanese Army checkpoint to get close enough to see the building.

What he saw brought tears to his eyes. It was as if the flesh of the building had been ripped away, revealing the frail skeleton beneath. Many of the survivors were still standing in small groups in front of the building, too dazed to move. As Fuad listened to their conversations, he pieced together a picture of what had happened.

The people inside the embassy had never heard the sound of the explosion. Their first sensation was a sudden flash of light, then a terrific force blowing in the windows and hurling them, still in their chairs, against the walls of their offices. It was like being in a centrifuge, the survivors said. Dust and shards of glass seemed to fly through the air in slow motion.

When things stopped moving, the first thought most people had was that the embassy had been hit by a mortar round. Several people, who had been through such attacks before, stayed on the floor awaiting another round. Others, their bodies pumping with adrenalin, pushed through the debris like Supermen in a half-mad effort to lock their office safes.

The lobby of the embassy was now a vision of Hell: a blackened wreck, dense with smoke and dust. Outside there was chaos as ambulances, fire trucks, Lebanese Army troops, and Marines from the airport converged on the bombed-out embassy. The Marines had established a defense perimeter around the building. The young soldiers, tense and hollow-eyed, fingered the triggers of their automatic weapons as they scanned the gathering crowd of Lebanese onlookers.

Behind them in the ruins of the embassy, rescue workers were picking pieces of bodies out of the rubble.

Fuad considered asking one of the embassy officials standing numbly in front of the building about Rogers, but decided against it. It would be a gross breach of security. And he wasn't sure he wanted to know the truth yet. So he loitered instead in the shadows. He felt a chill, so cold that he trembled for a moment there by the sea.

Fuad checked his hotel for messages, thinking that perhaps Rogers had left a coded signal, but there was nothing.

A last wisp of hope led him to the hotel where Rogers had been staying, an anonymous, out-of-the-way place off Hamra Street. He peppered the desk clerk with questions. Was Mr. Rogers in his room? Had he left any messages? Had he checked out? Had anyone been in his room?

The clerk refused to answer any questions until Fuad slipped 100 Lebanese pounds into his coat pocket.

Rogers had not come back, the clerk said. But an hour ago three men had arrived from the embassy in a great hurry. They entered Rogers's room, packed up all his belongings, and took them to a car waiting outside.

They paid the bill and said that Mr. Rogers had checked out.

PART II

Beirut; Fall 1969

1

Beirut; September 1969

Tom Rogers stepped off the Middle East Airlines plane into a vision of Oz. The new office towers and apartment blocks of West Beirut sparkled in the afternoon sun; the diminutive porters at the airport bustled to and fro, shouting and strutting as they hurled the baggage from place to place; in the distance, their horns blaring to wake the dead, a line of cars and trucks stood bumper-to-bumper along the airport road, bound for the enchanted city.

Rogers carried his two-year-old daughter Amy gently in his arms. She had gotten sick in Oman and was still weak. Rogers blamed the incompetence of the Omani doctor. But in Beirut, Rogers was convinced, Amy would get well. Behind Rogers, holding their eight-year-old son Mark by the hand, came his wife Jane. She was radiant, with jet-black hair and a creamy complexion, looking stylish even in the simple gray skirt and red blouse she had worn on the long flight.

The air was soft and fragrant, scented with traces of olive and mint. It was early fall, the start of that long, blissful season before winter. Rogers cradled his daughter against his chest and carried her to the red-and-white Middle East Airlines bus for the ride to the terminal. The other passengers smiled as they gave up their seats for Rogers's wife and children. A man offered Rogers's son a piece of candy.

"We love children," said the man in English, as if speaking for the entire Arab world.

"Shokran," said Rogers's son, using the Arabic word for thank you. The passengers beamed. How cute. How innocent.

Rogers listened to the buzz of Arabic voices on the bus: Lebanese accents, mostly; a few Palestinian; a few Egyptian. Most of them were talking about how good it was to be back in Beirut.

A fellow passenger might have guessed that Rogers was a college professor visiting Lebanon with his family to teach for a year at the American University of Beirut, or perhaps a journalist assigned to Beirut by one of the big American newspapers. He was tall and thin, wearing a worn corduroy suit. He had a slightly disheveled look: a shock of dark hair not quite combed, his white shirt fraying slightly at the collar, his suit jacket missing a button on the sleeve. He was wearing reading glasses to study the customs forms: they were half-glasses, made of tortoise shell, perched on the middle of his nose so that he seemed always to be looking over the top of them. As Rogers stared out the window of the bus toward the hills above the airport, he had a blank expression. The look of a man lost in thought, or perhaps lost in the absence of thought.

The bus deposited the passengers at the terminal. Rogers presented his diplomatic passport to the Lebanese policeman at passport control. The policeman looked at him and smiled the thin, corrupt smile of immigration officers around the world. Rogers could almost hear the click of the shutter as a camera somewhere took his picture. He studied the policeman's face and wondered, for an instant, how many different intelligence services had bought a piece of him.

Rogers hailed one of the sorry-looking yellow taxis outside the terminal. He told the driver in crisp Arabic that he wanted to go to the Sarkis Building in the Minara District, near the old Beirut lighthouse. That, he told the children, would be their new home.

"As you like," said the driver in English. He was shocked that an American—he had to be an American, he was so tall and he wore shoes with laces in them—could speak the language.

Rogers bribed the landlord the first day, in the precise

amount suggested by the administrative officer at the embassy. The man was effusively grateful and took to calling Rogers by the honorific, *Effendi*. Rogers also paid a small bribe to the doorman, who mattered a good deal more to the happiness and security of his family. He was a dark-skinned man who had come to Lebanon several decades ago from Assiut, in upper Egypt, and never left. He liked to be addressed by the Egyptian term for doorman: *Bawab*.

The apartment was vast and bright. It was laid out like a villa, with a large living room and dining room for entertaining, surrounded by bedrooms, a library, a playroom, and a maid's room. The center of the apartment was a large screened porch overlooking the Mediterranean. From the porch, you could watch the fishermen heading out to sea in their skiffs in the morning, and you could hear the crash of the waves against the rocky coast, 200 feet below. It was an apartment where a family could live richly and stylishly, in the Lebanese way.

Jane took the children on forays to scout out the neighborhood. There was Smith's market on Sadat Street, which seemed to have every spice and condiment—every canned, potted, and dried food imaginable—from around the world. A few doors down was the ice-cream man selling the Arab version of ice cream, sweeter than sweet, with a texture and flavor almost like pudding. In an alley was a tiny shop that sold coffee, mixed with spices in the Arab way, and on a summer day the whole of Sadat Street seemed to smell of cardamom.

Across the street was a florist, selling the most delicate flowers: orchid and rose, iris and gladeolus. The owner was a burly Sunni Moslem man, completely bald, who had the appearance and manner of a Turkish wrestler. It was an incongruous sight: this huge bull of a man, gently wrapping flowers for the fine ladies of Beirut.

The fall social season began in Moslem West Beirut soon after Rogers arrived. The shops in the Place des Canons twinkled with lights and the city was swept along by a tide of self-congratulation and good cheer.

It was the season for frantic partying: a prominent Lebanese doctor who worked for Aramco threw a farewell bash for himself at the Phoenicia Hotel; he was departing, poor man, for Saudi Arabia and received many condolences; in the Sunni neighborhood of Koreitem, the Moslem ladies of the Beirut College for Women were beginning rehearsals for their annual concert of Christmas music; in a similar spirit of ecumenicism, the International Women's Club of Beirut was planning its fall tour of churches and mosques.

Hamra Street, the grand boulevard of the new Lebanon, was crowded with shoppers, peering in the windows at the latest dresses from Paris, shoes from Italy, books from London and New York. This was the precinct of Lebanon's new money, where the middle class flocked to buy fashion, culture, respectability. The language in the shops was French, perhaps a little English, but certainly not Arabic, which represented a culture the Lebanese were rushing to escape.

"Les déracinées" was what the old feudal lords liked to call the young men who had come down from the mountains to build this new Beirut. The Uprooted. They inhabited a city that had slipped its old moorings and was drifting happily and obliviously into the future.

Beirut in 1969 was a border town, whose residents fancied their city as the last outpost of Europe, even though it stood on the landmass of Asia, at the frontier of Islam and the Orient. It was a city of confluence, where two cultures—East and West—met to produce a steaming and sensuous vortex, like the collision of two ocean currents.

Living on the border, the Lebanese felt the tremors of the 1960s from both directions. The Arabic papers were breathless with the latest impossible news from America: A man on the Moon. The Sharon Tate murders. Hippies. Vietnam. The headlines conveyed a sense of upheaval and rebellion at the center of the world, which gave people at the periphery a feeling of power and dread, like peasants watching the feudal manor burn to the ground.

Beirutis liked to call their city "the Paris of the Orient," but it often seemed more like the Hong Kong of Europe. Beirut had a quality often found in the Third World, a tendency toward ostentation and self-parody. A Lebanese host would provide his visiting Saudi friends with two voluptuous whores each, rather than just one. The Armenian tailor on Hamra Street learned that he could sell more suits by raising his prices, and calling each garment a "special" model, than by lowering them. On Lebanon's Middle East Airlines, the first-class seats were always sold out, while tourist class was nearly empty. The Lebanese national motto seemed to be: A thing worth doing is worth overdoing.

A headline in one of the local papers conveyed the national mood. It read: "Super Scheme to Turn Lebanon into Dream Country Aired; Project Said Easy to Achieve." The scheme in question was to build elevated highways to handle the crush of city traffic. It would cost a staggering $350 million, a hopeless sum for a nation that couldn't even raise enough tax revenues to collect the garbage.

It was all very exhilarating to the Lebanese. But outsiders saw the warning signs that most Beiruts ignored. The government bureaucracy had become so corrupt that it had difficulty performing the services for which officials solicited bribes. The old aristocracy had become so cynical that it was using radical rhetoric and gangs of armed thugs to maintain political power, and in so doing was unleashing forces that threatened to bring down the regime.

The Palestinians, everyone agreed, were a problem. They were the piece of the Lebanese mosaic that didn't quite fit. Their gunmen were becoming bolder in West Beirut, sitting in the cafés of Hamra Street with guns bulging from the tops of their blue jeans. It was a problem nobody quite knew how to handle, except to join in the Arab chorus of invective against Israel.

The Palestinian refugees, the uninvited guests at Lebanon's party of self-congratulation, lived in a string of camps around Beirut that were known as "the belt of misery." In the Lebanese way, two big Sunni landowning families named Sabra and Shatilla had found a way to profit from the influx. They offered derelict land near the Beirut airport for the refugees to build tin-roofed shacks and stucco houses.

The camps became a familiar sight for air travellers: the MEA jets would turn right from the Mediterranean, begin their descent above the shops and cafés of Hamra Street, and roar over the miserable camps of Sabra and Shatilla, so close that the frail houses seemed to shake, and then touch down their wheels in the Paris of the Orient.

2

Beirut; September 1969

Rogers had to wait a week before meeting the station chief, Frank Hoffman, who was away on a trip to Saudi Arabia. He was curious to meet his new boss, who had a reputation for being an outspoken character in an organization that prized discretion and anonymity.

Hoffman's secretary, a woman in her fifties named Ann Pugh, scowled at Rogers when he arrived at the station chief's office.

"You're five minutes late, Mr. Rogers," she said. Miss Pugh walked to a heavy oak door and knocked twice. There was a growl from inside. With an electronic buzz, the door swung open, revealing Hoffman at his desk.

Hoffman was short and stocky, with a meaty face and a bald spot in the center of his head. He looked—and talked—more like an FBI agent than a CIA man.

"So you're my new case officer," said Hoffman dubiously.

"Tom Rogers," said the younger man, approaching the desk with his arm outstretched. Hoffman grunted and shook hands.

"You look the part," said Hoffman, surveying his new case officer. Part of Hoffman's anxiety about being overweight was expressed by caustic remarks to anyone who wasn't.

"Sit down," barked Hoffman. Rogers sat on a fat, red leather couch.

"Now then . . . ," said the station chief, shuffling through the papers on his desk. "Your cover job is political officer."

"Much obliged," said Rogers. To maintain his previous cover, as a consular officer in Oman, Rogers had spent half his day processing visa applications. Before that, in Khartoum, his cover had been commercial officer, which required shuffling through import-export papers part of the day. Cover as a political officer was the easiest and best in any embassy, since the requirements of the nominal job weren't very different from those of an intelligence officer.

Hoffman took out a pack of Lucky Strikes.

"You don't smoke a pipe, I hope," said Hoffman. "I don't like professor types who smoke pipes."

"I'll take a cigarette," said Rogers.

Hoffman handed him a Lucky. Rogers took a wooden match from a box on the desk and lit it against the sole of his shoe.

"Is that how they light matches at Yale?" said Hoffman.

"I didn't go to Yale," said Rogers. Hoffman was beginning to get on his nerves.

"Good," said the station chief. "There's hope.

"It says here that you single-handedly penetrated the politburo in South Yemen," said Hoffman, staring at a piece of paper. "That right?"

Rogers smiled for the first time. It was inconceivable that any such information would be written on a piece of paper in an open file.

"I had several useful contacts," said Rogers.

"Cut the crap," said Hoffman.

"You have it about right," said Rogers. "I recruited one of the revolutionary leaders in Aden a few years ago. He turned out to be a gold mine. The closer he got to power, the more talkative he became."

"And why was that?" asked Hoffman.

"I don't know," said Rogers. "People like to talk."

"Bullshit."

"Maybe I was his insurance policy," said Rogers. "Maybe he hated the Russians. I don't know why, but he told me his life story. How he learned revolutionary strategy in Moscow. How the KGB taught him to establish a secret police force after taking power. He was a walking textbook on Soviet operations."

"Soooo?" asked Hoffman, still looking at the bogus file. "I mean, what's the point?"

Rogers paused. He thought of his Yemeni agent, who was now a senior official of the country that had been renamed the People's Democratic Republic of Yemen.

"There isn't any," said Rogers. "Except that the Soviets aren't as stupid as they look."

Hoffman squinted his eyes and looked closely at Rogers. Then he laughed.

"No shit!" said Hoffman. "That took you three years to find out?"

Rogers relaxed. The inquisition seemed to be over.

"Okay, my friend," said Hoffman. "You know your business. Let me give you an idea of what we're up to around here."

He handed Rogers a thick file marked "Top Secret," which carried the unlikely bureaucratic title, "Related Missions Directive." This document, prepared back in Langley, set forth the station's priorities.

"Read it later," said Hoffman. "I'll tell you what you need to know, which is the following: Beirut is a three-ring circus. We've got a little bit of everything here. We have a string of Lebanese politicians, the greediest bunch of bastards I ever met, who wouldn't be worth the trouble except that they seem to know everyone else in the Arab world. We have some third-country agents—Egyptians, Syrians, Iraqis—we run through the Beirut station. We have the usual cat-and-mouse game with the Soviet mission here."

Hoffman paused.

"We also have a few Palestinians, who have been on the books for years and who are the biggest bullshit artists in this entire, fucked-up part of the world.

"And that's where you come in," said Hoffman with a toothy smile. "When you get settled in, I'd like you to handle the Palestinian account."

At their next meeting, two days later, Hoffman was a little more relaxed. He was playing with a pen on his desk, absent-mindedly bouncing it in the air and catching it.

"Let's play a game," said the station chief.

"Assume that there's someone who wants to kill you. What do you do about it?"

"Kill him first," said Rogers.

"Wrong answer. In this part of the world, the guy's brother will come after you and kill you, so you still end up dead."

"Get somebody else to kill him," said Rogers.

"Better, but still wrong. The correct answer is penetrate! You got that? Penetrate!"

Rogers nodded.

"Find someone who knows the killer. Someone who can get very friendly with him, who'll know where he goes, who he sees, what he eats for breakfast. You follow me? And get *this* guy to tell you when the other guy is coming after you, so you have time to get out of the way. Get the picture?"

Rogers nodded. He was beginning to like Hoffman.

"My friend," said the station chief. "If you can play this little game in real life, then we're going to get along fine. Because that is precisely what we want to do with some of the undesirable elements around here who think that killing Americans is fun. Such as your friends, the Palestinians."

Already, Rogers noticed, they were "his" friends.

"Let's take a trip," said Hoffman, suddenly rising from his chair. "Show you around town."

He buzzed his secretary, grunted the word "car" into the phone, took Rogers by the arm, and led him out the door and down the stairwell. It was a comical sight: the short, pudgy Hoffman, dressed in a baggy blue suit, steering the tall young man by the arm. On the ground floor, Rogers headed for the front entrance. Hoffman yanked him by the arm and led him toward a side door where a black Chrysler was waiting.

"Take the day off, Sami," said Hoffman to the Lebanese driver. He slid into the front seat.

"Get in," he said to Rogers. When the doors were closed, Hoffman removed an automatic pistol from a shoulder holster and put it in the glove compartment. Rogers, who had never worn a gun in the office and never known anyone in the agency who did, concluded that Hoffman was an eccentric.

"I'd like you to meet a friend of mine," said Hoffman. "Another smart kid, like you."

Hoffman popped the Chrysler into gear and roared out of the alleyway onto the Corniche, heading west. He rounded the point beneath the lighthouse, passed the Bain Militaire on his right, and was spinning along the Mediterranean coast at 60 miles an hour, humming to himself.

When they reached an amusement park on the coast, Hoffman slammed on the brakes, swerved left onto a side street, and parked the car where it couldn't be seen from the Corniche.

"Get out," he said to Rogers.

There was a large Ferris wheel, turning lazily in the morning sun, and several smaller rides for children. The park was nearly deserted.

"Do you like cotton candy?" asked Hoffman. Rogers said he didn't.

"Too bad. It's very good here. A local specialty."

Hoffman walked ahead of Rogers toward a small building in the shadow of the Ferris wheel. It was a small, open-air café, empty except for an old man who was sitting at a table smoking Turkish tobacco from a hookah pipe.

When the old man saw his visitors, he dropped the pipe from his lips, walked over to Hoffman, and kissed him on both cheeks. Hoffman, to Rogers's surprise, reciprocated.

The old man disappeared into the back of the café. Not a word had been said.

"Smoke?" asked Hoffman, pointing to the pipe.

"No thanks," said Rogers.

"All the more for me," said the station chief, sitting down in front of the hookah and taking a big drag from the smoldering pipe.

Hoffman sat contentedly, puffing occasionally on the mouthpiece of the pipe but saying nothing.

After five minutes, the old man returned with coffee and then disappeared once again. The sun was warm and there was a pleasant breeze blowing in from the Mediterranean. Hoffman remained silent.

Rogers wondered if this was some kind of test.

They had been in the café about ten minutes when Rogers noticed a figure in the distance, walking alone on the beach. He was a young Arab man, smooth and compact, wearing sunglasses.

Rogers looked over to Hoffman at that moment and noticed

that the station chief had his hands clasped over his head, as if he was stretching. Or making a signal.

The young man slowly approached the seaside café.

"This is the fellow I wanted you to meet," said Hoffman. "His name is Fuad."

The young man entered the café. Hoffman welcomed him and made the introductions.

"Fuad, I'd like you to meet John Reilly," he said, pointing to Rogers.

"How do you do, Mr. Reilly," said the Arab. He seemed calm and almost unnaturally composed.

"Call me John," said Rogers. He hated work names, especially ones that were chosen for him by somebody else.

The Arab sat down and removed his sunglasses. Rogers could see a look of intensity, almost of hatred, in his eyes. Not hatred of the Americans, apparently, but of somebody.

"We first met Fuad when he was a student at the American University of Beirut," said Hoffman. "We have the highest regard for him."

Rogers nodded his head and smiled. Fuad nodded his head and smiled. It was all very Oriental.

"Fuad has been in Egypt for the last several years, working for a Lebanese trading company and dabbling in leftist politics." Hoffman panned his eyes slowly across the café and the beach beyond, making sure that nobody was approaching, and continued.

"While in Egypt, Fuad maintained occasional contact with our organization and provided a number of interesting reports. We especially appreciated his reporting on the activities of Palestinians in Egypt.

"Now Fuad is thinking of moving back to Lebanon," said Hoffman. "We think this is a fine idea."

Hoffman smiled at Fuad, who this time did not smile back.

There was silence. A cruise ship was slowly moving across the horizon.

Rogers spoke up, in Arabic.

"The Egyptians have a saying about travel by sea," Rogers said in colloquial Arabic, gesturing to the ship.

"They say: 'Better to hear the farts of camels than the prayers of the fishes.' "

Fuad cocked his head, as if he wasn't quite sure that he had heard right, and then smiled.

"The Egyptians are quite right," said Fuad.

"Bullshit," muttered Hoffman.

"The Egyptians have another saying that I like," continued Rogers in Arabic. "It's a warning for people who think they understand the Arab world."

"And what is that?" asked Fuad.

"'We expose ourselves to danger when we regard our own counsel as sufficient.'"

"Let's get serious here for a minute," said Hoffman. "Because I've got better things to do than listen to the two of you tell each other folk wisdom in a language that is not my mother tongue."

Rogers lit a cigarette, offered one to Fuad, and settled back in his chair, listening to Hoffman.

"Fuad, I'd like you to meet again in Beirut with Mr. Reilly for a serious talk about the Palestinians," said the station chief, all business now.

"I want you to do the same sort of thing for him that you did for me two months ago. Names, histories, political records, a Who's Who of the people you got to know in Cairo. I want Mr. Reilly to have as full a picture of the leadership of the guerrilla organizations as he possibly can."

Fuad nodded.

Hoffman pulled a 3 × 5 index card out of his pocket. On it was typed the address of an apartment in West Beirut, a time, and two brief sentences. He handed the card to Fuad.

"Go to this address three days from today, at ten in the morning. Mr. Reilly will be there, waiting for you. Say your code phrase, he'll respond with his, and then he'll let you in. If you're followed, or if you can't make the meeting for some other reason, go to the same address the next day, at four in the afternoon. Got it?"

Fuad nodded again.

"Have you memorized what's on the card?"

"Yes," said Fuad.

"Then give it back to me."

The young Arab took a final glance at the card and returned it to the station chief.

Hoffman rose from his chair. No one was invited to speak and no one did.

Fuad rose and shook Rogers's hand firmly.

The Arab turned to Hoffman. He placed his hand on his heart in a gesture of sincerity, shook Hoffman's hand, then turned and departed.

Watching the young Arab walk slowly across the beach, Rogers decided that he had the look of a born agent. His appearance was sleek and elusive: medium height, neither fat nor thin, with the sort of smooth, well-groomed face that you almost remember, but not quite. Some faces are a roadmap of character. Fuad's was a blank slate, a lustrous tan without lines or wrinkles, a picture of a journey across a desert that has left no traces.

Hoffman relit the pipe. After a few minutes more of puffing on the hookah, he put down the mouthpiece.

"Interesting fellow," said Hoffman. "He's convinced that it's America's destiny to liberate the Arabs! God knows why he has such faith in us, but he does."

"Is he reliable?" asked Rogers.

"That's for you to tell me, my boy. Because starting now, he's your agent."

Rogers laughed and shook his head.

"Does he know that he's on our books?"

"Sort of," said Hoffman. "Let's go."

They walked back to the car in silence. When the doors were closed, Hoffman turned to his new case officer.

"There's something you need to know about Fuad that isn't in the files," said the station chief.

"His father was assassinated a few years ago. He thinks the man who killed his father was a Lebanese Communist."

"Is that true?" asked Rogers.

"I have no reason to doubt it," said the station chief. "But who cares what I think? The fact is that Fuad believes it."

Rogers met Fuad in an apartment in Rauche, overlooking the sea, which served as one of the agency's half-dozen safehouses in Beirut.

The apartment was furnished in the garish style many Arabs enjoyed, derided by interior decorators as "Louis Farouk." Gilt-edged mirrors, overstuffed couches in pink and

yellow with tufts of material sprouting from the fabric, coffee
tables lacquered with enamel. Rogers arrived early and
scouted the apartment. It was hideous, the sort of decor that
might impress a Bedouin from the desert, but not an honors
graduate from AUB.

There was a knock at the door, and the ritual exchange of
passwords.

"Are you busy today?" asked Fuad.

It struck Rogers as a foolish code, hardly worth the trouble, but he went ahead with the prearranged reply.

"No, I have a few minutes now."

Rogers opened the door, shook Fuad's hand, and led him to
one of the pastel couches.

"Hello again, Fuad," said Rogers.

"Hello, Mr. Reilly."

Fuad moved across the room with the agility of a cat. He
was dressed today in the clothes of a young Lebanese playboy.
A jacket with wide lapels, pinched at the waist; linen trousers;
matching suede belt and shoes; and the inevitable Ray-Bans.
It was an outfit, Rogers reckoned, that must have cost Fuad a
month's salary.

The curtains in the apartment were drawn, and the room
was dark. As he sat down on the couch, Fuad removed his
sunglasses and stared at Rogers with the intense curiosity of a
man who is putting his life in another person's hands. There
were two striking things about Rogers. The first was the
American's size. He was over six feet, a giant by Arab standards, a size normally associated with Kurdish wrestlers or
Circassian bodyguards. The second was his informality. The
loose fit of his clothes, the frayed collars on his shirts, the
way he stared out the window when he was smoking a cigarette. The combination made him seem an embodiment of the
Arab image of America: big and relaxed, exuding power and
intimacy at the same time.

The housekeepers from the Beirut station had arranged the
room carefully. The plate on the table was full of packs of
cigarettes, three different brands, in an Arab gesture of hospitality. Fruit and drinks were in the pantry. Fuad took the pack
of cigarettes closest to him—a pack of Larks—and lit the
first of many cigarettes. Rogers poured sweet Arab tea into
two glass cups and made small talk. He asked about Fuad's

family, talked about his own wife and children, inquired about the political situation in Egypt. When they had finished the preliminaries, Rogers came to the point.

"Tell me about the Palestinian guerrilla leaders. Which ones should we try to get to know?"

"Excuse me, Mr. Reilly," said Fuad. "But the ones you should get to know are the ones who won't talk to you."

He's right, thought Rogers. But he said nothing and waited for Fuad to proceed.

"In Egypt, I met two kinds of Palestinians," Fuad continued. "There are the traditional leaders, the ones who can be bought, who are useless. And there is the new group—the fedayeen—who are not so easy to buy, and who are shaking the Arab world like a volcano. But you have a problem. The new ones are revolutionaries. They're getting training and guns from Moscow. Why would they want to talk to America?"

"Everybody wants to talk to America," said Rogers. "That's the one thing I have learned in this line of work."

"I am sure you are right, Mr. Reilly," said Fuad cautiously.

"Tell me about Fatah," said Rogers.

"It is the largest guerrilla group."

"Yes, yes. I know that. Tell me about the leaders."

"First there is the Old Man," said Fuad. "He is not really so old, but everyone calls him that. He is a very complicated and devious man. Perhaps a people with no country will inevitably select a leader like him, with no morals. The Old Man will say anything to anyone. He gets money from the Saudis and guns from Moscow. He tells his Saudi friends that he is a devout Moslem and his Soviet friends that his only god is the revolution. This man may look like a fool, but you should not underestimate him.

"Then there is Abu Nasir. He is the head of their intelligence organization. A very clever man. The Egyptian intelligence service, the Moukhabarat, were afraid of him. They tried to control Fatah intelligence by training a dozen of Abu Nasir's people. It didn't work. The training only made them more dangerous.

"And there are others. The man they call the Diplomat, who lives in Kuwait. He is smart, rich, well-connected in Saudi and Kuwaiti business circles. He thinks that he, rather than the Old Man, should lead Fatah, and he doesn't mind telling people so. Then there is Abu Namli, who runs the dirty operations. He is a clever politician but he talks too much. He does everything too much. Eats too much. Smokes too much. Drinks too much. This one is dangerous. He is a killer."

Rogers was jotting down notes, mostly for show. The tape recorder was running and he would read the transcript tomorrow morning.

"The most interesting person in Fatah is someone who you've probably never heard of," said Fuad.

Rogers put down his pen and listened.

"He's only twenty-seven, but he's already the Old Man's favorite. I met him in Cairo two years ago at a conference on Palestinian politics, and we talked half the night. I have heard since then that he is a rising star in Fatah.

"He's complicated. We would say in Arabic *mua'ad*. His father was a famous Palestinian fighter who was killed by the Jews. Part of him wants to be like his father—become a martyr and uphold the family name. But another part rejects the world of his father as backward and corrupt. That is why he is an interesting man. He is a modern Palestinian who wants to break out of the sickness of Arab culture. He loves Western things: cars, women, appliances. Anything that is modern."

Fuad paused a moment.

"Go on," said Rogers.

"You may not understand what I am saying, but he doesn't act like a Palestinian. He doesn't boast or brag. He doesn't tell lies like the Old Man and the rest of the Fatah leaders. He doesn't have the Arab sense of shame and inferiority about the Israelis. To him, they are the enemy, pure and simple.

"I saw him once in Cairo reading a copy of *The Jerusalem Post*. I don't know where he got it, but only someone very brave would do that. He told me that the Israelis were clever because they knew how to use the press to reach the Jews of Europe and America. The Palestinians should learn from them, he said. Nobody else in Fatah would dare to say such a thing.

"I had a strange feeling talking to him, as if I was playing chess with someone who had thought out his moves to the end of the game."

"What's his name?" said Rogers, trying not to sound too interested.

"Jamal Ramlawi."

"Perhaps," said Rogers, "you could renew your acquaintance with Jamal Ramlawi."

3

Beirut; September 1969

When the transcripts of the session with Fuad were ready the next morning, Rogers took them down the hall to Hoffman. He attached a cover letter, asking permission to do some initial scouting on a potential source inside Fatah.

"He's busy," said Hoffman's secretary, Ann Pugh.

"He ought to look at this today," said Rogers. "As soon as he has time."

Miss Pugh tilted her head to one side and gave Rogers a sardonic look that seemed to say: Who the hell do you think you are? She was the sort of CIA clerical worker who, in nearly twenty years with the agency, had handled more top-secret information than a dozen case officers. She was totally loyal to Hoffman, whom she regarded as a kindred spirit, and at war with anyone making demands on his time, especially newly arrived case officers. But a half hour later she buzzed Rogers and said that Hoffman was free for a few minutes. Rogers went immediately to his office.

"What's all this crap?" demanded Hoffman when Rogers arrived, waving the bulky interview transcript. "You don't expect me to read all this, do you?"

"No, sir," said Rogers. "I just want you to approve a little fishing expedition, based on something that Fuad told me yesterday."

"Will it cost me money?" queried Hoffman. CIA stations needed permission from headquarters for any operation costing more than $10,000.

"Nothing beyond the normal operational budget."

"Will it get me in trouble?" asked Hoffman.

"Absolutely not," said Rogers.

"I'm not authorizing anything that would require my authorization," said Hoffman. "Got that?"

Rogers said yes.

"If that's understood, then you have my authorization. Go see my deputy if you need anything special. And don't ask me to read any more God-damned paperwork. I have enough as it is."

Fuad called on Jamal two days later at a small office on the third floor of a building in the Fakhani district, just north of the Sabra camp. The neighborhood was in Fatahland, patrolled by commandos in tight blue jeans and Italian loafers.

He gave his name to an unshaven man in an outer office who appeared to be a secretary but for some reason had a gun thrust in his pants. Fuad sat down on a dirty couch and waited. In front of him on a coffee table was a huge ashtray, the size of a hubcap, filled with what looked like hundreds of cigarette butts.

Fuad was going to smoke but thought better of it and pulled out his worry beads. Inside the main office he could hear an occasional murmur of voices.

After a few minutes, the door of the main office opened and out walked a stunning blond woman, dressed in a leather miniskirt. A German, Fuad thought.

She was giggling and seemed to be fastening the top button of her blouse. Her breasts were loose and she was having trouble. The woman walked past Fuad, turned to him, and gave him a little wave. Clasped in her hand, Fuad noticed, was a pair of panties.

"You can go in now," said the man in the outer office.

Jamal was sitting in a chair with his hands behind his head and his feet up on his desk.

"Sorry to keep you waiting," said the Palestinian, swivelling his chair toward Fuad.

He looked, at first sight, like a European rather than an Arab. He was bright-eyed and clean-shaven, without the usual Arab mustache and beard. He was dressed all in black: black jeans, a black shirt open almost to the waist, and a black leather jacket slung over the chair.

Fuad began haltingly to introduce himself, mentioning that they had met in Cairo, but Jamal cut him off.

"I know who you are," said Jamal, rising from his chair.

The Palestinian grabbed his leather jacket, took a gun from his desk drawer, put it in his jacket pocket, and walked toward the front door.

"I'm hungry," he said. "Let's go out and have lunch." The man in the outer office, who turned out to be a bodyguard, trotted along behind.

Jamal told the driver to take them to a restaurant called Faisal's on Rue Bliss, across from the American University of Beirut. Fuad was delighted. He had spent much of his undergraduate career sitting in Faisal's, smoking cigarettes and talking politics with his classmates. Faisal's was famous in Beirut as the meeting place of the intellectuals who had spawned the Arab cultural renaissance of the 1930s. Leftists still venerated the spot as the birthplace of Arab nationalism.

Across the street were the AUB gates, bearing the inscription carved by the Protestant missionaries who founded the university a century earlier: "That they shall have life and have it more abundantly." A noble sentiment. Faisal's was a good spot, Fuad thought, to renew his acquaintance with Jamal and talk, as brothers, about the woes of the Arab nation.

"I think you work for the Americans," said Jamal quietly, when they were seated in the restaurant. Fuad felt his heart pounding in his chest but his face remained expressionless.

"Why do you say that?" responded Fuad evenly.

"Because it is the truth," said Jamal.

There was a long silence.

"When we first met in Cairo," said Jamal, "you told me you were a member of the Congress for Arab Cultural Freedom. I had never heard of this organization, so I asked a friend in the Egyptian Moukhabarat about it. He asked the Russians, who said it was an American front group. I found that interesting, but I said nothing to you. Why should I? Perhaps, I thought, this young Lebanese doesn't know who really runs his group.

"Then yesterday I heard that an old Palestinian man, who

everyone knows is an American agent, was asking around Fakhani for the location of my office. So I was expecting a visitor. I was very pleased that it was someone like you—a friend—and not a dirty dog like the Russians send after us."

Jamal pulled back a strand of his long black hair that had fallen over his eyes. He withdrew a pack of Marlboros from the pocket of his black leather jacket, offered Fuad a cigarette, and lit one for himself.

"I won't speak about it again," said Jamal with a twinkle in his eye. "Everyone in Beirut works for somebody. Why not the Americans? Don't worry. I haven't told my people. As the Egyptian proverb says: 'To us belongs the house and the talk therein.' "

Fuad changed the subject. He talked about the weather. He talked about Egypt. Anything he could think of. It was only many hours later that he concluded, with relief, that he wasn't going to be killed.

When Fuad reported the conversation to Rogers, the American was furious about the security breach. He made a note to have Hoffman fire the low-grade agent who had obtained Jamal's address. He also lectured Fuad about cover.

The more Rogers thought about the meeting, the more perplexed he was by Jamal's behavior. Why would an important Palestinian official, aware that he was talking to a CIA agent, join him for lunch and then promise to keep quiet about it? Why would he refrain from the usual Palestinian denunciations of American Mideast policy?

There seemed only two possibilities: either Jamal was a provocateur, trying to lure Fuad into an embarrassing situation, or he was inviting further contact. Rogers decided that it was worth the risk to find out which. He gave Fuad $5,000 in cash from the station's contingency fund and told him to rent an apartment near the Palestinian quarter of the city.

"Let's find out whether Jamal would like to make some new friends," said Rogers.

4

Beirut; October 1969

At the end of Tom and Jane Rogers's first month in Beirut, Sally Wigg, the ambassador's wife, called.

"Jane!" said the ambassador's wife. She spoke very loudly, with an enthusiasm that made clear how much pleasure she took in organizing the lives of other embassy wives.

"Yes, Mrs. Wigg."

"Jane! We're having a dinner next Saturday night! We'll expect you at eight. See you then!"

She rang off without waiting for an answer. A social secretary from the embassy called an hour later to say that the affair would be black tie.

Jane Rogers was a sensible woman. She had attended a good private school and Mt. Holyoke College. She knew that when the ambassador's wife calls in a post like Beirut, the world stops turning for a moment. So she did the sensible thing. She went out and bought a new evening dress, the fanciest she could find, from a designer on Hamra Street.

"A preemptive strike," said Rogers when Jane told him about the invitation.

Rogers, who mistrusted ambassadors and their wives, resignedly took his tuxedo out of mothballs. He had bought it a decade earlier, when he graduated from the agency's career training program, after a friend told him that a tuxedo was a must for a case officer overseas. Black-tie dinners were an ideal place to spot potential agents, the friend had advised.

That struck Rogers as preposterous, but he bought the tux-

edo anyway. It was a beautiful suit, with crisp, notched lapels
and a fine silk lining. Rogers had barely worn it in the years
since. Intelligence work, he had happily discovered, had very
little to do with attending dinner parties.

"You look smashing, my dear!" said Mrs. Wigg when she
greeted them at the door. "Good for you!"

Her tone was that of a girls' school principal, commending
a new girl who has just scored a goal in field hockey.

"And Tom! How *nice* to meet you!"

Mrs. Wigg batted her eyelashes as she greeted Rogers.
They were dark and crusted with mascara. She leaned forward
slightly as she shook his hand, revealing a good deal of her
bosom in the decolletage of her evening dress.

Rogers looked her squarely in the eye and thanked her for
the kind invitation.

Ambassador Wigg emerged from the bar to greet them,
holding a dark highball in his hand. He had bushy eyebrows
and a deep, resonant voice.

"So glad you could come," he said to Jane.

"Welcome to the family, Tom," he said to Rogers with a
wink. "In our embassy, I like to think that we *are* all one
family."

An ambassador who wants to be station chief, thought
Rogers as he shook the ambassador's hand.

"Let me introduce you around," said Ambassador Wigg,
escorting them into a huge living room.

"You know Phil Garrett, my deputy chief of mission, and
his wife Bianca." A flurry of handshakes.

"And Roland Plateau, the French chargé, and his wife
Dominique." The Frenchman kissed Jane Rogers's hand. His
wife gave a flirtatious smile.

"And I am pleased to present General Fadi Jezzine, the
chief of the Deuxième Bureau of the Lebanese Army, and
Madame Jezzine." Nods and bows all around.

"Mr. Rogers is our new political officer," said the ambassador, his eyebrows vibrating now at a very rapid pace.
Everyone around the room smiled knowingly.

Rogers, who wasn't eager to blow his cover the first month
in Beirut, tried his best to look like a debonair member of the
political section. He wished there was someone else from the

station to lend moral support, but he was alone. Hoffman, it seemed, didn't go to dinner parties.

Rogers's discomfort eased as he saw the French diplomat's wife ambling toward him. She was an attractive woman, dark-haired and sensuous, her age difficult to determine but somewhere in the long march between thirty and fifty. Her dress was open in the back, revealing a deep tan that was the product of months of determined sunbathing.

"Comme il fait beau aujourd'hui!" said Dominique Plateau, talking with very wide eyes about the weather. Yes, indeed, said Rogers. It was a beautiful day. He took a gin and tonic from a silver tray and decided to enjoy Beirut.

When the introductions were done, Mrs. Wigg gathered Jane and Mrs. Garrett, the DCM's wife, and led them to a corner of the room. They sat on a couch beneath a large painting, donated by a wealthy Lebanese American, which illustrated scenes from Khalil Gibran's *The Prophet*.

"Jane! What are your interests, my dear?" said the ambassador's wife. The DCM's wife, who seemed to be there in the role of vice-principal, nodded for emphasis.

"Reading, I suppose," said Jane. The two ladies were stone-faced.

"And the children, of course." They were glowering.

"And . . . tennis."

"Hmmm," said the ambassador's wife. Jane seemed to have come up with an at least partially correct answer.

"Doubles?" said Mrs. Wigg.

"Yes, quite often I do play doubles. Though in Oman it was usually so hot . . ."

"Tomorrow morning, then!" said the ambassador's wife, cutting her off. "Nine o'clock!"

Mrs. Wigg rose from the couch and smiled at Jane through clenched teeth.

"I'm so pleased," said Mrs. Wigg, and with that, she departed to attend to other guests, leaving Jane and Bianca Garrett together on the couch.

Jane waited for the older woman to say something, and when she didn't pressed ahead herself.

"Bianca . . . ," Jane began.

"Binky," the other woman corrected her. She was patting

her hair, which was lacquered in place around her head like a helmet.

"Have you been in Beirut very long, Binky? We've only just arrived."

"I must tell you that you're very lucky," said Mrs. Garrett.

"Oh yes," said Jane. "We love Beirut."

"I mean about the tennis," said the older woman. "You needn't worry about playing well, by the way. She's terrible. But it's a good start for you." There seemed to be a hint of jealousy in her voice.

"And you aren't even one of us, really," added Mrs. Garrett.

"Excuse me," said Jane. "I'm not sure I understand."

"Oh come now," said the other woman, leaning toward Jane in a conspiratorial whisper.

"Everyone knows that Tom isn't a foreign service officer. It's no secret, and why should it be? You're among friends."

Jane blushed so deeply and suddenly that she felt as if her cheeks were on fire.

"You're awfully lucky that Tom's boss isn't here. The fat one. Hoffman. He's a toad. And his wife, Gladys, is even worse. They tell me she has a degree from a secretarial school. Nobody in our crowd likes the Hoffmans. He's so *loud.*"

Jane cleared her throat.

"Say!" remarked Bianca Garrett to herself as if she had solved a riddle. "That's probably why you're here! Because Frank Hoffman isn't."

Jane Rogers, her discomfort increasing by the moment, signalled for a waiter.

"Let me tell you something, dearie," said Bianca Garrett in a whisper. "I used to work for you-know-who myself once, as a code clerk, in Lagos and then in Addis Ababa. That's how I met Phil." She winked and took another drink from the waiter who had arrived with his silver tray.

"So don't think I don't know the score," Binky continued. "And let me give you a word of advice. In a post like this, where socializing is half the fun, you really shouldn't keep to yourself and your little crowd from the fifth floor. Don't fight the ambassador. And for heaven's sake, don't fight his wife!"

Jane, who had never acknowledged to another soul outside

the agency what her husband really did for a living, mumbled a few words and changed the subject.

"We're looking for a good doctor for the children," she asked sweetly. "Can you recommend someone?"

Binky, with one more wink, recited the list of acceptable practitioners.

Eventually the bell rang, signalling that it was time for dinner. As Binky Garrett rose from the couch, she leaned unsteadily toward Jane and confided a last bit of advice.

"It all looks very civilized around here," she said. "But you and Tom shouldn't forget that there are Indians just over the hill. Looking for scalps. And white women!"

She downed her drink and was off.

Rogers was seated at dinner between the wife of the Lebanese Army general and the wife of the French chargé. Both turned to him nearly in unison when they were seated, both staring up coquettishly at the tall and attractive new American in town.

Protocol won out and Rogers turned to the wife of the Lebanese general. She was a flower of Lebanese Christian society: the daughter of one of the great families that ruled a part of Lebanese mountains; dressed in the style of East Beirut, like a fine china doll, elaborately coiffed and manicured; feminine and flirtatious in her conversation, but also smart and tough.

"So who is this Mr. Rogers who has joined the American Embassy?" she said, studying Roger's face.

Rogers smiled and adjusted his black bow tie. He told her a little about himself: where he had grown up, where he had served previously, what he liked about America.

"Tell me," demanded Madame Jezzine, "how is it possible to live in so democratic a country? That is what I have never understood. How can you organize things when there is no upper and lower, when everyone is the same? Isn't it very confusing?"

"Not at all," said Rogers. "We have no history in America. So we can invent ourselves in whatever shape we like."

Rogers smiled at the Lebanese woman and took a drink of his wine. Madame Jezzine, who had already emptied her glass, signalled the waiter for more.

"I think it sounds very tiring," she said. "Here in Lebanon it is very different, as you will see. Here we know exactly who everyone is. If a man tells you his name and his village, you know everything there is to know about him. And if you travel from his village to the next one over the hill, you enter a completely different world. A different religion, different customs, different accent, sometimes even different words.

"It is a great sport here in Beirut to imitate the accents of our rural cousins," continued Madame Jezzine.

"For example?" said Rogers.

"Take Zahle, in the Bekaa Valley. We have a friend from there named Antun—Tony—who speaks like a primitive. A cave man." The aristocratic woman had a mischievous look on her face.

"Here, I will show you," said Madame Jezzine. And in a loud voice, she proceeded to utter a vulgar Arabic expression as it would be spoken by someone from the district of Zahle.

Heads turned around the dinner table and there was a sudden silence.

Fortunately, Ambassador Wigg, who sat on the other side of the Lebanese woman, understood scarcely a word of Arabic.

"That sounds interesting!" he said loudly, eyebrows aflutter.

Madame Jezzine turned to him with a gracious smile and told him sweetly that it was a Lebanese folk saying, popular with rural folk, and had no meaning whatsoever. The ambassador laughed vigorously, to share in the joke, and then engaged Madame Jezzine in an earnest conversation about their respective children.

About that time, Rogers felt a slight brush against his leg. It was the French diplomat's wife, reaching for her napkin, which she seemed to have dropped. Rogers retrieved it for her and embarked on a pleasant and flirtatious conversation in French, in which the subject of children did not come up once.

Toward the end of the meal, Madame Jezzine turned again to Rogers.

"It is a scandal, don't you think, what the Palestinians are doing to my country?"

"I beg your pardon?" said Rogers.

"I said," repeated the Lebanese woman much more loudly, "I think it is a scandal that the Palestinians are taking over Lebanon."

There was dead silence around the room. The ambassador was too startled to say anything.

Rogers stepped into the void.

"The Palestinians are welcome to try, but I suspect even they would have difficulty taking over such a complicated country as this." Several people laughed nervously.

"No, I mean it!" continued Madame Jezzine. She was determined to have her say.

"No one will speak up about it. The Palestinians have bought the politicians. They have bought the journalists. Now they are buying the Lebanese Army!"

Sally Wigg rose from her seat.

"I believe coffee is ready for us in the living room," she said icily.

"It's true!" insisted Madame Jezzine above the commotion of people rising from their chairs and heading toward the living room. At that very moment, Bianca Garrett arrived and suggested to the Lebanese general's wife that they might go together to the ladies room and freshen up.

Rogers made small talk in the living room with General Jezzine, who headed Lebanon's intelligence service. He promised to call on the general when he was settled. The incident with Madame Jezzine seemed to be forgotten over brandy and cigars, but as the Rogers's said goodnight to their hostess, Mrs. Wigg gave Rogers a tart look, as if to say: This was your fault, young man. Attractive men who flirt with older women are courting disaster.

5

Beirut; October 1969

Rogers thought of his wife in the moments before sleep. He felt her lustrous black hair brushing gently against his neck and her breasts full against his chest. He liked so much softness. Other embassy wives seemed to Rogers as tough as shoe leather. They adopted the clannish manners of the girls' schools where most of them had been educated, gave lavish parties, drank too much, talked too much. They prodded their husbands for details of their work and gossiped to each other about embassy life.

Jane was different. She never ventured near Rogers's work. When someone from the embassy brought up the subject, or asked her what her husband was working on, she would laugh and say honestly: "I don't know. I never ask him."

They had met while Rogers was a student at Amherst in the 1950s. Jane was a student at Mt. Holyoke, an intense, hardworking girl who turned down dates so that she could study on weekends. She was an English major and liked, in those days, to talk to Rogers about such things as "the new criticism" and the different types of ambiguity in poetry, and whether Charles Dickens was, in fact, the greatest novelist who ever lived.

Rogers met her at a mixer and asked her out for a month before she finally accepted. She was a dreamgirl of the fifties: a slim waist, curvaceous figure, and the dark hair that seemed to make her skin look whiter than ivory. Rogers became infat-

38

uated with her on the first date and told his roommate that he had met the girl he would marry. She was a virgin, and Rogers pursued her lustily, half-disappointed when she removed his hand from beneath her dress and half-pleased.

Jane fell in love with Rogers, slowly and completely, with the passion of a woman who would fall in love only once. Rogers seemed to her older than the college boys she had dated. He was handsome, determined, occasionally taciturn, yearning for things outside the class-bound world of Amherst and New England, driven to succeed by forces that Jane couldn't understand. She teased him on one of their early dates that he was a new type of ambiguity. But gradually she grew to trust him, and her trust, once given, was total.

They were married the summer after graduation, on a perfect July day at an Episcopal church in Morristown, New Jersey. Though they seemed the perfect Ivy League couple—the dashing young man from Amherst and the chaste English major from Mt. Holyoke—the marriage bridged what in those days was still a wide social gap between Protestants and Catholics. He was an Irish Catholic, the son of a police captain from Springfield, Massachusetts. She was a Yankee Episcopalian, the daughter of a former Army intelligence officer who liked to be called "Colonel" and commuted to a stock brokerage firm on Wall Street. Parents on both sides were suspicious and prickly.

What drove Rogers was, in part, the insecurity of an Irish Catholic—a "harp," as the Brahmins of Boston liked to call them—who had gained admittance to the court of the Yankee elite. Rogers never lost his sense of being an outsider. The more time he spent in the world of the establishment, the more he felt that he was not of it. That yearning had pushed Rogers from Springfield to Amherst, as long and chilly a trip as swimming the Irish Sea. And it eventually pushed him into the Central Intelligence Agency.

Rogers's intelligence career began a few months after he was married. Like most of the recruits of the 1950s, he was initially spotted by a college professor and encouraged to contact a certain government official, whose title and agency were never precisely specified. He went to Washington full of enthusiasm, suffered through weeks of mumbo-jumbo about just who he would be working for and what he would be doing, and eventually was offered a job. It was 1958, a time when a new recruit could dream of using the enormous power of the United States, secretly and subtly, to make the world a better place. What's more, Rogers didn't know what else to do. He didn't want to go to law school. He didn't want to work on Wall Street or Madison Avenue. He liked the idea of travelling. So he became a spy.

Jane's father, the Colonel, sensed that something was up when Rogers visited Morristown the Christmas after he joined the agency training program. What sort of work are you doing? asked the Colonel.

"Government work," said Rogers.

"What agency?" asked the Colonel.

"What do you mean?" answered Rogers.

"I mean, where do you work?"

"Oh," said Rogers. There was a long pause. "Uh, the State Department."

"Balls!" said the Colonel. They never talked about it again, but the older man seemed delighted and gave Rogers his unqualified approval from that moment on.

Rogers began his CIA career with a mixture of ambition and idealism. The agency was a place, in those days, for doing good and doing well. Rogers had all the basic skills of a good case officer—the drive, the intelligence, the intuitive sense of how to manipulate others. And he had one thing more: the burr under his saddle, which left him never quite comfortable or content.

He fell into the Middle East almost by accident. The agency was offering a two-year training program in Arabic for interested new recruits. The only real qualification seemed to be a lack of prior involvement in the region. Rogers, knowing next to nothing about either Arabs or Israelis, was regarded as an ideal candidate. He leapt at the opportunity. The Middle East was as far from Springfield, Massachusetts, as he could imagine.

From the first, Rogers loved his work and excelled at it. His father, the police captain, had once confided to his son, as if it was a great secret, that every time he put on his uniform, he was an intensely happy man. It was a secret that Rogers shared. He regarded his work—the simple tasks of recruiting agents and gathering intelligence—as a sublime pursuit, combining duty and pleasure in equal measure. What more, Rogers occasionally asked himself, could a man want?

Rogers's marriage survived some difficult tests in the early years. The worst moment, etched in his memory, was their arrival in Khartoum in midsummer 1963.

Jane was weak and exhausted from a month of sleepless nights. She had given birth to their first child only four weeks before and wanted to wait until fall, when it was cooler, before travelling to Sudan. But Rogers had insisted that they couldn't wait. He was needed in Khartoum. There were rumors about a pro-Soviet coup. He was missing out on the action.

They had landed in Khartoum in the sweltering heat of July and unpacked their bags in an embassy house that didn't have an air conditioner. When they opened the door, a lizard was crawling on the living room wall and there were large bugs in the kitchen sink. Rogers remembered that first night in Khartoum—Jane nursing the baby in the intense heat, sweat pouring off her breasts as the infant sucked and cried—like a nightmare. He fell asleep that night to the sound of Jane sobbing in the bathroom and promised himself that he would try to make up for the awfulness of that first assignment. He never quite did.

Khartoum was the first child. Oman was the second. In those first few months in Beirut, Rogers and his wife still didn't like to talk about what had happened to their daughter in Oman. It was too painful, too much a symbol of what frightened Jane about the Middle East.

Jane coped. She learned to live with the privations of the Arab world. She studied Arabic, read and reread her beloved English novels, immersed herself in the world of her children. Surrounded by the deceit of the intelligence business, she somehow remained tender and vulnerable, as idealistic as she believed her husband to be.

As the years passed, Rogers's fascination with the Middle East became more intense. He was an Arabist in his heart, as well as his head. He spoke the language fluently, understood the strange rituals and nuances of the culture, grieved at the stupidity and suffering of the Arabs. He felt the Middle East like a physical sensation on his skin: from the moist, dank air of Jiddah on the Red Sea, where clothes hung from the body like wet rags in midsummer, to the dry deserts outside Cairo and the crunchy taste of sand in the mouth and throat during the winter dust storms.

Unlike many of his colleagues, who served their time overseas chiefly to advance their promotion prospects back at headquarters, Rogers wanted to stay abroad forever. He was happiest trekking through the wilds of Dhofar in Oman to call on a tribal leader, or sitting in a parlor in Aden, chewing qat, as he talked Arab politics late into the night with a Marxist revolutionary.

Rogers tried, not always successfully, to keep from romanticizing his work. He reminded himself that, at bottom, it was a struggle for control, over his emotions and those of others. But there was also a restlessness deep down in him—that burr under the saddle—which was part of why he had been drawn to intelligence work in the first place. There were so many layers of self-control in Rogers that people usually didn't see the yearning and the impulsiveness. But it was there.

Jane Rogers saw it and left it alone. If she worried about her husband, it was only that he worked too hard. She was the sort of woman who could not imagine character defects in someone she loved.

6

Beirut; November–December 1969

The CIA, which had a system for everything, had a lengthy procedure for assessing potential agents.

The first step, every young case officer was told, was "spotting" a potential agent who had access to useful information. Then came a sometimes lengthy period of "development," when the prospective recruit was watched and encouraged and bonds of trust were forged on both sides. Eventually there was "assessment," when the case officer had to decide whether to initiate a formal proposal to recruit the candidate as a controlled agent.

If the answer was yes, then a new bureaucratic procedure —known as the Headquarters' Operational Approval system, or HOA—took over. The case officer filed detailed biographical information on the recruit, including a two-part Personal Record Questionnaire, or PRO. Rogers suspected that this cumbersome routine was modelled on the Yale admissions process.

The Jamal operation was barely past the "spotting" phase. But before going any further, Rogers took some simple precautions to protect Fuad, himself, and the agency if things went sour.

He outlined for Fuad a new set of work rules. Fuad should stay away from the American Embassy or any known American official other than Rogers, his case officer. He should immediately adopt countersurveillance procedures at his hotel, in the street, and on the telephone. The station would monitor the Soviet Embassy for any sign that they had been tipped by Jamal to Fuad's identity. The station's liaison officer would also make a discreet check of the wire-tapping logs compiled by the intelligence branch of the Lebanese Army, known as the Deuxième Bureau.

Jamal's silence about Fuad's links with the Americans would be the best sign of his bona fides. They would proceed with the operation only if they were confident that Jamal hadn't blown Fuad's identity.

In the meantime, stressed Rogers, Fuad should live his cover. He was a Lebanese Sunni Moslem with strong leftist convictions. He had been living in Egypt but wanted to return to Beirut for family reasons. He was meeting with Fatah officials because he supported the Palestinian Revolution as the road to liberation for all the Arabs.

If the operation was blown at any point, endangering Fuad's status in Lebanon, Rogers pledged that he would arrange his relocation and termination in the United States. With the safety net out, Rogers felt more comfortable. He didn't like making mistakes, especially when they put his agents at risk.

The next step, Rogers decided, was to try for a second meeting with Jamal. If the Palestinian agreed to meet Fuad again, knowing of his links with the United States government, then they might have a live fish on the line.

Rogers sweetened the bait for the second meeting. With permission from Hoffman and the Near East Division back home at Langley, he gave Fuad a draft of the current U.S. peace plan for the Middle East and told him to give it to Jamal.

It was chicken feed. The same draft had already been circulated to the Lebanese, Egyptian, Jordanian, and Israeli governments. A version had even been leaked to *The New York Times*. Indeed, Fatah officials were already denouncing it on the grounds that it rejected their demand for an independent Palestinian state. But they hadn't seen the text. Rogers hoped that a leaked copy of the plan would convince Jamal that the Americans were willing to take the Palestinians seriously. Among revolutionaries, Rogers had noticed, the hunger for respectability was often nearly as strong as the drive for power.

Fuad and Jamal met this time at an Italian restaurant called Quo Vadis, near the Beirut red-light district.

The Palestinian arrived in a red Ferrari convertible, driven by the same bosomy blonde Fuad had seen emerging from the office in Fakhani. Jamal kissed her on the mouth while the poor Shia boy who parked cars looked on enviously. Then he strolled up the stairs and into the restaurant.

Fuad shook his head as he watched this grand arrival through the window. His Palestinian friend was not a man who seemed to value discretion. He's going to get himself killed, Fuad thought, as he watched Jamal strut into the dining room.

When they were seated and had lit up their cigarettes, Fuad got to the point.

"You were right, of course, about my friends," Fuad said quietly. He did not want to speak the word "Americans."

"Of course," said Jamal. He had his eye on a brunette across the room.

"I have a gift from my friends," said Fuad. He took from under his arm a copy of the morning edition of the pro-Egyptian Arabic paper, *Al-Anwar,* and placed it on the table. Inside it was the U.S. document.

Jamal picked up the paper and opened it enough to read the words "United States Department of State" written on the document. The Palestinian smiled like a boy with a new toy.

"Good news!" said Jamal, pointing to the paper. He called the waiter and ordered a bottle of wine.

They had a boisterous meal of spaghetti and veal. Jamal drank most of the bottle of Château Musar and told stories about his father's exploits fighting the Israelis. The Palestinian seemed ebullient, and when Fuad proposed that they meet again in a week, he readily agreed.

"What gives with this guy?" Rogers wondered out loud after debriefing Fuad later that day.

"Either your friend Jamal is recruiting himself—jumping into our arms—or he's running his own operation against us."

Rogers lit a cigarette. He had the nervous look of a man

who has just realized for the first time that someone may be setting him up.

"Jamal is flamboyant," said Fuad. "But he is not stupid."

Rogers paced the room. He stopped at the bar, poured a whisky, and then put it down.

"I wonder," said Rogers. "Is it possible that our new recruit imagines that he is recruiting us?"

Fuad clucked his tongue. That was how Lebanese answered questions for which they hadn't any answer.

"I'll tell you a secret," said Rogers. "The secret is that it doesn't matter what Jamal thinks he's doing. So long as he plays the game."

When he returned to the embassy that evening, Rogers set in motion some discreet inquiries about Jamal. The answers came back several days later from a Lebanese agent who worked in the registry of the Deuxième Bureau.

The Lebanese intelligence service, it turned out, had a thick file on Jamal Ramlawi. He was a security officer, with what appeared to be wide-ranging responsibilities. He was respected and feared by his subordinates. He was, just as Fuad had said, a favorite of the Old Man, who invited him to meetings with the senior Fatah leadership and solicited his advice. The Old Man, it was said, was cultivating Jamal as a leader of the younger generation of Fatah, someone who could work easily with the new wave of Palestinian exiles studying and working in Europe and the Arab world.

The evidence strongly suggested that whatever Jamal was doing, he had the Old Man's approval.

There was another interesting tidbit. Jamal was reputed to be sex-crazy. He was currently having an affair with a blond German woman who was the mistress of a very rich, but aging, Lebanese banker.

The third meeting, a week after the luncheon at Quo Vadis, was more discreet. They met at a prearranged time in a park on the grounds of the American University of Beirut. The smell of the sea mingled with the scent of the eucalyptus and pine trees.

This time, Jamal brought a surprise of his own. He proposed regular contact between himself, on behalf of Fatah, and Fuad, on behalf of the United States. The purpose would be to discuss "matters of mutual concern," a phrase as vague in Arabic as it is in English. He said the arrangement should be one of "liaison," like the contacts the U.S. Embassy maintained with other embassies and political organizations around town.

Fuad, who had been carefully coached for the meeting by Rogers, responded that he wasn't authorized to discuss substantive issues like the one raised by Jamal.

"I am here to listen," Fuad said. "Only to listen."

"That's not enough," said the Palestinian. "We are not interested in a one-way dialogue."

"Maybe what you are seeking is possible," responded Fuad. "But I cannot approve it. To make such an arrangement, you must talk directly with a member of the U.S. Embassy staff."

Now it was the Palestinian's turn to balk.

"Impossible! With an American agent? Do not ask for too much, my dear."

The Palestinian then delivered a brief lecture about the perfidy of the Zionists and the Imperialists.

Fuad listened patiently and eventually concluded the meeting with a well-rehearsed pitch.

The Americans had offered a sign of their goodwill by providing a document that dealt with issues of concern to the Palestinians. Now it was time for Fatah to reciprocate. Before proceeding further, Fuad said, the Americans would need some sign of Jamal's good faith.

The answer came on December 1, 1969, when Jamal delivered a public address to a gathering of students at the Lebanese Arab University. The local press was invited, and copies of their articles were sent the next day by the Beirut station to CIA headquarters in Langley, where they aroused considerable interest.

The speech was unusual in itself. Fatah officials, other than the Old Man, rarely spoke in public. But it was the tone of the speech that was most surprising. In those days, Fatah's pronouncements were usually ferocious blasts of revolutionary indignation. But Jamal's speech was something different. The young Palestinian seemed to be signalling that he was a responsible, reasonable man, willing to do business.

"The commando groups will respect the sovereignty of Lebanon," the newspapers quoted Jamal as saying. "Fatah will forbid our men to circulate in Lebanese cities and villages with their arms."

The analysts at Langley regarded this statement as an attempt to reassure the United States and its conservative Arab friends that the commandos weren't out to destroy Lebanon. The statement itself was demonstrably false. Fatah men were violating Jamal's edict about carrying weapons even as he spoke the words. But it was interesting that he said it, nonetheless.

"Because Fatah is the biggest commando organization, it has a big responsibility toward world public opinion," Jamal said. "We study every operation very carefully and make sure that it will not affect civilians." This seemed to be a vague promise—and not a very convincing one—that Fatah would seek to restrain terrorist operations abroad.

Jamal was asked by someone in the audience about Fatah's relations with Moscow. His answer was studied with special care back in Washington.

"The commandos don't deal with the Soviet Union as if we are affiliated with it," he said. No one back home was sure what that meant.

"Is this guy for real?" asked Hoffman when he read the transcript of Jamal's speech.

"What he said yesterday was mostly nonsense," responded Rogers. "But the man himself is serious."

"How do you know he isn't diddling us?"

"I don't," said Rogers. "But my instinct tells me he wants to do business with us."

"Your instinct? Listen, junior, don't tell me about instinct. Instinct can get you killed in this part of the world. Instinct isn't worth shit. So far, from what I can see, we're giving this guy documents and he's making speeches."

Rogers tried not to sound defensive.

"He did what we asked him to do. Which was to give us a sign of his bona fides. I'd like to try the next step."

"Which is?"

"Which is to explore the kind of relationship he's proposing, using Fuad as the intermediary."

"Okay, my friend," said Hoffman. "As we say in the espionage business, 'It's your ass.'"

Rogers nodded. He wanted to salute.

"By the way," added Hoffman. "In case it slipped your mind, we're going to need clearance from headquarters for this little stunt. You may have gotten away with this Lawrence-of-Arabia crap in Oman, but not here!"

Rogers thanked his boss.

"Have you talked to M&S?" asked Hoffman.

M&S was the agency's Directorate of Management and Services, a housekeeping organization that supported agency operations. It had its own field office in Beirut, mainly to handle covert financial transactions in Lebanon's foreign-exchange market.

Rogers said he hadn't.

"Well, you'd better, because if this little plan ever goes anywhere, you're going to need lots of help. Safehouses and surveillance equipment and couriers and travel funds. Not to mention whatever fat sum of cash it will cost to buy your little friend in Al-Fatah."

Rogers stared at the floor.

"It's an interesting scheme," said Hoffman. "I'll do my best to get it cleared."

7

Beirut; December 1969

The climate back home was cool to new operations in the Middle East. The agency's top officials were preoccupied with Vietnam and Laos. The senior analysts who prepared the National Intelligence Estimates regarded the Palestinian guerrillas as a passing phenomenon, irritating but ultimately irrelevant.

The real issues in the Arab world, the old hands insisted, were the same ones that had preoccupied the agency for the last fifteen years: Nasser of Egypt, known in the agency by the cryptonym SIBLING, and his endless flirtations with Washington and Moscow; the militant regime in Syria, which the United States had tried to topple in 1956 with Operation WAKEFUL, setting off a long string of coups and countercoups; and the King of Jordan, known in agency cables as NORMAN, who was sustained in part by CIA subsidies paid through a covert operation codenamed NOBEEF.

But the Near East Division chief, who regarded Rogers as a protégé, liked the idea. His name was Edward Stone, and he was a sturdy old ex-military man. In his many years of service, Stone had come to the view that when the analysts all agreed on something, they were nearly always wrong.

Stone asked Hoffman to send along a cable explaining why the agency should get more involved in collecting intelligence about the Palestinian guerrilla groups. With that, said Stone, he might be able to sell the project to the Deputy Director for Plans, as the head of the clandestine service was known.

Hoffman drafted a long cable, outlining the "objective factors" that made Fatah an appropriate target for high-level penetration.

First, said the station chief, the commandos were becoming an increasingly powerful force in Lebanon. The previous month the Old Man had met secretly in Cairo with the Lebanese Army commander and signed an accord that would give the guerrillas responsibility for policing the Palestinian refugee camps and allow them to conduct military operations against Israel from designated areas of South Lebanon. The "Cairo Agreement," as it was called, was a disastrous step for the Lebanese government, since it undermined Lebanon's sovereignty over the commando groups. There were rumors that some of the Lebanese Army officers who had helped negotiate the agreement had received payoffs from Fatah.

A corollary of the Cairo Agreement, Hoffman noted, was that the Lebanese intelligence service, the Deuxième Bureau, would be withdrawing its network of agents from the refugee camps and curtailing its operations against the fedayeen. That was also a disaster. The Deuxième Bureau, though controlled by Lebanese Christians, had agents in every Moslem sect and political faction. It had informants on every street corner in the Sabra and Shatilla camps. When they were withdrawn, warned Hoffman, the best source of intelligence about the Palestinians would be gone.

Second, Hoffman explained, there were diplomatic reasons why it made sense to have a back-channel line of communications open to Fatah. The United States was embarked on a serious effort to resolve the Arab-Israeli conflict through negotiations. The new administration had contact with all the parties—except the PLO.

Third, the station chief said, the guerrillas were becoming more dangerous. When it was founded in 1964, the PLO was a nonentity, a propaganda forum sponsored by the Egyptians to keep hotheaded Palestinians under control. The organization had been transformed by Fatah's ethic of revolution and guerrilla war. It had become, said Hoffman, a "loose cannon."

The PLO's guerrilla exploits thus far had been laughable, Hoffman stressed. Fatah's daily communiqués were works of Arab poetry, boasting of imaginary battles and nonexistent attacks against Israelis. But the Arab papers printed the communiqués, and the headlines enhanced the guerrillas' mystique. "Fatah Forces Wipe Out Israeli Patrol," "PLO Commandos Destroy Israeli Mobile Unit in Jordan Valley," "Commandos Down Israeli Jet, Attack Several Settlements." The Fatah propagandists were shameless. A few days ago, the station chief noted, they had taken credit for the death of an Israeli colonel, claiming that he had been killed by a Fatah land mine when, in fact, the poor man had died in a traffic accident.

The problem, Hoffman concluded, was that the PLO leaders weren't fooled by their own rhetoric. They knew that in the long run, guerrilla warfare against the Israelis was hopeless, and they were looking around for other weapons. The only one that worked, from their standpoint, was terrorism.

As an appendix to his cable, the station chief included the text of a recent communiqué issued by the radical Popular Front for the Liberation of Palestine, titled "Final Warning to the World to Stay Away from Israel." The document contained an unsubtle threat of airplane hijackings. It announced: "Don't Travel to Israel! Stay Neutral! Be Safe! Keep Away!"

"The DDP says he doesn't understand what he's being asked to approve," said Hoffman, when he had read the response to his cable. "Normally, I would tell him to go screw himself. But in this case, he has a point.

"To be frank, I'm not even sure I understand what we're asking him to approve, and I wrote the fucking cable! So bear with me while I belabor the obvious."

Rogers nodded.

"Is this an agent recruitment?" demanded Hoffman.

"No," said Rogers. "Not yet."

"Then what is it?"

"Our source is calling it 'liaison.'"

"Oh yeah? Well that's bullshit, and you can tell him I said so. In the meantime, what are we supposed to tell Langley we're doing out here?"

Rogers thought a moment.

"Tell them," said Rogers, "that we are in the development phase of what we expect will be a penetration of the senior leadership of the Fatah guerrilla organization. For now, we are using a Lebanese agent as talent spotter."

"Not bad," said Hoffman. "It sounds almost plausible."

And that was exactly what the DDP approved in early December 1969.

8

Beirut; December 1969

Christmas was only a few weeks away. Half the embassy, it
seemed, was planning to take home leave for the holidays.
The other half was scheming to take trips to Paris and London
on embassy business.

Ambassador Wigg gave a lavish Christmas party the first
week of December. It was a bit early, but the Wiggs were
among the many who were leaving the country for vacation.
Mrs. Wigg also organized some of the embassy wives and
their children to go caroling in early December. They mistak-
enly did so in a part of West Beirut that was entirely Moslem,
so the reception was less enthusiastic than hoped.

Jane made an appointment several days after the Wiggs'
party to see the ambassador's wife. She had come up with an
idea, and she wanted Mrs. Wigg's blessing. Jane wore her
best silk dress to the ambassador's residence and tried very
hard to make a good impression.

It was a modest proposal, really. Wouldn't it be a fine
thing, Jane suggested, if some of the embassy wives—rather
than staying cloistered in the wealthy foreign sections of West
Beirut every day—could play a more useful role in the community? Perhaps they could arrange to do some volunteer
work. Something like the Junior League back home.

"Where were you thinking of, my dear?" asked Mrs.
Wigg.

"The Makassed Hospital," said Jane. "I'm told that they
desperately need help."

"Where is that, exactly?" asked Mrs. Wigg.

"In West Beirut," said Jane, adding in a quieter voice, "near the Sabra refugee camp."

Mrs. Wigg didn't seem to hear.

"Isn't that a Moslem hospital?" asked Mrs. Wigg.

"Yes, I think it is."

"And who are the patients?"

"Moslems," said Jane. "Palestinians for the most part. They are the ones who can't afford private hospitals, you see, and are dependent on charity hospitals like the Makassed."

"Did you say Palestinians?" asked Mrs. Wigg, her voice rising.

"Yes, although I'm not sure why that matters."

"It's out of the question, my dear," said Mrs. Wigg with finality. "You should know better. Really."

Jane paused. She looked at Mrs. Wigg, deliberated a moment, and then spoke.

"Why?" she asked quietly.

"Why?" thundered Mrs. Wigg. "Why? I'm surprised you have to ask. Need I remind you that we are here at the sufferance of the Lebanese government. The Palestinian refugee problem is their affair, not ours. For all I know, the Lebanese government would rather not encourage these refugees to settle in Lebanon by providing them with free medical care at the Manhasset Hospital."

"Makassed," corrected Jane.

"Whatever."

"Forgive me," said Jane. "But that's just the point. The Palestinians have nowhere else to go. Their mothers and babies need medical care now, no matter what country they belong to."

"Not another word!" said Mrs. Wigg, cutting her off. "The answer is no."

Jane picked up her handbag.

"I hope you will reconsider," said Jane.

"I will not," said Mrs. Wigg. "Please do not raise the subject again. I would hate for this to interfere with your husband's career. But you have been warned."

"Bullshit!" said Rogers that evening when Jane recounted the conversation. "I'm glad you told the old bag off." As for

Mrs. Wigg's veiled threat to his career, Rogers assured his wife that it wasn't to be taken seriously. The only person in Beirut whose opinion mattered to Rogers's future in the agency was Frank Hoffman. And he detested Mrs. Wigg.

That was the end, however, of the Rogers's social career in Beirut. Thereafter, the Wiggs invited them to embassy functions only when it was absolutely necessary to do so. And if Mrs. Wigg learned about Jane's subsequent gifts of food and money to the Makassed Hospital, she said nothing about them.

Rogers spent the first week of December reviewing everything he could find in the files about Fatah, Jamal, the Old Man, Mideast politics, the history of the Palestinian guerrilla organizations. He was looking haggard: staying late at the office and going in early. Jane was wise enough not to ask him what was wrong. That was precisely the question that Rogers was driving himself so hard to answer.

Nothing was wrong, at least nothing that Rogers could see. But he kept looking and probing for the hidden flaw.

Late one afternoon, when Rogers had worked the problems through for what seemed like the hundredth time, he stopped by Hoffman's office. The secretary, mercifully, had left for the day.

"What can I do for you?" asked Hoffman. The onset of winter made his cheeks look almost merry.

"I have a question for you," said Rogers. "How do we know we can trust Fuad?"

"Don't ask me," said Hoffman. "He's your agent."

"Maybe. But I didn't recruit him, I didn't run him in Egypt, and I've only worked with him for two months."

Hoffman, who could see that Rogers wasn't in the mood for the usual sparring, moderated his sarcasm slightly.

"Okay. Fair question. How can we trust Fuad?"

"Don't misunderstand me," said Rogers. "I have no particular reason to suspect him. So far he has been a model agent. But there is something I don't quite understand about him. Something enigmatic, as if he is operating behind a mask."

"That's because he's an Arab," said Hoffman. "These people are born with masks on."

"Just the same," said Rogers, "I'd like to know more about him before we get in any deeper."

"When was the last time he was fluttered?" asked the station chief.

"According to the file, it was four years ago, before he went to Egypt."

"Jesus, Mary and Joseph! That's a long time. A lot can happen in four years."

"That's what I was thinking," said Rogers.

"Well, fuck him. Flutter him again."

The next morning Rogers invited the Lebanese agent to join him for dinner at the station's most lavish safehouse, a villa in the mountains overlooking Beirut and the sea.

The villa stood like an eagle's nest atop a steep road that ascended, in hairpin turns, the slopes of Mount Lebanon. Rogers drove himself in an embassy sedan. The car climbed the hills and ridges like the steps of a ladder, each one offering a broader and more picturesque view of Beirut, twinkling below in the darkness. As the vehicle climbed higher and higher, the air became moist and sweet with the fragrance of moss and pine trees.

A young woman from the Office of Security had already arrived at the villa and prepared dinner. The real reason for her presence was to administer a polygraph test. She had brought the machine in a discreet, cream-colored suitcase.

Fuad arrived precisely on time. He looked small and somewhat frail in the dark. His skin, which seemed so lustrous in the sunshine, looked pale at night.

Rogers greeted him warmly, but the Lebanese seemed to be on guard. As he entered the house, he caught sight of the cream-colored suitcase that was parked in the hall; then he noticed the woman from the Office of Security, who was standing attentively in the pantry.

"You do not trust me, Mr. Reilly?" asked Fuad.

"No more or less than before," said Rogers. He led Fuad to a large room overlooking the panorama of Beirut. Far below were the lights of Jounie, the ships at anchor in St. Georges Bay, and the starlit coast of West Beirut.

"Y'Allah! Let's go," said Fuad. "If it's time to use the

lie-detector machine again, I'm ready. I have nothing to hide."

Rogers lit up a cigar. He was relieved. He had half-expected that Fuad would refuse to take the polygraph, which would abort the operation right there.

"We'll do the test later," said Rogers. "Right now, I'd like to hear more about you, without any wires hooked up."

They talked until 2:00 A.M. Fuad unfolded the story of his early life, yard by yard. Rogers listened, puffing on his cigar, measuring Fuad's history against his own mental profile of what makes a reliable agent.

"We are like mirrors," said the Lebanese as he began his tale. "We reflect what is in front of us."

"I'm not sure I follow you," said Rogers.

"I mean that I am a product of my environment. My loyalties and hatreds were stamped on me a long time ago."

"Tell me," said Rogers.

Fuad took out his worry beads and then, deciding that they were a sign of anxiety and superstition, put them on the table.

"I was born in the village of Saadiyat al-Arab, twelve miles south of Beirut and two miles inland from the sea," he said.

"To call it a village overstates things. It was really no more than a gas pump and a store and a few dozen houses. The only thing that made it unusual, for Lebanon, was that it was in the wrong place. It was a Moslem outpost on a stretch of road between two Maronite Christian villages: Saadiyat, by the Mediterranean, and Dibbiye in the hills."

"With you in the middle," said Rogers.

Fuad nodded. He had an earnest look, as if he wanted Rogers very much to understand the story he was telling.

"When I was a boy, religion bounded my world like the four points of a compass. The Christians were on either side, in Saadiyat and Dibbiye. The Druse were over the hill in Jahiliyeh. The Sunnis, outside my village, were in Burjain atop another hill. The Shiites were to the south, in Sidon and Tyre. And in Beirut were the rulers, who cared not at all about our little Sunni enclave in the midst of a Christian area.

"The local political leaders seemed in those days to be fixed as eternally as the stars. Perhaps they were, for all of them are still here. We called them the *zaim*. The big men. They were all big crooks and liars.

"My father was an officer in the national police force, which we called the Internal Security Force to make it sound more grand. It was controlled by the Sunnis, and my father got his job through an uncle in Beirut. The headquarters for our district were in Damour, several miles up the coast. My father didn't even have an office in Saadiyat. Just his motorcycle and a khaki uniform. But he was still the most important man in our village."

Rogers wondered whether to tell Fuad that his father, too, had been a policeman, then decided against it. At this point, what was needed between him and Fuad was distance, not familiarity.

"Because of his job," continued Fuad, "my father became friendly with some of the Christian families who lived up the road in Dibbiye. On Sundays, my father would take me to the house of the richest man in Dibbiye, who we called Emile-Bey. It was a great mansion on top of the highest hill in the area. The fishermen from Saadiyat said they could see the red tile roof of Emile-Bey's house from many miles out at sea.

"Emile-Bey took an interest in my education. Perhaps because I was a poor Moslem boy and he was a wealthy Maronite who hated the sectarianism of Lebanon. Perhaps because he had no son of his own. I don't know why. But he tutored me in Arabic, French, and eventually English.

"When I was fourteen, he arranged for me to go to an English-language school several miles away in the village of Mishrif. He said the era of the French in Lebanon was over. The era of the Americans was beginning."

"Was he right, do you think?" asked Rogers.

"We shall see."

"Yes indeed," said Rogers. "We shall see."

"I loved that school," Fuad continued. "The other students were so much more sophisticated than I was. They wore fine clothes and some of them had travelled abroad. I loved to speak English with them. It became a kind of snobbery. When we were around poor Arab boys in Mishrif, we would always speak English. They must have hated us for it.

"By the time I was in high school, I loathed my village. I hated the moukhtar, the village leader, who had bad teeth and always had crumbs of food in his mustache. I was embarrassed by my sisters, who were married and already had too many children, and by my cousins, who were poor and stupid. Most of all, I was embarrassed by the backwardness of Arab village life.

"You cannot know what it was like to be a young Arab in that time, dreaming of the liberation of your people from so much stupidity. In school, that was all we talked about. We gathered around the radio to hear Nasser speak from Cairo on a station called the Voice of the Arabs. We skipped school when Inam Raad and Antun Saade, two famous Syrian nationalists, came to Mishrif and addressed a public meeting. That was when I began to think that America was the answer for the Arabs."

"Why?" asked Rogers.

"I don't know," said the Lebanese. "Perhaps because America seemed so pure. And so far away.

"For whatever reason, I decided then that I would go to the American University of Beirut. Emile-Bey encouraged me and offered to help pay the cost of my studies. And he did something else."

"What was that?" asked Rogers.

"He sent me to America, as a graduation gift, the summer after I finished high school. What a trip it was! The flight took nearly seventy hours by propeller plane. We stopped in Paris, Dublin, Newfoundland, and New York. I felt as if I had landed in another world."

"Where did you stay in America?"

"With an American family who were friends of Emile-Bey. A doctor's family. It was paradise. They had a swimming pool and fruit orchards. They took me to movies and camping trips in the mountains. Can you imagine what that was like? For an Arab boy whose childhood memories were of dust and mud and chickens in the yard? When I got back to Lebanon at the end of the summer, I was in love."

"With who?"

"With America."

Fuad paused. He looked away from Rogers and toward the window and the lights of Beirut beyond.

"Can I have a drink?" asked Fuad.

"Sure," said Rogers. "What would you like?"

"Whisky."

Rogers returned from the kitchen with two large tumblers of Scotch.

"You were talking about falling in love with America," said Rogers.

"Lebanon must have been jealous," said Fuad. "For it soon took its revenge."

"What happened?"

"In 1964, when I was a senior at the American University of Beirut, the dean of students called me into his office one day and told me that my father had been killed—murdered—in a political quarrel. He told me that it was too dangerous for me to go to Saadiyat-al-Arab and that I would have to stay in Beirut for a few days. He offered to help me."

"What did he do?"

"He gave me money."

"What else?"

"He put me in touch with someone at the embassy who he said could make inquiries about what had happened to my father."

"And did they find out anything at the embassy?"

"They found out everything."

"What happened?"

"It was all very Lebanese. There had been an argument between two local politicians—the representatives of the Druse and Maronite members of parliament from our district —about political patronage. The question was whether a Moslem or a Christian contractor would get the job paving the road between Saadiyat and Dibbiye.

"My father, though he was a Moslem, had sided with the Christian contractor. The man was a friend of Emile-Bey's and he was a good worker. The next day, when my father went to start his motorcycle, a bomb exploded. The government didn't want a scandal, so they hushed up the incident. They never caught the man who planted the bomb."

"Who did it?"

"That was where the American Embassy helped. They talked to their contacts in the Druse organization and identified the man who rigged the bomb. They even sent me a picture of the man. His name was Marwan Darazi."

Fuad paused.

"There is a part here that I'm not sure I should tell you," said the Lebanese.

"You should tell me everything," said Rogers.

"Okay. That was the first time that I met Mr. Hoffman. He was the one at the embassy who brought me the picture of Darazi, the man who murdered my father. Mr. Hoffman said that they had checked and learned that this man was a Communist."

Rogers felt his stomach tighten.

"Was he a Communist, this man Darazi?"

"Yes."

"How do you know?"

"Because Mr. Hoffman told me so."

"What else did Mr. Hoffman tell you?"

"He told me that I had a choice. I could get revenge in the Lebanese way, by killing Darazi. Or I could get revenge in the American way, by working to destroy the people who had created Darazi. The Communists."

"And what did you do?"

"A little of both," said Fuad. "Lebanese and American."

"You killed Darazi?"

"No. I only wounded him. But I cleared our family name of shame."

"What happened then? Didn't Darazi's people go after you?"

"Mr. Hoffman helped me to get out of the country, to Egypt. He found me a job there."

"And then?"

"You know the rest," said Fuad. "I am an agent. I work for you. I am at your service."

Rogers took a deep breath and exhaled slowly. He looked the young Arab in the eye.

"Is everything you have told me true?" asked Rogers.

"Yes," said Fuad.

"Are you working for anyone other than me?"

"No."

Rogers continued to look at him for what must have been fifteen seconds. Fuad did not blink. Rogers took his measure and finally looked away. You have to trust someone in this business, he thought to himself. Otherwise, what was the point?

"Trudie," Rogers called to the other room, where the technician was waiting with her polygraph machine.

"It's getting late. We'll flutter him another time."

Rogers shook Fuad's hand, thanked him, and said goodnight in Arabic.

9

Beirut; December 1969

The covert relationship between the CIA and Fatah's deputy chief of intelligence put down a first frail root in late December 1969. Even by the standards of the espionage business, it was an awkward and furtive contact.

Two things mattered to Rogers in planning this opening move. The Palestinian must understand that Fuad was an agent of the CIA and that Rogers was his case officer. And the Palestinian must signal his good faith directly to Rogers—even though he refused, for now, to meet with him.

A clandestine relationship had to begin as straightforwardly as possible, Rogers felt. Otherwise it soon became hopelessly tangled in the web of confusion and deception that was inevitably part of the secret world. Rogers also wanted to see Jamal in the flesh, to look in the eyes of this twenty-seven-year-old Palestinian and assess his character.

The arrangement was simple. Jamal and Fuad would meet at the sidewalk café in front of the Strand Theater on Hamra Street. They would sit down at a table together and order coffee. Rogers would walk slowly past the café.

As Rogers approached, Fuad would signal Jamal with a prearranged phrase, and Jamal would put his arm on Fuad's shoulder. It would be understood that this gesture would mean "Fuad is my contact" and would signify Jamal's willingness to deal with the CIA. The two sides were agreeing in principle to share information, but there was no commitment on the details.

Jamal asked that there be no surveillance of the meeting by either side, and he brought none of his own retinue of aides and bodyguards. In fact, he had told only one person about the meeting—a figure he referred to only as "the Old Man."

"Tough shit," said the station chief, when informed of Jamal's request that there be no surveillance of the rendezvous on Hamra Street.

"Tell him we agree to his condition and then screw him. If he thinks we're flying into this one blind, he's crazy." Rogers protested briefly but then gave up. He recognized that deceit was part of the business. Even so, it made him uncomfortable to begin a relationship of trust with a lie.

Hoffman assigned a small team of agents to cover the area. One would be positioned at a shoeshine stand across the street. Another would be in a café on the corner of Hamra and Rue Nehme Yafet, just west of the meeting place. Another would be just east, in a car parked on the corner of Hamra and Rue Jeanne d'Arc. The station chief insisted on photographing the rendezvous from several angles, so that there would be physical evidence showing Rogers, Fuad, and Jamal together. He arranged to have one photographer shooting from an office window across the street and one shooting from a parked car.

"We need a little control over this guy," Hoffman said matter-of-factly. "A little something in the bank if he ever decides to play games with us."

The rendezvous was set for two o'clock in the afternoon. Jamal was late, and Rogers worried that the operation had been blown before it started. But Jamal arrived at 2:20 p.m., sat down at the table with Fuad, and began chatting.

The Palestinian looked as sleek as ever. He wore the collar of his leather jacket turned up against the winter chill. But he left the top buttons of his shirt undone.

As Jamal talked with Fuad, his eyes panned Hamra Street. The Palestinian seemed to be as eager to lay eyes on Rogers as the American was to see him.

Rogers began walking slowly up the street, from the corner of Rue Nehme Yafet. He gazed up at the marquee of the Strand Theater, which was showing *Ice Station Zebra* that week, and then turned his head down toward the café.

Jamal had his arm firmly on Fuad's shoulder.

Then something happened that wasn't in the script. Jamal stared full into Rogers's eyes and nodded his head.

Rogers kept walking. As he rounded the corner of Rue Jeanne d'Arc, he let out a little shout of pleasure, restrained but audible.

PART III

January–March 1970

10

Washington; January 1970

The Director of Central Intelligence had held his job so long and survived so many bureaucratic wars that people simply called him "the Director," as if there had never been another. He was to the interagency conference room what Fred Astaire was to the ballroom. So smooth, so self-assured, so perfectly right in his role that even if he missed a step, you couldn't be sure that he had gotten it wrong. Perhaps the choreographer had made a mistake.

Part of the Director's charm was that he looked so precisely like what he wanted to be. Some people's appearance is at war with their self-image. Not so the Director's. He was a tall, patrician-looking figure, with thinning hair and a Roman profile, who had the useful talent of sounding disarmingly frank without saying anything injudicious. After a distinguished career in the agency, he had mastered the survival skills necessary to a DCI. He knew that his first priority was to maintain good relations with the president, the Congress, and the press, in that order. If those tasks were done, he reasoned, running the agency would take care of itself.

Though he was regarded as one of Washington's most powerful officials, the Director understood the limits of his authority. He served at the pleasure of the president. His job was to do the dirty work and take the blame when things went wrong. And, of course, to keep his mouth shut. These tasks he did to perfection. To some of his colleagues, he seemed like a bureaucratic version of the English butler: more intelli-

gent and better mannered than his master, yet always obe-
dient, respectful, discreet.

What the Director didn't like were surprises, especially
when they came at White House meetings. So he was particu-
larly uncomfortable in late January 1970, when the "cousins"
from British intelligence (as they liked to call themselves)
threw him a curve ball.

The occasion was a meeting of the National Security
Council attended by the British prime minister, who was visiting Washington that week. It was held in the Situation Room,
a cramped, windowless crypt in the basement of the West
Wing of the White House. The room featured a long teak
conference table, polished to a bright shine every morning by
a cleaning woman with a top-secret clearance; a dozen well-
padded executive chairs that would allow the nation's leaders
to plan World War III in comfort; communications and audio-
visual equipment that could provide information instantly
from around the world; and along the outer walls, chairs for
the aides who were allowed to attend the meetings, and did
much of the work, but were not privileged to sit at the big
table.

The British prime minister was a large man, whose face
and figure had been ravaged over the years by the finest wines
of Burgundy and Bordeaux. When it came time for him to
speak, he made a brief address about the specialness of the
special relationship, in which he managed to quote Winston
Churchill three times in less than five minutes.

To the Director's considerable surprise, the British official
then launched into a discussion of the crisis that was looming
in Jordan—the otherwise obscure Hashemite Kingdom of
Jordan—where the friendly, pro-Western monarchy was
threatened by Palestinian guerrillas.

"We feel that a *most* delicate situation has arisen in Jordan," said the prime minister.

Americans around the room looked quizzically at each
other.

"The King of Jordan has asked our advice, in the *most* urgent
terms. And we are quite frankly at a loss what to tell him."

The president nodded toward the Director at that point, as
if to say: Will you please explain what in the hell this is all
about?

The Director spoke up.

"The King is a worrier," he said. "I have been holding his hand for the better part of a decade, and I don't mind telling you that he is a worrier."

"A what?" said the president, who had been distracted by an aide whispering something in his ear.

"A worrier, and I will give you an example to prove it," said the Director. He loved telling secrets to those who were authorized to hear them.

"We have been working for two years to get the King together with the Israelis. Back and forth, yes and no. You can imagine. We finally succeeded in arranging a meeting aboard a speedboat in the Gulf of Aqaba between the King and the Israeli prime minister. Just the two of them. We provided the boat and, needless to say, we wired it for sound. Do you know what the King talked about most of the time? About how the other Arabs would try to kill him if he ever made a peace agreement. The man, as I say, is a worrier."

The president cleared his throat. It was a signal that he was impatient.

"Excuse me," said the president. "But the question is: Does the King have anything to worry about from the Palestinians?"

"Our judgment, at this point, is that he does not," answered the Director. He summarized in a few sentences the most recent intelligence estimate of the situation in Jordan. The gist was that the Palestinian guerrillas were a rag-tag, irregular group and would be trounced by the Jordanian Army if it ever came to civil war.

The British prime minister broke in again.

"We shared that opinion, until recently, when we obtained a most interesting set of documents."

The prime minister handed a copy to the president. An aide simultaneously handed a copy to the Director. It was a collection of several internal Fatah documents, translated from Arabic into English, outlining plans for a new government in Jordan. One of them was a handwritten note from the Old Man to a prominent Jordanian politician, offering him, in oblique terms, the post of prime minister in the new regime.

"What about all this?" asked the president, turning to the Director with a reproachful look.

"Our reporting is not dissimilar," said the Director, stalling for time. "I'm reluctant to go into the details of what we have, for obvious reasons, but I don't disagree with our British friends that the Palestinians are intent on overthrowing the King of Jordan. That information, if you will forgive me, is hardly a secret. To confirm it, all you need to do is listen to the radio. They proclaim it every day.

"The issue is what we should *do* about all this." The Director emphasized the word *"do"* to make clear that this was an area in which the British contribution was likely to be modest.

"Precisely," said the British prime minister. "Or to be more exact, what *you* should do, since we are in the process of withdrawing our forces east of Suez."

The president looked to an aide, looked at his watch, and cleared his throat.

"Stenographer," whispered the aide. A Navy enlisted man in a corner of the room took out his pad and pencil.

"The King of Jordan is a friend of the United States, and we intend to stand by our friends," said the president. He nodded his head abruptly, as if that settled the issue once and for all.

The meeting turned to a discussion of NATO strategy in Central Europe that left everyone bored and confused, even the attentive aides sitting along the wall of the Situation Room.

The Director walked out of the White House that day still steaming about the British sneak attack. Obviously the Brits had promised the King of Jordan that they would plead his case. Outrageous. The Director made a mental note to make life unpleasant for the M16 man in Washington. And he began composing in his mind the tart memo he would send to the Deputy Director for Plans telling him that he had *dropped the ball* on Jordan.

When he returned to his seventh-floor office at CIA head-quarters, the Director called for Edward Stone, the chief of the Near East Division of the clandestine service. He did so partly to snub Stone's boss, the DDP, and partly because he had grown over the years to trust Stone's judgment.

Stone was a tough old soldier, a warrior-intellectual in the George Marshall tradition, who had made his name in the

1940s as an intelligence officer in London, working with the British to unravel enemy intelligence networks. So many years of living in London had given Stone a British look: he had a ruddy face and silver-gray hair that was always combed in place; he dressed in heavy wool suits with cuffed trousers; he wore sturdy, well-shined Oxfords that he purchased every few years from a shoemaker on Jermyn Street in London; he carried an umbrella even when it wasn't raining. In his office, Stone had on the wall a paraphrased quotation from Nietzsche's *Beyond Good and Evil*, mounted in a simple wooden frame. It read: "Gaze not too long into the abyss, lest the abyss gaze back at you."

Stone arrived promptly at the Director's office and stood stiffly in front of his desk.

"I've just come from the White House," said the Director in a weary, pained tone of voice.

"I had to pretend to the president that I know what's going on inside the PLO, when in fact I don't know what's going on inside the PLO. I can assure you, I don't like being in that position."

Stone looked distressed.

"Do we have any penetrations of these guerrilla groups?" asked the Director.

"Nothing very useful," said Stone. "We bought a handful of Palestinians in Beirut and Amman years ago, but they don't provide us with much."

The Director was frowning and drumming his pen against the desk top.

"We have a promising operation starting up in Beirut," ventured Stone. "One of our best young officers out there is trying to recruit a senior man in Fatah. It could be a real catch, but it's the sort of thing that will take time to ripen."

"We don't have time," said the Director, raising his voice slightly.

"We must recruit one of these fellows," he said, talking as if he was describing a rival tennis team, "as soon as possible! I don't care what it takes, what it costs, or who gets mad about it!"

The division chief nodded his head.

"There is a slight problem that I must bring to your attention," said Stone.

"And what is that?"

"Our relationship with the Fatah official is currently structured as 'liaison.'"

"Liaison?" asked the Director incredulously. "Surely you don't mean intelligence liaison, like what we have with the British and French?"

"I'm afraid so," said Stone.

"That's completely mad. I don't want to share intelligence with these hooligans. I want an agent! Someone who is signed, sealed, and delivered!"

"That's our goal with the Fatah man, of course. But we aren't there yet. So far he is only dealing with us through intermediaries."

"Stone," said the Director, who retained a schoolboy habit of addressing people by their surnames, "I want a penetration. And soon."

Stone nodded.

"Right," said the Director. "Let's get on with it."

The Director congratulated himself on his performance when Stone had left the office. He imagined the wave of activity that would be set in motion by this brief conversation: the cables, meetings, and shadowy contacts that would eventually—if they were lucky—start a stream of information flowing back toward his office.

That was the real secret about the CIA, the Director believed. Not its exotic tradecraft, but the fact that it was very much like the rest of the federal government. It was a pinhead: a vast body controlled by a small brain sitting in the White House. The president issued an order—or perhaps, like today, expressed concern about something during a meeting—and it reverberated through the government like a roar of thunder. Directors summoned division chiefs, who cabled station chiefs, who summoned case officers—and so on until the huge apparatus of government was mobilized to deal with an issue the president had probably long since forgotten.

The Director turned to a more practical problem: How to keep any intelligence that might be obtained from the Fatah operation out of the hands of the Israelis.

He called the Deputy Director for Plans on the secure phone. After chewing him out for the Jordan fiasco, he got to the point. He had reviewed the Fatah penetration with Stone and wanted it to be a top priority.

"We're taking care of it," said the DDP, who didn't like the Director going behind his back.

"Not any more," said the Director. "Stone will report directly to me on this operation. He'll keep you briefed."

"I must protest . . . ," said the DDP.

"Don't waste your time," said the Director.

"One more thing. On this Fatah business, I want you to keep KUDESK at arm's length."

"Very well," said the wan voice of the DDP.

It was a polite way of saying: Keep the Israelis at arm's length. KUDESK was the cryptonym for the CIA Counterintelligence staff. In addition to their normal work of thwarting the KGB, the counterintelligence staff had the special assignment of maintaining CIA liaison with the Mossad. This peculiar division of labor stemmed partly from personal ties between the chief of KUDESK and Israeli intelligence officials that dated back to the 1940s. It was also a deliberate effort to compartmentalize information—to keep the CIA people who dealt with the Arabs separate from those who dealt with the Israelis —and thereby reduce the chance of leaks.

"We'll have quite a mess on our hands," said the Director.

"What mess?" asked the DDP.

"If the Israelis find out that we're running an agent at the top of the PLO."

"Yes, Director. Quite a mess."

"So let's make sure they don't find out."

The Director hung up the phone and put the PLO problem aside. An aide brought in an urgent cable from the Saigon station, summarizing the latest disaster in Vietnam. The lead Vietnamese agent in a CIA network that stretched into Cambodia had disappeared the previous week. The new intelligence report said that he had been spotted in Hanoi. The entire network had presumably been blown. The throat-slitting would come later.

Stone drafted an urgent cable for Hoffman. It said the Fatah project had the "highest repeat highest" support and should be put on a crash basis immediately. Headquarters' Operational Approval for the recruitment would be expedited,

Stone said, and all necessary paperwork should be forwarded as soon as possible.

"This is to be run as a controlled-agent operation, not liaison," Stone concluded. "Please advise soonest your plan for recruitment."

11

Beirut; January 1970

"This is classic!" said Hoffman the next day as he read the cable from Stone assigning the highest priority to the espionage operation against Fatah.

"One month they don't want to hear about the Palestinians, and we have to beat them over the head to get anything approved. The next month the PLO is the hottest thing since Oleg Penkovsky.

"You see," Hoffman confided. "That's why *they* are on the seventh floor, and we're out here shovelling shit. Because they *understand* these things."

"Why is the front office so interested all of a sudden?" asked Rogers. "And why so much emphasis on control?"

"Beats me," said Hoffman. "That's your problem. But I know a three-alarm fire when I see one, and this is a three-alarm fire! So take a friendly word of advice from your old pal: Don't fuck up!"

The words were still ringing in Rogers's ears several hours later as he pondered the case. He now had all the support he could dream of. The only thing he lacked was a plan that would lead promptly and surely to recruitment of Jamal Ramlawi as an American agent.

The problem, Rogers reassured himself, was a familiar one. He had faced it over the years with Saudis, Omanis, Yemenis, Sudanese. How do you get a potential agent to cross a line that he doesn't want to cross? How do you impose your will on him and establish control? Do you buy him? Break him down, find his weaknesses and exploit them? Or do you try to establish a bond of trust and personal commitment?

Rogers thought back over his own career. For all his training in deceit, his successes as a case officer had most often come from being open and straightforward. The true marvel of the intelligence business, in his experience, wasn't the gadgetry or the shadowy operations. It was the simple fact that people like to talk. The old politician wants to tell war stories. The young revolutionary wants to explain how he plans to change the world. They shouldn't tell you these things, but they always do. And all of them, all over the world, want the ear of an interested American. That was what made the business fun.

That gentle approach, unfortunately, didn't seem to be what Langley wanted in this case. They wanted something quick and dirty. Rogers decided to have a chat with Hoffman.

"Let's go out and have a drink," suggested Hoffman when Rogers stopped by his office late that afternoon. "I know just the place. The Black Cat!"

The Black Cat was a sleazy strip joint on a narrow side street off Hamra. It was dark inside, and it took Rogers a few seconds to adjust to the red lights and clouds of cigarette smoke. When his eyes had focused, he saw a long bar, with a half-dozen overweight European women in various stages of undress sitting on the bar stools. On the stage, glowing under a blue stage light, was a woman—completely naked—careeessing a rubber snake.

"The virtue of this place," said Hoffman, pushing his stocky frame past one of the chubby bar girls, "is that nobody would think to look for us here.

"The other virtue," he added in a whisper, "is that we own it. Don't ask me why, but a few years ago it seemed like a good idea. That means nobody will overhear us. Except us."

There were a few other patrons, mostly Arabs in long white gowns. One of them was sitting in a corner, drunkenly trying to undo the bra of one of the bar girls.

"Saudis!" said Hoffman scornfully. "Blackmailing Saudis is so easy it's pathetic."

The arrival of the two Americans had roused the woman on stage to more aggressive courtship of the rubber snake. She pulled it slowly between her legs and then caressed each breast with the serpent's tongue. The blue light showed on the woman's head. She was naked, Rogers noticed, except for a small black veil covering her face. The mysterious East.

"Jesus!" said Hoffman, looking at the row of tired women propping up the bar, each making half-hearted gestures of seduction in their direction.

"These girls should be wearing feedbags! Remind me tomorrow about hiring a new team."

They ordered drinks, refusing an offer by several of the bar girls to join them. The women retreated to the bar and resumed gossiping among themselves.

"Now what did you want to talk about?" asked Hoffman.

"The case," said Rogers.

"Which case?"

"You know," said Rogers. *"The case."*

"Oh. Okay. Shoot."

"I think we have a problem," began Rogers. "The guy we're going after is a patriot. He's not interested in working for us. He wants to work *with* us. For the good of his people."

"So make him interested," said Hoffman. "Find a handle!"

"I'm not sure that's the way to go."

"Look, my boy," said Hoffman. "This business is easy. Don't make it complicated. You find somebody you think can help you. You grab him by the balls. Then you squeeze real hard. It's simple."

Rogers was silent.

"Give me a break!" said Hoffman, gesturing to the stage. A new dancer had arrived, leading a large dog on a leash.

"That's disgusting!" said the station chief, turning away from the stage after a minute or so of rapt attention.

"Christ! Where do we get these girls?"

Hoffman lit up a cigarette before realizing that he already had another one going.

"I agree with you that the business is easy," said Rogers, picking up where they had left off. "But I look at it a different way. Recruiting someone is about getting him to do what you want, rather than just forcing him to do what he doesn't want. I learned a long time ago that it's easy to manipulate people —if you know what you want from them and don't tell them why you're being so friendly."

Hoffman straightened up in his chair and cocked his eye toward Rogers.

"Say that again," said the station chief.

"For me," continued Rogers, "getting a hold on somebody works like this: You go see a prospective agent once, talk to him about his life, his family, his politics. He's flattered. You're an American, from the embassy. He's still on his guard, because you might be a spy, but you play it low-key. You're polite, discreet. You bring a present for his child.

"Then you go back and see him a second time. He's nervous about seeing you again. But what can he do? He's an Arab. He has to be polite. You see him a third time. And then you do· him a favor. Nothing spectacular, but a nice gesture. He's in your debt. He knows it, but neither of you say anything about it. It's just friendship, hospitality. Then you see him a fourth and fifth time, and a little business begins to flow his way. He's comfortable. He likes dealing with you."

"Right," said Hoffman. "And then you bust his balls!"

Rogers laughed, despite himself.

"Can I tell you a story?" asked Rogers.

"Sure. So long as it doesn't involve dogs."

"A few years ago, during the civil war in Yemen, I needed information very badly. There was a sheik I thought could give it to me, but he was supposed to be totally hostile to the West and unrecruitable.

"I thought I would give it a try anyway, so I trekked two days into the desert to meet him. I went alone and unarmed. I wasn't even sure why I was going at all. When I arrived, I was exhausted. The sheik gave me coffee, fed me. It was the least he could do. We began to talk. He couldn't believe that I spoke Arabic fluently. He kept calling his aides over to marvel at me. Apparently the Russians always used translators. Anyway, we stayed up all night talking and chewing qat. By morning this guy—without ever realizing it—had become a CIA asset. He provided me with goodies for more than a year."

"There's a name in the trade for what you're talking about," said Hoffman. "It's called 'rapport.'" He said the word daintily.

"I take it you don't approve," said Rogers.

"To be honest, 'rapport' sounds to me like a limp dick. But it's your case."

"What do you recommend?" asked Rogers.

"That we try to get a handle on your man. Do a little surveillance, some taps, some pictures. See what we're dealing with. If there's a hook, grab it. If not, then we'll see."

Hoffman looked again at the tawdry cast of characters in the Black Cat.

"I have a suggestion," said the station chief. "Let's get out of this dump."

Hoffman busied himself, arranging the surveillance of Jamal. He insisted on managing the details himself, despite Rogers's protests.

Hoffman loved surveillance. He regarded it as the purest from of intelligence, a street ballet whose beauty lay in its precision and economy of motion. He delighted in seeing how few people he could use in a surveillance team and still maintain adequate coverage of the target. He would sit in his office with a map of the stake-out area, studying it like a chess problem, seeing if he couldn't replace a body here or there. He would draw little diagrams illustrating the most efficient way to cover a suspect who entered a store with several exits, or to track a suspect who took taxis and buses and changed directions frequently to throw off his pursuers. Hoffman regarded himself as a maestro of the streets.

To Rogers, it was pure pedantry. The part of Hoffman that made him seem most like an FBI agent.

The surveillance on Jamal was gradually put in place. Loose coverage of his movements day and night, to get a general picture of where he went and who he saw. Tight coverage of his office, audio and video. A special team, flown in from Europe, tapped the phone line and placed a microphone in the ceiling. And by drilling through an empty office next door, they managed to plant a tiny camera in one wall, no bigger or more prominent than a speck of dirt, which took excellent pictures.

Rogers said nothing to Fuad about the surveillance or the new urgency of the operation. Instead, in his twice-weekly meetings with the Lebanese agent, he focused on basic tradecraft. They agreed on the location of dead drops in downtown

Beirut where messages could be passed quickly and discreetly. They reviewed extraction procedures for getting Fuad and Jamal out of Beirut in an emergency. Rogers urged Fuad to deepen his cover as a pro-Palestinian Lebanese businessman by spending time with other Fatah officials. Every additional Fatah man in Fuad's circle of acquaintance, he stressed, was additional protection for Jamal.

The surveillance reports began to accumulate. The trackers who were following Jamal described the subject as an Arab playboy. He stayed out late at discos and nightclubs, almost always in the company of a beautiful woman. He woke up late in the morning, often in the bed of a young lady, went back to his apartment to shower and shave, and arrived at the office around 11:00 A.M.

He was rootless and almost bohemian in his lifestyle, drifting among the offices and apartments of friends, co-workers, and lovers. He ate nearly all his meals in restaurants and always had a fat roll of banknotes. The oddest thing about his routine, the trackers reported, was that he would occasionally go to the library of the American University of Beirut in the afternoon and read. Just read! Science books, news magazines, pop-music tabloids. Books about America and the Soviet Union. Even books about Israel.

There was a final detail, said the trackers. He loved to buy presents, the more expensive the better. On his way to an appointment, he would often stop in a store and buy for his host some fruit, or flowers, or candy, or books. Sometimes he would stop at fancy women's shops on Hamra and buy gifts in bulk for his girlfriends: bottles of perfume; a dozen silk scarves; a half-dozen pairs of gold earrings.

"I can tell you one thing about our boy," said Hoffman, after the surveillance had been in place for several weeks.

"What's that?" said Rogers, suspecting that he already knew the answer.

"This guy loves pussy!"

Rogers groaned.

"No really, come here. Take a look at these pictures. When this guy tells people he put in a hard day at the office, he really means it!"

Spread out on Hoffman's desk were a dozen glossy photographs, culled from hundreds that had been taken by the camera hidden in Jamal's office wall.

"Check this out," said Hoffman. "This is babe number one."

He handed Rogers a picture that showed a blond woman with very large breasts lying spread-eagled on top of a desk. Her blouse was open and her skirt was pulled up to her waist. On top of her was Jamal.

"What a unit!" said Hoffman. "That girl's got a pair of Hogans!"

"Hogans?" asked Rogers, who had never heard the expression before.

"Yeah, wise guy. Hogans. Bigger than big."

Hoffman picked up another picture and studied it.

"Blow job!" announced Hoffman. "Yesirreee. No question about it. The woman is playing the skin flute! Eating tube steak!"

"I get the point," said Rogers, taking the picture from Hoffman. It showed the blond woman kneeling on the floor, performing fellatio on the Palestinian, who was smiling and had his eyes closed.

"Don't swallow it, lady! It might explode!" shouted Hoffman.

"Are you aware that we already have a file on this woman?" said Rogers, who felt foolish looking at dirty pictures.

"Hubba! Hubba!" responded the station chief.

"She's a German girl," continued Rogers. "She drives a red Ferrari and keeps house for a Lebanese millionaire. This is how she gets her kicks."

"Outstanding young woman," said Hoffman. "Sensational. No wonder the Germans lost the war. They were exhausted."

He went back to the pile of photographs and pawed through them until he found the one he was looking for.

"Okay. Here's babe number two," said the station chief.

"First, we have a little get-acquainted shot." The photograph showed a dark-haired woman in a fashionable dress with her back to the camera. She was passionately kissing Jamal, who had his hand under the woman's skirt.

Hoffman was already looking at the next picture. "Woof, woof!" barked the station chief.

He handed the photo to Rogers. It showed the dark-haired woman completely naked, kneeling on a desk chair. Jamal was entering her from behind. The woman was slender and her body was darkly tanned. She seemed to be a European, but her head was down, which prevented any clear identification.

"Smile! You're on Candid Camera!" said Hoffman, handing Rogers yet another picture.

This showed the same woman, the same scene. Except this time she was looking up. Her head was turned toward the wall so that she was gazing, without realizing it, directly into the camera. Her eyes were wide open and her lips were curled seductively.

I've seen that face, thought Rogers. I know I've seen it.

"More!" shouted Hoffman, but Rogers ignored him.

Rogers saw in his mind's eye another image. It was the face of a woman looking up at him coyly as she picked up her napkin from the floor at a dinner party.

"My God!" exclaimed Rogers. "That's the French chargé's wife!"

Hoffman was jubilant.

"I love this job," he said, smiling from ear to ear. "It is a humbling reminder of the breadth of human folly and depravity. People really are capable of the most *amazing* things!"

Hoffman called in his deputy, who doubled as chief of operations, for a brief meeting to discuss the new piece of intelligence.

"Okay, boys and girls," said Hoffman. "The first question is: Have we got anything we'd like to know from the Froggies? Because we've got a perfect chance to burn a certain French diplomat who might be a bit embarrassed to know that his wife is getting banged by a Palestinian terrotist in a black leather jacket."

"And loving it," said the chief of operations, studying the picture.

"I think we might let headquarters in on the fun," said Hoffman. "Send these back home via diplomatic pouch, pronto."

"Definitely," said the operations chief. "In the meantime, I don't suppose you have this woman's phone number?"

"Grow up," said Hoffman.

"The second question," continued the station chief, "is what we do about donkey dick."

"Jamal," interjected Rogers, who was becoming increasingly dismayed by the course of events.

"Right. Because we have a serious problem on our hands. Either this guy is going to fuck himself to death, or he's going to get killed by a jealous husband. Either way, he's not a very good security risk."

"Is he married?" asked the operations chief.

"No," said Rogers.

"Too bad," said the operations chief. "That makes him harder to blackmail."

"Does the Old Man care whether he's screwing every European broad he can find in West Beirut?" asked Hoffman.

"I doubt it," said Rogers.

"How about his mother?"

"Chief," said Rogers. "Can I talk to you privately for a minute?"

"Yeah, sure," said Hoffman. He turned to the operations chief.

"You don't mind stepping outside for a minute, Pete? Mr. Rogers has something 'private' he would like to discuss with me."

The deputy glowered at Rogers and left the room.

"Shoot," said Hoffman when he had gone.

"I think we ought to be careful about using these photographs. They'll tip off the French that we're running surveillance on Jamal. And by the time the whole mess is over, we may find that we've caused more trouble for ourselves than for the French diplomat. As for Jamal, if you think you can blackmail him with dirty pictures, you're crazy. He'll just show them to his friends."

"Now wait a minute!" said Hoffman. "I hate to break the news to you, but photos like these are the mother's milk of our particular line of work. I'm not about to throw them away."

"I'm not asking you to do that," said Rogers. "But I'd like you to go slow."

"So that you can do what?"

"So that I can make personal contact with Jamal. As soon

as possible. That's the only answer. Otherwise we're whis-
tling in the dark."

"Hmmm," said Hoffman. For once, he actually looked
pensive.

"Hasn't Jamal already told you he won't meet you?" asked
the station chief.

"Yes," said Rogers.

"Well, he isn't going to change his mind just because you
ask him politely. This is what I have been trying to explain to
you: You need a handle on him!"

"Let me try it my way," said Rogers. "I've got some
ideas."

"Okay," said the station chief after a moment's delibera-
tion. "As we say in the personnel-management business, it's
your ass."

12

Amman, Jordan; February 1970

Roger's first plan was simple: trickery. He decided that he would wait for the next scheduled meeting between Fuad and Jamal, a few days hence, and crash it. He would be there in the safehouse when Jamal arrived, sit him down on the couch, and insist that he had to deal directly with an American. The worst that could happen was that the relationship would break off right then and there. Which would be better than waiting months before finding out that Jamal wasn't willing to play ball.

The appointed day arrived. The meeting was set in an apartment in Ramlet el-Baida, near the seacoast. Rogers went early to the safehouse, waited for Fuad, and told him that there had been a slight change in plans. They would both be meeting with Jamal that day. He didn't explain why, and Fuad didn't ask.

Rogers and Fuad sat in the cheerless apartment for five hours, smoking cigarettes and waiting for the Palestinian. He never showed up.

Rogers suspected a double-cross. His fears were relieved by a bit of intelligence that arrived the next day. The Beirut station had learned from a source in the Deuxième Bureau that a number of senior Fatah officials, including Jamal, had gone urgently to Amman, where some sort of crisis was brewing between the PLO and the Jordanians.

Details of the crisis emerged in the cable traffic from the CIA station in Amman. On February 9, the king had issued a decree banning the Palestinian commandos from carrying weapons in public in Amman. The decree also required the commandos to carry identity cards and put license plates on their cars. The king's demands sounded modest enough. But in the supercharged atmosphere of Jordan, where the PLO commandos had become a virtual state-within-a-state, they amounted to a declaration of war.

It's a bluff, thought Rogers as he read the cables. It has to be a bluff. The king doesn't want a showdown yet.

The Fatah leadership seemed eager enough for a confrontation. The Foreign Broadcast Information Service, the CIA's radio-monitoring unit, picked up a communiqué the night of February 9 from Fatah Radio in Cairo. In the tormented syntax of the Revolution, it declared: "The time has come for the masses to act and act quickly, not only to stop the new conspiracy, but to inflict final defeat on the conspirators."

That meant that if the king wanted war, he would have war.

When Rogers put the pieces together in his mind, he saw that the crisis in Jordan might provide a useful opportunity. It represented movement, and movement of almost any kind was beneficial. Movement altered the field of play and created space in which to operate. A political crisis of this sort was better still, since it provided openings that, in normal times, wouldn't exist.

The trick was to contrive the right moment, Rogers told himself. The moment when your target had no choice but to walk through the door you were opening for him.

Rogers decided to follow Jamal to Amman. He sent Fuad separately by car and booked an MEA flight for himself in the name of Edwin Roberts. The same name was on the Canadian passport that Rogers carried in his briefcase.

In a saner world, the MEA flight from Beirut to Amman would take about thirty minutes. The plane would fly due south from Beirut, enter Israeli airspace over the northern Galilee, pass over the biblical towns of Nazareth and Tiberias, then glide across the Jordan River near the town of Ajlun and land in Amman. But in the actual world of the Middle East in

1970, Arab maps didn't even identify Israel by name, let alone overfly its airspace. The maps called it "Occupied Palestine" and the Beirut-Amman flight made a long detour through Syria.

Rogers scanned the bleak Jordanian landscape through the window as the plane approached Amman. Jordan was a dry, dusty country at the best of times, with rocky hills and arid plateaus alternating with sandy deserts. It was worse in the winter, when dust storms blew across the unprotected countryside and biting winds swept the hilltops. Amman was bitterly cold that day, and the air was so full of dust that it began to make a little sandpile in the bottom of Rogers's throat soon after he stepped off the airplane.

As Rogers rode into Amman by taxi the afternoon of February 11, he found the city in an uproar. The commandos were openly defying the king's ban on carrying weapons and had set up roadblocks at the entrances to the Palestinian camps that ringed the city. The Jordanian Army, for its part, had established checkpoints on the four major roads leading into the city. They were stopping Palestinian commandos and refusing to let them pass unless they turned over their guns. Rogers waited more than an hour in a long line of traffic at one checkpoint on the airport road.

Amman is a city built on seven hills. The souks and mosques of the old Arab quarter lay in a valley at the center of town. The residents of the city, many of them Palestinians, lived on the surrounding hills, in houses of white stone that seemed to have been carved like steps out of the rocky hillsides. The international quarter, which housed the fancy hotels and shops and the American Embassy, was on a hill known as Jebel Amman. The Palestinian headquarters stood atop the next hill, called Jebel Hussein. It adjoined the sprawling Al-Hussein refugee camp.

Rogers headed for the safehouse in Jebel Hussein that night. He got past the Palestinian checkpoint at the entrance to the fedayeen quarter by showing his Canadian passport and a business card that said he was a construction contractor. He gave the address of a small engineering concern in the neighborhood, where he said he had an appointment.

The safehouse was a small, white stone villa on a road that skirted the hillside of Jebel Hussein. The road was called Jaffa Street, after the coastal city in old Palestine, and it was several blocks from the Fatah military headquarters.

Fuad was already there when Rogers arrived. He had his sunglasses off and he was sitting on the stone floor of the nearly-empty house, relaxing. He had a serene look, like someone who has finally begun a task he has anticipated and dreaded for a long time.

This is Fuad's graduation day, thought Rogers. He is in a dangerous place, helping his case officer run an operation. He has made the team.

"What's for dinner?" asked Rogers.

"Tuna fish and crackers," said Fuad, who had already examined the meager provisions in the house.

"I'd like tuna fish and crackers please," said Rogers. He scouted around the pantry and found a few cans of Foster's Australian lager. Drinking the beer, he wondered who the previous users of the hideaway had been, and why on earth they had left behind cans of beer from the other side of the world.

There was a radio in the house. Rogers tuned in the BBC World Service.

The Old Man was visiting Moscow to discuss joint Soviet-Palestinian action in the Middle East, the radio said. Fuad muttered something derogatory about the Palestinian leader in Arabic.

That's bad news for the king, thought Rogers. The Old Man has upped the ante by going to see his patrons in Moscow.

"And in Munich today," continued the broadcaster, "a taste of Palestinian terror as three PLO commandos tossed hand grenades at a group of passengers awaiting a Lufthansa flight, killing one person and injuring twelve."

Rogers turned up the radio. Things are getting out of control, he thought to himself.

"The Munich police captured an unusual message written by the leader of the group, which he planned to read to the passengers of the Israeli jet.

"According to police sources in Munich, the message read: 'Good evening, ladies and gentlemen. This is the deputy commander of the 112th unit of the Martyr Omar Sastadi Division of the Action Group for the Liberation of Palestine. In the name of the Palestinian Revolution, we are taking command of this aircraft and renaming it Palestine II.' According to German police, little is known about the Sastadi group."

"Bullshit," said Rogers over the sound of the radio. "Nothing is known about the group because there is no such group."

"My dear Mr. Reilly, you do not understand the Arab mind," said Fuad. "We think that if we announce that there has been an operation by the 112th unit of an organization that no one has ever heard of, then people will assume that this organization must have at least 111 other units. No Arab would believe it, of course. No Arab believes anything that anyone tells him. But we think the rest of the world is stupid."

"And now for the soccer results," said the radio newscaster. "In the fourth division, Hartlepool nil, Wigan nil. Doncaster two, Cardiff one."

"Turn it off," said Rogers.

"And in the Scottish League, Patrick Thistle nil, Queen of the South, one. Aberdeen two, Celtic two. Hibernians nil . . ."

"Turn it off," said Rogers again. The radio went silent

At 8:00 P.M. that night, they heard the sound of gunfire coming from the eastern part of the city, near Jebel al-Taj. It seemed to be a clash between the Jordanian Army and the commandos.

An hour later, the neighborhood of Jebel Hussein shook with the sound of heavy-caliber machine-gun fire. Rogers could see from the window a volley of tracer bullets coming from the rooftop of the headquarters of the Jordanian Ministry of Interior. It was answered by a rattling barrage from two machine guns positioned within Jebel Hussein.

"Now we know why Jamal was in such a rush to get here," said Rogers as he peered over the windowsill.

Below him on Jaffa Street, Rogers saw a jeep fitted with a machine gun, careening up the street at breakneck speed. A dark-haired Palestinian commando stood in the back, legs apart and hips swaying with the motion of the vehicle, holding the trunk of the machine gun in his hands and rotating it on its turret. It was a sensual, almost erotic embrace of a deadly weapon, and it was an image that Rogers came to associate with the guerrillas; the posturing of a vain but ultimately powerless people.

"Come watch the show," Rogers whispered to Fuad. "The fedayeen are in heaven."

"They are children," said Fuad. "When I want to watch children, I go to the playground."

The sound of automatic weapons rattled on through the night but tapered off toward dawn.

When he awoke, Rogers set in motion the plan he had devised over the previous two days. He wrote out a message in neat Arabic script, sealed it, and gave it to Fuad.

The message read: "A friend with important information will be in Nasser Square at noon. If you want the information, follow him."

Rogers turned to Fuad and spoke to him carefully and deliberately.

"Take this letter to 49 Ramleh Street and knock on the door. A bald Arab man will answer the door. Tell him you have a message for Jamal Ramlawi at the Fatah military headquarters at Nasser Square, on the corner of Khaled Ibn Walid Street."

"What if he asks me who the message is from?" queried Fuad.

"He won't ask."

"Who is he?" asked Fuad, wanting to understand every detail.

"A friend who has maintained contact with us for many years, who travels easily among the commandos."

"But won't it be dangerous for Jamal to receive the message?"

"No," said Rogers, smiling at all the questions that were tumbling out of the usually taciturn Fuad. "Jamal is an intelligence officer, and intelligence officers are supposed to collect information. That's their job."

"What if something goes wrong?"

"It won't," said Rogers. He put his two large hands on Fuad's shoulders, as if to brace him for the task ahead.

"When you have delivered the message, return to

Beirut," said Rogers. "Here's five hundred dollars for the trip." He handed Fuad the money and walked him to the door. The Lebanese walked out into the chilly February morning. He walked deliberately, Rogers thought, with the confidence of a man who, with each step, feels that he is fulfilling his destiny.

Rogers tidied up the safehouse. He collected a few bits of paper that might identify the occupants of the apartment as Americans—a matchbook cover with advertising for a restaurant in New York, a well-thumbed copy of *The International Herald-Tribune*—and burned them in the kitchen sink. He checked his wallet to make sure it contained only documents that supported his Canadian identity.

At eleven-thirty, Rogers left the house. He walked slowly and deliberately, his head down, along Jaffa Street. The city seemed to have calmed down after the previous night's gunplay, and some of the roadblocks had been removed.

As Rogers crossed a side street, two teen-aged Palestinians shouted at him. Rogers's heart pounded like a hammer against an anvil. He shouted out in Arabic, "Death to the traitor King and all his family!" One of the boys roared back a similar epithet and they continued on their way.

At the edge of Nasser Square, the scene of the machine-gun exchange the previous night, Rogers saw a half-dozen small children creeping along the sides of the stone buildings that lined the street, darting out every few steps to retrieve small objects from the ground. They were scavengers, gathering spent cartridges from the previous night's battle. The copper linings from the spent shells would bring a few piastres in the souk.

Just before noon, Rogers arrived at the entrance to Nasser Square. There was still a smell of powder in the air. The streets were nearly empty. At noon exactly, he emerged from Ameena Bint Wahab Street, walked halfway across Nasser Square, and sat on a stone bench. Directly across from him was a tin-roofed building that housed the Fatah military command.

He felt conspicuous and wished there were more people and noise around him. He saw a man walk out of a building and disappear down Khaled Ibn Walid Street; 100 yards away he saw another man, a blind vendor selling smuggled American cigarettes. At the edge of the square a woman with a shopping bag was sitting and resting. Every twenty seconds or so, a car or truck rumbled past.

Rogers looked toward one of the upper windows of the Fatah headquarters, fifty yards away. He thought he saw a figure, all in black, staring out the window. He stood and walked a few steps closer to the building. He counted slowly to ten, feeling his pulse beat against his closed eyelids. Then he turned and walked back the way he had come, across the square and into Ameena Bint Wahab Street. Had Jamal gotten the message?

Rogers walked very slowly. When he reached the shadow of a building, he stopped and turned around. There was nobody following him. He waited fifteen seconds in the shadows, then walked another half block. He was afraid to turn around. Afraid not of who would be there, but of who wouldn't. He took a cigarette from his pocket and turned around to light it.

And there, ambling toward him, was a man in a black leather jacket.

Bingo! said Rogers under his breath.

Jamal approached Rogers and asked him if he had an American cigarette.

"Marlboro," offered Rogers.

The Palestinian took the cigarette and lit it.

"What information do you have for me, friend?" said Jamal.

"Come back with me to a quieter place, where we can talk," answered Rogers.

"No. Here." He sounded like he meant it.

"Very well," said Rogers. "The message I have for you is this: The King will rescind his decree about carrying weapons."

"The King will back down?" asked Jamal dubiously.

"Yes," said Rogers. "He will back down."

Jamal looked at him suspiciously. He brushed a strand of hair out of his eyes.

"When?" demanded the Palestinian.

"I don't know."

"How do you know this information?" asked the Palestinian.

"Because I know it," said Rogers. "I can't say any more than that."

The Palestinian took a long drag on his cigarette. If we stand here any longer, thought Rogers, we will become conspicuous.

"There are other important things I must discuss with you," said Rogers.

"Not here," said the Palestinian. "Not in Amman."

"Where?"

"Somewhere else."

"Where?" demanded Rogers.

"I will send you a message."

"When?"

"When I return to Beirut."

He took another cigarette and was gone.

Rogers, tired but elated, was back in Beirut that night.

Two days later, the king held a press conference and announced that he was "freezing" his order banning the fedayeen from carrying weapons in public. The confrontation had been the result of a "misunderstanding," the Jordanian monarch explained. "Our power is their power and their power is our power," he said of the fedayeen.

The king had capitulated.

A week after that, back in Beirut, Jamal sent word through Fuad that he would meet Rogers in early March in Kuwait.

Hoffman listened to Rogers tell the story of the encounter in Amman, and then asked him to repeat it.

"I have one question for you, hot dog," said Hoffman, after he had heard the explanation for the second time. "How in the hell did you know that the King was going to back down? I didn't see that in any of the cables."

Rogers looked sheepish.

"To be honest, I didn't know it. But it seemed like a safe bet."

"You're shitting me!" said Hoffman. "You mean you risked this operation on a hunch?"

"It was better than a hunch," said Rogers. "It was a strong probability."

Hoffman looked at his young case officer with a combination of puzzlement and new respect.

"You're crazier than I thought," said Hoffman. "In fact, you're almost as crazy as I am."

Rogers took it as a compliment.

"So Jamal thinks the CIA helped to pressure the King to stop the crackdown?" asked the station chief.

"Perhaps," said Rogers with a trace of a smile. "But I doubt he's that gullible."

Hoffman called Rogers into his office several days later.

"Guess who's packing his bags and leaving sunny Beirut?" said the station chief, his eyes twinkling.

Rogers shrugged his shoulders.

"A certain French diplomat."

"Oh shit," said Rogers.

"Hold on. It's not what you're thinking. The wife did it!"

"What?" said Rogers. "Why?"

"It seems," said Hoffman, "that Madame Plateau got angry at her husband one day for being such an asshole and told him the whole story. How she was fucking her brains out with one of the Palestinian guerrillas and loving it, and what did he think of that? Apparently she didn't tell him who, because the thugs from SDECE are making inquiries all over West Beirut trying to find out. The chargé got so angry that he beat her up. They had to take her to the hospital. It's the talk of Beirut."

"What's going to happen to them?" asked Rogers.

"The French Ambassador is mucho embarrassed. Frenchmen are supposed to screw other people's wives, not vice versa. Anyway, it doesn't look good for Mr. and Mrs. Froggie. They're being recalled for extended consultations back home. Looks like bye-bye, Beirut."

"And the photographs?" asked Rogers.

"I didn't have the heart to give them to the Frenchman. The guy is miserable enough as it is. He didn't need to see the smile on his wife's face. Anyway, there wasn't much we could have squeezed from him. Even if we had threatened to run the pictures in *An Nabar*.

"One more thing," added Hoffman.

"When you see your Palestinian friend, tell him to keep his pecker in his pants for a while. People take sex seriously in this part of the world. Around here, if you touch the merchandise, you've got to buy it."

13

Kuwait; March 1970

Rogers arrived in Kuwait three days early. He wanted to get the feel of the place, to look over the safehouse, prepare the food and drinks, ready himself emotionally for the encounter. It was a bit like practicing before a basketball game. The exercise probably didn't improve your aim, but it steadied the nerves.

Kuwait was a flat little smudge of sand at the western end of the Persian Gulf. It had three distinguishing features: a vast reservoir of oil, which was transforming the sheikdom into the richest country per-capita in the world; a class of merchants and traders that dated back several centuries, which gave Kuwait the semblance of a mercantile elite and spared it the indignities of Bedouin culture; and a huge influx of Palestinian migrant workers, which made Kuwait an important staging ground for the Palestinian Revolution.

Kuwait was in many ways an ugly country, made more so by the oil boom. It was ferociously hot in the summer—over 120 degrees in July—so hot that the air seemed to burn your lungs and had to be breathed in small gulps. Kuwait City was on the coast, and the heat there wasn't the dry baking heat of the desert, but the humid heat of a steam bath. The temperature wasn't so bad now, in mid-March, during the brief Kuwaiti spring. But in all seasons, the place seemed to smell of oil, which was so plentiful in Kuwait's vast Burgan field that it bubbled out of the ground on its own, without a pump.

As Rogers drove in from the airport, he saw a spasm of

spending and construction. Everywhere there were new buildings, erected as fast and cheaply as the British and American contractors could build them. Along Fahad al-Salem Street, approaching downtown, there was a traffic jam of bulldozers and cement mixers and dump trucks, all caught in the rush to build more ugly new buildings. He noticed that the Kuwaitis were all driving big American gas-guzzlers. Cadillacs, Lincolns, Oldsmobiles, Buicks, the bigger and gaudier the better.

Kuwaitis seemed to understand that these automotive behemoths were the mother of their prosperity. Though the country lacked modern highways, it had nearly as many cars as people, and the downtown area resembled a vast parking lot. As the traffic slowed to a halt, the Kuwaitis sat in their velour-upholstered cars, power windows up and the air conditioning on full blast, enjoying the accident of geology that had made them, at least momentarily, the richest people on earth.

Soon after arriving, Rogers stopped by to see the local station chief. His name was Egbert Jorgenson and he ran a small, three-person shop—himself, an operations officer, and a code clerk—in a cluttered wing of the embassy.

Jorgenson's cover job was agricultural attaché. It was a silly cover, since there wasn't any agriculture to speak of in Kuwait, but that seemed to be the least of Jorgenson's problems. He was a small, intense man with a loud voice and a look of perpetual harassment.

"Hey, great to see you. How's the family? What are you doing in Kuwait?" asked Jorgenson in one long sentence as he ushered Rogers into his office.

"I can't tell you that, Bert," said Rogers amiably. "Sorry."

"Yeah sure, I know. Okay," said Jorgenson. He looked hurt.

"How about you?" asked Rogers. "What's cooking?"

"Are you kidding? Plenty! You know the Sovs have an embassy here now? I'm going crazy! Never been so busy. Day and night."

Rogers asked what particular battles of the Cold War were being waged in Kuwait these days.

"Media!" said Jorgenson emphatically. "The Sovs have got people on the payroll at all the local papers. Indians from Kerala who do the editing and make-up. The KGB resident

feeds them articles—written by some clown in Moscow—
and they run the stuff as is. Verbatim. Word for word. The
Kuwaitis don't know the difference. They don't read the
newspapers anyway. But the Palestinians love it.

"You gotta see this shit. You won't believe it!" said Jorgenson.

He scurried over to his file cabinet, unlocked the top
drawer, and pulled out a thick file of clippings.

"Look at this!"

He handed Rogers an article headlined: "Kremlin En-
deavors to Give People More Homes."

"Can you believe that? Isn't that a gem? Look at this one."
Jorgenson pulled out another article, headlined: "Afro-Asian
Peoples Protest American Mideast Policy."

"Unbelievable! Who writes these headlines? Joe Stalin?
Wait! There's more," exclaimed Jorgenson. He was considerably agitated now, handing Rogers story after story with headlines like "Kim Il-Sung Strongly Supports Anti-Zionist Armed
Struggle" and "Imperialism Behind Food Shortage in Sudan."

"The Sovs are shameless!" said Jorgenson, bursting with
indignation. "And the Keralites print this crap for a few dinars
a week. It's pathetic. No wonder we're in trouble around the
world.

"Fortunately," said Jorgenson with a sly smile, "I've got a
few Keralities of my own. We're getting into this game, toe to
toe. Want to see some of what we're putting out?"

"Are you sure you should be telling me this?" asked
Rogers.

"Yeah, sure. Who gives a shit?"

Jorgenson removed another folder from the file cabinet,
much thinner than the first, and opened it with a flourish.

"Check this out," said the Kuwait station chief.

He handed Rogers an article headlined: "Hard Facts About
Air Pollution." And another titled "Alaskan Oil Potential
Enormous," and a long feature piece titled "Will U.S. Shift to
All-Volunteer Army?"

"This stuff is subtle," said Jorgenson. "I'm getting it from
Langley. A little pro-American spin for a change. What do
you think?"

"Great," said Rogers, almost speechless. "Really great."

Kuwait was a study in hypocrisy, Rogers decided. It was

an Islamic country, where it was technically forbidden for
people to drink alcohol. Yet when Rogers passed Kuwaitis in
the hotel lobby, slumbering on the couches, he could smell the
whisky on their breath. In the evening along Arabian Gulf
Street, he could see swarms of drunken migrant workers from
India and Ceylon.

Islamic Kuwait was officially prudish about sex. Yet
Rogers learned from a garrulous hotel desk clerk that airline
stewardesses, on a stopover from London, could make $1,000
a night entertaining Kuwaiti gentlemen. Even the local English-language newspaper seemed to be sex-crazy. Every day
on page 8, it ran pin-up pictures of half-naked women. The
day Rogers arrived the page 8 girl was a bosomy blonde in
garters and black silk stockings with the caption: "It's back to
belts!"

The only people who seemed diligent and disciplined were
the Palestinians, who did most of the work in Kuwait's government ministries, schools, and hospitals. The Palestinian
population was thought to number about 200,000—the Kuwaiti Emir was too nervous to publish precise census data—
and it overwhelmingly supported Fatah. The commando group
demanded two things from the skittish Kuwaiti government:
the right to levy a tax of 7 percent on the incomes of all
Palestinians working in Kuwait; and denial of Kuwaiti passports to all but a few of the Palestinians, so that the rest would
remain stateless and militant.

Fatah, in fact, had been born in the diaspora of Kuwait.
The Old Man had worked in Kuwait during the 1950s. So had
the Diplomat and Abu Namli. Rogers had Jorgenson check
with a police source at the Ministry of Interior and learned
that Jamal, too, had sojourned in Kuwait. He had come there
from Cairo in the mid 1960s to join the movement. Now, the
movement had matured and Jamal was returning.

A day before the meeting, Rogers received a cable from
Langley via the Kuwait station, marked with the highest security classification. It was a message from the operations
chief of the Near East Division, an aggressive young careerist
named John Marsh, who regarded Rogers as a rival.

The cable was full of gratuitous advice. Rogers should use
the Kuwait meeting to lay the groundwork for a future "con-

trolled-agent operation," the cable advised. To establish a basis for control, he should probe for the agent's pressure points.

After the meeting, Marsh directed, Rogers should recommend to NE Division the suitability of two options: financial recruitment, with suggestions as to the amount of money that would be necessary; and blackmail, through a threat to disclose tapes and photos documenting the agent's contacts with the CIA.

"Control is the essence of this operation," admonished Marsh in his concluding paragraph.

Rogers tore the cable in two, burned it, and flushed the ashes down the toilet. He had the code clerk transmit a brief response to Langley. It read: "C/NE/OPS. Msg text unreceived. Transmission garbled. Pls resend. Rogers."

He checked out of his hotel, rented a car in the name of Frank Worth, and headed for the safehouse, where nobody—not even the wizards of Langley—would disturb him.

14

Kuwait; March 1970

Rogers departed the hectic confusion of Kuwait City, driving a big American car that floated gently on its springs like a boat on a crest of water. As he reached the outskirts of the city, he stopped the car, made a U-turn, and then doubled back again to see if he was being followed. He wasn't. One of the benefits of working in the Middle East, as opposed to Europe, was that surveillance was loose or nonexistent. In the Arab world, the Soviets seemed to be as lazy as their clients.

He turned on the radio. A local Arabic station was playing a song by Fayrouz, a Lebanese singer adored throughout the Middle East. The song told the story of a girl who waited forlornly by the roadside for a lover who never arrived.

"I loved you in the summer . . . I loved you in the winter," Fayrouz sang in her tremulous voice. It was the sound of the Arab world, Rogers thought. A sentimental story about unkept promises.

As he headed south along the Persian Gulf coast, Rogers saw a breathtaking change in the landscape.

Stretching to the western horizon was the Arabian desert, undulating slightly like the sea on a calm day. But rather than the blank white of midsummer, the desert was a thin carpet of green, dotted with the blue flowers of thistles and the yellow of daisies. The effect was like a pointillist painting, with tendrils of herbs and shrubs dabbed against a sandy background.

It was spring in Kuwait. The brief season between the rain of February and the heat of May when the desert burst into bloom. In this brief springtime, Kuwaitis liked to flee the city and emulate their Bedouin ancestors. Every few miles Rogers saw the billowing flaps of a camping tent, often with a shiny new RV parked alongside, which marked a Kuwaiti family on a desert holiday. Further from the highway were the ragged tents of a few real-life Bedouin nomads, lost in time, wandering with their sheep and camels across the ocean of sand.

The radio crackled with static. Rogers fiddled with the tuning knob trying to find a clearer station. Eventually, he heard a familiar radio voice, speaking in perfect, modulated, American English:

". . . and it is well known that the peoples of Africa and Asia are resolutely opposed to the plans hatched in Washington for further warfare against the peoples of Indochina. According to certain circles, the American monopolists, as is well known, are achieving super-profits from this military adventure. A concrete analysis of the situation . . ."

Radio Moscow! Rogers changed the dial. It was remarkable, he thought to himself, that no matter where you were in the Middle East, Radio Moscow was always the loudest broadcast signal. As he fiddled with the dial, Rogers mused about the phrase "concrete analysis." What did it mean, exactly? Certainly not an analysis made of concrete.

Rogers eventually found another station. It was a voice speaking loudly in Arabic, with the cadence and intonation of someone shouting through a bullhorn.

". . . Zionism is a political movement organically associated with international imperialism and antagonistic to all action for liberation and to progressive movements in the world. It is racist and fanatic in its nature, aggressive, expansionist, and colonial in its aim, and fascist in its methods. Israel is the instrument of the Zionist movement, and a geographical base for world imperialism placed strategically in the midst of the Arab homeland to combat the hopes of the Arab nation for . . ."

Radio Baghdad.

Rogers turned off the radio.

A few miles past the town of Mina Abdulla, he slowed the big car and turned off the main highway onto a sandy road that ran along the beach. The road skirted an irregular row of beach houses, which prosperous Kuwaitis and westerners used as retreats during the Moslem weekend of Thursday and Friday. "Chalets" is what Kuwaitis liked to call these cottages by the steamy Persian Gulf.

Rogers parked his car outside one of the houses—a modest gray bungalow that belonged, on paper, to a senior executive of the Americo-Kuwaiti Oil Co.

Inside, it was neat but slightly faded, like an old motel. Behind a small leather-topped bar, someone had neatly arrayed bottles of whisky, gin, vodka, and brandy; in the refrigerator, Rogers found heaping platters of Arab and American food; on the kitchen table was a basket piled high with fresh fruit. On the stove was a fresh pot of coffee.

There was a musty smell in the house. Rogers opened the windows to let in the sea breeze. Then he walked into the main bedroom, opened a compartment that was hidden behind a wall painting, and checked the taping system. It was a voice-activated Wollensak that automatically recorded anything said in any room of the house. There was a second recorder, hidden in a separate place, which served as a back-up, and Rogers checked that too.

Eventually, he settled into an easy chair in the living room and fell asleep reading a book called *Arabian Sands,* the memoirs of an obscure British Arabist.

When he awoke the next day, Rogers dressed for the meeting with Jamal in his favorite corduroy suit. But instead of his normal shoes, he wore a pair of fancy cowboy boots that his wife had given him years ago, and which he had decided in subsequent years were his good-luck boots. Then he sat in a chair and waited for the Palestinian.

Jamal arrived late that afternoon. He was driving a red Buick LeSabre that threw up a great cloud of dust as it came to a stop outside the beach house.

Rogers, expecting Jamal to be in his usual black leather, was surprised to see him clothed in a neat brown business suit. His long black hair, usually touseled, was brushed straight back from his forehead and combed tightly against his head. He looked like a young college graduate going to a job interview.

Jamal approached the door warily. Rogers saw in his face a shadow of hesitation and doubt.

"Come on in," said Rogers, shaking the Palestinian's hand and pulling him inside. Having waited months to meet with Jamal, he wasn't about to lose him to last-minute indecision.

"Kadimta ahlan wa wata'ta sahlan," said Rogers, using the formal Arabic greeting that means: You come as a member of the family, you walk on friendly ground. As he spoke the words, he put his hand over his heart.

Jamal made no response. He carefully eyed the room.

"Sit down. Make yourself comfortable. Let me take your coat."

The Palestinian shook his head no. Rogers looked at him carefully and noticed a slight bulge in the jacket under the left armpit.

"Please," said Rogers quietly. "No guns."

He waited for Jamal to remove the gun. When he didn't, Rogers spoke again evenly.

"This is a bad way to begin a friendship, to come into my house with a gun. Especially when I have no weapon to threaten you."

Jamal narrowed his eye, as if measuring Rogers. The American looked even taller than usual in his cowboy boots.

Rogers held his breath.

Jamal removed his coat, slowly, revealing the shoulder holster and an automatic pistol.

"I am sorry," said the Palestinian. He removed the gun carefully from the holster. The pistol was now pointed directly at Rogers. For an instant, it occurred to Rogers that the Palestinian might shoot. But then he laid the pistol gently on the table.

"I am sorry," repeated Jamal. "I always carry a gun. It becomes a habit."

Rogers relaxed. He offered Jamal a cigarette. The Palestinian insisted that Rogers take one of his. They both sat silent for a moment, smoking their Marlboros.

"Now I must ask you a question," said Jamal. "Is there a tape recorder in this house?"

Rogers thought a moment before responding. Without honesty, he told himself, there is no possibility for trust.

"Yes," said Rogers, looking his guest straight in the eye. "It is a standard practice."

"Disconnect it, please," said Jamal.

Rogers deliberated another long moment.

"I can't," he replied finally. "I could pretend to turn it off, but in doing so I would automatically activate a second system, which is installed for situations like this. There is no point in trying to deceive you. The tape recorder is part of our business."

Jamal was silent for a long time. He turned away and faced the sea, so that his face was hidden from Rogers. Eventually he turned back.

"Let us go for a walk in the desert," said Jamal.

"A reasonable compromise," said Rogers. He gathered a blanket and a thermos of coffee.

"I have brought something for you," said Jamal when they were seated on the sand a half mile from the house.

He passed Rogers a sheet of paper bearing a neatly typed list of five Arab names. Beside each was a second name and a number.

Jamal looked away from Rogers as he handed over the list. The transaction embarrassed him, just as it had embarrassed him to enter the safehouse. He was pulled in two directions: his head told him that meeting the American intelligence officer would serve the Palestinian cause; his heart told him that it was treason.

"I am providing you with this list of names because I have been authorized to do so," said the Palestinian in a flat tone of voice.

"Who are these people?" asked Rogers, studying the names and numbers. The list was typed on plain white paper, with no markings that might disclose its source.

"They are members of the group that tried to hijack the plane in Munich last month. They are accomplices of the three who were arrested. The five accomplices were travelling on false Iraqi passports. The list shows their real names, their false names, and the passport numbers."

"Are they members of Fatah?"

"No," said Jamal. "They are all members of the Democratic Front for the Liberation of Palestine."

Rogers nodded. The DFLP was the commando group with the closest ties to the Soviet Union.

"You said you were authorized to give me this list," said Rogers. "By who?"

"The Old Man."

"Why?"

"Because Fatah opposes international terrorist operations. They are the tactic of madmen and provocateurs. Terrorism harms our cause."

Rogers looked at him curiously. He found Jamal's embarrassment more convincing than his speech.

The two men sat side by side on the blanket, legs crossed beneath them, staring west toward the setting sun. The springtime moss was turning a deeper green in the fading light.

Rogers poured Jamal a cup of coffee. The smell of the coffee was intoxicating in the desert air. As he poured a cup for himself, Rogers tried to decide whether to believe the Palestinian. He knew what the specialists back at Langley would say about the list of terrorists. That it was a throwaway. That the Palestinians must have assumed that the Munich police had already obtained the same information during interrogation of the three bombers. That it was an obvious ploy, which made Jamal more suspicious, rather than more trustworthy. Rogers knew the arguments the specialists would make because he had heard them in dozens of other cases. Usually, in his experience, the specialists were wrong. Sitting in Langley, they didn't see the nervousness on an agent's face as he met a case officer for the first time, or the look of distaste in his eyes as he took the first steps toward cooperation. They didn't understand the nuances that made one person believable and another an obvious phony.

Rogers watched Jamal's discomfort and wanted to say something reassuring. He recalled a passage from an Arab poet named Al-Moutannabi that he had memorized a decade ago while he was at language school.

It was about fate, and he recited it for Jamal in classical Arabic, the language of the Koran:

"'We have walked along the path of life that was laid down for us, as must men whose steps have been ordained.'"

Jamal stared at Rogers. He looked tense and unhappy, as if he was about to explode.

"I am not a spy!" said the Palestinian suddenly. "I am not your agent! That is not my fate!"

"Of course not," said Rogers.

"I am instructed in everything I do by the Old Man."

"I understand," said Rogers.

"Good," said Jamal.

There was silence. The Palestinian, having vented his frustration, seemed to sit a little easier.

"Does anyone else in Fatah, other than the Old Man, know that you are here?" asked Rogers eventually.

"No," said Jamal.

"That is sensible," said Rogers. There was another interlude of silence. Okay, thought Rogers. At least it's clear what he thinks he's doing. He is an emissary from the highest level of the PLO to the United States. A conduit for information, not an agent. If that explanation makes him feel better, let him believe it. Rogers remembered some advice that an instructor had given him a decade ago. It doesn't matter whether an agent is a double or a triple. So long as you know which.

"You shouldn't be ashamed to talk with us," ventured Rogers. "We're not quite as bad as you may think."

The Palestinian smiled for the first time.

"How can I not feel ashamed? Meeting with an American spy in secret in the desert. It is shameful. But do not worry. We Arabs have grown used to shame. It is like our mother's milk. We live on it."

The afternoon light was fading.

"Where were you born in Palestine?" asked Rogers.

"I was born in Iraq. My father went there in 1941 to work with the Germans."

"There is an Arab saying," said Rogers. " 'If she gets pregnant in Baghdad, she will give birth in Beirut.' Perhaps that is your story."

Jamal laughed. "You know too many Arab proverbs. Is that part of your spy training?"

"A hobby," said Rogers.

Jamal lit up a cigarette, cupping the match in his hands to shield it from the wind of the desert. He ran his hand through his jet-black hair so that it blew in the desert breeze.

He is a vain man, Rogers thought to himself. Handsome. Clever. A born operator.

"I am a man who has barely seen his own country," said Jamal, resuming his story. "We returned to Palestine from Iraq

in 1945 but didn't stay very long. My father was killed in
1948 by an Israeli bomb and my mother and I fled, first to
Beirut, then to Cairo. I graduated from Cairo University in
1964. I have been moving ever since: to Kuwait, to Beirut, to
Amman, to Europe. I am like the Bob Dylan song. A rolling
stone."

"You listen to Bob Dylan?" asked Rogers.

"I am a child of the 1960s," said Jamal. "A flower child."

My ass, thought Rogers. But he was right in a way. There
was something about Jamal that captured the spirit of the
time. The long hair, the sexuality, the worldliness that he
seemed to have soaked up during his years of travel in the
Mideast and Europe.

"Let me ask you a question," said the Palestinian. "Why
are you going to so much trouble to meet with me?"

Rogers thought for a moment. Tell him the truth, he said to
himself.

"The United States Government wants to establish a direct
line of contact with you. They authorized me to take whatever
measures I thought were appropriate."

"But why did you go to Amman during the fighting? You
might have been kidnapped or killed."

"Do you want an honest answer?" asked Rogers.

"Of course."

"Because I felt that without some personal gesture by me,
something that would challenge your assumptions about my
organization, the operation would fail. Anyway, it wasn't
really dangerous. Nobody in the Middle East would dare harm
a representative of the United States."

"This is what I like about Americans," said Jamal. "They
are so naive. And so sincere."

Rogers smiled.

"It is true," he replied. "We are naive. But in this part of
the world, where everyone is so worldly, perhaps that is not
such a bad thing."

"What do you mean?" asked Jamal.

"I've spent ten years now in the Arab world," answered
Rogers. "I've watched things go from bad to worse. I've seen
the Arabs turned into cripples, humiliated by their enemies,
mistrusted by their friends. Always blaming the Israelis for
everything that goes wrong."

Jamal nodded. It was true. Who could deny it?

"But the Israelis aren't to blame for the tragedy of the Arabs," continued Rogers. "I blame the Arabs themselves. They have become corrupted. By money, by the Russians, by too many lies. I truly believe that the only answer for the Arabs—above all, for your people, the Palestinians—lies with the United States. And I believe that we—you and I—can alter this story."

Jamal clucked his tongue.

"I am serious," said Rogers.

"What are you saying?" demanded Jamal.

"I am telling you that you and I, personally, can help change the story of the Middle East."

"How?" answered Jamal. "Impossible!"

"I mean exactly what I said. I believe that a secret relationship between you and me—between Fatah and the United States—can change the history of this part of the world."

"Your words may be sincere," said the Palestinian. "But the dream is impossible."

The sun had set now and the desert was turning chilly. The two men rose from the blanket and walked together back to the beach house.

"Do you have any whisky in the house?" asked Jamal. "I am a corrupted Arab."

Rogers poured a double Scotch for Jamal and one for himself. He thought for a moment about the tape recorder and decided the hell with Langley. He turned on a radio, near the microphone in the living room. That should drive the transcribers crazy, he said to himself. Hours of Arabic ballads and chanting from the Koran.

"Come out on the deck," he said to Jamal.

The Palestinian appreciated the gesture. He brought with him the bottle of whisky.

"So how do we change history?" asked Jamal, sipping his whisky and looking at the play of moonlight on the calm waters of the Gulf.

"By making peace," said Rogers.

"On whose terms? Ours or the Zionists'?"

"Neither," said Rogers. "Those of the United States of America."

"For you Americans, the word 'peace' is like a narcotic. It lulls you to sleep, and you think it will do the same for everybody else. But it won't!"

"There is an American peace plan on the table," said Rogers. "I sent you a copy."

"Yes, and the Old Man was pleased to receive it. But the Soviets told him when he was in Moscow last month that the American peace plan is dead."

"They may be right, about the current version," said Rogers.

Jamal looked at him with genuine astonishment. In the Middle East, such candor was rare indeed.

"The situation isn't ripe yet," continued Rogers. "The Egyptians and Israelis are telling us privately that they are interested in negotiations. But they are also in the midst of a war of attrition along the Suez Canal. For now, they would both probably rather fight than make peace."

"That is what the Old Man says," answered Jamal. "He is waiting for the next war."

"So are we," said Rogers. "That is the sad truth about the Middle East. The opportunities for creative diplomacy come after wars."

"People who are humiliated in war cannot make peace," said Jamal. "The Arabs must win this time."

Rogers poured another glass of whisky for Jamal and one for himself.

"Let us suppose that after the next war, there are peace negotiations," said Rogers. "Would Fatah agree to join in discussions?"

"That depends," replied the Palestinian.

"On what?" pressed Rogers.

Jamal laughed.

"You are asking questions as if I was a foreign minister," he said. "But I don't even have a country."

They stopped for food and more drink. The bottle of whisky was soon gone and they opened another. It was past midnight when they turned to the most delicate topic: the looming conflict in Jordan between the king and the commandos.

Jamal probed to understand the American position.

"If there is a real civil war in Jordan, will the United States stay out?" he asked.

"I can't answer that," said Rogers.

"Suppose there was a constitutional monarchy, with a Palestinian prime minister. Would America recognize such a government?"

"I can't answer that either," said Rogers.

"Well, what *can* you tell me?" demanded Jamal.

Rogers spoke very carefully. He had been briefed in detail on how to respond to queries about the situation in Jordan.

"The United States believes that the problems of the Palestinian people shouldn't be solved at the expense of Jordan. The King is a loyal friend of America, and the United States will support him in taking appropriate measures to protect his kingdom. We hope that Fatah will act responsibly to avoid a confrontation. Fatah shouldn't doubt American resolve on the Jordan issue."

Jamal listened intently. Rogers suspected that he was trying to commit the statement to memory.

"Would you like that in writing?" asked Rogers.

"Please," said the Palestinian. He looked embarrassed, as if he had been caught in the midst of his own espionage operation.

Rogers retreated to the bedroom and retrieved from his brief case two sheets of paper. He handed Jamal the one that contained the Jordan position, nearly word for word identical to what he had just said.

Jamal read the text several times.

"It looks to me as if you are telling us to go to hell!" said the Palestinian.

"No," said Rogers. "But perhaps we are telling you to go to Lebanon."

"And then?"

"On behalf of the President, I give you a commitment that the United States respects the legitimate rights and aspirations of the Palestinian people and will seek a just solution to the Palestinian problem in all its aspects, based on the principles set forth in United Nations Resolution 242."

"Copy, please."

Rogers handed him the second sheet of paper, stating the American position on the Palestinian problem.

"What does this statement mean?" asked Jamal.

"We shall discover that together," said the American, more than a little curious himself.

The sun rose in a quick burst of pink at the eastern rim of the Persian Gulf, and then climbed majestically in the sky amid deeper tones of red and gold. Rogers and Jamal watched this splendid sight from their chairs on the deck of the beach house, where they sat drinking Turkish coffee.

"What do you want from me?" asked Jamal as he sipped his coffee.

"We want security assistance. We want to know about terrorist operations that endanger the lives of Americans. We want more of what you just brought me: names, dates, passport numbers, work names. You say that you oppose international terrorist operations. Then help us!"

"What is the benefit for Fatah?"

"The promise of American help in resolving the Palestinian problem. If you are honest, you will realize that this provides the only realistic chance of achieving your goals."

"How will you protect me from the Israelis?" asked Jamal.

"We won't. That's your problem. But we do guarantee to keep the fact of your contact with us secret. If you agree to continue meeting with me, your identity will be known by only four people: me, the chief of station in Beirut, my division chief, and the Director of Central Intelligence. All of us will do our best to protect this operation."

"And if you make a mistake?"

"We don't make mistakes," said Rogers. "I haven't lost an agent in ten years."

"I'm not an agent!" said Jamal sharply.

"Of course not," answered Rogers quickly. He thought for a moment that he had blown it.

Jamal rubbed his eyeballs. In the soft morning light, he looked younger and more vulnerable than he had the previous day.

"Will you work with us?" said Rogers. He was a salesman now and it was time to close the deal.

"It's not my decision alone. I have to discuss it with the Old Man."

"That's not enough. I need an answer!"

"You already have it."

"What is it?" said Rogers, raising his voice.

"It is not no."

"Say it!"

"Yes," said Jamal at last. "I will work with you. If the Old Man approves."

"Will you tell him everything about our meeting?"

"Almost everything. But not everything. There are some things he wouldn't understand."

"Then we have a deal," said Rogers, shaking Jamal's hand.

He sat back in his chair, put his lucky cowboy boots up on the railing of the deck, and watched the sun climb upwards in the heavens.

PART IV

March – May 1970

15

Yakov Levi noted Rogers's return to Beirut on a file card in a box he kept at the office. Levi entered the dates of the trip and the notation: "Kuwait." The entry followed one marked: "Amman." The information came from a contact at the airport who provided passenger lists and, when necessary, photographs of passengers.

It was a puzzle, Levi thought to himself. Why was Rogers taking these trips? What was he doing? Who was he meeting?

Levi fretted about such puzzles, and about most things. He was a short, wiry man, with dark features and a look of perpetual uneasiness. His family was from Marseilles, he told friends, with a few distant relatives from Corsica. He was a nervous man with a bad stomach, who chewed antacid pills through the day in the vain hope that they would relieve the tension that was eating away at his gut.

Yakov Levi's problem was that he didn't exist. Not in Beirut, at least. There was no one in the city by that name. There was instead a Frenchman, an import-export trader named Jacques Beaulieu, and Levi lived inside his skin. The worldly Monsieur Beaulieu worked in an office on the Rue de Phenice in West Beirut, several blocks from the St. Georges Hotel. The brass plaque on the door said "Franco-Lebanese Trading Co." It was a busy little import-export firm, quite profitable, it was said, staffed by a handful of bright young men and women who were well-mannered, spoke French, English, and Arabic, and had a wide circle of acquaintances in

Lebanon. Members of the firm travelled extensively in the
Arab world and had a reputation for paying generous commis-
sions on business deals.

Levi's import-export firm was, in reality, the Mossad station in Beirut. His family had indeed lived in Marseilles once,
but no longer. The survivors now lived in Israel. All except
for Yakov Levi, who called himself Beaulieu. He was a Jew,
living secretly in the midst of Arabs who wanted to kill him,
and he was perpetually frightened. A fear so deep and con-
stant that it had entered his body and flowed in his veins. He
had been in Beirut for three years, burning out his circuits day
by day. A few months ago they had promised him a fancy
desk job back home at the end of the year, but he didn't
believe them. It was a lie, told to keep him living a few more
months in Hell.

The Mossad station in Beirut, the very fact of its existence,
was one of the few true secrets in a town where gossip and
spying were a way of life. The station had been in operation,
in various locations, since 1951. The Americans hadn't a clue
where it was, nor had the Deuxième Bureau, nor had anyone
else. The Israelis who worked for Franco-Lebanese Trading
didn't tell a soul their true identities or what they were really
doing.

They were Israel's eyes and ears in the Arab world. They
serviced dead drops, acted as couriers, spotted potential
agents, scouted the terrain. They might recommend the recruitment of a particular Lebanese or Palestinian, but they
never did the actual recruiting or handling. That was too dangerous. One false move would blow the station's cover. They
left such tasks to Mossad officers in Europe, who could meet
agents easily in Paris or Rome, receive their information, pay
them their stipends. In Lebanon, the handful of Mossad officers were under a cover so deep that they didn't like to talk,
even to each other, about their real work.

Watching the Americans was part of Levi's job. Identifying
the intelligence agents among them, tracking them, trying to
understand what they were doing in secret in the Middle East
behind the veil of America's public policy. Levi was perfect
for the job. He believed almost nothing that anyone said, least
of all the Americans.

Levi had been watching Tom Rogers for more than six

months. He was convinced that he was a CIA case officer, but that part was easy. All you had to do was study the diplomatic list and look for the odd man out. The person whose résumé didn't quite make sense: who had been a consular officer one place and a commercial attaché somewhere else and was now a political officer. Or you could look for social quirks: a political officer who didn't attend the Christmas party given by the head of the political section at the embassy. Or if you were still stumped, you could look at the State Department's foreign service list, published in Washington. With chilling precision it listed the CIA officers under diplomatic cover as "reserve" officers of the foreign service—"FSRs," they were called—rather than as full-fledged FSOs.

Some cover! thought Levi. The Americans could afford to be so sloppy. They were rich and powerful. And they were not Jews.

Walking to his office on the Rue de Phenice, Levi could see the grand facade of the American Embassy on the Corniche. He would look to the fifth floor, where the CIA officers worked, and try to imagine what they were doing and thinking. It was easy with some of them. The case officers who handled Lebanese politicians were so clumsy they left footprints all over town. Others, like the new man Rogers, were more careful. They looked, from a distance, as if they were almost clever enough to be Mossad officers. That worried Levi, and it made his stomach hurt.

Watching the Palestinians was the other part of Levi's job. In some ways that was easier than watching the Americans. It was almost too easy, with too many tidbits of information in the air and too many tracks to follow. The Palestinians were braggarts. Rather than trying to conceal their military and intelligence operations, they boasted about them. And they fought over who would control them. Levi made it a practice to check out gunfights in Fakhani, because they often involved rival Fatah officers dueling for control of units, or operations, or money.

Levi despised the Palestinians. That hatred was part of what kept him going. The Palestinians were so thoroughly corrupt. And they were spoiled by the other Arabs, who were terrified of them. To become rich, all a PLO official needed to do was gather up a band of scruffy refugees in a place like

Qatar or Abu Dhabi, let the local Emir know that trouble was brewing, and wait for the payoff to arrive. It was so easy to buy PLO officials that Levi wondered whether the solution to the Arab-Israeli conflict might lie, not in another war, but in a takeover bid.

He watched the Palestinians with a horrid fascination, hating what he saw, his hatred in turn feeding his curiosity about the nature of his enemies. He was fascinated by their sexual habits. The Old Man, for example, had never been known to sleep with a woman. Who, then, did he sleep with? Levi wanted to believe that he slept with little boys. That would be exactly, perfectly right. Levi wanted evidence to support his theory, but where could he look? He couldn't very well ask young boys in Fakhani whether they had ever been molested by a man in guerrilla fatigues.

And then there were the playboys, the young men in Fatah's so-called intelligence service. There was Abu Namli, who bought his whisky by the case and frequented the whorehouses of Zeituny with a fat roll of dollar bills, buying two or three girls at a time. There was Abu Nasir, cool and austere, who liked to use women for other tasks, such as planting bombs.

And there was Abu Nasir's assistant, a flamboyant young man named Jamal Ramlawi. Levi was convinced that Ramlawi was the mystery Palestinian in the recent scandal involving the French diplomat's wife. There was no proof, but there were many rumors. Agents had even seen a dark-haired European woman near Ramlawi's office in Fakhani. It had to be Ramlawi. He was notorious in Beirut as a ladies' man. He had been seen in every nightclub and bistro in town. He was almost reckless in his behavior. So reckless that Levi wondered, as he thought about it, whether the young Palestinian's disregard for what most people liked to keep secret might conceal a deeper secret. That was a possibility. Levi made a note to open a new index card in the Palestinian file. And to start checking Ramlawi's travels more carefully.

Levi could remember dimly the time when he hadn't been scared. That was before he joined Mossad, when he was just a simple solider. When all he was required to do for the state of Israel was to risk the chance of dying once, in war. As an intelligence officer, he had already died a thousand times.

Levi liked to remember how he had joined the Israel intelligence service. It was a way of pinching himself, reminding himself that he had once had another life.

He had been serving in the army. That wasn't unusual. All Israelis join the army. But he was very fit and very clever, so he was allowed to join the paratroops, which made his parents proud. And he was so good in the paratroops that they asked him to join the special operations unit, where he was a team leader.

Perhaps the fear began then. Levi had made a jump into southern Sudan, with a team of Israelis who were helping to foment a civil war there between the Moslems of the north and the Christians of the south. The Israelis provided guns and training for the southerners, on the theory that if the Moslem-dominated regime in Khartoum was pinned down by internal strife, it couldn't do much to help Nasser in Egypt make war on Israel. That assignment was only frightening for the few minutes before the jump. After that it was easy. Either you died or you didn't.

After a year in special operations, he left the military and attended university. It was enough, he had done his service. A few months later the phone rang. Go to an address in downtown Tel Aviv tomorrow. No explanation, except that it was for the army. They spent four days asking questions, assembling every detail of his life history. The family's background in France. Old addresses and telephone numbers in Marseilles. Old passport numbers and the names and addresses of dead relatives. A former girlfriend called to ask whether he had done anything wrong, because an investigator had just spent the entire day asking questions about him.

And then the ruse. He was called back to the army for more training. A three-month advanced intelligence course. Okay. Fine. No problem. Everyone in Israel is in the army. Then another course. A more advanced intelligence course, at a much higher salary, the salary of an Israeli Army captain, which was a small fortune in those days. By this time it was becoming obvious what was happening. The subjects covered in the course included covert communications, demolition, small-arms training, how to operate inside urban areas.

And finally the graduation ceremony. He was roused from

bed in the middle of the night and taken to the airport, where he was given a false French passport and $10, put on a plane, and flown to Frankfurt, West Germany. Leaving the plane they gave him an address and told him to be there in ten days. Until then he was on his own, speaking no German, with $10 in his pocket. He had to survive in a strange country for more than a week without giving away his identity.

So what did he do? He survived. He stole a car and drove around Germany. He was a French student on holiday, he told people. He lived by stealing money. Purses, wallets. It helped that he hated Germans. He arrived ten days later at the address they had given him driving a brown Mercedes, with a new set of clothes and the lipstick of his German girlfriend still on his cheek. He was one of the few recruits who made it. Some of the other boys had slept in the bushes near the airport, eaten food from trash cans, and called the Israeli Embassy in desperation after two days. They were not survivors, like Levi. Perhaps they were not scared enough.

They said, Okay. You have survived. You are one of us. Go to France, to Marseilles. Settle down. Disappear. Take classes at the university. Build an identity. Apply for a passport. It's legal; you were born in France. Here are the supporting documents. Money arrived every month at a numbered bank account in Nice. It was like a long vacation, until the French passport arrived in the mail. A few days later came a message from a Mossad case officer, and the beginning of the awful fear.

Levi went to work as a courier, making runs behind the Iron Curtain. He travelled as a French businessman, servicing dead drops and agents in Warsaw, Prague, Lithuania, Kiev, Moscow. He carried money, messages, assignments for Mossad agents in the East. They were Jews, nearly all of them. People as frightened and determined to survive as Levi was. He would collect their information in a quick meeting at a railway station in Warsaw, or in a brush pass in a Moscow subway station, or by retrieving a set of documents from a metal can hidden in the spout of a rain gutter in Bratislava. he travelled on a precise itinerary, pre-programmed down to the minute. Each contact set for a precise time, with a fall-back twenty-four hours later in a different place if the agent didn't show or the dead drop was empty.

All he could really remember about those trips was the fear. The perspiration dripping down his shirt as he stood in the line for passport control, the struggle to control his voice when a policeman stopped him on the street on his way to meet an agent and asked him where he was going. So scared that he worried he would shit in his pants. So scared that he couldn't think of anything else except surviving and staying alive. And when he had crossed the frontier at last, and made it out alive, he would go back to Marseilles and wait, like a condemned man, to do it again.

He was very good at it. One of the best. That was Levi's curse. It had landed him in Beirut.

We are pushing at the seams, the chief of the Mossad station in Beirut liked to tell his young officers. Pushing at the seams of a garment that is unravelling. The Arab world is a myth. There are no Arabs. There are Christians and Moslems; Palestinians and Syrians and Lebanese; Sunnis and Shiites and Druse and Maronites and Melchites and Alawites and Copts and Kurds. They live in make-believe countries that were created by the colonialists of Europe. The fabric is ready to break, the station chief would say. The false thread of Arabism won't last another generation. Just look, he would say, at Lebanon.

The chief of station was a man named Ze'ev Shuval and Levi was in awe of him. He became convinced, in the way that a junior officer can, that it was Shuval who kept them all alive. But for the station chief, Levi thought, they might all walk through the streets of Beirut singing the Israeli national anthem, the Hatikva. Shuval was restless, thoughtful, playful, and furtive. He had translucent skin, a face that was slightly reddish and freckled, and a balding head with the few remaining strands of hair combed carefully over the top. He looked like a prim and proper French businessman. His French was nearly flawless, but there was a hint of another accent—perhaps Dutch—from long ago.

Shuval invited Levi to dinner one night in the spring of 1970. Did Levi remember, as he rang the doorbell that evening, that there was anything special about that particular night? And was he surprised to see several other people from the station at the chief's house? The other guests included a young woman who worked as a courier when she wasn't typing letters and weigh bills, and a couple in their mid-forties who handled bugs and cameras and other surveillance gear.

Levi did not realize what was happening at first that night at Shuval's apartment. He saw Shuval's wife go to the window and close the blinds tightly, but that was normal enough. He noticed that there was one extra place at the dinner table, but maybe they were expecting someone else for dessert. It was only when he looked carefully at the table itself that he realized what Shuval had done. Laid out on the table were a plate with three pieces of matzoh; a roasted shank bone; a sprig of parsley next to a dish of salted water; the top of a horseradish root; a boiled egg; and a paste made of apples and nuts.

Shuval is mad, thought Levi. It is too dangerous to celebrate Passover here. Someone will see us. Someone will hear us. But Shuval emerged from the kitchen smiling broadly. He had on his head a yarmulke and presented one to Levi and the other male guest.

"Will someone please turn on the radio," said Shuval. Levi turned the knob. The radio was turned to the Voice of the Arabs from Cairo, which was repeating a week-old speech by President Nasser. The Egyptian leader was talking in a monotone about the efficiency of Egyptian industry.

"Thank you," said Shuval.

The lights were dimmed and Shuval's wife went to light the candles. With tears streaming down his face, Levi listened as Shuval recited the traditional blessing of the candles in a voice that was quiet, just above a whisper, but still rising above the drone of Nasser's speech.

Barub Atab Adonai Eloheinu . . .

"In praising God, we say that all life is sacred. In kindling festive lights, we preserve life's sanctity."

Levi was crying. So was the code clerk. But Shuval's voice was strong and full of hope.

"With every holy light we kindle, the world is brightened to a higher harmony. We praise thee, O Lord our God, majestic sovereign of all life who hallows our lives with commandments and bids us kindle festive holy light."

"Sit down, everyone," said Shuval's wife.

Levi looked at the table. The matzoh, because there had been no time fleeing Egypt to make leavened bread. The tender herbs of spring, the green of hope and renewal, to be dipped in the salt water of tears. And the maror, the bitter horseradish root, standing for the bitterness of life in Egypt, and the greater bitterness and pain of the 2,500 years of exile in the Diaspora. And the sweet paste of apples and honey, the mortar with which we build our dreams.

For once, Levi felt that he understood what he was doing in Beirut and remembered that he was part of a very long journey indeed.

16

Beirut; March 1970

Rogers returned home from Kuwait to find Hoffman in an especially cranky mood. A few days earlier, a crisis had erupted in Lebanon between the Christian militia and the Palestinian commandos.

Like so much else in Lebanon, it was a game of tit for tat. Christian gunmen had ambushed a Palestinian funeral procession as it passed through the village of Kahhaleh along the Beirut–Damascus highway. The Christians claimed that the mourners were carrying weapons illegally. Palestinian commandos in the Tal Zaatar refugee camp retaliated by attacking a neighboring Christian suburb. Gunfire had spread to other parts of the city and there were fears that the fighting would escalate.

The lights were still on in Hoffman's office when Rogers stopped by the embassy on his way in from the airport. The station chief looked exhausted. He was sweaty and unshaven, with a cigarette in his mouth, a cup of coffee in one hand and a telephone in the other.

"How nice of you to join us," said Hoffman with elaborate politeness when he got off the phone.

Roger sensed that he was in the doghouse, but he wasn't sure why.

"If it wouldn't be too much trouble," continued Hoffman, "perhaps you could help us with a little intelligence collection, before this whole fucking country goes up in smoke!"

Roger began to apologize, but the station chief cut him off.

"Save it for the chaplain," said Hoffman.

"What in the world is going on?" asked Rogers.

"That, my dear boy, depends on who you talk to. If you ask the Ministry of Interior, there are 'unreliable rumors of civil disturbances in certain areas.' If you ask people in Dikwana, there's a God-damn war going on. So, take your pick."

"Need some help?" asked Rogers.

"How thoughtful of you to ask," said Hoffman, reverting to his earlier tone of sarcasm. "If it's not too taxing after your travels, maybe you could contact your little friend in Fatah and find out what in the name of Jesus is going on over there. Seeing as how we're on the verge of a civil war. If it wouldn't be too much trouble, that is."

"Consider it done," said Rogers. "As soon as I can reach him."

"There's one more thing, hotshot," growled Hoffman. "Headquarters is complaining about a smart-aleck cable that you supposedly sent from Kuwait. Stone has written both of us a polite note in agency-ese. Here's a brief translation: If you ever pull a stunt like that again, he'll have your ass! Got it?"

Rogers obediently nodded. So that's why Hoffman is so agitated, he thought to himself.

"By the way," called out Hoffman as Rogers was halfway down the hall. "How was your trip?"

Jane Rogers was sitting in the living room, reading to the children, when her husband returned home. She was wearing a tweed skirt and a pullover sweater. In the light of the reading lamp, her face had the stark contrast of a chiaroscuro: the hair black and deep in shadow, the skin white and luminous.

Jane was overjoyed to see her husband. Rogers hadn't called to tell her when he would be coming home. He usually didn't, for security reasons. She gave him a long hug and, when it was time to let go, she hugged him again.

"We were a little nervous the last few days," she said when the children were out of earshot.

"I gather from Frank you've had some fireworks," said Rogers, already beginning to feel guilty.

"We heard gunfire on the Corniche two days ago. The bawab downstairs said it was just a wedding party, but they always say that. Then Binky Garrett from the embassy came by and warned that we should stay indoors at night and stock up on food."

"Binky is an idiot," said Rogers.

Rogers noticed then that the apartment had the look of an air-raid shelter. The curtains were drawn tight and the pantry was piled high with canned goods. Stacked in the hall were three cases of mineral water.

"I probably overreacted," said Jane.

Rogers tried to say that he was sorry, but no words came out. He was mute, silenced by remorse for leaving his family alone and in danger.

"Kids okay?" asked Rogers eventually.

"Fine," said Jane.

"Mark?"

"He's fine. He missed his daddy."

"And Amy? How is Amy?"

Rogers's heart was racing as he asked the question. The one thing on earth that truly frightened him was the health of his two-year-old daughter.

"She's better," said Jane. "The doctor says she's doing much better."

"Thank God!" said Rogers. He felt for a moment a sense of lightness, as if a weight had been lifted from his body. But he couldn't quite believe the good news, and his doubt showed on his face.

"She's in the other room," said Jane. "Go see for yourself."

Rogers walked toward the children's playroom, brightly painted and cluttered with toys. He carried with him a bag of gifts he had brought from Kuwait.

"Daddy's home," called out Rogers in the direction of the play room.

"What did you bring us?" shouted Mark.

The boy raced toward his father. He was dressed in a Boston Red Sox baseball cap and a T-shirt that said "Amherst 198?"

Amy followed, more slowly. She was a beautiful child: curly blond hair, an easy smile, red cheeks, wearing a white summer dress embroidered with flowers. She ran with the choppy, bowlegged steps of a toddler. Halfway to Daddy, she tumbled on the carpet.

Rogers winced. He picked her up and gave her a hug.

"She's not perfect yet," explained Jane. "But better."

"Amy," said Rogers. "Here's a present for you."

He reached into the bag and gave her a handmade doll he had bought in Kuwait, dressed Arab-style in harem pants and a veil. The baby took the doll in her hands and began to remove its clothes. As she was removing the pants, the doll slipped from her fingers and dropped to the floor.

Rogers picked up the doll from the floor and handed it back to his daughter gently.

"You'll see," said Jane. "She's really much steadier."

Rogers gave his son a poster advertising the Kuwait national soccer team. It showed a camel kicking a soccer ball and bore the legend: "Our Camel Is a Winner!"

"Wow!" said Mark, who was already something of a soccer buff.

Rogers hadn't the heart to tell his son that the 1970 Kuwait soccer team was one of the worst in the world. Bad even by the modest standards of the Persian Gulf. Their camel, in point of fact, was not a winner.

"So who's leading the Lebanese Soccer League?" Rogers asked his son, who studied the league tables every morning in the paper.

"The Druse!" said the boy. "By one point."

"What about the Shiites?" asked Rogers. When he left they had been leading the league.

"Third place," said his son.

What a country, thought Rogers. Religion was so embedded in the life of the nation that it even dominated athletics. If you asked any soccer fan—even one in grade school, like Mark—he would break down the first division of the Lebanese Soccer League by religious sects: a Druse Moslem team; a Shiite Moslem team; two Sunni Moslem teams from West Beirut; three Maronite Christian teams from East Beirut; a Greek Orthodox team; a Sunni team from Tripoli; a Maronite team from Zgharta; and two Armenian teams, one leftist and one rightist. (Mark looked at his father apprehensively.)

"Daddy, will they keep playing soccer if there is a war?"

"Don't be silly," said Rogers. "There isn't going to be a

war in Lebanon. Who put that idea in your head?"

"Nobody," said Mark. He looked relieved.

When the children had gone to bed, Rogers gave Jane a bracelet he had bought in the gold souk in Kuwait. He put it on her wrist as tenderly as he could.

"Let's have a drink," said Jane.

Rogers returned with a glass of vodka and orange juice for his wife and a tumbler of whisky for himself. He sat down on the couch. Jane curled up next to him.

"I feel guilty about leaving you alone," said Rogers.

"That's good. You should. You were a shit to leave us alone."

She frowned, and then kissed her husband gently on the cheek.

"Where did Mark pick up all this war talk?" asked Rogers.

"It's everywhere. At school. In the market. That was the scary part, actually. As soon as the fighting started, everybody automatically seemed to think things would get much worse."

"What did people say?"

"Rumors, gossip. You know the Arabs, how they're always talking. Well, this time they really had something to gossip about, and they couldn't stop. The flower man on Sadat Street said the Moslems in the Lebanese Army wouldn't fire on the Palestinians if it came to a fight. He said they would refuse to obey orders from Christian officers. I asked him how he knew and he just winked. And the Christian ladies at Smith's grocery were the same way. They all claimed to have friends in East Beirut who knew someone in the Christian militia. When I asked what was going to happen, they would cluck their tongues. What does that mean?"

"It depends," said Rogers. "In this case, it probably meant they didn't know anything but didn't want to admit it."

"They say the crisis isn't over yet," said Jane.

"Who says?"

"The ladies in Smith's."

"Ahhhh." Rogers laughed. "Reliable sources."

"It's strange," she continued. "I think of this country as so calm and friendly and modern. I didn't realize there was so much tension under the surface, until these last few days."

Rogers hugged her. This seemed to be a night for hugging.

"Let's go to bed," said Jane.

They made love tenderly, Rogers trying to express in bed the things he had wanted to say, but couldn't. They were nearly asleep when Rogers spoke.

"What did the doctor say about Amy?"

"I told you," said Jane drowsily. "She's getting better. And in a few months she'll be as good as new."

"Do you believe him?" asked Rogers.

"This time I think I really do," said Jane. She was warm against Rogers's side, like a cat.

Rogers lit a cigarette and thought about Amy.

"Do you forgive me for what happened?" asked Rogers. There was no answer. Jane had fallen asleep.

For Rogers, what had happened to Amy was a metaphor for what was worst and most frightening about the Middle East. It started as a mysterious disease that nobody seemed to understand or know how to treat. Rogers had never in his life felt more helpless or scared.

It began one day in Oman, when Amy was nearly eighteen months old. She had been having trouble walking—she was much slower at it than Mark had been—and was only gradually learning to creep around the room. And then one day she fell down. She picked herself up, and fell down again. At first it seemed funny—helpless and cute—but it happened over and over again, and by the next day it was obvious to Rogers and his wife that something was wrong. Then Amy started to drop things. Cookies, toys, her bottle.

They went to see their pediatrician. His name was Dr. Abdel-Salaam Fawzi. He was an Egyptian who had been living in Muscat for many years. All the wealthy Arab and European families took their children to him.

Rogers remembered every detail of the awful day when they had gone to Dr. Fawzi's clinic and heard his diagnosis. It was hot and the waiting room smelled of garlic and cigarette smoke. The nurse had called Rogers and his wife into the doctor's office as if they were prisoners awaiting their sentences. On Dr. Fawzi's wall, Rogers had noticed, was a medical degree from the American University of Beirut, along with plaques from various Omani medical organizations and a personal testimonial from the Emir of Abu Dhabi.

"Please sit down," said the doctor. He was a stiff man, dressed in a three-piece suit despite the summer heat. He reminded Rogers of old pictures of Ottoman officials at the turn of the century: dignified and proper, wearing their fine clothes like uniforms of respectability, at once ennobled and embarrassed by their Arab roots. The doctor needed only a red fez to complete the picture.

"I have conducted a series of neurological tests on your daughter," Dr. Fawzi said solemnly. "Let me explain to you the range of possibilities that could account for her difficulties.

"The simplest explanation is that she is having a slowdown in development. This occasionally happens with children. Some do not walk until they are three or four, but they do quite well as adults. Quite well. So this could be a temporary problem that will disappear."

Jane took a deep breath. Rogers tried to steel himself for what was coming.

"There are other possibilities," said Dr. Fawzi.

"What are they?" asked Rogers.

"Well, let me see," the doctor said, stalling. Like many Arabs, he disliked giving bad news.

"The possibilities are several. They include polio. Which, of course, these days, is curable."

"Amy has been vaccinated," said Rogers.

"Yes, of course," said the doctor. "That rules out polio."

"What else?" asked Rogers.

"Well, in cases like this, where there are unexplained motor difficulties, we cannot rule out some of the more serious diseases."

"Such as?" pressed Rogers.

"Muscular dystrophy," said the doctor. Jane shuddered.

"What else?" said Rogers.

"A tumor," said the doctor.

"A brain tumor?"

"Yes, it could be a brain tumor. Possibly."

Jane looked as if she was going to faint.

"What about something infectious?" asked Rogers. "Or something that she ate?"

"I don't think that's very likely," said the doctor quickly. "Not in the Middle East today. That sort of thing is really much more prevalent in Asia or Africa than in the Arab world."

Remembering the doctor's vain and defensive manner, Rogers became angry all over again.

Amy got worse. Dr. Fawzi's demeanor grew more and more solemn. The symptoms, he said, suggested that there was a serious neurological problem. They asked friends at the embassy what to do and nobody had good suggestions. Dr. Fawzi was, after all, everybody's favorite pediatrician.

It was about then that Rogers began to think: This is my fault. I brought my family here, put them in this miserable place while I played at saving the world. My work will come to nothing, and my little daughter is going to die.

In desperation, Rogers had gone to the local hospital in Muscat. He looked at the names of the residents, and asked where they had done their training. He eventually found a young Omani, Dr. Tayib, who had gone to medical school in America, at Boston University. He went to see the young man, introduced himself as an official at the American Embassy, and explained what was happening to his daughter. Would he be willing to come back to the house and take a look at her, Rogers asked.

Dr. Tayib came that night. He was a reserved young man, the son of an Omani army officer, who had done well at medical school. It was difficult to practice medicine in the Arab world, he said, because people so often were dishonest about their symptoms.

He examined the baby. There were neurological problems, without doubt, he said. But there was a relatively simple possibility. Had the other doctor mentioned it?

"What's that?" said Rogers.

"Visceral larva migrans," said the doctor.

"What is that?" asked Jane.

"Roundworms," said Dr. Tayib. "That is the common name for them. They invade tissues and can remain alive for months. Even for years. If they aren't treated, they can go to the brain. That may be happening to your daughter."

Rogers wanted to vomit.

"How could she have gotten them?" asked Jane.

"By eating dirt, usually," said the doctor.

"Dirt?" asked Rogers.

Dirt. The dirt of the Middle East, of the barren, benighted region of the globe where Rogers had chosen to spend his life.

"Does she play outside?" asked the doctor.

"Yes," said Jane.

"And do dogs frequent the areas where she plays?"

"Yes," said Jane. "She goes looking for them. She loves dogs."

"And is it possible that the dogs have defecated where she plays?"

"I guess so," said Jane.

"It is possible that this is the explanation," said the Omani doctor. "Visceral larva migrans. We will have to run tests, of course. A biopsy of the liver. That will be a nuisance, but I would strongly suggest it."

"Yes, please," said Rogers.

"I can arrange for your regular doctor to supervise the tests," said the Omani.

"No!" said Rogers. "Absolutely not. I want you to treat my daughter."

The Omani protested that transferring the case would be awkward. But Rogers pressed him and he eventually agreed.

"Doctor," said Jane warily. "Can roundworms be cured?"

"Oh yes," said the doctor. "Quite often there is a complete recovery within six to twelve months."

Jane Rogers collapsed into her husband's arms. Rogers was still too scared to let himself believe the good news.

The Omani doctor's diagnosis proved right. Amy was suffering from roundworms. The doctor prescribed the appropriate medicine, and she began to respond to the treatment.

But there were complications, of a political sort. Dr. Fawzi, the Egyptian, was furious at the young Omani doctor for interfering in his case. He petitioned the local medical society to withdraw the young doctor's license. Later, as the Rogers were leaving Oman for Beirut, they heard that Dr. Fawzi was bringing pressure on the local hospital, through some of his wealthy patients, to have the young doctor removed from his residency.

Rogers was enraged. But the American Ambassador in Muscat insisted that he shouldn't get involved any more deeply. It was a local matter.

Now, in Beirut, Amy was getting better. It was like a re-prieve. Like one of the Old Testament stories where God devises a terrible punishment but in the end, for reasons that are unfathomable, relents.

The next morning Rogers left early for the office to send a message to Jamal. He showed a draft to Hoffman, who in turn showed it to the ambassador, who cabled the State Department desk officer. When the brief message had been cleared by the various layers of the bureaucracy, Rogers typed it on a blank sheet of paper and put it in a plain white envelope.

The message read: "The United States is urging the leaders of the Lebanese Christian militia to show restraint in the current crisis. The United States urges Fatah to show similar restraint."

Rogers attached a cover note to Fuad, instructing him to pass the message to Jamal for delivery to the Old Man. He also asked Fuad to press Jamal for details on the military situation in Beirut.

The message was simple but the process of delivering it was complicated by security procedures. An embassy courier took the letter and dropped it in the mailbox of "Trans-Mediterranean Forwarding Agents," a fictitious company that maintained a one-room office in the Starco Building downtown. A Lebanese contract agent carried it from there to a dead drop in an alleyway in the Souk Tawile. The courier then called Fuad from a public telephone and, using a prearranged code, told him that a message was waiting.

Fuad retrieved the message and called Jamal. Using another prearranged code, he set up a meeting an hour later at a crowded café. Three layers had been interposed between the American case officer and the Palestinian. If the system worked, the links in the chain were invisible.

Fuad reported back to Rogers twenty-four hours later. They met in an apartment off Hamra Street, entering the building fifteen minutes apart through different doors. Fuad handed Rogers a brief message from Jamal written in neat Arabic script, quoting the text of an Arabic proverb that was unfamiliar to Rogers.

The message read, in its entirety: "They came to milk the goat. He broke wind." •

"What in the hell is this supposed to mean?" demanded Rogers.

Fuad looked reproachfully at his case officer. He removed his sunglasses.

"I assume it means that this particular goat has no milk for you."

"I still don't get it," said Rogers. "Translate for your American friend."

"I believe Jamal means that you asked the wrong person for information about the Kahhaleh incident, and so you are getting a rude reply," Fuad said gently.

"Great!" said Rogers. "That's very helpful. Anything else?"

"We talked for a few minutes about the situation," answered Fuad.

"What did Jamal say?"

"He said that he talked to the Fatah military leaders after he returned to Beirut. They told him that Fatah wasn't to blame. The Christians provoked the crisis. He said that Fatah has shown restraint from the beginning and doesn't need advice from the Americans."

"That's the party line," said Rogers. "I could have read that in the newspaper."

"Jamal says it's true. He said one other thing. One of the PLO splinter groups is trying to exploit the situation. They fired mortar rounds on Christian areas of the city last night and they will try to do it again. He said that the Old Man is opposed to the extremists, and that they are the ones you should worry about, not Fatah."

"If it's just the crazies, this will die down," said Rogers.

"Probably," agreed Fuad.

"Was Jamal angry at my message?"

"He was until he thought of the proverb about the goat. Then he stopped being angry. He said that you should add it to your collection."

Rogers briefed Hoffman on the intelligence report and drafted a cable for Langley. The crisis in Lebanon would blow over, the cable said. The PLO group with the most firepower, Fatah, didn't want a confrontation. Other Palestinian factions were trying to exploit the situation, but without Fatah's support they could be contained easily by the Lebanese authorities.

"Not bad," said Hoffman. "Maybe your little operation isn't entirely worthless, after all. But loverboy had better be right about this one. Because if he isn't, we are in very serious trouble. There are people on the Christian side screaming bloody murder. They want to pound the refugee camps into rubble, and we're telling them to cool it."

"I trust our man," said Rogers. "Besides, he's all we've got."

"Send the cable," said Hoffman.

The Beirut station looked good the next day when the gunfire around the Tal Zaatar refugee camp stopped and the Lebanese prime minister, a Muslim, issued a statement declaring that the crisis was over.

17

Beirut; April 1970

It took Rogers several weeks to complete the Personal Record Questionnaire, or PRQ, formally proposing that Jamal be enrolled as an agent. The real work was already done. The contacts had been made in Beirut, Amman, and Kuwait. Jamal, whatever his status, was already providing timely information. But none of that mattered to the bureaucracy. Their triumph was to reduce the mysterious and often sublime relationships of the intelligence world to an orderly flow of paper.

Rogers loathed this sort of paperwork. The PRQ was a lengthy document that was itself compartmentalized for security reasons. Part I was a seven-page biographical summary, much like the résumé that a normal job-seeker might present to a prospective employer. It included the subject's name, birth date, and home address; the names of his parents, his educational background, his hobbies; it also summarized his drinking habits, drug usage, and sexual history. Part I used true names throughout.

The PRQ Part II had the juicy operational details. It explained how the subject had been spotted and assessed, how the information about him in Part I had been gathered, and most important, how the case officer intended to use him. It was a sort of operational game plan, outlining how the agent would be run and what intelligence he would be expected to provide. Part II referred to the agent only by a cryptonym. The segregated parts of the PRQ went into the agent's basic file in the central registry, known as the "201 file." In theory, the people who had access to the real names of agents hadn't any access to their operational records, and vice versa.

The agency had borrowed many of these bookkeeping practices, along with so many other details of running a secret service, from the British. The British, however, took the business of secrecy far more seriously than the Americans. In the early days, they didn't even like to use code words in their operational records and preferred, where possible, to use numbers. Rogers had read of an SIS man who had been reprimanded for a security breach years ago. His crime was that in a message home he had identified Berlin as the capital of the country known in SIS jargon only as "1200."

A six-letter cryptonym was assigned to the case. Agents in Lebanon all had code names that began with "PE." Jamal Ramlawi became, in agency-ese, an agent with the code name PECOCK

The portrait of PECOCK that emerged from the biographical material suggested that he had the makings of a quite remarkable agent. Indeed, the Americans could not have invented a better target for recruitment.

PECOCK, the documents explained, was a sort of Palestinian aristocrat, with the self-assurance and disdain for conventional manners that are typical of the children of prominent families around the world. In 1964, after graduating from Cairo University, he had attended the founding session of the Palestine Liberation Organization in East Jerusalem. At that meeting he accosted some of the leaders of Fatah, then a small underground network based in Kuwait, and asked to join them. Several of the elders tried to convince him to go to graduate school instead, but he would have none of it. He moved to Kuwait in 1965. Because of his easy bearing and his knack for languages, he was used often as a courier in Europe.

Like so many aristocrats, the young man gravitated toward intelligence work. Perhaps the visible world bored him. He moved to Amman in 1967 and worked under Abu Namli, vetting new recruits to Fatah. The next year, the Egyptians quietly offered to help Fatah form a security service. PECOCK was among the ten members of Fatah who went to Cairo in mid-1968 for a six-week training course in intelligence. The course covered recruitment and control of agents, surveillance and interrogation techniques, and the preparation of intelligence reports and estimates.

The ten Cairo graduates, who returned to Jordan in late 1968, formed the nucleus of a new Fatah intelligence organization, known as the Jihaz al-Rasd, or "Surveillance Apparatus." Like many security services, it was divided into two parts: one responsible for counterintelligence and the other charged with collecting information and conducting special operations. The chief of the Rasd, from 1969 on, was Mohammed Nasir Makawi, known as "Abu Nasir." PECOCK was one of his three top assistants. He was thought to be the most influential because of his relationship with the Old Man, who treated the handsome young Palestinian like a son.

Why had the Old Man placed such trust in Jamal? Rogers asked himself. Why had this relatively junior intelligence officer been singled out and given responsibility for Fatah's most sensitive operations? Perhaps because the Old Man couldn't trust anyone his own age, who might be a potential rival.

Suspicion was the universal sentiment of the Arab world, Rogers believed. This was the land of the stab in the back, a culture that believed the admonition: "Fear your enemy once, fear your friend a thousand times." The bond of friendship among Arab men was intense, but it never lasted. Confidences were always betrayed, pledges of trust and fidelity always broken. Look at Islam. Within a few years after the death of the Prophet Mohammed, his followers were at daggers, hatching assassination plots against each other. The same had afflicted Arab politics ever since. The suspicions and rivalries were so intense that it was difficult to trust anyone long enough to build something solid, like a political party or a nation. An Arab man trusted only one other man completely: his son. Even his brothers were potential rivals. The Old Man had no son. But he had Jamal.

The rest of the PRQ Part II summarized operational details. It was obvious that agent PECOCK had access to Fatah's most important secrets. The only question was how to run him.

Here Rogers made a recommendation that he knew would upset headquarters. PECOCK should be regarded initially as an asset, rather than a controlled agent. He should be encouraged to believe that the CIA accepted his definition of the relationship—as "liaison" between two potentially cooperative intelligence services—and didn't view him as an American agent. Rogers drew on the conversations in Kuwait. He noted that the young Palestinian had been directed by the Old Man himself to work with the United States. The agency should appear to accept this approach. It should enhance PECOCK's stature and encourage the fiction of a two-way relationship, by providing him with a regular flow of low-level intelligence that might be useful to Fatah. There was a strong chance that PECOCK could eventually be recruited in the usual way, paid a stipend, and run as a controlled agent. But only if the agency was patient.

"We shouldn't get greedy," Rogers stressed in a cable to Stone that accompanied the PRQ. "The operation may collapse if we insist at the outset on complete control and reliability. We should make no effort to buy or compromise PECOCK, and we should not, at this point, ask him to submit to a polygraph."

For now, recommended Rogers, the Palestinian should be handled discreetly. The Lebanese contract agent who had spotted him and helped develop the case should continue as the courier and intermediary. His cover as a Lebanese leftist with strong pro-Palestinian sympathies would give him easy access to Fatah without arousing suspicion. Rogers should meet regularly with PECOCK, but outside Lebanon whenever possible.

Rogers included, as appendices, summaries of his sessions with Jamal in Kuwait, along with summaries of Fuad's meetings in Beirut. He gave the bulky file to Hoffman, who reviewed it and sent it to Langley.

"You're going to lose on this one," Hoffman warned Rogers before sending the PRQ on its way. "You have me half-convinced that you can recruit an agent who isn't really an agent. But you're not going to convince them."

"Why not?" asked Rogers. "What I am proposing makes perfect sense. It will give us what we want, without the risk of blowing the operation."

"Because they are stupid," said Hoffman. "In the way that only very smart people can be stupid."

"Why?" asked Rogers, genuinely puzzled.

"Something happens to people at Yale, I think," answered Hoffman, picking at his teeth with a wooden match.

"They become convinced that it's only because of a few people like them that the world isn't a hopeless mess. They think the world's problems stem mainly from the fact that there aren't enough rules and regulations—and well-educated gentlemen to enforce them. That's where they come in. They are the rulemakers, standing guard against chaos and disorder. And that's why they're going to say no to your proposal."

"Why?"

"Because it violates the rules."

"But what I'm recommending makes sence."

"Don't waste your breath on me, sonny," said Hoffman. "I just work here."

18

Rogers was summoned to Washington three weeks later. The Operational Approval branch didn't like his plan of action. Neither did John Marsh, the operations chief of the NE Division, who urged Stone to recall Rogers for "consultations."

It was the first real rebuff Rogers had faced in a career that, until then, had been a steady progression of successes and commendations. Hoffman tried to assure him that being summoned home was part of the game, a rite of passage in mid-career. They didn't take you seriously in the front office until they had hauled you on the carpet and given you a lecture. Anyway, Hoffman said, if Rogers wanted to play it safe, he should have chosen another career.

Hoffman was kind enough not to add: I told you so. But Rogers could hear him thinking it anyway.

Rogers dreaded the trip. He was edgy at home with Jane, distant in their final few nights together, restless and temperamental even around the children. He didn't like being second-guessed, especially by people who hadn't recruited an agent of their own in years. He also didn't like to be reminded that he was in mid-career, no longer a prodigy, exposed to attack from people back home who regarded him as a threat or a rival. Rogers liked to keep his life in neat compartments. The biggest one, called work, had suddenly passed out of his control.

* * *

Rogers tried to relax on the airplane. He had a few drinks. He thought of his athletic exploits in high school. He reminisced about old girlfriends. He reviewed in his mind some of the intelligence operations for which he had been commended in the past.

On the Paris–Washington leg of the flight, Rogers struck up a conversation with an attractive French woman, blond and blue-eyed, in her mid-thirties.

She was carefully coiffed and dressed in an expensive tweed suit. When she moved, Rogers thought he could hear the rustle of her undergarments.

Rogers asked the woman why she was travelling to America. Business or pleasure?

"Pleasure," said the woman, drawing out the syllables of the word. Rogers heard the sound of silk and satin as she adjusted herself in the seat.

"Any plans?" asked Rogers.

"We shall see," said the woman.

She was the wife of a French industrialist, she explained. A flat on the Isle Saint-Louis, too many parties, too many responsibilities. She was tired of Paris and wanted a holiday in America.

Rogers found the woman overwhelmingly attractive. When she leaned forward to talk to him, he could see the fine white powder of her makeup, the gloss of her lipstick, and the fullness of her breasts. She had the perfect manners of a woman kept for the pleasure of a refined and wealthy gentleman.

As they were leaving the plane, Rogers, without quite knowing why, asked for the name of her hotel.

The woman blushed and averted her eyes but said quietly, "The Madison." She handed him a card with her name: Véronique Godard.

"Shall I call you?" asked Rogers, taking the card.

"As you like," said the French woman, closing her eyes as she spoke.

Rogers was staying at a cheap hotel in Arlington where the agency booked people who were home on TDY. He checked in, called several friends to announce his arrival, and took a stroll across the Key Bridge to Georgetown.

He sat in a bar debating whether to call the woman from

the plane. It felt strange even to be asking himself the question. He was monogamous, for reasons of personal sanity as well as security. The conviction that he was happily married was central to his sense of well-being. But he felt a restlessness, a pull toward adventure and doom, an impulse like the feeling one gets occasionally on a high balcony looking out over the edge of the railing.

Jump, said Rogers to himself. He saw the French woman in his mind's eye, arrayed on a bed of soft pillows and white linen.

He went to the phone and dialed the number of the Madison.

I'll invite her to dinner, Rogers told himself. Who knows what will come of it? We'll have a meal together. An innocent flirtation.

"Good evening, the Madison," said the hotel operator.

"The room of Madame Godard, please," said Rogers. He felt as nervous as a teenager on his first date.

Ring-ring, ring-ring.

What would he say when she answered? Hello. I am infatuated with you. I can't get you out of my mind. No, obviously not that. He would think of something when she answered.

Ring-ring, ring-ring.

Rogers's palms were sweating. He heard a voice. It was the operator.

"I'm sorry, sir. There's no answer."

Rogers went back to the bar and had another whisky. He waited thirty minutes and called the hotel again.

The same nervous wait. Again, no answer.

He decided to have dinner at his favorite French restaurant, Jean-Pierre on K Street. When he arrived and saw the soft banquettes and the delicate watercolors on the wall, he called the hotel again.

"Madame Godard, please."

"One moment," said the operator.

Ring-ring.

"Allo...."

It was a man's voice. Rogers thought he could hear a woman's voice in the background, singing.

"Allo?"

The man had a French accent.

Perhaps it's just the bellhop, Rogers told himself.

"Hello," said Rogers. "Is Madame Godard there?"

"Un instant," said the man in French.

"Hello," said a woman's voice.

"Véronique," said Rogers. "This is Tom, the man from the plane."

"Who?" said the voice.

"The man from the plane," repeated Rogers.

"Oh yes. Hello," she said in a lower voice. She sounded embarrassed.

"I thought perhaps you might be free for dinner this evening," said Rogers.

She lowered her voice almost to a whisper.

"Not tonight. I am busy. Perhaps another time."

"Yes, perhaps," said Rogers, knowing that he wouldn't call again.

"I am glad that you called," said the woman in a voice that was barely audible. Rogers pictured her standing in a bathrobe, talking on the telephone in a whisper while her boyfriend jealously paced the room. It was a perverse sort of satisfaction, but not very lasting. The Frenchman, after all, had Madame Godard.

"I think you are beautiful," said Rogers. What did it matter now? He could say whatever he wanted.

She gave a slight laugh that was, at once, a protest of modesty and a further seduction.

"Goodbye," said Rogers.

He looked at the phone fondly, a last remnant of the woman, before hanging it up.

"C'est dommage," Rogers said to the headwaiter as he returned to his seat. The waiter smiled indulgently.

Rogers ordered medallions of venison with chestnut puree, a house specialty. After drinking down most of a bottle of Burgundy, he wondered if perhaps there was an angel in heaven with the task of keeping him faithful to his wife, despite his own flights of desire. He tried to remember the priest's admonition in school long ago. Was the adulterous wish the same in the eyes of God as the act itself? Surely not. But he couldn't quite remember. Perhaps he was getting old.

A shuttle bus arrived at the hotel at 9:00 A.M. It had

smoked windows, so that any KGB agents who happened to be crusing along the George Washington Parkway couldn't be sure just who was taking the exit for the Central Intelligence Agency. The bus deposited Rogers in the basement of the building. He passed through security and took the elevator to the wing where the DDP and his minions planned their global escapades. A secretary in a distant outer office welcomed Rogers, gave him coffee, and took him down the hall.

The agency's headquarters looked so clean and wholesome. Someone had once told Rogers that it had been designed to look like a university campus. A place where people smoked pipes and went to seminars. How distant that image was, Rogers thought, from the world that he inhabited.

"The problem with your operational plan is that there isn't any plan," said John Marsh.

Rogers listened impassively. He was seated in a conference room with Marsh and Stone. The room was decorated with photographs of past heads of the clandestine service. A gallery of chiselled features, measured judgments, stiff upper lips.

"I had thought these issues were resolved a month ago, only to find that they were not," continued Marsh.

Marsh made an interesting contrast to Rogers. He was shorter, neater, tighter, meaner. Where Rogers looked relaxed and informal in his corduroy suit, Marsh was dressed fastidiously, like a salesman at a Brooks Brothers store. He wore a blue pinstripe suit, a white shirt with a button-down collar that rolled just so, a yellow tie, striped suspenders, and a pair of black tasseled moccasins. His hair was combed back tightly against his head. If someone had told Marsh that his head looked as smooth and hard as a bullet, he probably would have felt flattered.

"At the risk of sounding immodest," Marsh went on, "I must point out that the central problem in the PRQ is the same one that I tried to bring to Tom's attention in the cable to him in Kuwait. Which was, shall we say, mislaid." He chided Rogers in the curt, bloodless way that a schoolteacher corrects a dull pupil.

"It shouldn't be necessary to remind someone of Tom's experience and standing . . ."

Rogers noted that he was being discussed in the third person. He had a momentary desire to punch Marsh in the face.

" . . . that the essence of any successful intelligence operation is control.

"An uncontrolled agent is like an unguided missile," continued Marsh. "We have no hook, no handle, to manipulate his behavior. The uncontrolled agent can go running off in whatever direction he pleases, talk to whomever he likes, do or not do what we request—as it suits his fancy. In my opinion it's better not to deal with such a person at all, regardless of how well placed he may be, because the potential for mischief is so great. I regard it as essential, especially in an organization like Fatah that is already thoroughly penetrated by the Soviets, that we work only with people who are under discipline."

As he finished his discourse, Marsh took a white linen handkerchief from his breast pocket and dabbed it against his mouth. Rogers decided he had been right in a judgment he made several years ago: Marsh was a pompous ass.

Rogers offered a brief defense of his recommendations in the PECOCK case, repeating the same arguments he had made in the PRQ. He spoke calmly and carefully, trying to sound like himself and not a misshapen version of Marsh.

"Control would certainly be preferable," said Rogers, "if it were possible. But I don't think it is in this case. At least not yet. We're dealing with someone at the top of his organization, who believes in his cause. He isn't a defector. He isn't a crook. He isn't a pervert. If we want control, we should go after somebody who is less important and more vulnerable. Somebody who will be more susceptible to pressure."

"That's defeatism," said Marsh. "You are assuming you can't recruit the agent through financial incentives when, by your own admission, you haven't really tried."

You fool, thought Rogers. You wouldn't know a potential agent if he walked up and bit you on the ass.

Rogers turned to Stone.

"All I can do is ask you to trust me," Rogers said. "That may sound unprofessional. But I know this case, and I know what will work with this agent, and I hope you'll trust my judgment."

Stone, who had been listening silently to the two younger men, eventually spoke up.

"This isn't an easy case," the division chief said. "We all have an enormous regard for Tom's work, and we also have a pressing need for the intelligence he can provide about the Palestinians. But our need isn't so pressing that it makes sense for us to launch an insecure operation."

Marsh nodded.

"I want to take a day or so to consider the issues that we have discussed and talk to a few people who are wiser than I am," concluded Stone. "I'll let you know my decision as quickly as possible."

The meeting ended.

Stone asked Rogers to stay behind a moment.

As Marsh walked out of the conference room, he could hear the division chief inviting Rogers to join him for dinner that night at his club.

Dinner with Stone was a ritual, born of his early days in the officers' mess of the prewar Army, nurtured in London during the war, sustained in the years since then at dinner meetings around the world with agents, case officers, and friends. Stone regarded dinner as a play in three acts and liked each detail of the production—each dish, drink, and morsel of conversation—to be precisely right.

Rogers arrived at the Athenian Club promptly at seven-thirty. It was a brick building in downtown Washington, squat and solid like a broad-beamed Victorian banker.

"Can I help you?" said the doorman, discreetly stopping Rogers at the foyer. The doorman had memorized several thousand faces. He knew everyone who was a member. More important, he knew everyone who was not, and each person in this latter category was greeted with the same polite but firm query: "Can I help you?" The doorman in this case helped Rogers to the lobby, where Stone was seated in a leather chair by the fire, reading a newspaper.

Stone rose and escorted his guest up a grand stairway to the drawing room on the second floor, where another fire was blazing and two big leather chairs awaited them. An old black waiter in a white coat arrived and took their drink orders.

"A dry gin martini," said Stone.

Rogers, swept along by the tide of the encounter, ordered the same. They made small talk for forty-five minutes, talking about their respective families, current events, low-level agency gossip.

A waiter brought menus and both men ordered steaks. Stone selected a bottle of Bordeaux from the wine list. At eight-fifteen exactly, the older man rose from his chair and led his guest to the fourth-floor dining room, past acres of starched white linen, to a corner table. Dinner conversation was slightly more focused, touching on events in the Middle East, life in the Beirut station, the agency's ups and downs.

"How is my old friend Frank Hoffman?" asked Stone after the two had eaten their steaks and drunk most of the wine.

"I didn't know you were friends," said Rogers. He found such a friendship hard to imagine.

"Yes indeed," said Stone. "Frank saved me once from making a very bad mistake in Europe. I am still grateful to him."

"What was the mistake?" asked Rogers.

"The details are a little fuzzy now," said Stone. Like many CIA officers, he had a selective memory. He could recall with precision the specific facts that were required to deal with the problem at hand, and forget everything else.

"Tell me," pressed Rogers, "I'd like to know."

"We were in Germany together after the war," explained Stone. "Frank was my security man. He had switched over not long before to CIA from the FBI."

"So he really was in the FBI."

"Oh yes. Didn't you know? That's why he makes such a point of wearing a gun."

"He doesn't talk much about his past, at least not to me," said Rogers. "What happened in Germany?"

"We were trying to reconstruct some of the Abwehr networks in Eastern Europe. The Germans had had an especially good fellow in Prague. We managed to get him to the West for a chat. Hoffman and I spent an evening with him.

"I came away very impressed. He was an immensely clever man, who had wide contacts and appeared to despise the Russians. He seemed like a good bet to me. But Hoffman didn't like him."

"Why?"

"He wouldn't really say at first. He just kept repeating that the agent didn't smell right. Finally he explained that he thought the Czech agent was unreliable because he was unpatriotic. Any Czech who had worked for the Nazis was a dubious character, Hoffman claimed. If he had betrayed his own people once, to work for the Germans, then he could just as easily betray us. I disagreed. I thought we could use him for our purposes."

"Who was right?"

"Hoffman, of course. The Czech was a bad apple. Because of Frank's concern, we didn't use him for any sensitive operations. But we kept him on the payroll for a year or so, until we learned from a KGB defector who had served in Prague that this same Czech had made a pass at them. We were very lucky. The whole thing could have been disastrous. Hoffman refused to take any credit. He said it had just been a lucky guess."

Rogers pondered the story and deliberated a moment before asking his question.

"What would happen today?" Rogers asked cautiously.

"What do you mean?" queried Stone.

"What would happen today if someone objected to an operation because it didn't smell right?"

"Ahhhh," said Stone. "A good question. In all probability he would be called home immediately, for consultations."

Rogers wasn't sure whether Stone was joking.

"Times have changed," said Stone. "The small and inexperienced organization that Hoffman and I joined doesn't really exist anymore. It has been replaced by a bureaucracy, quite a large one, with its own rules and rhythms. In the old days it was possible to trust one's instincts and hunches, because we didn't really have anything else to go on. There was no body of cases and experience to draw on. Today there is.

"The sad part," continued Stone, "is that it doesn't do any good to regret the changes. It's like regretting the passing of time. As organizations grow, they change in character. They develop their own systems and routines. A bureaucratic culture emerges, with rewards for people who play by the rules and punishments for those who don't."

"Unfortunate," said Rogers.

"Unfortunate, but inevitable. This is the life cycle of a

bureaucracy. Supple in youth. Rigid in middle age. Weak and decaying in old age. Organizations are like any other sort of animal. Their strongest instinct is to survive and reproduce themselves. It may be that the problems are greater in a secret organization like ours, where the bureaucratic culture is sealed off from the outside. But they aren't fundamentally different."

"What do you suggest?" asked Rogers.

"Take risks. Lean against the wind," said Stone. "Listen to correct advice and ignore incorrect advice."

"How do you know the difference?"

"Let us order dessert, shall we?" said Stone.

When the dessert dishes had been cleared, Stone finally got down to business. He led Rogers to a small private room on the third floor, ordered two brandies from the waiter, and closed the door. He offered Rogers a cigar—a Cohiba, Castro's brand, smuggled from Cuba—and lit one for himself. It was a signal that the serious part of the evening was about to begin.

"I regard you as the ablest case officer we have in the Middle East at present," Stone began warmly. "I also regard you as a kindred spirit and an example of what is best in our business. For these reasons, I very much want you to succeed in your current operation.

"The course of action you are proposing is unorthodox, as our friend Mr. Marsh took such pains to demonstrate this morning."

Stone raised his eyebrow slightly when he mentioned the name, as if to say that he, too, found his operations officer a bit of an ass.

"Without endorsing Marsh's conclusions, I think it's important that you understand why he spoke as he did about control. He was right. Control is the soul of what we do. Perhaps you recall the passage in *King Lear* where Edgar observes that 'Ripeness is all'?"

Rogers nodded yes.

"Well, in our business, we might well say: 'Control is all.' Control of ourselves and others.

"Let me tell you a brief story that will illustrate my point. It is about one of our illustrious British ancestors in the SIS, Commander Mansfield Cumming, the man who first took the designation of 'C.' He has come to be regarded as an eccentric, an oddball who signed his correspondence in green ink and tapped absent-mindedly on his wooden leg."

"His wooden leg?"

Stone nodded and continued.

" 'C' rarely told people how he had lost that leg, but the tale was recounted years after his death in a friend's memoir. One day in 1915 in France, the old man and his son were taking a drive. Their car hit a tree and overturned, mortally wounding the boy and pinning 'C' by the leg. The father heard his son's cries for help, but he could not free himself from under the wreckage of the car to help the boy. In desperation, he took out his pocket knife and hacked at his leg—his own leg—until he had cut it clean off."

"With a knife?"

"With a pocket knife. Then he attended to his dying son."

Rogers took a deep breath. Stone took a drink from his snifter of brandy.

"I think of that remarkable story of courage and self-discipline whenever I consider the requirement for control in intelligence operations. We must control ourselves—and to the extent possible, our agents—as completely and cold-bloodedly as 'C' did that day."

Stone drained his brandy glass and rang for another round. When it arrived, he closed the door firmly and settled back into his chair. He turned to the next stage of his argument, as neatly as if he was turning over a card in a game of blackjack.

"Control is not the only virtue, however," said Stone with a smile. "Reliability is also essential, and it isn't the same thing as control. I think some of our 'purists' often forget this distinction.

"Let me give you an example. In this business we have to deal with a spectrum of people . . ." Stone spread out his hands wide in front of him—". . . from the man over here who refuses to work for you until you force him to cooperate, to the man over there who talks to you because he is your friend and he trusts you. You 'control' the first and not the second. But which one is more reliable?"

Rogers pondered the question. He thought he knew the answer.

"In our world," continued Stone, "reliability is inevitably a

question of many different shades of gray. To simplify our
task in making judgments about people, I often recommend
two sorts of yardsticks.

"The first is the quality and accuracy of the information the
agent is providing. If it's good information, people will
usually overlook the operational details of how it was obtained. The second measure is to set practical tests that can
establish an agent's bona fides. Ask him to do something particular for you. Tell him you need a certain piece of information that only he can obtain. If he does what you ask, then you
will develop confidence in him."

Stone smiled contentedly and turned over his last card.

"This brings me to the question at hand, regarding your
agent in Fatah. The information we have received from him
thus far is solid stuff. Very promising. As you say, control
may be impossible at this stage. But how can we answer Mr.
Marsh's concerns, and my own, and gain a greater measure of
reliability and trust?"

"By testing him," said Rogers.

"Just so. I believe we should set a small test for your man
and see how he responds. It should be something that is in the
interest of his organization as much as ours, so that he won't
feel like a traitor."

"Any suggestions?" asked Rogers.

"Actually, yes. I do have a suggestion. From what I have
read in the agent's 201 file, I believe an appropriate target
exists in the Democratic Front for the Liberation of Palestine.
Here we have a radical pro-Soviet group, staging terrorist
operations that undercut Fatah and challenge its position in the
PLO. Your man evidently shares our view, because he has
already passed along information to you about this group.
Now I think you should tell him that we wish to go further.
We want to plant a microphone in the offices of the DFLP in
Beirut and we need his assistance."

"It's worth a try," said Rogers. "But I have to tell you I
think it's a long shot."

"That is not an adequate reason not to make the effort,"
said Stone.

"Yes, sir," answered Rogers. "How long will it take the
Technical Services people to make the arrangements?"

"Actually," said Stone with a slightly apologetic tone, "the arrangements are already being made. I asked several people from TSD to study the problem. They have a first-rate scheme. A paperweight in the shape of a map of Palestine that would contain a microphone and transmitter. Irresistible for anyone in the PLO, they reckon.

"All your man has to do is put this device in the office of the fellow who heads the DFLP. He can give it to him as a present, or leave it behind by accident after a meeting, or sneak it into his office. Whatever he likes. It's really quite a simple operation. Almost risk-free. Far less than we normally ask agents to do."

"What if he says no?" asked Rogers. He didn't want to hear the answer.

"Then we will have a bit of a problem," said Stone. "Marsh will recommend that we make a more direct attempt to establish control." Stone paused and gave a sad smile. "I will probably support his recommendation."

"Understood," said Rogers. "I'll do my best."

"You can pick up the little gadget tomorrow morning," said Stone, his three-act play finally complete.

19

Cairo; May 1970

Holding the next meeting in Egypt was Jamal's idea. Rogers thought it was crazy. Why hold a supposedly clandestine meeting in the heart of enemy territory, surrounded by thousands of gumshoes from the Egyptian Moukhabarat? Why travel to the center of Soviet influence in the Middle East?

Jamal insisted that Egypt would be safe. He knew the Egyptian security service from his training there, he told Fuad. He knew how they tapped phones and how they conducted surveillance. They were incompetent. Rogers shouldn't worry. It was almost as if Jamal wanted to demonstrate his proficiency as an intelligence officer. Rogers reluctantly agreed to meet in Cairo and packed his bags once again.

They set the meeting for early May, when Jamal had to be in Cairo on Fatah business. Fuad gave Jamal the address of a CIA safehouse in the Cairo suburb of Heliopolis. It was an apartment on a quiet street in a Coptic Christian neighborhood where the Nasser regime had few friends. Jamal should proceed to the apartment, use the agreed password, and enter. If no one answered, he should return the next day, an hour earlier, and try again. Avoiding surveillance on his way to the meeting would be Jamal's problem, Fuad said. Jamal scoffed at the precautions.

Rogers arrived in an Egypt that was hobbling along in the waning days of Gamal Abdel Nasser. It was like visiting the locker room of a baseball team that has lost twenty straight games. The Egyptians were surviving on their good humor.

The dreams and illusions of Nasser's revolution had been shattered by the 1967 War, when Nasser's boasts about Arab military power had been revealed as puny lies. Yet the good-natured Egyptians forgave their leader everything. When he spoke, the masses still chanted: "Nasser! Nasser!" The name translated as: "Victory! Victory!" Perhaps they meant it as a joke.

A thin veneer of Nasser's socialism overlay Egypt, but it was warping and peeling at the edges. Beneath were the residues of so many other cultures—British, French, Ottoman, Bedouin, Roman, Greek—left behind by each wave of invaders that had sojourned in Egypt since the days of Pharoah. Walking around Tahrir Square downtown, Rogers felt as if he was suspended in several centuries at once. Above him were the French-style facades of the old commercial buildings, their ornate moldings and capstones barely visible under the grime of the city; ahead were the modern Egyptian bureaucrats and businessmen in their sharp suits, mopping their brows in the Cairo heat; below, in the shadows, were the *fellabin*, the peasants from the villages of the Nile Delta, ragged and barefoot, relieving themselves in alleyways and on doorsteps, laughing and telling crude jokes. All around was the incessant noise of cars honking their horns and merchants peddling their wares' and pedestrians bantering in musical Egyptian Arabic.

Rogers was staying at the Nile Hilton, a grand American hotel along the river that had become, paradoxically, the favorite haunt of President Nasser. It was an island of sanity and efficiency in the middle of chaotic Cairo. Egyptian novelists came to the air-conditioned Coffee Shop to write their books in the cool and calm; Moslem brides held their wedding receptions in the crowded lobby, blushing as a chorus sang tales of the wedding night. It was the place where all Cairo met and socialized.

Rogers arrived a day before his meeting and practiced losing the Moukhabarat surveillance teams, the little men in baggy suits who waited in clusters outside the hotel. He found that it was easy and wondered whether perhaps Jamal had been right.

The day of the meeting, Rogers slipped out the back door

of the hotel and walked several blocks up Kasr el-Nil Street to Talat Harb Square, where he hailed a taxi. He had the taxi drive to Dokki, across the river. He stopped there, checked for surveillance, and took another taxi back toward the center of town. He shifted cars one more time before heading to Heliopolis. When he finally arrived in the neighborhood of the safehouse, he had the taxi drop him a block from his true destination and walked the rest of the way, stopping twice to check for little men in baggy suits.

Jamal arrived on schedule an hour later. Rogers barely recognized him. He was dressed like a *bawab*, a humble doorman, in a dirty gray gallabiya, muddy leather sandals, and a turban-like scarf that covered his head and most of his face. It was a discordant sight: the dark lustrous hair and fine features of a movie star, wrapped in the rags of a beggar. Rogers found the outfit faintly comical and said so.

"I count on the snobbery of the secret police," said Jamal. "They would never imagine that anyone dressed like this would be worth following."

"I hope you're right," said Rogers, walking toward the window.

The drapes were closed to prevent surveillance from across the street, leaving the room nearly dark at midday. Rogers opened the drapes slightly. The street looked quiet. In the building across the way he saw women and children. In one apartment, a young man was sitting alone reading a newspaper and looking idly out the window. He looked harmless. Rogers closed the drapes.

He offered Jamal a whisky. The Palestinian smiled and said no, tea would be fine. They made small talk for only a few minutes. Jamal seemed eager to do business. From the folds of his dusty gallabiya, he removed two sheets of paper covered with dense Arabic writing and handed them to Rogers with a flourish. The shyness of Kuwait had vanished.

"The Old Man sends greetings to the United States," Jamal said.

Rogers touched his heart in a sign of gratitude.

"What's in the papers?" Rogers asked.

"Part of our security cooperation," said Jamal, still beaming.

"Tell me," said Rogers. The tape recorder was going. He wanted a record for Stone.

"We are giving you the names of eight people who are attending a training camp in South Lebanon. There are four Palestinians, two Germans, and two Italians. They are studying techniques that could be used in airplane hijackings. The Popular Front for the Liberation of Palestine organized the camp, but one of the trainers works for us."

"Why are you giving us this information?" asked Rogers.

"The Old Man doesn't like the fact that the Europeans are involved," explained Jamal.

It struck Rogers as an odd sort of racism, the notion that it was all right for Palestinians to blow airplanes out of the sky but not Europeans. But he kept his mouth shut.

"The second page is the most useful," said Jamal with the knowing smile that a lawyer or accountant might use in briefing a client.

The second page gave details about the passports that had been prepared for the eight by the PFLP's documentation bureau. The four Palestinians would be travelling on real Algerian passports, the two Germans and two Italians on false ones from their home countries. The names and passport numbers were listed neatly.

"Thank you," said Rogers.

Rogers was more pleased than he wanted to admit. The document was a bonanza. It would allow Western intelligence services to track the terrorists as they left the training camp in Lebanon, monitor their contacts with other operatives in Europe and the Middle East, and apprehend them before they killed anybody.

The American dreaded what he had to do next.

"The names and passport numbers are fine, as far as they go," Rogers said in a measured voice.

"But they don't tell us all that we need to know. They tell us who will try to hijack airplanes and discredit the Palestinian Revolution. But they don't tell us when or where. For that, we must go further. I am sorry to push you, Jamal, but we must move to a new level of security cooperation."

Jamal looked at him suspiciously. The enthusiasm had drained from his face. His lips were tight and his nostrils flared.

Rogers removed the paperweight from his pocket.

"This is a simple device that can help us save many lives. I'll explain how it works . . ."

"Aaacchh!" Jamal cut him off with a sharp cry. It was almost a scream, a noise that someone might make to block out another sound he didn't want to hear.

"Impossible! It is absolutely impossible! I told you in Kuwait that I will not be your spy!"

Jamal was almost shouting. Rogers was torn between concern for the Palestinian and worry about the racket he was making.

"Shhh!" said Rogers.

He walked to the darkened window again and pulled the curtain back a hair to see if the noise had roused anyone. After no more than a second he let it fall back in place.

Rogers groaned and bit his lip. He turned to Jamal and spoke in an eerily calm voice.

"My friend," said Rogers. "Your problems are just beginning."

In an apartment across the way, Rogers had seen the same man he had glimpsed before. Still in the same spot, still pretending to read a newspaper. It was so obvious. Why hadn't Rogers realized it before? The man across the street was a watcher, and he was watching the safehouse. Somehow, despite all the precautions, the Egyptian Moukhabarat had them under surveillance.

Rogers took a deep breath and exhaled slowly. He turned to Jamal.

"There is an escape plan," Rogers said coolly. The apartment had been provisioned with this sort of contingency in mind. He led Jamal to a bedroom and pointed to the simple business suit and broad-brimmed hat that were in the closet.

"Put them on as quickly as you can," said Rogers.

The Palestinian wordlessly obeyed.

"There are sunglasses in the pocket of the jacket," Rogers said. "Put them on."

Rogers looked at his feet and saw that he was still wearing the peasant sandals. There were no shoes in the closet. Never mind. It would have to do. Rogers led the Palestinian toward the front door.

"Listen to me carefully and do exactly as I say. If you

follow these instructions precisely, there is no reason that anyone should identify you as having been here.

"Take the stairs down two flights to the basement. At the bottom of the stairwell is a door. Open it. The door leads to a tunnel that passes underground to the basement of the next building. When you come out of the tunnel, walk calmly up the stairs to the front door. It opens on a busy street where the Heliopolis streetcar line makes a stop. The stop is thirty yards from the building. Wait in the doorway until you actually see the streetcar coming. Then walk out quickly and catch it.

"When you get downtown, take a bus from Tahrir Square toward Giza. Stop at one of the clubs along the Pyramids Road where the whores work all day long. Go in and stay with one of the girls as long as you can. Give her a big tip so she'll remember you. There should be some money in the jacket.

"When you get back to Beirut, Fuad will make contact with you. In the meantime I'll try to find out what happened here.

"Any questions?"

Jamal looked at Rogers as if for the first time. He shook his head silently. In his eyes was a look of professional respect and deference, the look of a junior officer obeying his superior. Rogers opened the door quickly and peered down the corridor. There was nobody.

"Move!" he said, and Jamal was gone.

Rogers waited fifteen minutes and repeated the same escape procedure himself. Except that he didn't go to the whorehouse on the Pyramids Road for his alibi. He went to the U.S. Embassy.

Four days later, the Cairo station managed to debrief its best agent within the Egyptian Moukhabarat about the incident in Heliopolis. The damage was less than Rogers had feared. It was the apartment that had been under surveillance, not Rogers or Jamal. Because of a lapse on the part of the Cairo station, the "safehouse" wasn't so safe.

The Moukhabarat had photos of everyone who had gone into the building. They had made a tentative identification of Rogers, who the Egyptians remembered from the old days in South Yemen. But they were having more trouble with the other person who had been dressed in simple Arab garb and shielded his face. The pictures of him were fuzzy.

The Egyptians had tentatively concluded that Rogers had been meeting with a member of the "Ikhwan Muslimin," the Moslem Brotherhood that bitterly opposed the Nasser regime. A half-dozen members of the Ikhwan had been arrested in the last twenty-four hours in Cairo and Alexandria. They were being tortured for information about the group's contacts with the CIA. Several had died protesting their innocence.

Rogers didn't like mistakes. The botched meeting in Heliopolis wasn't his fault, but that was little consolation. He had been unlucky. Rogers, who believed in luck, didn't like feeling accident-prone.

The worst part about a botched operation was the postmortem that inevitably followed. The Heliopolis incident produced a string of inquiries, memos, and recommendations. Marsh himself flew to Beirut and Cairo and spent a week querying and admonishing everyone in sight. The counterintelligence staff sent its own man to conduct a separate investigation. He was a tall, cadaverously thin man who was unusually secretive and kept talking at odd moments about trout fishing. It was assumed that he prepared a report of his own, but nobody ever saw it.

By late May, the dust had begun to settle. The damage was considerable, but Rogers hoped it wasn't enough to kill the operation.

The first question the specialists addressed was whether Rogers's own usefulness as a case officer had been destroyed by the tentative identification of him in Heliopolis. The answer was no. The Egyptians and Soviets had tagged Rogers years ago as an intelligence officer; now they simply had more evidence.

The second question was whether Jamal's contact with the CIA had been exposed. Every bit of evidence the agency could gather indicated that the Egyptians genuinely believed Rogers had been meeting with a member of the Moslem underground in Egypt. The Moukhabarat's inability to find confirming evidence of the relationship only seemed to make them more worried about it.

The third question was how the location of the safehouse

had been blown. That was Cairo's mistake. Bad tradecraft. An Egyptian support agent had rented the apartment, it turned out, from a man who had a cousin in the security service. A junior officer under commercial cover in Cairo, who had supervised the rental of the safehouse, was rumored to be packing his bags.

Rogers didn't escape criticism. He even provided his inquisitors with the evidence they needed. As he fled the apartment in Heliopolis that day, he had grabbed the tape recording of his aborted session with Jamal. During a postmortem in Cairo, Marsh played the tape over and over, especially the brief passage at the end when Rogers proposed the bugging operation.

"You sound almost apologetic," said Marsh as he listened to the tape. "You don't have to make any excuses about asking someone to work for the United States! This is a hard-nosed business and there's no room for sentimentalists."

Rogers kept his mouth shut. But he winced, later, when he heard Marsh, dressed in a seersucker suit, repeat one of Hoffman's favorite lines.

"It is time to grab this Palestinian by the balls and start squeezing!" said the man from Langley. Coming from Marsh, it sounded nastier, and also less believable.

Rogers couldn't quarrel with Marsh's basic point: an effort to plant a bug had failed because the case officer didn't have control over his agent. The agent felt free to say no!

Rogers urged a few more months of patience. "We need to wait for the scars to heal," he told Marsh. "The relationship needs time to ripen. More pressure now may sever it altogether."

But Rogers was becoming bored by his own arguments. He had made them a dozen times already. By now, they sounded weak and ineffectual even to him. Admit it, he told himself. You've failed.

Marsh listened with the aggravating politeness of someone who knows that he has won his bureaucratic battle and doesn't need to gloat.

You bloodless bastard, thought Rogers, as he listened to Marsh thank him politely for all his time and hard work building the foundations of the case.

* * *

Eventually Stone cabled the bad news. The evaluation of PECOCK would be frozen temporarily, pending a review by senior staff of the Near East Division and the DDP. They would handle further development of the case.

The next step would be a meeting between the agent and a senior member of the NE Division staff. Beirut should handle the arrangements. The meeting should take place in a controlled environment, preferably a NATO country. The case officer involved in the initial phase of the case—meaning Tom Rogers—would not be present at the next meeting with PECOCK.

PART V

June–September 1970

20

Beirut; June 1970

The Lebanese election season had begun by the time Rogers returned to Beirut from his misadventure in Cairo. A new president was to be elected in August, and both sides were prophesying the destruction of Lebanon if the other side won. To a disturbing extent, both sides were right.

The Lebanese electoral system mirrored the national condition. It was based on an unwritten "understanding" that had been reached among the leading politicians in 1943, when Lebanon became independent from France. The agreement was a menu for sectarian government. It provided that the Christians would get the largest slice of the pie—the presidency and a majority of the seats in parliament—and that every other religious group would get at least a small sliver, too.

The ballot allocated seats in each parliamentary district by religious sect. Voters in the Shouf district southeast of Beirut were required to select three Maronites, two Sunnis, two Druse, and one Greek Catholic. Voters in Zahle, in the Bekaa Valley, had to select one Maronite, one Sunni, one Shiite, one Greek Catholic, and one Greek Orthodox. Similar formulas prevailed for every district of the country. Religious discrimination was not simply permitted by the parliamentary system, it was required.

The Lebanese system for electing a president married the sectarianism of parliament to the other great Lebanese political tradition: corruption. The president was elected by parliament, not the people, which meant that every six years there was a carnival of bribery as the eager parliamentary deputies auctioned off their presidential votes. What made the 1970 election ominous was that the most popular bribes that year seemed to be shipments of weapons and ammunition for the illegal militias that were springing up around the country.

Rogers spent several listless weeks at the office, busying himself with routine work. Tasks that he normally ignored or delegated to others now seemed to preoccupy him. He arrived early each morning and read the overnight cable traffic from Washington, a tedious and generally unrewarding job. He spent hours auditing the accounts of agents under his supervision. He checked and rechecked the station's watch lists and surveillance reports. Had anyone asked him whether he was depressed, he instantly would have denied it.

At home he was restless and short-tempered, even with his son. The boy's games of roughhouse and ball-playing, which Rogers usually enjoyed, now gave him a headache. Mark would quiz him about who was leading the Lebanese Soccer League and Rogers would answer dully, "I don't know."

Rogers would go into his study immediately after dinner to read. But when the door was closed, he often found he had the energy only for reading newspapers and magazines. Depression was a stranger to Rogers, which was why he found the encounter with it so disorienting. His career had left him unprepared for failure.

Jane Rogers, who had never seen her husband in such a prolonged melancholy, was uncertain how to deal with it. Over cocktails, she would wait for him to light the spark—to speak about a small event at work, or something he had seen on the way home, or a trip they would all take to the country, or some other flicker of conversation. But the spark didn't come, leaving Jane sitting in silence with a drink in her hand, wondering what was wrong. She didn't ask, of course. That was against the rules.

Jane eventually tried various gambits to bring her husband out of his gray mood. She embarked on conversational jaunts of her own, chatting about plays and novels and the latest news from the ladies at Smith's grocery. She experimented in the kitchen, cooking elaborate Lebanese dishes with garlic and yogurt. She even bought a manual of sexual instruction from a bookstore on Hamra Street and, following its advice, picked up her husband one evening after work dressed in a raincoat with absolutely nothing underneath. In the car on the way home, she unbelted the raincoat and let it slip open till it revealed the curve of her breast and her bare thighs. They made love lustily that night, beginning in the stairwell on the way up to the apartment, and Jane thought she had found a cure.

But the next morning the emptiness and sense of failure returned for Rogers. Jane wished that he would be less polite and scream out his unhappiness. But that was against the rules, too.

What saved Rogers from utter despair in those weeks was his daughter Amy. Her health preoccupied Rogers. He took her to the doctor, checked her temperature and pulse every morning, tested her reactions with a silver mallet. And he rejoiced when the signs from all these tests confirmed what the doctor said. She was getting better. Rogers found that some days his daughter was the only person in the world he truly wanted to see. He would sit with her in his lap in the evening and rock her slowly to sleep. Sometimes he would even bring her with him into his study after dinner and let her play on the floor while he read. It was as if her physical illness and Roger's spiritual wound had combined in Roger's mind and become extensions of each other.

Jane resolved to see the difficult period through. She gave Rogers room to brood, made few demands on him, and waited for the clouds to clear.

As she lay awake in bed on one of these somber evenings, Jane thought of a boat in the fog. It was a boat her parents had chartered one summer, and they were cruising off the coast of Maine. In the thick fog she could hear the sound of waves breaking against the rocks on the shore, and the sound of foghorns from other boats, and the occasional clanging sound of a buoy marking the channel. But she couldn't actually see anything beyond a few feet, the fog was so dense. She saw her father, staring at the ship's compass, glancing from time to time at a chart, steering a course toward the next mark. He was muttering to himself as he tried to keep the boat on its compass heading.

I know where I want to be, her father had grumbled, but I don't know where I am.

That muttered remark in the fog off the Maine coast was the very heart of the truth, Jane thought to herself. You could hear and feel the world around you, but you couldn't see anything clearly. You did your best to steer a course by dead reckoning, with no certainty even that you were heading in the right direction.

Rogers ignored Fuad. The Lebanese agent was part of an operation that was dead, as far as Rogers was concerned. Rogers approved his expense vouchers and signed a weekly report for the auditors, but otherwise he left Fuad alone. Eventually, after a few weeks, Fuad became restless and left a message in one of the dead drops requesting a meeting with his case officer.

"Have I done wrong?" asked Fuad when they met. "Why do you ignore me?"

"I'm sorry," said Rogers. "I've been very busy."

Fuad nodded. Rogers was, for him, such a towering figure that it would not have occurred to him that the American might have problems of his own. It would have been easier for Fuad to imagine the sun not rising.

"I am at your service," said Fuad. "If there is any project you would like me to undertake, I am ready."

Rogers heard the eagerness and loyalty in Fuad's voice and felt ashamed. Agents are like children, he thought to himself. They are utterly dependent on their case officers for work, protection, meaning, survival. They cannot live alone. The part of them that was independent has been destroyed by the process of recruitment.

"Fuad," said Rogers in as commanding a voice as he could summon. "There is one thing I would like you to do."

"What is that, Effendi?" asked Fuad. He already looked a little happier.

"I am going to be very busy with other work for a while. So I won't be able to meet with Jamal. I've asked other people to help out on that."

Fuad nodded. He was disappointed, but trying not to let it show.

"I would like you to keep an eye on Jamal for me," Rogers

continued. "Make sure that he is adequately protected. That he has enough bodyguards, that he isn't spending money too wildly. That he isn't leaving himself vulnerable to anyone. Do you understand me?"

"Yes, Effendi," said Fuad. His posture had changed. He was a man restored.

Rogers was not. After rousing himself to deal with Fuad, he fell back into his numbness. Indeed, the brief discussion of Jamal only made him sorrier that his role in the operation had ended in failure.

Hoffman, who had been watching Rogers's melancholia mount day by day, eventually decided that he had had enough. There was room in the station for one prima donna, and that post was already filled by Hoffman himself. One afternoon in late June, the station chief called Rogers into his office.

"Sit down, my boy," said Hoffman when Rogers arrived. "Listen to me carefully, because I'm going to tell you three crucial words that will matter a great deal in your career."

"Yes, sir," said Rogers dutifully.

"Illegitimi non carborundum," said Hoffman, reciting a Latin phrase.

"What?" asked Rogers.

"Illegitimi non carborundum," repeated Hoffman. "Those are the three words."

"What do they mean?" asked Rogers.

"They mean: 'Don't let the bastards get you down.'"

"Where did you learn that?" asked Rogers, rousing himself slightly.

"Harvard," said Hoffman.

"Harvard?" said Rogers sitting up straight in his chair. "I didn't know you went to Harvard."

"I didn't," said Hoffman. "I went to Holy Cross. But we used to play Harvard in football."

"So?"

"So when we played in Cambridge, I made a practice of listening to the Harvard band. They were the smart ones, you see, and they liked to sing in Latin just to show everybody how smart they were. When everyone else sang 'Ten Thousand Men of Harvard,' they sang their Latin number, 'Illegitimi non carborundum.' Would you like me to sing it for you?"

"No thanks," said Rogers.

Hoffman started singing anyway, bobbing his large head until Rogers finally cracked a smile.

"Gaudeamus igitur," sang Hoffman vigorously.

"Veritas, non sequitur!" His hands were gesturing in the air like a conductor's.

"Illegitimi non carborundum. Ipso, facto!" He bowed slightly in Rogers's direction when he had finished.

"Not bad," said Rogers.

"Don't let the bastards get you down," repeated Hoffman.

There was a brief interlude of silence. Hoffman resumed his tune, humming it sotto voce.

"God damn it!" said Rogers, raising his voice above the sound of Hoffman's humming, finally allowing himself to get angry at something, in this instance Hoffman's relentless good humor.

"What's bugging you, anyway?" asked Hoffman.

"What's bugging me?"

"Correct," said Hoffman. "You."

"Isn't that obvious?" answered Rogers. "They're trying to take my case away from me!"

"My boy, they are not *trying*," said Hoffman. "They *are* taking your case away from you. It's done. Over. Finished. Kaput. So wise up, and stop feeling sorry for yourself."

"Thanks," muttered Rogers. "That makes me feel a lot better."

"It could be worse, my boy. They could have fired you."

"They probably should have," said Rogers. "I let them down—especially Stone."

"Forget Stone."

"He tried to help. When I went back to Washington a few months ago, he took me to dinner at his club and gave me a long lecture about control and self-control. He was on the mark."

"Did you say he gave you a lecture about self-control?"

"Yes."

"In this little lecture, I don't suppose he told you his story about the Brit—'C'—and how he cut off his leg with a penknife, did he?"

"As a matter of fact, he did," said Rogers. "What of it?"

"Oh, Jesus."

"What?"

"Nothing," said Hoffman. "Except that the story is total bullshit."

"It is?"

"Yup! 'C' lost his leg in a car wreck all right, but he didn't cut it off himself. That's a legend the Brits have been circulating for fifty years. Stone tells it to everybody. It's his favorite story. But it ain't true. So wise up. Nobody's perfect. Not 'C'. Not Stone. Not you."

Rogers shook his head. He had no idea who was telling the truth: Stone, Hoffman, or perhaps, neither of them.

"Do you want my advice?" asked Hoffman.

Rogers didn't answer.

"My advice is, fuck 'em. The whole lot of them."

"That's helpful," said Rogers.

"Seriously," said Hoffman. It was a word Rogers hadn't heard him use. "I think you need a break from the Palestinian account. Change of scene. Catch your breath. Forget about how your colleagues in the front office are mistreating you. Let them screw things up for a while. How does that sound?"

"I don't want a vacation, if that's what you're asking."

"Look, smart ass, if you think I can spare my best man just because he's having an identity crisis, forget it."

Rogers's face showed a flicker of interest.

"What I had in mind," continued Hoffman, "was that you spend some time on the other side, in East Beirut with the Christians. Prowl around. Make some contacts. See what's out there. Something's going on with them, or my name isn't Nathan M. Pusey."

"Like what?" Rogers asked.

"Like some kind of secret underground movement."

"What in the world does that mean?"

"If I knew, I wouldn't need you, would I?"

"Don't you already have people on that account?"

"Second-raters."

"I don't know," said Rogers, still wary.

"Well, I do! Anyway, it isn't a suggestion. It's an order."

"Yes, sir," said Rogers. As he spoke, he was already making a mental inventory of what would be necessary for the task Hoffman had described.

"I'll need access to the files. And I'll need to know who's already on our payroll, so we don't buy the same people twice."

"Permission granted," said Hoffman.

"Thank you."

"But I can save you a lot of trouble by telling you the simple truth, which is that our agents in East Beirut are a bunch of flaming assholes who are good at only one thing, which is stealing money."

"So where do I begin?"

"If it were me," said Hoffman, "I would begin with our esteemed colleague in the Lebanese Deuxième Bureau, General Fadi Jezzine."

"Why him?" asked Rogers. His image of General Jezzine, from dinner at the ambassador's house months ago, was of an elegant, austere man in a tuxedo who seemed, to Rogers, to typify the political and economic system that was strangling Lebanon.

"Because the general knows where all the bodies are buried on the Christian side," said Hoffman.

"Who owns a piece of him?"

"Everybody," answered Hoffman. "And nobody. The good general sells information to us, the Israelis, the Syrians, the Egyptians. He's a regular supermarket. He's got something for everyone. Which means he's never completely in the bag for any one customer. What's more, he understands the first rule of the intelligence business."

"Which is?"

"Which is: Don't give anything away for free. When you have a piece of information, sell it, or trade it. But don't give it away."

"How am I going to get anything new out of him?"

"That's your problem," said Hoffman. "By the way, if you strike out with the general, try his wife. She's a firecracker."

"I know."

"You know the lady?"

"Slightly," said Rogers. "I sat next to her one night at a dinner party when she got drunk and denounced the Palestinians."

"Excellent."

Rogers turned and began to walk out of the office.

"Guadeamus igitur!" called out Hoffman.

"What does that mean?" asked Rogers.

"Let us make merry."

21

East Beirut; July 1970

Rogers embraced the new assignment as if he was starting a new life. He spent his days in East Beirut, among the Christian elite, making new contacts and renewing old ones. Several weeks after his conversation with Hoffman, he had wangled an invitation to lunch at the Jezzines' house in the mountains northeast of Beirut.

The luncheon took place on a bright summer day that seemed hot when Rogers left his apartment in West Beirut. He was dressed casually, in a light summer suit and open-necked shirt, and his cowboy boots. When he reached the mountains near the Jezzines' village, the air was chillier and Rogers wished he had brought a sweater.

The village, on the slopes of Mount Lebanon, had been tidied up for the arrival of a special visitor. There was a string of lights across the main street, shining dully and almost invisibly at midday, and Lebanese flags were fluttering from many of the stone houses. As Rogers drove down the road, he noticed that in the windows of some of the houses were faces, staring silently at him.

The village was the ancestral home of the Jezzine clan. Their villa sat atop the highest hill, sheltered in a grove of cedar trees. As Rogers neared the house, he saw a barricade ahead in the road. It was manned by peasant boys dressed in black and carrying automatic weapons. They stopped him, asked to see his passport. When they had established that he was the important American visitor who was expected that day, the gunmen insisted on driving Rogers the remaining one hundred yards to the house.

The Jezzines kept him waiting, inevitably. Rogers amused himself smoking cigarettes and reading the magazines from Paris on the table in the salon. Eventually, precisely thirty minutes after Rogers had arrived, General Jezzine emerged from the private quarters of the mansion to greet him. The general was dressed in a white linen suit and smoking a Havana cigar.

"How good of you to come," said Jezzine. "It is an honor to have a distinguished member of your organization in my home." His voice was precise and measured. He had a way of talking that allowed his mouth to form words while the rest of his face remained utterly immobile. Especially his eyes, which seemed to stare at Rogers without blinking.

They made small talk for a few minutes. Jezzine showed Rogers his collection of guns, mounted in a case on the wall. Then he strolled to the large picture window that dominated the salon and pointed out, in the distance, the valley where he had hunted with his father when he was a boy, and where he now hunted with his own sons. The general glanced momentarily at Rogers's boots and looked away in disdain.

A servant eventually arrived with tea, served in small glass cups that were half-full with sugar.

"Have you ever heard of 'Le Dactylo,' Mr. Rogers?" asked the general, sipping his tea.

Rogers shook his head.

"It means 'The Typewriter' in French. But here in my country it has a special meaning. Do you perhaps know what that is?"

"I do not," said Rogers.

"It is a nickname that Lebanese journalists have for the Deuxième Bureau. The name has a certain logic. Sometimes, you see, I will summon the owner of one of the Lebanese newspapers to my office in Yarze, and I will give him a bit of information. I will say that the bank owned by Mr. So-and-so, the Palestinian millionaire, is in trouble, or that a particular ministry has exceeded its budget because of financial irregularities. The newspaper owner, if he is a sensible man, will take this information to his editor and tell him to run it in the newspaper. If the editor asks where it came from, the owner will say: 'Le Dactylo.'"

"From 'The Typewriter,'" said Rogers.

"Yes. Precisely. Everyone knows what that means. It means the story comes from me, from army intelligence, from the secret police. And that will be that. The story will run, praising one politician who is acting in the interest of the nation, condemning another one who is not."

Rogers nodded. He wasn't sure where Jezzine's recitation was leading.

"Sometimes," continued the general, "The Typewriter will supply the newspapers with information that originated, not with us, but with the American Embassy. Le Dactylo types it out, just the same, and it appears in the Beirut papers. And from here, it can be sent by news services around the world."

"An efficient system," said Rogers.

"Indeed it is. And one that is possible, I would immodestly add, only because of the efficiency and skill of the Lebanese intelligence service."

"And the pliancy of Lebanese editors," said Rogers.

General Jezzine's mouth smiled. The rest of his face remained frozen. "That also reflects the efficiency of the Deuxième Bureau," he said.

"How?"

"Because Le Dactylo understands its clientele. We know that all Lebanese have a common weakness. To put it bluntly, they can be bought. It is a fact of life. We are a small, poor country with few resources. Our people live by their wits. They sell their most valuable asset, which is their loyalty, to the highest bidder. It is not our most admirable trait, perhaps, but it is understandable.

"Unfortunately we in the Deuxiène Bureau cannot afford to buy the loyalty of all our citizens. But we have learned a little secret: You do not have to bribe someone yourself, so long as you know the identity of the person who *is* bribing him. Do you understand what I am saying? Knowledge truly is power. This is our technique, and in this way we can control nearly everyone."

"I'm not sure I understand," said Rogers untruthfully. In fact, he understood the bureau's methods perfectly well. It rigged elections, manipulated newspapers, and tapped telephones. It ran Lebanon.

"I will give you an example," said Jezzine. "Several years ago, the president of the republic held a meeting with the editors of all the major newspapers. He gathered them around the table and turned to them one by one, addressing them by the names of the Arab rulers who sent them money.

"'How is President Nasser?' he said to the editor of the paper that received a secret bribe from the Egyptians. 'How is President Assad?' he said to the editor who received a stipend from Syria. 'How is King Faisal?' he said to the editor whose payoffs came from Riyadh. And then he came to the editor of our most respected and incorruptible newspaper."

"And what did he say?" asked Rogers.

"He said, 'How is the whole bloody world?'"

Rogers laughed at the joke. Jezzine smiled and squinted his eyes, which for him was the equivalent of a belly laugh.

"So you see," continued Jezzine, "as long as we know who is paying whom in our corrupt little country, we have a handle on nearly everyone."

"But not everyone?" queried Rogers.

"Alas, there are fanatics among us whose motives are not so clean. They hunger for something other than money. They want dignity, justice, things that are difficult to provide on this earth. They are a more difficult problem."

"Forgive me for asking an impolite question," interrupted Rogers. "But why are you telling me all this?"

"You are aware, no doubt, that we have a presidential election coming soon," said the general.

"I am indeed aware of that," said Rogers.

"In our view, this election will determine the future of Lebanon. It will be a contest between the bloc we call the *'Nahj'* —a term that refers to the 'method' of our president, which has guided this country successfully for twelve years—and the forces of corruption and anarchy that would succeed him. If we lose, the forces of anarchy will assume power—the corrupt bureaucrats and traders, the Moslem hooligans, the Palestinians. We stand for stability and order. Our opponents stand for change and disorder. It is appalling to imagine what might happen if they win."

The general looked to Rogers for a nod of agreement or support but received none.

"Perhaps you do not understand," said the general. "We in the Deuxième Bureau have devised a formula for governing this riotous little country. We propose to run it like the army. The generals are Christians, yes, it is true. But many of the other officers are Sunni Moslems and Druse Moslems. And for soldiers, we have the Shiite Moslems, who ask only to be led. In an army, who thinks about religion? We are all Lebanese in the army, with one common purpose."

The general again looked for a nod of encouragement from Rogers. But still there was none.

"Do you know what our president calls these little men of the opposition who propose to take the country away from us?"

"What?" asked Rogers.

"The *fromagistes*—the cheesemen. That is what you will have if they win the election. A nation run by the cheesemen."

Rogers smiled. So it's the cheesemen versus the rats, he told himself.

"What do you want from us?" asked Rogers.

The general sighed.

"Support. Encouragement. Money. I have already explained the details of what we need to Mr. Hoffman."

"And what has he told you?" asked Rogers.

"That it is the policy of the United States to remain neutral in the election."

"That is also my understanding of our policy."

General Jezzine clucked his tongue in exasperation.

"You cannot expect me to believe that."

"But it is true," said Rogers. "We are neutral. We aren't providing money to either side, I assure you."

"Then I am offended," said the general icily. "I am perturbed that you care so little about us."

Rogers cocked his head.

"Wait a minute," said the American. "Are you telling me that you are disappointed in America because we aren't trying to fix your election?"

"Precisely," said the general. He looked genuinely hurt.

Rogers wanted to laugh out loud but feared that he would offend his host even more.

"Do you know what your Mr. Hoffman told me when I raised these issues with him?" asked the general.

"No," said Rogers, wondering what pearl of wisdom the station chief had offered.

"He said: 'Take a walk, Charlie.' Those were his precise words. Tell me, please, what does that mean?"

"It means no," said Rogers. "It's an emphatic way of saying no."

There was an awkward silence.

"When you called me and suggested that you pay a visit," continued the general, "I hoped that perhaps it was Mr. Hoffman's way of apologizing and showing that he had changed his mind. But I gather that is not the case. You are not coming to offer support in the election?"

"No, I am not."

"Pity," said the general.

He stood and walked to his gun case, took out a shotgun, and pointed it toward the valley.

"I have come here for a different reason," said Rogers.

"What is that?" responded the general diffidently from the window, aiming his gun at unseen targets.

"I will explain," said Rogers. He rose from the couch and walked over to where the general was standing. He spoke carefully, in a confidential voice.

"Sir," began Rogers. "The embassy is worried about the growth of underground militias among the Christians. We are worried that these organizations are part of a cycle of violence in Lebanon that may eventually become impossible to control. We assume that you know about these organizations."

"Of course I do," said the general. "That is my job."

"We hope that you share our concern."

"That is a different matter," said Jezzine. "My concern is for the future of Lebanon."

"May I ask you a question?" said Rogers.

The general nodded his head.

"Why do these organizations exist?" pressed Rogers. "What is their purpose?"

"They exist because of the dangerous prospect I spoke of a moment ago. The prospect that the power of the army, repre-

sented by the Deuxième Bureau, will be destroyed in the next
election, leaving this country at the mercy of its enemies. In
that event, it will be necessary to supplement the power of the
army with private groups. Groups that can do things that the
army, in a divided country like ours, cannot do."

"What things?" pressed Rogers.

"I will leave that to your imagination. Let us simply say:
things that are part of the reality of warfare, but cannot be
publicly admitted."

"That sounds dangerous to me."

"You are not a Lebanese."

"Let me put my cards on the table," said Rogers. "The
embassy wants to know more about these Christian underground groups. I have come to make a request: that you share
with us whatever information you have on this subject."

"Why don't you just steal it from us?" asked the general.
"We know you have your own agents inside our service. You
won't even need to steal it. We'll probably give it away free."

"I'm not talking about what we can get from file clerks,"
said Rogers. "We don't need any more telephone taps or sto-
len documents. We want what isn't in the files. The things
that people won't talk about on the phone or put in writing but
will tell you privately, because they trust you."

"Impossible," said the general.

"Why?" asked Rogers.

"Because I don't agree with what you are doing. Why
should I help you analyze the symptoms when I want to cure
the disease?"

"What do you mean?"

"If you want to prevent the growth of underground terrorist
organizations among the Christians, then help our side in the
election. We are the alternative to that sort of anarchy."

"We cannot do that," said Rogers. "I have already explained that our policy is to remain neutral."

"Then I refuse to help you destroy the secret weapons that
we may need someday to protect Lebanon."

Rogers began to speak again, making the same request in a
different way, but General Jezzine cut him off.

"We will not speak about this subject again," said the general coldly. His manner changed, as quickly and completely as
if he had changed his clothes.

"I believe it is time for lunch," said the Lebanese intelligence officer, leading Rogers through two large oak doors into a formal dining room.

Rogers took his place at the long dining table, which was set with the heaviest silver knives and forks he had ever hoisted. On his right was Madame Jezzine. She was wearing a black dress with a plunging neckline and a heavy gold necklace. The gold ornament gleamed above her bosom like a mark of ownership.

Madame Jezzine was as charming and flirtatious as Rogers had remembered. She resumed the conversation they had begun nearly a year ago at the ambassador's house, as if the intervening months had been no more than a trip to the powder room.

"We were talking of the differences between my country and Lebanon," said Madame Jezzine.

"You have a good memory," said Rogers.

"I thought later," she continued, "of one difference that would perhaps help you to understand all the others."

"I would like to hear it."

"The best way to explain it is for me to ask you some questions. Yes?"

"Yes," said Rogers.

"In America, what kind of houses did your pioneers build?"

Rogers thought a moment.

"Wood, mostly," he answered.

"Of course! That is what we read in all our histories of America. Your famous pioneers exploring the vast continent, building their famous log cabins. Living in one for a few years and then moving on to build another log cabin somewhere else. That is our picture of America: a land of fields and forests and houses made of wood. Is it accurate?"

"Yes, I suppose it is," said Rogers. He found the Lebanese woman irresistible.

"Now," she continued, "what kind of houses do we Lebanese build?"

Rogers looked at the walls of the Jezzine house, and through the window at the houses of the village. Every single one was built of the same material.

"Stone," said Rogers.

"Correct!" said Madame Jezzine. "Now what does that tell you about the Lebanese? It tells you that we build our houses to last forever. A Lebanese man builds the house that he will die in, that his sons and grandsons will die in. He may go away to work in Africa or even America. But he will always come home to that stone house. For him, there is nothing else on earth except his house and his village."

"I see your point."

"Do you?" asked the Lebanese woman. "Are you sure that you do? Imagine for a moment what this man in his stone house will feel if he suddenly sees other people in his midst, who have come into his country and are building houses of their own in the shadow of his village. Do you think he will feel threatened?"

"Who might these newcomers be?" asked Rogers, already knowing the answer.

"The Palestinians, of course!" said Madame Jezzine. "As I told you once before, they are destroying my country."

Their conversation was interrupted by an attractive woman sitting across the table, next to General Jezzine. She was a cousin visiting for the day, and she was dressed in the most exquisite summer outfit of silk and jade and pearls.

"Did you hear the news on the radio this morning?" asked the woman slyly. There was a look of pure malice on her face.

"No," said Madame Jezzine.

"There was a bomb in one of the Palestinian refugee camps."

"Was anyone killed?" asked General Jezzine.

"Malheureusement, no," said the cousin. "Perhaps next time." That was her joke. She laughed and put one of her long slender fingers delicately on the strand of pearls around her neck.

A waiter arrived with a tray piled high with roast quail, which had been shot by one of the general's sons. Madame Jezzine turned to Rogers and said quietly: "Do you see what I mean?"

Rogers nodded.

There was gay banter around the table. Rogers got into a conversation with a young man seated on his left, who was married to the well-dressed cousin. He was a smooth, carefully groomed young businessman who was working in Saudi Arabia. His name was Elias, and he seemed to have many political contacts in Lebanon and abroad. He made rude comments about the Saudis and their backwardness through much of the lunch.

When the meal was nearly done, Rogers turned back to his hostess. He spoke quietly, so as not to be overheard by General Jezzine.

"Suppose I wanted to understand better the views of the Lebanese Christians," said Rogers. "Who would you suggest that I go see?"

Madame Jezzine deliberated for a moment.

"My confessor," she said softly. "Father Maroun Lubnani."

"Where is he?" asked Rogers.

"Kaslik!" boomed a voice from across the table. It was the voice of General Jezzine. The usually stone-faced man was smiling.

22

Beirut; July 1970

Rogers travelled several nights later to the University of the Holy Ghost at Kaslik. It was a spectacular drive up the coastal highway, through East Beirut and the harbor of Jounie. There was a full moon out, painting a silvery beam across the Mediterranean and casting faint shadows within the dark stone cloisters of the university. It was an eerie landscape, drawn in shades of black, like a photographic negative come to life.

Kaslik was a symbol of Lebanon's troubles. Once a sleepy religious institution, the university had in recent years become a center for militant Maronitism, a place where priests and students met to discuss Christian political tactics rather than theology. The issue was Christian survival, argued the firebrands of Kaslik. The Palestinian commandos had tipped the political balance in Lebanon toward the Moslems, endangering the protected status of the Christians. Some of the Maronite theorists went further and advanced the ultimate Arab heresy: the Lebanese Christians were like the Jews of Israel! Both were tiny islands in a hostile sea of Islam and Arabism. Before it was too late, the Christians should emulate the Jews and vanquish their enemies.

Father Maroun Lubnani met Rogers at the gate and escorted him to his monastic cell, a simple room that contained a narrow brass bed, a desk, two chairs, and a crucifix. Father Maroun was a sturdy man, built like a football linebacker. He wore a simple cassock with a rope belt, as if to say: I am a humble friar. Rogers didn't beleive it. He introduced himself to the Lebanese cleric discreetly, identifying himself only as a representative of the U.S. government who worked at the embassy.

Father Maroun gestured with his hand as if to say: Come now. Do you take me for a fool? The priest appeared surprised when Rogers spoke to him in Arabic. He said he would prefer to speak in French.

"Are you acquainted with the history of our Church in the Middle East?" Father Maroun asked.

Rogers didn't answer, but it seemed that no response was required. Father Maroun had a prepared text.

"It is a history, I may say, of survival. It is the story of a mountain people who would not surrender their faith or their liberty." As he spoke, the priest gestured with his large, thick fingers.

"Our ancestors sought refuge in Mount Lebanon thirteen hundred years ago, following a theological dispute in which they sided with Rome against Byzantium. They were driven from northern Syria into these mountains, and their ancestors have remained here ever since."

The priest paused.

"Fighting for survival," ventured Rogers.

Father Maroun looked at him with the pained expression of a professor whose lecture has been interrupted by an over-eager pupil. He arched his eyebrows and continued.

"The Maronites were never warriors. We were montagnards who fought only to protect ourselves. We welcomed other persecuted minorities into our midst: Greek Orthodox, Melchite and Syriac Christians, Druse and Alawite Moslems.

"As the centuries passed, we saw the rise of Islam and the periodic slaughter of Christians in the Middle East. The Armenians in Turkey, the Copts in Egypt, the Greeks in Anatolia. We saw people driven from their land. The Armenians lost their ancient kingdom. The Palestinians lost Palestine. The Jews themselves left Israel and were gone for nearly two thousand years! But we did not leave. We stayed in our mountains and created a nation—the Lebanon—that embodied our belief in freedom and religious tolerance."

The priest paused and poured a glass of water for himself and one for his guest.

"Lebanon is under attack," he continued. "The battle is just beginning, but the dimensions of the conflict already are clear. The Palestinians, who understand that they cannot regain their land from the Jews, have decided that they will take our land instead. The Lebanese Moslems, who are afraid of their Arab brothers and secretly dream of ruling an Islamic state, are encouraging the Palestinians to destroy Lebanon. Our corrupt government has nearly surrendered. They have given the fedayeen control over South Lebanon and allowed the gunmen to parade their weapons on the streets and highways. No true nation would tolerate such things! Even the King of Jordan, a frightened little man, will find the courage to expel these bandits from his country.

"And what will Lebanon do?" asked Rogers. As he listened to the priest, Rogers had in his mind an image. He saw a colorful sweater, frayed at the edge, and a man tugging at one of the loose strands of yarn.

"Make no mistake!" said Father Maroun, his voice rising. "We Christians will destroy Lebanon before we surrender! If the Lebanese government will not support us, then we will defy the government. If the Lebanese Army will not defend us, then we will form our own army! You Americans cannot stop us. Do not imagine—ever—that we will stand aside so that others can solve their problems at our expense."

"Surely there is a way to save your country without committing suicide."

The priest looked at Rogers and shook his head ruefully. How foolish you Americans are, his expression seemed to say.

"We are in mortal danger," said the priest. "We look to you for help, as a child looks to his father. We are disciples of the Church of Rome. We are an island of freedom and democracy in the Moslem Arab world. We look to the West. A father who does not fight to protect his children is unworthy of respect!"

"And if the West doesn't help you?" asked Rogers.

"We have other friends, closer to home, who understand our cause and are prepared to help us."

"What friends?" asked Rogers.

"Our friends are discreet, and they expect us to be discreet also."

The priest was exhausted. His face was red and his thick

fingers were trembling. Rogers felt he owed the old man some
sort of response.

"I cannot speak for my government," said Rogers. "But I
must tell you honestly, speaking for myself, that what you are
describing worries me. I worry that in creating private armies,
you will weaken the institutions of the Lebanese state, on
which your people depend for their security."

"Leave me," said the priest. "I am tired. Especially I am
tired of friends who say they care about us, but not enough to
help us defend ourselves. Perhaps we need new friends."

"Can I come to visit you again, Father?" asked Rogers.

The priest nodded.

Rogers left him in his cell with his head bowed in prayer.

Yakov Levi travelled the same coastal road toward Kaslik
not long after Rogers. He was on a business trip for Franco-
Lebanese Trading Co., to see a client in Jounie. If he made a
stop along the way, and waited in a park in Ashrafiyeh, what
of it? It was a lovely summer day. And if he chanced to pick
up a newspaper that had been left on the park bench, that was
no crime. And anyway, on such a pleasant day, who would
notice?

Levi drove slowly into Jounie, a port town that hugged the
shore of a magnificent half-moon bay, a few miles north of
Beirut. He parked his car, walked along the quay, and looked
toward the Casino du Liban, which rested on top of a hill at
the far end of the bay. Perhaps I will go to the Casino after
lunch, thought Levi. Perhaps I will be lucky today.

Levi looked innocent enough: a small, wiry man with curly
hair, a bit tense perhaps, but who was not these days? He
walked through several stores, browsing, but keeping his eye
on the door. He walked down the main street and then, as if
he had forgotten something, changed direction. When he was
convinced that he wasn't being followed, Levi headed toward
the outskirts of the town. Eventually, he came to a small dirt
road that skirted a grove of olive trees. He stopped at a small
religious shrine along the road. It was a terra cotta likeness of
the Virgin Mary, hand-painted by a local artist so that she
looked Lebanese. Arrayed below the figure of Mary, like a
little altar, were candles enclosed in glass and prayers written
on tiny scraps of paper. Levi felt embarrassed. The dead drop

hadn't been his idea, but the suggestion of an agent he had never seen.

Levi left a piece of paper under the right edge of the terra cotta statue. It was a handwritten note that included times, dates, and places.

"24 September, Paris. 10:00." September 24, the day that a flight would be leaving Paris for Tel Aviv.

"8 October, 9:15." The return flight from Tel Aviv to Paris.

"331-74-26-85." The number of the Israeli Embassy in Paris, to be called only in case of an emergency.

Levi checked his watch. It was exactly 11:25 A.M. He looked over his shoulder once more and then crossed himself, in case anyone was watching. He felt ridiculous. A Jew, crossing himself before a Catholic shrine, on a dusty lane in an Arab country. It was too absurd. He continued on his way and eventually arrived back in Jounie in time for his business meeting.

The Israeli intelligence officer had left behind, in the roadside shrine, a message for a contact who, he had been told, was active in the Maronite Church. The message was an abbreviated itinerary for a trip the contact would be making to Israel in two months. The trip had been arranged at a level of the Israeli government far higher than Levi. The nominal purpose would be to visit the handful of Maronite religious institutions that still existed in Israel. But the Maronite cleric would be attending other meetings, with a range of Israeli government officials. It was a promising sign, the Mossad officials told each other, that the Maronite priest wanted to keep the contacts secret. That meant he had something to hide. Which suggested, in turn, that he was a serious man.

At noon, a lone figure appeared on the dirt road. He was dressed in a black cassock, wearing a gold cross. He carried in his hand a breviary, which was stamped in gold with his name: "Père Maroun Lubnani—L'Université du Saint-Esprit de Kaslik." The priest walked to the shrine, removed a piece of paper, said a brief prayer, and, after making the sign of the cross, turned and walked back down the road.

There was a blizzard of cables from Langley that summer, so many that Rogers gave up trying to read them. All hell was breaking loose in Jordan. In early June, Palestinian commandos had ambushed the king's motorcade and nearly killed him. Heavy fighting had erupted across Amman. The next day, the Popular Front for the Liberation of Palestine had seized the Intercontinental Hotel, across the street from the American Embassy, and held eighty-eight hostages at gunpoint.

The crisis passed, but the Americans were becoming frantic. The king seemed paralyzed and unwilling to order the Jordanian Army to crush the guerrillas. The new Jordanian cabinet was said to have a pro-fedayeen majority. There were rumors that the Old Man was meeting openly with leading Jordanian politicians and sounding them out about becoming prime minister in a PLO government, once the commandos had toppled the Hashemite regime.

CIA headquarters was more eager than ever to recruit a top-level agent in Fatah. Marsh himself had assumed operational control of the recruitment of Jamal, following the botched meeting in Cairo. He was going to meet with the Palestinian—himself—and set things right.

Marsh cabled Hoffman in early July with details of the meeting with Jamal. They would rendezvous at a hotel in Rome. A support agent from the Beirut station should accompany the Palestinian. There would be a new arrangement for running the operation after the Rome meeting, once control had been established.

Hoffman asked Rogers to meet one last time with the Palestinian and brief him on the details of the Rome meeting.

They met at the safehouse in Ramlet el-Baida, on the coast. Jamal arrived without his black leather jacket, in deference to the midsummer heat. He wore a white T-shirt and blue jeans, which made him look even more than usual like Marlon Brando.

Rogers shook the Palestinian's hand. Jamal kissed him on both cheeks. He seemed genuinely pleased to see the American case officer again, for the first time since their aborted meeting in Egypt.

"The last time I saw you," said Rogers, "you were running down the stairs in a pair of sandals and a suit that didn't quite fit. Evidently you survived the ordeal."

"I enjoyed it!" said Jamal. "It was like a cowboy movie."

"I didn't enjoy it," said Rogers. He looked at his watch.

"I don't have much time, so listen to me carefully," continued the American. "A very senior official of the American government wants to meet with you. He would like to continue the discussions you and I have begun."

"Fine," said Jamal. "If he understands the arrangement that you and I have reached, why not?"

Rogers said nothing. He took a piece of paper from his pocket and handed it to Jamal.

"This is the address of the hotel in Rome where he will meet you and the time and day of the meeting. Fuad will go with you. He will give you money for the trip and arrange any other details."

"When will you arrive?" said Jamal, lighting a cigarette and taking a deep drag.

"I won't," said Rogers. "I'm not coming to the Rome meeting."

"Why not?" asked Jamal.

"I'm busy with other work. And I think it's important that you and the senior official have a chance to talk alone." Rogers sounded almost convincing.

Jamal nodded his head, but he wasn't pleased.

"I would prefer that you be there," said Jamal.

"That isn't an option," said Rogers.

"Why not?" asked Jamal. "What has changed?"

"Nothing," said Rogers. "Don't complain about meeting someone from headquarters. It's a sign that we're serious."

"But my understanding was with you, not the American government."

"It's the same thing," said Rogers.

"What about your promises in Kuwait?"

"Stop it!" snapped Rogers. "You may thing the world revolves around you and the Old Man, but it doesn't. There are lots of other things going on, and I have other responsibilities. I'm not a babysitter."

Jamal was stung. His expression had turned from enthusiasm to concern, and now to an angry silence. Rogers hated to wound him, but saw no other way to make the break that was necessary.

Jamal rose from his chair. He put the sheet of paper with the instructions on it in the pocket of his blue jeans and headed for the door. He had his hand on the door knob when he stopped and turned back toward Rogers.

"Will we meet again?" asked Jamal. There was something of the child in his voice.

"Of course," said Rogers. "Don't be melodramatic."

"I have another Arab proverb for you to add to your collection," said Jamal.

"What's that?" asked Rogers.

"'Entertain the Bedouin and they will steal your clothes.'"

Jamal let himself out the door. Rogers sat alone in the apartment for a few minutes and then went back to the embassy and his paperwork.

23

Rome; July 1970

Rome was hot and sticky. The vines on the stone walls in the Villa Borghese looked wilted. The shops on Via Frattina closed early for the afternoon siesta. Even the lizards on the Palatine Hill hid beneath the rocks until it was dark.

Marsh made a point of not minding the heat. He believed that physical sensations, like fatigue or fear or heat itself, could be overcome by an exercise of will. With this in mind, he had purchased a pair of sunglasses when he arrived in Rome: the kind with thick black frames that the Italians liked. They made him feel cooler. So did his suit, a blue suit of tropical wool made by the tailor in Hong Kong he had befriended when he was stationed there. Many of his colleagues had left Asia in the 1960s with bullet wounds. Marsh had left with suits.

"Anyone for tennis?" Marsh asked his luncheon companions. They were eating at Il Buco, a small outdoor restaurant on Via Sant'Ignazio near the Pantheon. The other luncheon guests, sweating in the midday heat, looked incredulously at the visiting American. Except for a vivacious young Italian woman named Anna Armani. She was married to one of the generals who headed the Servizio Informazione Difesa, as the Italian intelligence service was then called.

"Andiamo!" said Anna. Let's go! Her husband gave her a wink.

The general's wife collected Marsh an hour later at the

Excelsior Hotel on the Via Veneto and drove him to a tennis club north of the city. It was an elegant Roman establishment, with red-clay courts and street urchins in white shorts acting as ball boys. As they began to warm up, a look of disappointment showed on Anna's face. Her American guest, though dressed in expensive tennis clothes from head to toe, was a player of modest skills. After they had played a set, Marsh proposed that they take a breather. As they walked toward the clubhouse, Anna Armani noticed that her guest was limping slightly.

"War wound," said Marsh.

It was true. He had sprained his ankle badly once in Saigon running along the pavement during a rainstorm. The general's wife nodded sweetly and led him to the clubhouse. She rubbed the tender ankle and held an icepack against it. The American's spirits improved markedly.

"What a wonderful country!" said Marsh as he sat on the clubhouse patio, gazing out at the courts and the Roman hills beyond. He was sipping a Campari soda. The midday heat had passed and the courts were beginning to fill up with Italians: members of parliament, prominent journalists, executives of the Italian national oil company, ENI. Anna Armani explained that the club was frequented mostly by people connected with the Socialist Party.

"Do you know what I love about Italy?" said Marsh grandly. "You can buy anything here. Clothes. Ideas. People. That's why this country is so stable beneath the surface. Because everything has its price!"

"Everything?" asked Anna coquettishly.

"Everything but love," answered Marsh. He imagined that he was being charming.

"Perhaps you will live here someday, since you love Italy so much."

"Perhaps," said Marsh. "But my area of expertise lies a bit further east."

"I hope you will come to Rome. My husband says you are a clever man."

"Oh does he really now? He should be more discreet."

"Come now!" said Anna. "It is not a secret that you are a clever man."

She adjusted the icepack on his ankle. Marsh chided himself, Don't be so uptight. Her husband already knows enough about the CIA to fill a book.

"Will you be in Rome long?" asked Anna. "We would love to have you to dinner."

"I'm afraid it's just a short trip. Just one meeting, really. I'll probably be leaving in a day or so."

"What a shame!" said Anna. "To come so far."

There was a lull in the conversation. They gazed toward the tennis courts and watched the players, chattering in Italian as they batted the balls back and forth on the red clay. Marsh noticed a tall Arab playing on one of the courts. He was a distinguished-looking man, with long legs and a slice backhand.

"Who's he?" asked Marsh.

"I don't know," said Anna. "One of the Arabs."

"Are there many Arabs living in Rome these days?"

"They are everywhere!" said Anna disgustedly. "They are ruining prices in the stores. Soon the signs in the shops on Via Condotti will be only in Arabic."

"And Palestinians?" asked Marsh, thinking he might gather a little intelligence. "Are there many Palestinians in Rome?"

"I don't know," answered Anna. "They all look the same to me."

"Do you find them attractive?" asked Marsh.

"Ugh!" said Anna Armani. "I am one of those things in Italy that Arab money cannot buy."

Marsh was in heaven. He chatted for more than an hour with the Italian woman. She seemed fascinated and besides, Marsh told himself, she was practically one of the family. But despite her ministrations with the icepack, his ankle still hurt. On the way back to the hotel, Marsh stopped in a store near the Via Veneto and bought himself a carved wooden cane.

Marsh sometimes struck people as a fool, but he wasn't. Shy by nature, he had taught himself to be outgoing and enthusiastic by an act of will. Like many insecure people, he sometimes behaved with a certain pomposity and braggadocio. But he cared as much about the agency as any of his colleagues. He simply had a different style.

Marsh was more cautious and less instinctual than some of his fellow officers. He was one of those people who believe that slow and steady would win the race, who regarded himself as the tortoise in life's never-ending contest with the hare. He brought this methodical approach to his handling of agents. He was determinedly uncreative. Creativity got people killed, Marsh told himself. Playing by the book kept them alive.

In the world of recruiting agents, playing by the book meant contracts that were clearly understood by both sides, ones that imposed on the slippery and deceitful world of espionage some of the order of the legal world. Marsh liked relationships that were clear and straightforward. I buy your services for an agreed-upon price; you agree to deliver certain material in exchange; we both profit by the relationship. He understood that sort of arrangement, and he believed in it. Each side knew the risks and rewards. It was a transaction between adults. What troubled Marsh were relationships that were more complicated, where subtler and less orderly motivations prevailed. Those relationships—based on frail human emotions like friendship, respect, and loyalty—were the dangerous ones. And perhaps also less moral.

Anna reported her conversation with Marsh to her husband that night. He rubbed his eyeballs and lit a thick French cigarette.

"How long is he here?" asked General Armani.

"Long enough for one meeting. Perhaps only a day."

So he is meeting an agent, the general thought to himself.

"What was on his mind?" asked the general.

"Let me see," said Anna. "He talked about buying things. He talked about Italy. He asked about an Arab who was playing tennis. He asked whether there were many Palestinians in Rome. He asked whether I found them attractive. He seemed interested in Arabs."

"He has Arabs on the brain," said the general.

"Yes, maybe. And me. He has me on the brain, too. I think maybe he wanted to sleep with me, but he was too shy to say so."

"Thank you, my dear," said General Armani, giving her a kiss on the cheek and a pat on the bottom. He lit another cigarette and went to the phone.

"The American is in Rome to meet an Arab agent," said

General Armani in crisp Italian to one of his colleagues. "We could arrange surveillance, but what does it matter? He isn't meeting an Italian!"

He hung up the phone. General Armani had done his duty and notified the appropriate authorities.

But nothing in Italy is ever quite that simple. The SID at the time was split into two factions. One was pro-Arab, the other pro-Israeli. General Armani was part of the latter faction. He made it a practice, from time to time, to pass along to the Israelis bits of information he thought would interest them. They reciprocated with information that was useful to the general. It was a trade, the universal commerce of the intelligence business.

"I'm going for a little walk, darling," said the general. He strolled to a pay telephone several blocks away and dialed the number of an Israeli friend. The general knew the phone was tapped—his own people did the tapping—so he muffled his voice and arranged a quick rendezvous in a bar near his house.

When the Israeli arrived, General Armani came quickly to the point: A CIA man named Marsh was in town. He hadn't said why, but it was a safe bet that he had come to meet an agent. It was also a good bet that his trip involved an Arab. Perhaps a Palestinian, the general said. He thought the Israeli government would like to know.

The Israeli asked where Marsh was staying and what name he was travelling under. But the general begged off. There were limits, he said.

The information went into the Mossad files in Tel Aviv. It was one more bit of evidence to support a thesis that the Israeli intelligence analysts had speculated about often enough, but never explored in detail: the possibility that the Americans had secret contacts with the Palestinian terrorists. The subject raised the most awkward sort of question. If a friend has dealings with your enemy, is he still your friend?

Fuad arrived in Rome that night with Jamal in tow. He had reserved a suite at the San Marco Hotel, a modern and anonymous establishment on Monte Mario, overlooking the city. When the two Arabs pulled up to the entrance, the lobby was nearly empty and Fuad got nervous about security. He preferred a crowd. He told the taxi driver to take them into the city for dinner.

"Where you go?" asked the driver. Jamal spoke up, answering in Italian that they wanted to go to Sabatini in Piazza Santa Maria di Trastevere. It seemed that Jamal had been in Rome before.

They returned to the San Marco just before midnight. Jamal sat in the cocktail lounge, listening to a guitarist named Carlo Mustang, while Fuad checked in and went to the room. Thirty minutes later the Palestinian called Fuad on the house phone and discreetly made his way upstairs. The hotel, thinking that Fuad must be an Arab oil potentate, had sent up baskets of fruit and an arrangement of flowers.

The concierge called and asked in broken Arabic if the Pasha would like female company. Jamal answered the phone and said yes enthusiastically.

"Quattro, per favore!"

Fuad overruled him. Business before pleasure, he admonished his ward. Deprived of women, Jamal fixed himself a whisky and soda from the mini-bar and turned on the television, which was broadcasting American cartoons dubbed into Italian.

At eleven the next morning Marsh arrived and knocked twice on the door. "Is this Mr. Anderson's room?" he asked.

"No," said Fuad. "But Mr. Jones is here."

Marsh, who liked tradecraft, had cabled the passwords to Beirut the previous week.

The American solemnly entered the suite, leaning on his new wooden cane and nodding to Fuad as if he was the maître d' in a fancy restaurant. Jamal stood in a corner of the room, wearing his usual black shirt and trousers. His hair, still wet from the shower, was combed back slick against his head. Marsh cleared his throat and extended his hand.

"I represent the National Security Council," said Marsh. "I bring you greetings from the President of the United States."

Jamal said nothing. Fuad suggested that everyone sit down.

"My government is very pleased with the work you have done for us," Marsh began.

Jamal cut him off.

"I haven't done any work for your government," said the Palestinian.

Marsh peered at him over the rim of his glasses and then continued as if he hadn't heard.

"My government hopes that our relationship can become stronger and more clearly defined." He looked toward Jamal and smiled.

"Shu al haki?" said Jamal angrily to Fuad. What is this guy talking about?

Fuad excused himself for a moment and asked Jamal to join him in the bedroom. They talked noisily for a minute or so. An Arabic speaker could have heard Fuad repeating several times an expression that means: Calm down. Eventually they returned and the conversation resumed.

Marsh pressed on as if nothing had happened.

"We would like to hear your assessment of the situation in Jordan," Marsh said. Jamal turned toward Fuad and answered the question in Arabic. It was intended as a sign of disrespect to the American, but the gesture was lost on Marsh. He assumed that the Palestinian spoke English poorly.

"The road to Jerusalem passes through Amman," translated Fuad. "The King should go back to the Hejaz. If America isn't worried that the King is finished, then why are you here, talking to a man from Fatah?"

"Hmmmm," said Marsh. "That isn't very helpful." He posed another question, this time about Fatah's contacts with Soviet intelligence. Again Jamal gave a vague and elliptical answer.

Marsh then asked the number of people under Jamal's command in his section of the Rasd, the Fatah intelligence organization. He sounded like a man at a cocktail party who is running out of things to say.

"Very many," said Jamal in English, smiling at the American.

"One hundred?" pressed Marsh.

"Perhaps. Perhaps more, perhaps less. I don't know."

The discussion meandered in this way for forty-five minutes, producing little of value for either side. Jamal asked several questions about American policy toward the Palestinian problem, eliciting long and ponderous answers from Marsh. As the discussion progressed, Jamal concluded that the American—though evidently a fool—was probably harmless. He missed Rogers.

Lunch was ordered. Fuad intercepted the waiter at the door to prevent him from glimpsing his two guests. Jamal poured himself a double whisky from a bottle in the bedroom and drank it down in several gulps.

Marsh proposed a toast to the future of U.S.–Palestinian cooperation. Jamal responded with a Lebanese toast—*Kaysak!*—which literally means: "Your glass!" Then he smiled and repeated the toast, changing the pronunciation slightly. Mispronounced in this way, the word meant: "Your cunt!"

When lunch was done, Marsh turned to Fuad and asked him to leave the room. "We have some matters to discuss," the American said. Jamal protested, but Fuad was already out the door.

Marsh removed from his pocket a device that looked like a small tape recorder and turned it on. It made a babbling noise, like the sound of five conversations taking place at once.

"Security," said Marsh with a wink.

Jamal clucked his tongue.

"Let's talk business," Marsh began. "As you may have guessed, I am an intelligence officer. I am familiar with the details of your case and I have read the full transcripts of all your previous meetings."

Jamal winced.

"Oh yes!" said Marsh, nodding his head for emphasis. "We have all of those meetings on tape!"

Jamal lit a cigarette and seemed to disappear in the clouds of smoke. Marsh pursued him intently.

"I must also advise you that I am a senior official of my agency, unlike the people you have dealt with previously, and I am thus familiar with the broad aspects of this case."

"What case?" muttered Jamal. He was slumped in his chair, like a teenager listening to an especially unwelcome parental lecture. His head was tilted so that he looked at Marsh out of half-closed eyes.

"Am I going too fast for you?" asked Marsh.

"No," said Jamal, slumping even deeper in his chair.

"Good. Now then, I believe that our relationship with you has gotten off to a bad start because we haven't clarified in a businesslike way the nature of our dealings. We are in the business of acquiring information. You have information that is of value to us. Therefore, a basis exists for a relationship that is mutually beneficial. But there must be no mistake—I repeat, no mistake—about who is running the show. There will be severe consequences for you if you fail to live up to your side of the bargain. Would you like me to detail those consequences?"

Instead of answering, Jamal sat up in the chair and spit on the rug.

"Stop that!" said Marsh. Control your agent, he reminded himself.

The American picked up a leather attaché case he had brought with him and placed it on the coffee table in front of Jamal. He turned it toward the Palestinian and popped the locks. The case was filled with $100 bills, neatly stacked and bound. The money, gathered covertly from a half-dozen banks in Europe, was dog-eared and dirty.

"I hope we can reach a businesslike agreement," said Marsh. "There is $100,000 in that briefcase as an initial payment. You may count it if you like." He picked up a wad of bills and rifled them with his thumb.

"As in any business arrangement, I must request that you sign a contract." He removed a sheet of paper from his inside coat pocket and placed it face up on the table, next to the money. From another pocket he removed an ink pad, to take the fingerprint that would form his receipt.

Jamal lit another cigarette. His face had the tight surface tension of a balloon that is nearly ready to explode.

Marsh was oblivious. In his own nervousness, he had barely looked at the Palestinian.

"As you will see from the contract," continued Marsh, "we propose to pay you a sum of three million dollars over the next five years. The balance will be paid in regular installments to a numbered bank account in Switzerland. We have taken the liberty of opening the account already.

"Three million dollars!" Marsh repeated the sum like an incantation. With this final, gross invitation to bribery, the balloon burst.

Jamal rose from his chair, muttered an oath in Arabic, and kicked the attaché case—dumping the neat stacks of bills on the floor. He loomed over Marsh's chair. His hands were shaking with rage. Hundred-dollar bills were scattered on the rug in front of Marsh.

"You bastard!" said the Palestinian. "If I had a gun I would shoot you!"

With that, Jamal went to the bedroom and began packing his bag.

Marsh, suddenly frantic, walked to the bedroom and began making blackmail threats. He talked about photos, tapes, incriminating evidence that would be sent to the Soviets, warrants that would be issued for Jamal's arrest in Italy, Lebanon, and Jordan. When it was obvious that these threats were having no effect, Marsh picked up the phone and called a number that reached the switchboard of the Rome station. With a few prearranged code phrases, he signalled that he had a problem and needed a backup team in a hurry.

Jamal ignored the American. When he had finished packing, he walked briskly past Marsh to the door. He took the stairs to the ground floor and slipped out a side entrance, escaping into the heat of the Roman summer.

PART VI

September 1970 –
June 1971

24

Rogers was shattered when he heard about the Rome meeting.
He felt mute and helpless, like a father hearing the news that
one of his children has died while in the custody of someone
else. In the first several weeks he tried to reestablish contact
with Jamal. He came up with various stratagems, but nothing
worked. It was difficult to locate somebody if you couldn't
acknowledge that you knew him.

The Palestinian remained silent and invisible. The Lebanese had no record of his returning to Beirut. Indeed, nobody
had any record of his going anywhere. He had vanished. It
was then that Rogers began to suspect that he had underesti-
mated Jamal.

Rogers's immediate problem was Fuad. The Lebanese was
disgusted by what had happened, and for a time he disappeared, too. He eventually sent a message to Rogers from
Greece—a postcard from Skiathos—but Rogers let him be.
Fuad's anger toward the United States would help reinforce
his cover, Rogers assured Hoffman. Eventually, Fuad returned
to Beirut and threw himself into the whirl of Lebanese leftist
politics. He went to meetings of the Progressive Socialist
Party, the National Syrian Socialist Party, the Independent
Nasserite movement. He watched, he gathered information,
he reported at regular intervals to Rogers. And he wondered,
in his idle moments, why it was that the Americans were so
accident-prone.

The PECOCK file went dead. There were meetings and discussions. The DDP's office conducted a review of Marsh's handling of the Rome meeting and concluded that he had badly bungled the case.

Much as Rogers disliked Marsh, he felt sorry for him now. His career was in limbo. He asked for a transfer to the newly formed staff that was handling congressional relations. It was said to be a growth area for the agency. There was some debate about the wisdom of that move, but Stone vouched for Marsh's integrity. Rogers was pleased that his own arguments about how best to run the case had been vindicated, but that did him little good now. The agent had bolted.

In August, Stone made a swing through Beirut. Without ever admitting that his own recommendations had been wrong, he commended Rogers for his patience and good judgment. He also advised him that he would receive a promotion and advance to a higher pay grade as of September 1. It was Stone's way of saying that he was sorry.

Jamal found the disastrous meeting in Rome oddly comforting. It clarified matters for him. The Americans seemed, once again, to fit the stereotype. They were arrogant and manipulative, interested in the Arabs only to the extent that they could get something from them. Jamal was also relieved to have broken off the ambiguous relationship he had begun with Rogers. He liked blacks and whites better than grays.

The Old Man was not so pleased when he received a coded account of the meeting from Jamal through the Kuwaiti diplomatic pouch from Bonn. The Old Man regarded the American channel as a project of the highest importance. He sent Jamal a return message advising him to continue building his network in Europe. He should forget about the Americans for now. Fatah would maintain contact with them through other intermediaries in London and Amman.

Though the Americans didn't know it, Jamal was under their noses. He had remained in Europe, staying mostly in Rome, where the Fatah security service maintained a secret base of operations. The Fatah intelligence service, the Rasd, had safehouses there and secret sources of funds and even a local documentation office that produced forged travel documents. Jamal travelled occasionally through the summer, especially to Germany and France.

He was building an infrastructure. The Rome center operated under the cover of a bar called Il Principe Rosso near the Via Veneto. It was financed by wealthy Palestinians in Kuwait and provided the Rasd a discreet way to move large sums of money. The Italian authorities, had they been curious, would have believed it was nothing more than another Roman establishment cooking the books and cheating on its taxes. On his trips to Paris and Munich, Jamal broadened the network. He developed local contacts and used them to rent apartments, open bank accounts, spot local talent, and do the thousands of other mundane things that provide a base for clandestine operations.

Jamal didn't ask what it was all to be used for. The Old Man had told him that the movement might need such a network someday and dismissed further questions with a wave of his hand. Making his rounds in Europe, Jamal felt sometimes like a squirrel storing up nuts for a long winter whose advent nobody could predict.

The crisis in Jordan had been building for months. But the final confrontation was triggered by an act of terrorism so foolish and inflammatory that even Jamal wondered later whether it had been a deliberate act of provocation.

The Popular Front for the Liberation of Palestine launched a terrorist "spectacular" on September 6 by simultaneously hijacking two airplanes. They landed at an airstrip in Jordan that PFLP propagandists dubbed "The Airport of the Revolution." On September 9, the PFLP hijacked another plane. The group held nearly five hundred hostages, many of them Americans.

The hijackings were like pointing a blowtorch at a pool of gasoline. The flames exploded from several directions at once. The United States, which had been urging the king for months to crack down against the fedayeen, moved the Sixth Fleet toward the Eastern Mediterranean. The king—who had been taunted in recent months by Bedouin officers who put brassieres on their tank antennas to signal their doubts about his resolve—finally ordered the army to crack down hard. There was the usual comic interlude of mediation by the Arab

League. But the king finally gave the order to his army on September 17 to open fire with their tanks and heavy artillery.

The military pretensions of the guerrillas were quickly demolished. The Jordanian Army captured the Fatah headquarters on Nasser Square in minutes. The Old Man fled deeper into Jebel Hussein, then to the hilltop of Ashrafiyeh. In the first hours, the Fatah leader spent his time frantically calling his Jordanian political contacts to try to arrange a ceasefire. Fatah had no battle plan, no secure headquarters, no reliable communications other than open radio transmissions.

The one-sided battle lasted barely more than a week. It ended when the Old Man ignominiously slipped out of Amman, disguised in Bedouin robes as a member of a Kuwaiti mediating delegation. The Jordanians continued for more than a year mopping up what was left of the resistance until they eventually slaughtered the last band of die-hard fighters who had remained in the woods near Jerash and Ajlun in northern Jordan.

The Old Man had believed nearly to the end that he would win in Jordan. His folly was documented in stacks of handwritten memos and documents that were captured by the king's Bedouin troops during the Battle of Amman.

It was a touching collection. A hand-drawn plan of Basman Palace, roughly sketched as if by a child, showing how the fedayeen could attack the Hashemite monarch in his chambers. A crude map showing how to attack a Jordanian military encampment on a road between Amman and Salt. Another rough sketch showing how to penetrate Jordanian barbed wire. Lists that endlessly detailed the responsibilities of various chiefs and subalterns in this most bureaucratic revolution. Handwritten notes from the Old Man himself that showed him scheming, double-dealing, manipulating, and playing politics—assuring the king all the while that the fedayeen hadn't any designs on his throne.

After it was all over, the king gathered the most incriminating documents into a simple booklet called *The Activities of the Fedayeen in Jordan, 1970*. The booklet was printed only in Arabic and was never distributed in the West. But the king sent a copy to each of the twenty-one Arab heads of state. It was a catalogue of the Old Man's perfidy and helped explain why, for years after, the other Arab leaders paid lip service to the Palestinian cause but didn't fully trust the PLO chairman.

"Black September," as the dazed Palestinians called the events in Jordan, seemed at first like a finale, but it was really only a prelude. It was a hurricane, which swept through the cracks and crevices of the Arab political world and left the foundations weak and vulnerable. One of the Fatah leaders who supervised the Rasd's intelligence activities wrote later of a warning that he secretly transmitted to the Jordanian king after the events of Black September:

"If you strike the fedayeen in their last holdouts in Jerash and Ajlun, I'll follow you to the end of the earth, to my dying breath, to give you the punishment you deserve."

It must have sounded like a vain and idle threat. But it was the beginning of a nightmare that took the codename "Black September."

25

Beirut; Fall 1970

Hoffman came into the office the morning after the Lebanese election waving a copy of *An Nabar*, the leading Beirut newspaper. A banner headline across the top of the page proclaimed: "The Voice of the People Has Spoken." Beneath it was a front-page editorial, lauding the victory of the new president, who had been elected by parliament the previous day by one vote.

"Can you believe these assholes?" said Hoffman to his four senior officers as they sat down in the conference room for one of their infrequent staff meetings. Hoffman was in a bad mood: red-faced, mean-tempered, a menace to anyone unlucky enough to get in his way. He brandished the newspaper at Rogers.

"The guy wins by one fucking vote and they're calling it the voice of the people!" said Hoffman. "Imagine what they would be saying if he had won by *two* votes."

"Sore loser?" asked Robers.

"Hell, yes," said Hoffman. "It cost us plenty to buy the old gang of thugs. Now we've got to start all over again."

"It's a bit more complicated than that, chief," said the station's senior political analyst. He was a beady-eyed man who looked as though he should be wearing a green eyeshade.

"No doubt," said Hoffman. "Everything seems to be more complicated than I think it is. All I want to know is who won and who lost."

"That's just the problem," said the analyst. "It's very hard to tell. The old political establishment has been swept out of office, to be sure. But that doesn't mean there are clear winners and losers. The Sunni Moslems might seem to have won, since the new president has the support of most of the Sunni leadership. But the new president also has the support of some of the Christian militia leaders who were being squeezed by the old regime. So you see, it's really rather complicated."

"Bullshit," said Hoffman.

"May I suggest the real problem with this election?" ventured Rogers.

"Oh please," said Hoffman. "Absolutely. By all means."

"The real problem with this election was that both sides couldn't lose."

Hoffman tilted his head, squinted his eyes at Rogers, smiled with elaborate politeness, and silently clapped his hands. Rogers looked at the round-faced station chief. Sitting in his comfortable, overstuffed leather desk chair, he looked like Humpty-Dumpty.

"Now then, boys and girls," said Hoffman. "Since you're all such political experts, perhaps you can help the United States government figure out where we stand with the new leaders of this miserable excuse for a country."

There was silence.

"Any volunteers?"

"Yes, sir," spoke up a new member of the station named York Harding. He had arrived in Beirut two months earlier, following a stint in Vietnam, and he wore his hair in a crew cut. York Harding was what grade schoolers call an "eager beaver."

"Yes, Mr. Harding," said Hoffman.

"The election of the new president offers us a real opportunity for political action . . ."

"The election of the Squirrel," interjected Hoffman.

"The Squirrel?" queried Harding, totally mystified.

"That's what I call the new president, Mr. Harding. And do you know why?"

"No, sir," said Harding.

"Because he looks like one, you idiot! He's a furry little bastard whose cheeks always look like they're full of nuts. Don't you agree?"

"Yes, sir."

"Sorry I interrupted you, Mr. Harding. Pray, continue."

"I think the election of, uh, the Squirrel gives us a new opportunity to find a middle ground in Lebanon. A third force, between the Christians and the Moslems."

"A third force, eh?" said Hoffman, stroking his chin.

"Yes, sir."

"How long were you in Vietnam, son?" asked the station chief.

"Eighteen months, sir," said Harding.

"And you were a political action officer out in the countryside. Teaching the peasants about farming and medicine and self-government, and maybe a little throat-slitting on the side. Am I right, Harding?"

"Yes, sir."

"Well, spare me your Vietnam bullshit, will you, Mr. Harding? We may have problems here in Lebanon. But we are not yet at the total monumental fuck-up stage. You get me?"

"Yes, sir," said Harding.

"And if I ever hear the words 'third force' again, I'm going to throw you out the window."

"Yes, sir."

"And don't call me 'sir,' you cross-eyed little son of a bitch."

Rogers looked at Harding. The young case officer's eyes were moist. Rogers decided it was time to draw the bull away before he further wounded his young prey.

"Chief," said Rogers, "I think Harding has a point. There are opportunities created by the election of a new president. Let's face it. The incumbents were running a glorified police state. The country was under the thumb of the Deuxième Bureau, which made life easy for us. But the Lebanese, evidently, got sick of it."

"Sooooo?" said Hoffman.

"So we shouldn't shed any tears for the old gang."

"That's very touching," said Hoffman. "I'm ashamed that I've been so insensitive."

Rogers ignored Hoffman's sarcasm and pressed ahead.

"The problem is polarization," Rogers continued. "If extremism continues among Christians and Moslems, the whole country will begin to unravel. Harding is right. The only hope lies in some kind of middle ground. What we should be discussing is whether we—the embassy—are ready to get serious about creating an alternative to extremism."

"I can answer that for you right now, boys and girls," said Hoffman. "The answer is No. N-O. No fucking way."

"Then that makes it simple," said Rogers. "If we aren't going to intervene to help the good guys, then we should at least try to keep track of the bad guys—the militias, terrorist cells, secret organizations. Find out what they're doing, and to whom."

"Motion proposed," said Hoffman. Without waiting for anyone to respond, he pounded the table with his fist.

"Agreed!"

Hoffman turned to other subjects: details of the station's operations; plans for making contact with members of the new government; guesses about who the new president would appoint to run the Deuxième Bureau; discussion of what Hoffman should tell headquarters in the cable he had to send later that day; and finally, a new scheme that Hoffman had devised for conducting surveillance in crowded areas that would, in theory, eliminate one person from each surveillance team. Eventually the station chief pushed his overstuffed chair back from the table and adjourned the meeting.

"Thank you very much, boys and girls," said Hoffman. "Class dismissed."

The Squirrel, as Hoffman called him, took office in September and immediately began a purge of the Deuxième Bureau. The first thing he did was change its name. It was no longer the Deuxième Bureau, simply the Military Intelligence Office.

A symbolic house-cleaning came several months later when the new prime minister, a moon-faced Sunni Moslem who smoked big Cuban cigars and wore a fresh carnation in his lapel every day, led a raid on the Deuxième Bureau's telephone-tapping facility. The tappers, housed in the central PTT building in downtown Beirut, had run a notorious operation that regularly monitored several thousand telephones. It was an outrageous violation of civil liberties, everyone agreed. Dismantle it! In the enthusiasm of the new regime, nobody thought to mention that the government was losing its best means of keeping track of the deadly political germs that were infecting Lebanon.

At the end of the year, the Squirrel took the inevitable last step. He replaced General Jezzine as head of the Lebanese intelligence service and quietly (though not so quietly that it wasn't the talk of Beirut) instructed the Ministry of Justice to begin investigating whether the general had violated the law in certain practices of the Deuxième Bureau.

General Jezzine, whatever his faults, was not stupid. He left the country a week after he was fired for what was described as a vacation in Geneva. Since it was well known that he maintained a house there and a large bank account, it was assumed that the general wouldn't be back any time soon. Rogers visited General Jezzine in his village the day before he left. He came to make a simple request. The American Embassy wanted access to Jezzine's files.

The general was curt and evasive. His files had all been confiscated by the new head of the intelligence service, the president's man, he said. Jezzine himself couldn't even get access to them now. He had taken a few personal papers with him, to be sure. Nothing of any importance. And those already had been shipped to Geneva. So there was nothing, alas, that he could do to help his dear friends, the Americans.

"I am touched by your concern," said the general sardonically as he ushered Rogers to the door. "Pity that it did not come a bit sooner."

The Squirrel's regime soon became mired in corruption. It was the revenge of what the former president had called "the cheesemen." A health minister who tried to reduce drug prices ran into a wall of opposition from friends of the president who monopolized the drug trade. The pharmaceutical magnates simply withheld drugs from the market—public health be damned!—until the minister gave up and resigned.

A public works minister who attempted to rebuild the country's primitive road system lasted only fifteen weeks. A finance minister who advanced the novel theory that the government should collect taxes and audit its books was rebuffed. The president's own son was installed as telecommunications minister and began soliciting bribes that were enormous, even by Lebanese standards.

It was get-rich-quick time in Lebanon. Rapid inflation turned peasants into land speculators and created a new class of overnight millionaires. The government became a free-for-all. In this climate of ambition and avarice, the Lebanese lost what little respect they still had in public institutions. The public stopped believing that what was left of the Deuxième Bureau would maintain order, or that the army would keep the Palestinian commandos in check. Instead, the Lebanese turned increasingly toward the private militias that were forming ranks throughout the country.

26

Beirut; April 1971

Jane Rogers was sitting in the doctor's waiting room with her daughter when she noticed a familiar face. The attractive Lebanese woman on the next couch, wearing an expensive silk dress, looked very much like a woman she had met at a party many months ago.

Jane was on the verge of introducing herself, but then thought better of it. The woman was wearing dark glasses and reading a magazine. The French edition of *Vogue*. Perhaps she didn't want to be disturbed. Better not to pry, especially not at the doctor's office.

Jane turned instead to her daughter Amy, who was playing with trinkets from her mother's purse. The child had recovered dramatically during the last few months. The worms had disappeared entirely, their Lebanese pediatrician assured them. So had the symptoms of neurological distress. Amy was cured.

Jane glanced again at the Lebanese woman and noticed that she wasn't wearing a wedding ring. Perhaps it wasn't the same woman, after all.

"Madame Jezzine," called out the nurse. The attractive Lebanese woman closed her magazine and rose from her seat.

I was right, thought Jane. She watched Madame Jezzine walk into the doctor's office. The elegant woman emerged five minutes later folding a piece of paper on which the doctor had written a prescription. She slipped it into her purse.

"Mrs. Rogers," called out the nurse. Jane, holding her

daughter by the hand, began walking toward the doctor's office. She had gone only a few steps when the Lebanese woman approached her.

"Jane," said Solange Jezzine with a warm smile. "I am sorry that I did not recognize you before. How pretty you look."

"Hello, Solange," said Jane.

The Lebanese woman greeted Jane fondly, kissing her on both cheeks. Jane felt slightly awkward at her transformation, in the space of several minutes, from total stranger to dear friend. But never mind. She kissed the Lebanese woman warmly. As she did so, Jane could smell the scent of an expensive perfumc behind each ear.

"And what a lovely little girl," said Solange, patting Amy on the head.

"Will you be long in there?" asked Solange, nodding toward the doctor's office.

"Only a minute," said Jane. "I'm just getting a prescription refilled."

"Good," said the Lebanese woman. "Then I'll wait. We'll have lunch together, my dear."

"All right," said Jane, trying to sound friendly. She glanced at the baby and hoped that Madame Jezzine didn't have in mind a fancy restaurant where a toddler might not be welcome.

Jane was in the doctor's office just long enough for him to write out a refill prescription for the birth-control pills she had been taking ever since Amy got sick. She had resolved then that she wouldn't have any morc children until they left the Middle East. The doctor liked his patients to come by in person to pick up their refill prescriptions rather than phoning the pharmacy. Perhaps he imagined it was more discreet that way. Jane found it the opposite. But never mind. Jane had folded the prescription and put it in her wallet by the time she returned to the waiting room.

Solange Jezzine gave Jane a little wink. She rose from the couch and greeted the American woman almost conspiratorially, putting her arm in Jane's. As they were walking out of the office, she whispered in Jane's ear.

"It's liberating, isn't it?"

"What's that?" asked Jane.

"The pill, my dear," said Solange. "Isn't that why you're here?"

Jane nodded shyly. She wondered whether she should explain that she wasn't taking birth-control pills to facilitate a love affair, as Madame Jezzine's whispered conversation implied, but for another reason. She decided to say nothing. It was pleasant, in a way, to be regarded by another woman as a secret co-conspirator. And she found that she rather liked Madame Jezzine's frankness. It seemed very Lebanese.

"It will transform the world," whispered Madame Jezzine. "Especially the Arab world."

On the curb outside the doctor's office stood a gleaming red Mercedes-Benz with white leather seats. A burly man, who had the disinterested air of a chauffeur, was sitting in the driver's seat. Next to him was an Asian woman dressed in a black skirt and a white apron, who appeared to be a maid.

"This is my car," said Madame Jezzine. "Come, get in."

Jane entered the car, which smelled of leather and perfume and the smoke of the driver's cigarettes. She set the baby on her lap, in the same motion checking her diapers to make sure they weren't wet.

"Chez les Anges," Madame Jezzine told the driver.

Jane recognized the name of the restaurant. It was a chic French bistro on the waterfront in West Beirut, not far from the embassy. It was reputed to be the most expensive place in town.

"I'm not sure that's a good spot for a toddler," said Jane.

"It isn't," said the Lebanese woman. "We'll leave her with Sophie." She gestured toward the maid.

Jane was going to say no, that's all right. Another time. That was the appropriate thing to say, after all. You couldn't very well leave your three-year-old daughter in the custody of someone else's maid. But she hesitated, and the reason was that she very much liked the idea of eating with a rich Lebanese woman at the fanciest restaurant in town.

"She'll be fine, won't she, Sophie?" said Madame Jezzine.

"Yes, madame," said the woman. She seemed to Jane to be Indian, or perhaps Sri Lankan. She looked responsible enough.

"Perhaps we could drop her off at our house," said Jane. "Would you mind that, Sophie? My cleaning lady is there, and she can help you look after the baby." Sophie nodded compliantly.

"Perfect!" said Madame Jezzine. "Tell the driver your address."

Jane directed the Mercedes-Benz to their apartment building in Minara. She took Amy and Sophie upstairs and explained the contents of the baby's kit bag. Extra diapers, favorite toys and books, a bottle filled with apple juice.

"If she cries, be sure to call the restaurant," said Jane.

"Yes, madame," said Sophie, wobbling her head in the submissive gesture that is characteristic of the Indian subcontinent.

Jane left the baby playing happily in her nursery and returned to Madame Jezzine. As she bounded down the steps and toward the car, she felt a giddy sense of adventure, and of momentary liberation from the routine of loyal wife and mother.

They arrived a few minutes later at a small building near the St. Georges Hotel. The driver parked the car and scrambled to open the door for Madame.

"Go get your own lunch, Antun," she said to the driver. "We'll be several hours."

The restaurant's plain white facade masked an exotic interior. The back wall was all glass, providing a breathtaking view of the Mediterranean. The main room was full of tables of businessmen, conversing intently about work and money. A smaller room, beyond, featured a series of booths set along the oceanfront windows, each with very high backs so that they were almost like private rooms. There seemed to Jane something slightly scandalous, and delicious, about two women dining alone in a restaurant like this.

"Do you have a booth, perhaps, Joseph?" the Lebanese woman asked the maitre d'hotel in French.

"Oui, Madame Jezzine," came the answer. Evidently she was a regular.

They walked through the main dining room, drawing appreciative glances from several of the men, and entered the smaller and more intimate room. Walking past the booths, Jane noticed that in most of them, men seemed to be dining with very young and attractive women. Jane thought she saw one man stroking the breasts of his luncheon companion through the thin fabric of her blouse.

When they were seated, Madame Jezzine leaned across the table and spoke to Jane in the same conspiratorial tone she had adopted at the doctor's office.

"Surely you know this restaurant?" said the Lebanese woman. "This is where the men of Beirut bring their mistresses to show them off. And sometimes, to do a bit more." She nodded toward the nearby booth where the man had been petting his date.

Solange Jezzine ordered a kir. Though it was midday, too early to drink, Jane did the same. This was an adventure, she told herself. When Solange offered a cigarette, she accepted, even though she hadn't smoked one in years. She coughed after the first puff, and Solange laughed at her inexperience.

"I'm afraid I am a novice," said Jane.

"You'll learn," said the Lebanese woman.

Jane felt embarrassed and wanted, for a moment, to retreat into her ordinary identity of wife and mother.

"Do you have any children?" Jane asked.

"Yes," said Solange. "Years ago. It seems like another lifetime." They talked amiably about children for several minutes, until the drinks arrived.

"I thought that you were leaving Beirut," ventured Jane as she raised her glass. The cassis was swirling through the wine and darkening it like a sudden thunderstorm.

"Why? Because of my husband's legal difficulties?" answered Solange bluntly.

"Well, yes," said Jane. "I read in the paper that he was expected to stay in Switzerland. So I assumed . . ."

"That as a loyal wife, I would go there with him," said the Lebanese woman, finishing the sentence.

"Yes."

"Not yet," said Solange. "Perhaps I will go eventually. Certainly I will go eventually. But not now. It is spring and the most beautiful time of the year in Lebanon. It snowed last week in Geneva, did you know that? I will go later. But not now. There is so much to do here."

She smiled in the most charming and coy way. Looking at her, Jane concluded that men must find her absolutely irresistible.

"And how is *your* husband?" asked Solange, arching her eyebrows.

"Fine," said Jane. "Wonderful, actually."

"You are a lucky woman, to have such a handsome husband. I am sure everyone gives you the same warning: Watch out!"

"No," said Jane. "To be honest, people don't tell me that. Why should I watch out?"

"If you need to ask, take another walk past these booths."

Jane wanted to say, No, my husband isn't like that. But she said nothing.

"What do you think of Lebanese men?" asked Madame Jezzine.

"I find them very charming," said Jane.

That's not a very honest answer, Jane thought to herself. She took another sip of her kir, and then spoke again.

"I find them very charming and very sexy, but they don't seem very reliable."

"Ahaa! Then I think you must know them very well," said Madame Jezzine with a wink.

"Not at all," said Jane. "Or hardly at all. But I would like to understand them better. Perhaps you can explain what they are like."

What am I saying? Jane thought. Why am I doing this?

"I can tell you a great deal," said Solange. "But first let us order some lunch." She pressed a buzzer under the table and a waiter arrived promptly to take their orders. Clearly she was no stranger to the booths, either. The waiter recited the list of specials. Jane ordered the filet of sole Duglère, poached and served with a sauce of white wine and grapes. Solange ordered a lobster, broiled. And a bottle of white Burgundy.

"And salads," called out Solange as the waiter was walking away. "And potatoes!"

Heads turned in the quiet room. Madame Jezzine smiled and lit another cigarette.

"Let me tell you about Arab men," said Solange Jezzine quietly. "This is a topic on which I am something of an expert."

"Goody," said Jane. She giggled as she said it. This was like a dormitory party at Mt. Holyoke.

"Do you want to know *everything?*" asked Solange, taking a drink from her wine.

"Yes," said Jane, still feeling girlish and giggly. This must be what it's like in the harem, she thought. Women who barely know each other exchanging confidences about the men who rule their lives.

"The first thing to understand about Arab men is that they grow up sleeping with everybody. Men, women, uncles, brothers, sisters, aunts. It's very hot in the Middle East and people don't wear much clothing. So things happen. It is nature."

"Come now," said Jane.

"It is true," said Solange. "One of my lovers, a man who is famous throughout the Middle East, told me once about how he was seduced by his aunt. It happened during the afternoon siesta, when the wind was blowing through the curtains. The poor woman denied that it happened. She said that she had been asleep and unaware of what was going on. But my lover told me that she came to his bed and took his penis in her hand and stroked it, and then straddled his body and put him inside of her."

Jane was blushing. Her cheeks felt hot. All she could think of to say was: "My goodness."

"Am I embarrassing you?" asked the Lebanese woman.

"No," said Jane. "You are answering the questions I would never dare to ask."

"Good," said the Lebanese woman. "Now, the second thing to understand is that the most important person in every Arab man's life is his mother. Not his wife, not his mistress, but his mother. Most Arab men see their mother every day. They all want to be on their own, men of the world, but they also want mothering. From every woman they find."

"I think most men are that way," said Jane.

"Perhaps, but in the Arab world everything seems more extreme, doesn't it?"

"It does," said Jane. She looked for the waiter, who was nowhere to be seen. Rather than ring the bell, she picked up the wine bottle from its ice bucket and poured another big glass of wine for herself and Solange.

"What is the third thing?" asked Jane.

"The third thing is . . . I am ashamed to say it."

"I don't believe that," said Jane. "I can't imagine that you would be embarrassed by anything."

"The third thing is that Arab men are afraid about their penises."

"What?" asked Jane, pretending that she hadn't heard.

"They are afraid because of circumcision. You see, in the Arab world, men traditionally are circumcised when they are seven, not at birth. By that age it can be quite painful. And it is a public ritual, at least for the Bedouin. I had one lover, a very rich Saudi prince, who told me how he watched them do it to his older brother and listened to his screams of pain. When it came his turn several years later, he ran away from the sheik who was trying to apply the blade of the knife. I'm not sure the poor boy ever got over it."

Jane looked so wide-eyed and innocent as she listened to these tales that the Lebanese woman suddenly wondered if her American companion, birth-control pills or no, was really very experienced.

"My dear," said Solange. "Have you ever had an Arab man for a lover?"

Jane dropped her head sheepishly.

"Actually, no," said Jane.

"Would you like to know what they are like?"

"In bed?" whispered Jane.

"Yes," said Solange.

"I suppose so. Yes, I suppose I would."

"They don't make any noise when they make love!" said the Lebanese woman.

"What?"

"They never say a word. They don't moan. They don't call your name. You never know when they're finished."

"Why?" asked Jane. "Why are they so quiet?"

"I think it is because they are ashamed. Arab men are very clean, you see. They get it from the Koran, which goes on and on about how to wash yourself. And maybe they think sex with women is dirty."

"Dirty?"

"Yes. Because as soon as they are done, they go wash themselves."

"They do?" Jane was more astonished with every word of the conversation.

"Yes."

"And what about, you know, before . . . ?"

"Foreplay?" volunteered Solange. "They've never heard of it. It doesn't even occur to them."

"It doesn't?"

"No," said Solange.

"Well, then, excuse me for asking this, but why does any woman in her right mind take an Arab for a lover? It doesn't sound like much fun."

Solange smiled. It was the look of secret warmth and pleasure that cats have when they are purring.

"There are a few Arab men who are different," said Solange.

"And what are they like?"

"Aaah, my dear," said Solange. "How can I tell you? They are God's apology for the shortcomings of all the rest. They are like men and women at once. Hard and soft, strong bodies and gentle hands. They have dark eyes the color of the sky on a night when there is no moon. And they are tireless. They will sleep all day to have energy for the night."

Solange closed her eyes, and her voice trailed off. She is thinking of last night, Jane thought. For the first time she could remember, she felt a touch of envy for another woman.

The food arrived. The two women were both ravenous. Jane, normally a light and dainty eater, found that she was picking the white grapes off the sole with her fingers and dropping them, one by one, in her mouth. Solange devoured the lobster, a morsel at a time, cracking each claw, extracting the meat delicately with her fork, dipping it in a silver cup of clarified butter. The waiter tied a large red napkin around her neck to protect the silk dress, which only made her look more exotic and abandoned.

"Do you know what bothers me about Arab men?" said Jane. "They are crazy about sex, but they are afraid of women."

"It is possible," said Solange. She was sucking on one of the thin spiny legs of the lobster.

"I was thinking about it the other day," said Jane. "I was watching some men on Hamra Street who were swooning over a Western woman. She was wearing a fitted blouse and a tight dress. I think she was an airline stewardess. But it was the longing on the faces of the men that frightened me."

"Why?" said Solange. She had put down the lobster and was patting her mouth with her napkin.

"Because I thought to myself: This is what the Arabs want from us. From the West, I mean. They want to have sex with us. That's why they are so eager for the modern world. Smoking our Marlboros and drinking our whisky. Because they think they'll have more sex that way."

"They are right," said Solange. "They probably will."

"Yes. But what happens when Arab culture becomes modern enough that the women have more sex, too? Or at least begin to think about it. I'm not sure that Arab men will be able to handle that part of modern life very well, because they're so afraid of women to begin with. What will happen then?"

"They will go the other way," said Solange.

"What do you mean?"

"Back into the dark ages," said Madame Jezzine. "The Arabs will embrace just enough of the modern world to become terrified by it, and then they'll run the other way."

Jane finished the last bites of her sole. The busboy arrived from nowhere and cleared away the dishes. Solange offered Jane a cigarette. She took it and inhaled deeply and pleasurably.

"Tell me about your husband," said Solange.

"Oh my goodness," said Jane. "What can I tell you? It will sound so sentimental. He is a good man. A strong man. He loves his work. He adores the Middle East, but he also loves his family."

What am I saying? thought Jane. Am I going too far?

"And do you think," asked Madame Jezzine delicately, "that your husband has ever had an affair?"

Jane put her hand to her forehead. She had said too much. She had drunk too much wine. She had allowed the conversation to stray into the forbidden zone.

"No," said Jane brightly, raising her head and smiling. "I don't think that he ever has."

"Lucky girl," said Solange Jezzine. "Lucky girl."

Jane excused herself and went to the bathroom. She tidied herself up, applied new lipstick, brushed her hair, and returned to the table. When she got back, Solange had gone.

Jane peered down the room and saw that she was seated in one of the other booths, talking to a handsome Frenchman. Though the Frenchman was seated across from a younger blonde, he had his arm around Madame Jezzine.

Solange returned in a few minutes. They talked some more, about less exotic topics, and eventually drank their coffee and paid the bill. Solange insisted that they should meet again in several weeks.

"Next time," she said, "I want to hear more about your husband. He is the only attractive man in Beirut."

Jane felt flattered at this praise of her husband and nodded politely. Later that day, she wondered if there was anything in Madame Jezzine's manner that should cause concern. Anything that she should mention to her husband. No, she concluded. She is simply a charming, gossipy Lebanese woman who is mad for sex.

27

Beirut; April 1971

As the Deuxième Bureau crumbled, the CIA station tried to pick up useful pieces of the debris. There were so many angry and frustrated officers that the hardest problem for Hoffman and his colleagues was deciding which of them was worth trying to recruit.

Hoffman ignored most of them. He had a rule about buying members of another intelligence service: Don't recruit the ten people in the field who are gathering information. Recruit the one man at the top who runs the network. With the surge of walk-ins, Hoffman added another rule: No more Lebanese agents at all, unless they had vital information or access to it.

For Rogers, the top priority was getting access to the Christian militias. He focused his attention on a bright young army officer named Samir Fares. Though only in his mid-thirties, Fares had gained a reputation as one of the Deuxième Bureau's ablest intelligence officers. He had the look of an intellectual: balding, smoking a pipe rather than the ubiquitous Lebanese cigarettes. But he was a tough operator. His current assignment, Rogers had learned, was to recruit agents from among the militias and secret political organizations of Christian East Beirut.

Rogers decided to set up a meeting with Fares. He asked Elias Arslani, a retired history professor who had been Fares's mentor at AUB, to arrange a meeting at his country home in the mountains near Jezzine, in southern Lebanon. Dr. Arslani was the sort of person the American Embassy called on to make discreet introductions: a distinguished academic, a pillar of the Greek Orthodox community, a man who believed in the establishment of a modern and liberal Arab world. He was not an agent, not even an "asset." He was simply and forthrightly a friend of the United States.

Rogers drove south on a spring day, navigating the hairpin turns that looped up and down the steep hills like thin strands of yarn, till he reached the village of Watani and the professor's large, red-roofed villa. The professor, known to the villagers as "Sheik Elias," greeted Rogers at the door. He was a gaunt, erect old man, dressed in the uniform of a Levantine gentleman: a crisp white shirt, a well-tailored gray suit, and a red fez. Standing next to him was Samir Fares, dressed in a baggy seersucker suit and looking more than a little uncomfortable.

Dr. Arslani apologized to his guests for making them travel to the mountains. He rarely went to Beirut anymore, he said. He found it too depressing. His goal as a professor had been to help train a modern civil service in Lebanon, the old man explained. But when he went to Beirut now and saw what had become of the Lebanese bureaucracy, he felt that his life's work had been a failure.

"They are pickpockets," Dr. Arslani said scornfully.

In his lapel, the old man still wore the fading emblem of the Order of Lebanon, awarded years earlier for his services to the republic. Looking at him, Rogers felt he was seeing a remnant of a vanishing era. Dr. Arslani excused himself after a few minutes and left Rogers and Fares alone to talk.

The conversation began awkwardly, since neither man wanted to admit, at this early stage of their discussion, what they had come so far to talk about.

"How is the new regime treating you?" asked Rogers.

"Well enough," said the Lebanese Army officer. "They pay my salary."

"Is it much different from the old?"

"We do the same things," said Fares. "But we have stopped believing in them."

"Why?"

"Because our job has become absurd," said Fares. "We are charged with protecting the security of a state whose citizens no longer trust the state to do anything. So we are protecting something that is, in reality, nothing."

"Why is this country unravelling?" asked Rogers, posing the question as much to himself as to the other man.

"Ask Dr. Arslani," answered the young Lebanese. "He's the professor."

"You were his student," continued Rogers patiently. "What do you think he would say?"

"He gave me a book once, years ago," answered Fares. "It was a history of the Weimar Republic in Germany. It tried to explain how democracy collapsed in Germany. Inflation, demoralization, the growth of extremism. It was a story of how a country lost its center and collapsed from within. When Dr. Arslani gave me that book fifteen years ago, I wondered why. What could this possibly have to do with Lebanon? Now I'm beginning to understand."

"What should a sensible German have done?" asked Rogers.

"If he had known what was coming?"

"Yes."

Fares smiled thinly, almost grimly. He could see where Rogers was leading.

"He would have worked to strengthen the political institutions of his country," said Fares.

"And if that was hopeless?" pressed Rogers.

"He would have left."

"Where, do you suppose?"

Fares laughed.

"To America," he said.

"Yes," said Rogers. "I agree. That is what a sensible German would have done."

Rogers decided then that he liked the young Lebanese and, what was considerably more, that he trusted him. The two men talked for another hour, still in vague and general terms, before emerging from the closed drawing room and joining Dr. Arslani for a pleasant lunch on a terrace overlooking the mountains and the sea far beyond.

Rogers and Fares met twice more before they concluded an arrangement. Fares was a professional, and he had no illusions about what he was doing. It was treason. The only mitigating factor, he told Rogers, was that the way things were going, in a few more years there wouldn't be a Lebanese nation left to betray.

Rogers explained what he wanted: access to the underground movement that was developing among the Christians of Lebanon.

"Let's be clear on one thing," said Fares. "All I can do for you is to make introductions. I have my own network of agents in East and West Beirut, and I hope that they can help me to penetrate these organizations. But it won't be easy. The militias are very secretive and their members are intensely loyal to each other. It is like trying to recruit one member of a family to provide information about his brothers. So don't get your hopes up."

"We need to see inside the cave," said Rogers. "We're seeing shadows on the wall, but we don't know whether they are made by a giant or a dwarf."

"I know what you want," said Fares. "You want to know who makes the bombs."

"Yes," said Rogers. "But I also want to understand why he is doing it."

"Those are good questions," said Fares.

To Rogers, that sounded like a deal.

"I insist on two things," said Fares, when they were down to the final bargaining. He was puffing on his pipe, releasing a cloud of fragrant smoke into the air with each puff.

"First," said Fares, "I want an annuity that will allow my wife to live comfortably abroad and my children to complete their studies in America if anything happens to me. And I want it done in a way that neither my wife nor my children ever know that you are providing the money."

"That shouldn't be a problem," said Rogers. "We do this more often than you might imagine. We have accountants who can buy the annuity and establish a trust fund for your children, and brokers who can manage the money, all very quietly. We even have our own offshore banks and mutual funds in the Caribbean to handle the paperwork. What's the second request?"

"It's more complicated," said Fares. "You may find this strange, given what I am doing, but I still love my country."

"I don't find that strange," said Rogers.

"Good, because then you will understand what I am asking," said Fares. "Several years ago, my commanding officer told me that someday I would run the Deuxième Bureau."

"I hope he's right," said Rogers.

"Personally, I doubt it. But if it should ever happen, I want your promise that the agency will terminate me immediately as a controlled agent and allow me to serve my country honorably."

Rogers thought a moment.

"I can make you that promise," said Rogers. "What matters is that you believe me."

Fares looked at him warily.

"We've been down this road before," Rogers said matter of factly. He explained that the issue came up surprisingly often. People recruited by the agency when they were young men, studying in the United States or serving in junior positions in their governments, inevitably rose in the ranks. Some of them rose to the very top. The agency had dealt with the problem often enough that it even had a phrase for agents who did so well that it became embarrassing. They called it "the prime minister syndrome."

"So you will never betray me," said Fares.

"That's right," said Rogers.

"I suppose I should find that reassuring," said Fares, extending his hand toward Rogers. "But even America cannot suspend the laws of human nature. Let us say that you will never betray me unless it is absolutely necessary."

28

Beruit; May 1971

"There is someone I would like you to meet," Fares told Rogers a month later over lunch at Le Pêcheur restaurant near the port. Rogers had finished eating and was smoking a cigarette as he gazed out across St. Georges Bay at the tramp steamers lying at anchor and the small boats used by the smugglers and fishermen. He had removed his tie and his open shirt was blowing in the sea breeze.

"Who's that?" asked Rogers, turning to Fares. The Lebanese intelligence officer was wearing a tweed coat, which made him look all the more like a junior professor.

"He is a young agent I have recruited from a secret organization in East Beirut. He came to me because he is troubled about something. He won't tell me the details, and he refuses to meet with anyone else from the Deuxième Bureau. He says that we're penetrated by his people from top to bottom, and I suspect he's right. But he is willing to meet with an American. I think he regards it as a sort of insurance policy. Any interest?"

"Definitely," responded Rogers. "But I'm not putting any militiamen on the payroll."

"I don't think this fellow is interested in money," said Fares. "It's more complicated than that."

"What kind of a Lebanese is he?"

"Confused," said Fares. "He's a bright young man, one of the top students at the Université de St. Joseph, who has seen something that terrifies him. His name is Amin Shartouni."

"How did you meet him?" asked Rogers.

"His brother is married to my wife's sister," said Fares.

"How Lebanese," said Rogers.

"I can arrange a meeting in a week or so," said Fares. "But I warn you, he's an odd fellow."

"La puissance occulte!" whispered the tormented-looking young man. "They never teach us about it in school, but it is the secret history of the Middle East!"

Amin Shartouni spoke in a raspy, breathless voice—as if in a fever—at an apartment in Ashrafiyeh. He was a thin man with short curly hair and a look of intense concentration. His skin was the color of parchment and was drawn tightly across his face. As he talked, he wagged his finger at Rogers and Fares.

"What do you mean by *'la puissance occulte'*?" asked Rogers cautiously. "Is that some sort of organization?"

"No, no, no! Of course not!" said Amin in exasperation. "Are you a fool? It is not a single group. It is the hidden power behind all of the groups and leaders."

"I'm still not sure I understand," said Rogers gently, not yet certain whether he was talking to a lunatic or a useful intelligence asset. He prodded the young man. "Perhaps you could explain what you mean in more detail."

"Very well," said Amin. "I will give you an example. A new leader named Hafez Assad came to power in Syria last year. There is a story about the name. Should I tell it?"

Fares nodded.

"Very well. The name of his family was 'al-Wahash,' which means 'the Beast.' So he was Hafez the Beast. But he changed it to Assad, which means 'the Lion.' So now he is Hafez the Lion."

"What about *la puissance occulte?*" said Rogers.

"I'm coming to that," said Amin. "The question is, who is the real power behind Hafez the Lion? Is it the Syrian Arab Baath Party? No, of course not! Preposterous!" He snorted at the absurdity of the thought.

"The real power lies elsewhere, shrouded in mystery and deceit: Assad is an Alawite, and the hidden force behind him is the Alawite tribal council. Officially, there is no such council. Any Alawite will tell you that it does not exist. In Arabic, we even have a word for the lies we tell to protect such secrets. We call it *taqiyya*. But here is the truth. Assad's father was a member of the Alawite council, and it was this council that selected Hafez as leader of the Alawites and ultimately as president of Syria! Do you understand?" He looked hopefully toward the American.

"Continue," said Rogers.

"Ahaaa!" said Amin, pleased to have an audience. "Next, consider the Druse. Everyone assumes that the Jumblatt family controls the Druse, yes? But that is an illusion! The real power is not Kamal Jumblatt, but the secret council of Druse notables that chose him as leader. This council includes the Sheik al-Aql and others and maintains secret relations with the Druse of Israel and Syria. It is another example of *la puissance occulte*."

"Tell me more," said Rogers. He was becoming fascinated by this little dervish of a man.

"Yes, certainly," said Amin. "Consider the Shiites. People imagine that the most powerful Shiite leader in the world is the Shah of Iran. Why not? He is the Shah of Shahs! He has money and palaces and tanks! But the reality is entirely different. The Shah rules at the sufferance of a humble man in Najf, who is the highest authority in Shiite Islam. He leads the ayatollahs of the Ulema, the Shiite religious council. If the ayatollahs ever decide to make trouble for the Shah, then poof! He is finished. Do you begin to understand what I mean by occult power?"

"I'm beginning to," said Rogers. "But I would like another example. What about the Lebanese Christians? What is the hidden power that guides their decisions?"

An uneasy look came over Amin's face. Rogers immediately wished he hadn't asked the question. The young man's hands fidgeted on the table and his eyes darted back and forth between Rogers and Fares.

"I cannot talk about that," he said, shaking his head.

The meeting lasted thirty more minutes, but the young man had become wary. Rogers played for time by asking him simple questions: Where was he from? Where had he gone to school? Where did he work? Amin gave polite, cautious answers. When he opened his clenched palms, they were covered with sweat.

"We've talked enough for today," said Fares. He suggested that the three get together again in two weeks. Amin nodded his head almost imperceptibly.

Before the next session, Fares spent several hours alone with Amin. Calming him, reassuring him, coaxing him. Fares felt like a doctor treating a patient who has been so traumatized by an event that he can't bear to discuss it. They arrived together at the safehouse, doctor and patient.

"I think that Amin is ready to tell us more about *la puissance occulte* today," said Fares. "Isn't that right, Amin?" The young Lebanese nodded.

"Please tell our American friend about the organization that you joined in East Beirut."

Gently, gently, said Rogers to himself. The curtains were closed and the lights were dim.

"Yes, I will tell you about the group," said Amin. "Not all about it, but some."

Rogers nodded and the young man began.

"The name of the group is Al-Jabha. The name is supposed to be secret."

"Al-Jabha?" asked Rogers.

"Yes," said Amin Shartouni.

"And what does that mean?" asked Rogers. He knew the answer, but that wasn't the point.

"It means 'The Front,'" said Shartouni.

Rogers nodded. He believed that interrogations had a kind of rhythm. Make someone answer a first question, and then a second, and a kind of rhythm develops, like a trance.

"Please continue," said Rogers.

"Al-Jabha was founded sometime in the late 1960s, I don't know when. I don't even know who founded it. Once I asked the man who recruited me and he just laughed.

"What did he say?"

"'Les cinq illustres inconnus!' The five illustrious unknowns. A doctor, several lawyers, an engineer, an insurance man. All professional people. But he wouldn't tell me their names. His tone of voice made me think there must be others —bigger and more powerful—behind these people."

"How were you recruited into the organization?" asked Rogers.

"It happened gradually. First I heard from one of the other students at St. Joseph about a group that was training people how to use weapons in case of trouble with the Palestinians. Then a friend from my neighborhood in Ashrafiyeh approached me. He said that I should do something for Lebanon and told me about the organization. When I said I was interested, he took me to meet a man who owned a bookstore near my house. This man told me that Al-Jabha had been watching me for some time and asked if I was interested. I said yes."

"And what happened then?" asked Rogers. Gently, gently.

"He gave me a number—611—and said that from then on that was my only identification in the group. He said I should never write the number down. Just memorize it. The bookstore owner's number was 138. My friend's number was 457. We were a cell, the three of us. That was it! I was in. There were no meetings, no papers, nothing."

"Tell us about your training," said Fares.

"It started right away. The bookstore owner told me to be ready the next Saturday. He said I should go to the Sin el-Fil roundabout and look for a car that had on the rear window a map of Lebanon and the words: 'Lebanon for the Lebanese.' He said I should follow this car up into the mountains."

"Was that a slogan of the group?" asked Rogers.

"Yes," said Amin.

"Were there other slogans?"

"Yes. There was one other. 'The first responsibility is to the nation. Everything else comes second.'"

"And where did you go from Sin el-Fil?"

"We went deep into Kesrouan, to an abandoned convent in a remote valley that I had never seen before. We were very far up the mountain, and completely hidden from outsiders. As we got near the training site, the road signs were covered over with paper so that we couldn't be sure where we were."

Rogers nodded. Come on, come on.

"There were about forty people there. They seemed to have come from all over Lebanon. I thought I recognized a few faces—one from school and another from the law faculty—but I didn't say anything to them because it was supposed to be secret. There was an instructor—his number was 808—who drilled us in hand-to-hand combat and taught us to shoot automatic rifles. It was like the Boy Scouts, except it was more serious."

Rogers nodded again. Fares sat close by, puffing his pipe.

"We met like that each Saturday for the next six weeks, each time following a car to that hidden place in the mountains. I would tell my parents that I was going hunting."

"Did they believe you?"

"At first they did. To keep up my alibi, I would stop on the way home and buy some birds that somebody else had shot. Eventually I think they realized something was going on. But they never said anything, not even to this day."

"What did the instructor tell you was the purpose of Al Jabha?" asked Rogers.

"During the first six weeks, they just talked in general terms about fighting the Palestinians. They said that foreigners were trying to take over our country and change its identity so that it would be like the rest of the Arab world. It was always in terms of Lebanese against foreigners, but we knew what the instructors meant."

"What did they mean?" asked Rogers.

"That the Palestinians were Moslems and they wanted to kill the Christians."

Fares now sat forward in his chair. He had been through this debriefing once already, without Rogers, and it had stopped at this point. They were now about to cover new ground. He wondered if the frightened young Lebanese would continue.

"What happened later in the training?" asked Rogers gently. Amin looked warily at Fares.

"What happened later?" repeated Rogers.

"There was another kind of training," said Amin.

"And what was it?"

"After the first round, the instructor—202—took me aside and said that he wanted me to enter a special course for the inner circle of the group."

"What did you tell him?"

"I said that I would. I was very flattered that he asked me. It seemed like a very great honor. It was only in this later training that it became clear to me what the group was doing. That was when I began to understand about occult power. You see this secret organization—Al-Jabha—was really just a cover for another, even more secret group."

"What was the more secret group called?"

"It was called 'The Guardians of the Mountain.'"

"Can you tell us about this inner group?" asked Fares.

"I don't think so. They made us swear on the gospels that we would not reveal what we learned."

"I want you to tell me," said Rogers firmly.

"I can't," said Shartouni. "It is too dangerous."

Rogers was wise enough to back off before the frightened young man broke completely from the thin tether with which they held him.

"Perhaps another day," said Fares.

"Perhaps," said the young Lebanese.

Having begun the process of confession and absolution, Amin wasn't going to stop. He met again with Rogers two days later. Again, Fares spent time with the young Lebanese before the meeting, stroking his wounded psyche and encouraging him to tell the rest of his story. They gathered at an apartment near Jounie, in a complex overlooking the sea. The session began in the late afternoon, as the sun was beginning to set on the western horizon of the Mediterranean.

"Today, Amin would like to continue his story by telling us about the inner circle of Al-Jabha," said Fares. "Isn't that right?"

"Yes," said Amin Shartouni.

"Amin has promised that today, he will tell us everything about the group," said Fares.

Shartouni nodded. Rogers settled back in his chair. Fares lit up his pipe. Amin sat on a couch facing the sea.

"The purpose of the inner circle was to do the things that the Lebanese Army could not do," the young man began. "The leaders told us that because of political problems in the army, especially the friction between Moslem and Christian officers, it was no longer possible for the army to take the measures that might be necessary to defend the republic. That would be our job. They called it 'special operations.'"

"What did they teach you in this second round of training?" asked Rogers.

"They taught us to make bombs," answered Amin. His lips

were crinkled into an odd smile that Rogers hadn't seen before.

"Please tell us about it," said Rogers.

"Very well. We had a new instructor in the inner group, who knew everything about making bombs. He had travelled around the Arab world and knew the secret tricks of warfare."

"What was his name?" asked Rogers.

"He didn't have a name," said Amin. "We just called him 'the Bombmaker.'"

"And what did he teach you?"

"First he taught us how to make homemade explosives."

"Tell me," said Rogers.

"They were the simplest kind at first, which you could make by mixing a pesticide with a fertilizer. The Bombmaker said that the nitrogenous compound in the fertilizer, combined with the acid of the pesticide, would produce a powerful explosive. But he recommended against using this mixture."

"Why?"

"Because it was unstable. It would explode if you shook it, or dropped it."

"I see," said Rogers.

"The Bombmaker recommended what he called 'nitrocotton.' He had me mix it in the bathtub. We took pure cotton and mixed it very slowly, very gently, with nitric acid. The Bombmaker warned us that if we mixed nitrocotton too fast, it would explode right there in the tub!"

"And you made nitrocotton?"

"Yes," said Amin. "It was difficult for me at first, because my hand was shaking so much that it was churning up the acid. But I learned how."

"What came next?" asked Rogers.

"Detonators. The Bombmaker taught us how to make a simple detonator. You start with gunpowder. You can get it from any bullet. Then you take a flashlight bulb, break the glass, put the gunpowder around the resistance wire, and recap the bulb with wax. When you run electricity to the bulb, Boom! You have a detonator!"

Amin smiled that peculiar smile again. Rogers wondered if he was a lunatic after all.

"But those were just the basics," continued Amin. "We moved on to real explosives: gelignite and melignite and plastique. The Bombmaker said the simplest way to get these fancy explosives was to steal them from the military. He said that tons of explosives disappear from NATO stocks every year, and if we wanted some, we should bribe an American soldier in Europe who would steal what we wanted. If we didn't need the high-quality military explosive, the Bombmaker said we should just buy dynamite from the people who sell it to construction companies. All we would need to make it legal was a construction license! The Bombmaker also told us about another way, but he said it was very dangerous."

"What was that?"

"To buy explosives from the Palestinians."

"What?" asked Rogers, unsure that he had heard correctly. "Why would the Palestinians sell explosives to the Christians?"

"I don't know," said Amin. "That's just what the Bombmaker told us."

"What else did he tell you?"

"He taught us how to make remote-control detonators. That was really the most interesting part."

"How do you make a remote-control detonator?" asked Rogers. He felt his stomach beginning to tighten.

"You start by buying a simple radio-control kit, like the kind that children use for model airplanes or boats. You can buy them in any big toy store. The Bombmaker warned us that we should buy only one kit in each store. Otherwise, people would get suspicious."

"How do they work?" asked Rogers.

"In each kit, there is an emitting device and a receiving device. One for the ground controller, if it's a toy airplane, and one in the plane itself. Mind you, when you use the kits to make detonators, you must change the frequency and select a new one that isn't used by model builders or amateur radio operators. Otherwise, the bomb might explode in your hands because of a child who is playing with a model airplane nearby and sets it off by mistake!"

Rogers nodded.

"The kits usually have two frequencies, one to regulate the speed of the toy plane and one to control its direction. That's the kind that you want, because it gives you two keys on the detonator. A simple electronic transmission on the first frequency opens one key; an audio signal—a voice, let's say—opens the second key."

"And then?"

"Then, BOOM! Remote-control detonator."

"Amin," said Rogers softly. "What were these bombs and detonators to be used for?"

Amin ignored the question. "Would you like me to tell you the most frightening part of the training?" he asked.

"Yes," said Rogers.

"It was connecting the electric battery to the detonator. And do you know why? Because of static electricity! Sparks can jump from the battery to the detonator, even when the switch is off. Then, BOOM! The Bombmaker taught me a safety trick. Before you get the battery wires near the detonator, touch them together and make them spark. That removes the static electricity."

Rogers nodded. Who is mad, he wondered, this poor man or his country?

"I hated attaching the battery," said Amin with a shudder. "The Bombmaker made me do it over and over, and my hands trembled and shook. But he said it was necessary. Everyone had to do it."

Remembering the experience, Amin trembled once again.

"The rest of the receiving device was easy," he continued. "You just attach the detonator to the aerial."

"The aerial?"

"Yes. The car aerial."

"Amin!" said Rogers loudly. "Why did they need an aerial? What were they going to use the remote-controlled bombs for?"

"Don't you know?" said Amin, tilting his head. "Isn't it obvious?"

"No," said Rogers.

"Car bombs!"

Rogers felt sick. He could not ask the next question.

"Why did your group need car bombs?" asked Fares.

"Because the other side had them. The Palestinians."

"How did you know that?"

"Because the Bombmaker told us."

"Yes, but how did he know?"

"He knew because . . ." Amin began to laugh. "It's sort of funny, really."

"How did he know?"

"He knew because a few months before he came to us, he had been working for the Palestinians. Teaching them how to make bombs. That was his job, you see. Teaching people how to make bombs!"

The young Lebanese continued to laugh. It was a nervous giggle—like the sound of a frayed nerve vibrating—that masked emotions Amin could not express.

"And who were the targets?"

"What?"

"Who were the targets?"

The question produced another stutter of laughter from Amin. Then there was silence, and a look of pain and exhaustion that distorted his face.

"That was what bothered me," said the boy, his face frozen. "The Bombmaker told us that it didn't matter! We could decide about all that later. He said it would be easy. With car bombs, we wouldn't need specific targets!"

"Why not?" asked Rogers, almost in a whisper.

"Because we would only need an address."

"An address?"

"Yes. A street address. Where to park the car."

The apprentice terrorist looked at Rogers. He put his head in his hands. Was he crying? Was he laughing? It didn't matter. Fares embraced the boy.

"Do you have any more training sessions scheduled with the Bombmaker?" asked Rogers.

"Yes," said Amin. "One more."

"Good boy," said Rogers. "You are very brave to have come here and talked with us. Go to your next session. Behave normally. And don't be frightened. We will make sure that no harm comes to you."

The young Lebanese nodded. Fares escorted him to the door, speaking gently to him in Arabic. Rogers watched him walk out the door, into the Christian heartland of Kesrouan, and then turned to Fares.

"Follow him," said the American.

29

Beirut; June 1971

They followed Amin Shartouni until he led them, several days later, to the Bombmaker. Then they followed the Bombmaker.

Hoffman organized the surveillance. It was, he said, the most interesting and complicated surveillance problem he had encountered. How do you track someone, with the utmost discretion, when you can't use your usual trackers? Borrowing people from the Deuxième Bureau was out of the question. Most of the other agents available to the CIA station would be too obvious. It was like trying to play chess without chessmen.

Eventually, with Fares's help, they put together a small team, gathered mostly from Ankara, that could maintain loose surveillance on the Bombmaker. They also obtained photographs of him and some of the people he met. The results of this exercise were as startling as anything that Rogers had come across in more than a decade of intelligence work. When the evidence was ready, he took it to Hoffman and briefed him in detail.

Hoffman was standing at his open window when Rogers arrived for the briefing. The station chief was feeding bits of a chocolate eclair to a pigeon that had landed on the window sill.

"Show-and-tell time?" asked Hoffman.

"Yes, sir," said Rogers.

"Awaaay we go!" said Hoffman. He scooted over to his desk with a dancelike motion similar to the one made famous by the comedian Jackie Gleason. Looking at him, Rogers wondered whether perhaps the station chief was becoming more eccentric than a government official could afford to be.

"This is the man known as 'the Bombmaker,'" began Rogers.

He handed Hoffman a grainy photograph taken from a distance with a high-powered lens. It showed a heavyset Arab man with a stubbly beard and a mustache. He had a bald spot on his head and was wearing thick glasses. There were bags under his eyes and a look of perpetual sleeplessness. He was wearing what appeared to be an expensive silk shirt, open at the neck. Because he was overweight, the fabric was pulling at the buttons. Around his neck, matted in the hair on his chest, was a large gold ingot.

"So this is the face of evil," said Hoffman. "He looks to me like your average fat slob."

Rogers handed Hoffman the next photograph.

"This is a picture of the apartment building where he lives," said Rogers. The photo showed a modern building, with clothes hanging from some of the balconies and children in the courtyard.

"Where is it?" asked Hoffman.

"West Beirut," said Rogers. "Off the Corniche Mazraa, near the Palestinian camps."

"But I thought you told me this guy was a Christian," said Hoffman.

"He is," said Rogers.

"Well, then, why in the Sam J. Hill is he living in the middle of a bunch of Palestinians?"

"Because he's a Palestinian."

"Now listen, Rogers. Don't fuck with me. I'm warning you."

"I'm not," said Rogers.

"Well, then, what is he? A Christian or a Palestinian?"

"He's both. That's what I'm trying to tell you. He's a Christian Palestinian. His family is from Bethlehem."

"Oh," said Hoffman.

"His real name is Youssef Kizib. He studied electrical engineering at Cairo University ten years ago and he was the best student in his class, by far. His teachers still remember him. He was the student who could build anything. He was

working on his doctorate when he got in trouble with the
Moukharabat in Egypt. They thought he was working with
one of the Palestinian underground groups. He fled to Lebanon in 1964 and has been here ever since, except for occasional trips to Cannes, where he lives like a pasha."

"Attractive fellow," said Hoffman.

"Now here's the interesting part," said Rogers. He handed
Hoffman another grainy, telephoto-lens picture. It showed the
Bombmaker in a dimly-lit room. Standing near him were
Amin Shartouni and several other young Lebanese.

"This is the Bombmaker with his Lebanese Christian
pupils," said Rogers. "We tracked them to the place where
they do their training in the mountains. This picture shows
him giving his final lesson."

"What's that?" asked Hoffman.

"How to make bombs that are hidden in the lining of a
suitcase, that will explode when an airplane reaches a certain
altitude."

"Why in heaven's name do the Lebanese Christians need to
know that?" asked Hoffman.

"They probably don't," answered Rogers. "But it's part of
the curriculum."

"Asshole," said Hoffman, looking again at the heavyset
face with the stubbly beard.

"Guess where this next picture was taken?" said Rogers as
he handed Hoffman another photograph. This one showed the
gray exterior of a modern office building on a hill overlooking
Lebanon. In the foreground of the picture was a short man
dressed in an army uniform.

"I give up," said Hoffman without looking at the picture.

"It's the headquarters of army intelligence, formerly known
as the Deuxième Bureau. The man in the foreground is a Lebanese Army major who happens to be a cousin of the president."

"The Squirrel?"

"Yes, sir."

"So what?" said Hoffman.

Rogers handed him the next picture. It showed the same
Lebanese intelligence officer sitting in a café talking with the
Bombmaker, Youssef Kizib.

"We photographed them together a week ago. Then we

bcgan to look around. It seems that Kizib maintains regular contact with several members of army intelligence. They know exactly what he's up to with the Lebanese Christians and, in fact, they seem to have given him their blessing. That's how he gets some of his explosives."

"Now let me get this straight," said Hoffman. "We've got a Palestinian who's training a bunch of Lebanese Christians to kill other Palestinians, with the blessing of the Lebanese Army."

"More or less," said Rogers. "But the best is yet to come."

Rogers handed another black-and-white photo to Hoffman. This one showed the Bombmaker walking down a narrow street, framed by rough cinderblock buildings.

"This was taken in Tal Zaatar refugee camp," said Rogers. "Our man is paying a secret visit to another set of his friends. Guess who they are?"

"In Tal Zaatar, they must be Palestinians," said Hoffman.

"Correct," answered Rogers. "He's visiting one of the men who handles logistics for Fatah. We think he went there on behalf of his friends in East Beirut to buy rocket-propelled grenades—RPGs—for one of the Christian militias. This was just four days ago, so we're still checking out some of the details. But as near as we can reconstruct the deal, the Fatah man agreed to sell Kizib one hundred RPGs, at eight hundred Lebanese pounds each. All out of Fatah's stores of ammunition."

"You're shitting me," said Hoffman. "A Palestinian from Fatah is selling grenades to the Christians to use in killing Palestinians!"

"You got it," said Rogers.

"Humor me," said Hoffman. "Explain to me why the Bombmaker is doing these odious things."

"For money," said Rogers. "And fun."

There was silence.

Rogers had a mental picture of the arsenals that were being assembled in basements and warehouses across town. Homemade cluster bombs for residential neighborhoods; RPGs to shoot across the boundaries of East and West Beirut; car bombs for mosques and churches; sniper's rifles to attack innocent civilians who happened to be the wrong religion; pistols with silencers to remove obstinate politicians; and the militias training in secret while the scoundrels who ran the country tried to squeeze the last piastre of graft from the dying system. And in the middle of it all, at the eye of the hurricane that was destroying Lebanon, stood a small group of professionals like the Bombmaker, who saluted all flags but sailed under none, who disdained ideology and sold their services to whoever was willing to pay the price.

"The question," said Rogers, "is what we do about it."

"That is indeed the question," said Hoffman. "And I fortuitously have the answer."

"Which is?"

"That we do nothing about it."

Rogers looked at him, dumbfounded.

"You can't mean that," said Rogers.

"Wanna bet?"

"But for God's sake, Frank," said Rogers, his usually calm voice becoming insistent. "We should do something before things get out of control."

"Like what?"

"Simple things. A media program to bolster moderate political opinion. Security assistance for what's left of the Deuxième Bureau. Contacts between Palestinian and Christian leaders. Recruit more people who can keep tabs on the gangs of thugs out there. Anything. But we should do something."

"My boy," said Hoffman. "Forgive me for saying this, but that's a very American response. You see a problem on the horizon. Ergo, you want to solve it. I understand completely. I share your concerns. But forget it! Uncle Sam isn't going to solve the problems of this fucked-up little country! So let's not waste our time trying."

"But this is serious!" said Rogers. "A friendly country is falling apart. Surely there is something we can do?"

"Yes, as a matter of fact there is," said Hoffman. "We can stay the fuck out of the way! We can do our best to see that when this little papier-mâché democracy falls apart, as few Americans as possible get hurt."

Rogers looked away glumly.

"We aren't the Salvation Army," Hoffman continued. "Some of our colleagues tend to forget that sometimes. Like a few years ago, when people got sentimental ideas about saving democracy in another little turd of a country. Remember where?"

Rogers didn't answer.

"I'll give you a hint," said Hoffman. "The capital is Saigon."

"What about the Bombmaker?" asked Rogers quietly. "Isn't there something we can do about him?"

"You tell me," said Hoffman. "What can we do about him?"

There was a long silence. The words were on Roger's lips: Kill him. Deprive the demented bastard of his ability to build any more bombs. Just kill him. But he couldn't say it, and he knew in that moment that Hoffman was right. There was nothing that they could do except stay out of the way.

"Saving the world isn't our job," Hoffman said gently to the younger man. "We aren't priests and we aren't assassins."

Rogers thought of a Lebanese proverb he had heard from a Druse friend. It was becoming a kind of Lebanese national prayer, and perhaps it was Rogers's prayer as well. The proverb said: Kiss the hand you cannot bite, but call upon God to break it.

Rogers was sitting at home one night late that summer, reading a book. There was a knock at the door, then the sound of something heavy dropping to the floor, then the sound of footsteps running away down the stairs and out the door of the apartment building.

Jane was closest to the door. She had risen from her chair to answer the knock but Rogers stopped her and went himself. He looked carefully through the peephole but saw nothing. Curious, he unbolted the door to make sure nobody was there.

"Oh my God," muttered Rogers.

He closed the door and told Jane to go into the nursery immediately with the children and stay there. He placed a quick call to the security officer at the embassy. Then he went back to the front door.

There on the floor of the landing was the body of Amin Shartouni. The face was horribly distorted, caught in what seemed a final scream of anguish. Dried blood covered his mouth and chin and was crusted on his shirt. There was something on the floor next to the corpse. In the dim light of the hallway, Rogers could barely see it at first. It looked like a piece of meat, rough and red. He bent down and looked at it carefully and then felt a surge of nausea.

It was the boy's tongue, which had been cut from his mouth and left as a warning.

The war of the bombs began a few months later, when a series of explosions rocked Beirut. The bombers hit a wide range of targets, from a pharmacy owned by the leader of the right-wing Phalange Party, to the offices of a leftist, pro-Iraqi newspaper.

What frightened the Lebanese was that the attacks were so random and anonymous. The Palestinians seemed the most likely perpetrators, since they had an interest in destabilizing Lebanon. But there were other theories. Some blamed the Jordanians, who wanted to force Lebanon to crack down against the fedayeen just as the king had done. Others blamed the Israelis, who also wanted to push the Lebanese to take a tougher stand. But the ominous fact was that nobody knew for sure who had done it and nobody was ever brought to justice. The bombings created a feeling of instability throughout Lebanon, a sense that something frightening was happening in the shadows.

30

Damascus; June 1971

Yakov Levi's last run was to Syria. They told him to service four dead drops: one in Aleppo, one in a remote village south of Homs, two in Damascus. It was the assignment that members of the Mossad station in Beirut dreaded most. Levi had been hoping—praying—that his tour in Beirut would end before he had to do it again. But he was unlucky.

Shuval, the station chief, took Levi out to dinner the night before he left for Syria. They drove in separate cars to Chtaura, halfway to the border, and ate at a Lebanese restaurant there. It was the chief's way of holding Levi's hand as long as he could before letting him go. They talked in French through the dinner. Shuval laughed and told jokes about the life Levi would be leading in a few months, when he went back home. The girls on the beach. The loud talk and laughter in the streets. All the sights and sounds and fellowship of that other place, which the chief never named.

The organization had promised Levi the moon. When he got back to Tel Aviv, he would be a senior deputy in the section they called *Tzomet*—Junction—that handled the collection and analysis of intelligence. His specialty would be analyzing information about the Palestinian guerrilla groups. With a nice raise in pay, and a down payment for a new apartment in Herzliya. How did that sound? Didn't that make it all a little more bearable? What they were really saying was: Hang on. Keep it together for a few more months and you can put your Maalox away in the drawer. We're bringing you home.

Levi picked at his food in the restaurant in Chtaura. He pushed the humous back and forth on his plate with the pita bread. He cut his kibbeh into smaller and smaller pieces, but ate only the pine nuts and the spiced-lamb filling. He looked awful. Tired, frayed nerves. And he hadn't even started the run yet.

The station chief embraced Levi when the dinner was over. "See you in a week," he said.

"Insha 'Allah," said Levi, not really meaning it as a joke. If it pleases Allah.

The chief drove back to Beirut. Levi went to his room in a small tourist hotel in Chtaura and slept fitfully. He rose at dawn to the sound of two taxi drivers arguing over a fare. They were screaming at each other so loudly and angrily that Levi worried, as he shaved, that one of them might start shooting. A policeman arrived and the fight ended. Levi breakfasted and headed for the border.

Levi reached the border before 9:00 A.M. Syrian customs officers dressed in khaki uniforms were questioning drivers and searching their cars. They weren't the problem. The dangerous ones were the security officers at passport control.

Levi went through his final checklist as he braked the car near the checkpoint. He was Jacques Beaulieu, totally and completely. He saw the images of his cover identity in his mind as if he was looking at snapshots. His imaginary parents, brothers and sisters, friends from Marseilles. He knew what each of them looked like. Hair color, eye color, height, and weight. It was a game he played, like a blind man inventing the shapes and colors of his world.

Levi's commercial cover was easier, because it was all real. The man carrying the passport in the name of Jacques Beaulieu traded goods throughout the Mediterranean, there were hundreds of people who could attest to it. He was coming to Syria to negotiate a contract for exporting agricultural products. It was true, he had the papers in his briefcase, the contract typed and ready to sign. He was a trader. That's all he was. Who could prove otherwise? His identity fit as smoothly and tightly as a silk glove.

Levi parked his Citroën sedan. He got out and walked to the passport-control office at the border. He stood in the shortest line. In a minute—too quick—he was standing at the window. His knees felt weak when he looked at the passport-control officer. He steadied himself by remembering the snapshots of his fictitious father and mother.

"Papers!" growled the Syrian officer. He was unshaven and had a cigarette dangling from his lips.

Levi handed the Syrian officer his French passport and his Lebanese residency card. In theory, the residency card allowed him to come and go in Syria at will. That was one of the benefits of the Baath Party's claim to sovereignty over Greater Syria. They didn't recognize, officially, the existence of a separate nation of Lebanon. But that was only in theory.

The border guard looked at Levi suspiciously. Don't panic, Levi told himself. They always do that. The guard was looking in a thick book covered with Arabic writing. Shit! Why the delay? What was he looking for? Was Levi on a watch list? The security man looked at Levi again through hooded eyes. Despite himself, despite all his preparation, Levi was trembling. He bit his lip hard and put his hands in his pockets so the guard couldn't see them shaking. I'm not going to make it, Levi told himself. This is one trip too many. I'm a dead man.

The guard was writing something down in a book. Levi looked away. Shit. Shit! Here it comes.

But Levi was wrong. The guard was handing him back his papers and waving him on. The man behind him in line was pushing toward the window. Levi apologized in French. *Pardon, pardon.* He returned to his Citroën and drove it to the customs-inspection line. The hard part was over, he told himself. The customs men were cheap thugs. Sometimes they wanted a bribe. But they didn't want to kill Levi.

Levi got through easily, letting the customs man "confiscate" a carton of French cigarettes. He always carried extra cartons, more than he needed, as a distraction for wayward policemen. And then he was off. Levi relaxed in the overstuffed seat of the Citroën, feeling the sweat from his armpits drip down his sides. He had survived another hour in his eternity of fear.

Levi drove east toward Damascus, then north on the main

highway to Aleppo. He was a French businessman, on a business trip. He smoked cigarettes, one after another, and turned his car radio on loud. It was a Syrian station, playing a ballad by Fayrouz about how the Arabs would someday recapture Jerusalem. "The gates of Jerusalem will not remain closed to us," sang Fayrouz. "We will rebuild you with our own hands. Jerusalem, we salute you." Levi knew the tune. He sang along.

Levi had a momentary fright, outside Homs, when he flipped the radio dial and caught the sound of a Hebrew voice on Israeli radio. It was a jingle for a new bank. It was a catchy tune, and Levi found himself singing it in Hebrew. That's what made him panic. In that idle moment of singing, his true identity had ruptured through the fine membrane of his cover. He willed himself to forget the tune, forget the words, forget the Hebrew language itself, for another few days.

He stopped for lunch in Hama, in a small outdoor café by the River Orontes. He sat by the stream, eating a veal cutlet, looking at the old waterwheels that lined the banks. Out of the corner of his eye, he noticed a military officer, dressed in the camouflage uniform of the internal security forces, examining his car. It's normal, he told himself. They check all cars with foreign tags. It's routine. The officer took out a pad and wrote something. Probably the license number. The officer continued walking and stopped at another car with Lebanese tags, this one a Mercedes. He wrote down the license numbers of that one, too. That was the peculiar advantage of operating in a police state, Levi decided. They were watching you always, it was true. But they were watching everyone else, too.

Levi reached Aleppo that night and checked into the Hotel Hovsepian. It was a fine old pile of a hotel, built by a distinguished Armenian family that had come to Aleppo in the late nineteenth century. Levi sat in the bar and swapped stories with the owner, not telling too much about himself—that would seem odd—but revealing just enough to embellish his cover when the Sûreté stopped by that night to inquire about the names on the hotel guest list.

Levi was awakened the next morning by the sound of the muezzin. He had read once in a guidebook that Aleppo was called the city of a thousand mosques. This morning, it sounded as if all one thousand were just outside his hotel room. He bathed, ate a leisurely breakfast, and asked the concierge for tips on local sightseeing. Then he left the hotel to collect the first of his four drops.

Aleppo seemed to Levi that morning like the most remote spot on earth. There wasn't another Jew in 100 miles. Levi felt he had reached the edge of the planet. In the streets he saw the dark faces of Turks, Circassians, Armenians, Kurds. The rough faces of the merchants and nomads and farmers who dwelled in this edge of the world, so very far away from anything else. The morning was quickening. The streets were filling up with people, and the air was fragrant with the smell of bread baking and coffee brewing. An entire city of people Levi had never seen before that day and, God willing, would never see again. He passed an orphanage for Armenian children. My God! he thought. That is the very farthest exile from the garden: to be an Armenian orphan in Aleppo.

Levi walked to the souk, which was about a mile from his hotel. With its maze of narrow alleys and and its many entrances and exits, it was an easy place to spot surveillance, and to get lost. He stopped often, looking for familiar faces. He bought a lacquered wooden box in one of the stalls. After thirty minutes, he was certain that he was clean. There was nobody following him.

He left the souk through a small alleyway and headed for the Crusader castle that overlooked the city of Aleppo. It was a massive pile of stone, gray and forbidding, dominating the city. The castle testified to the peculiar Syrian disinterest in the past. Though a spectacular monument, it was usually deserted.

Levi stopped at the gate, paid his ten piastres to a guard who looked half asleep, and entered the ruins of the fortress. He turned to his left and walked two hundred paces, just as the instructions had said. Then he stopped and looked for a parapet with a chalk mark, which was a sign that the drop had been filled. The chosen mark was a swastika, which seemed to Levi like a sick joke but must have struck someone as good tradecraft.

There was writing on many of the parapets. Arabic names and slogans written right to left, the chiselled names of a few lovers. But no mark. Perhaps he had miscounted the number of paces. The castle was still deserted. Should he start again?

Then he saw it. A tiny swastika, drawn with white chalk. There was nobody in sight.

Levi walked exactly twenty-five more paces—strolling, ambling, gazing out over the city the way a tourist would. Then he stopped. He saw it hidden in a crack in the stone, just where the instructions had said it would be. A small brown envelope containing four rolls of microfilm of Syrian military documents, taken by a disgruntled Sunni military officer who believed that he was working for the Turks. Levi looked around. Still nobody. It was too easy. He slipped the envelope into his pocket, turned, and continued his slow stroll around the perimeter of the castle.

Levi returned to the hotel, packed his bags, and checked out. He gave a generous tip to the bellhop, who bowed and called him "Effendi." He apologized to the owner that he was leaving so soon, but he was due for lunch at the home of a Syrian agribusinessman who lived thirty miles southeast of Aleppo. The Syrian was interested in exporting tomatoes to Europe, and Levi had the contract in his pocket. He relaxed slightly on the road south from Aleppo. One down and three to go.

The second drop was in the village of Sednaya, in the mountains between Homs and Damascus. The village was carved out of the rocky cliffs of the mountains, and in the dry and dusty climate of central Syria, it resembled the cave dwellings of Pueblo Indians in the American Southwest.

The residents of the area were Syriac Christians, an off-shoot of the Eastern Church. They maintained a convent just outside of the village, which made the village a tourist attraction, at least by Syrian standards. But the true pride and joy of Sednaya was something quite different. The men of the village, fathers and sons, were truck drivers, and they regarded themselves as the finest smugglers in the Arab world. Guns, hashish, whisky, whatever the market required. They knew hidden roads that traversed the peaks of Mount Lebanon, which no customs man had ever seen. They knew tracks in the trackless deserts of Arabia. The men of Sednaya made ideal agents, since they went everywhere and saw everything, but they were also dangerous. A smuggler, after all, is always ready to consider a better offer.

Levi's agent was supposedly reliable. Ten years on the payroll and never a mistake. Providing purloined military and government documents, unaware that he was working for the Israelis. A man in it purely for the money. A man, thought Levi, who would probably sell his mother for the right price.

The drop was in a wooded area about a mile from the village. Levi approached it very carefully. Careful to avoid surveillance, careful to scout the terrain.

What terrified him, on a run like this, was the possibility that the agent had somehow been caught and turned. That he had been tortured and confessed that on this very day in this very place, the agent of a foreign intelligence service would be retrieving information that had been left in a hollowed-out log. That at the very moment Levi put his hand into the log to retrieve the packet, a dozen security men would emerge from hiding and arrest him, and take him to a prison where they would torture him, break his bones one by one, until he confessed that he was an Israeli Jew.

Levi felt in his pocket for the tiny metal case that contained the poison tablet. He put it in his hand as he approached the drop. He had no doubt that he would take it if he was captured. That was part of being a coward. Preferring quick and certain death to the excruciating uncertainty of torture.

Levi retrieved the packet. He closed his eyes. There was dead silence. He looked around. Nothing. Empty space. Two down.

Levi was nearing the city center of Damascus when he noticed the traffic lights. Big and bright on nearly every street corner. That was remarkable enough in the Arab world. But the miracle was that the Damascene motorists actually stopped at the lights, yielded at the intersections, gave way to incoming traffic at the circles. Perhaps they were too scared not to obey the traffic regulations.

This was a country, Levi had been told, in which one in ten citizens was an informer for the secret police. It was a nation where the ruling Baath Party instructed the masses at election time with a huge neon sign on a mountain overlooking Damascus. The sign had just one word—"NAM"—the Arabic word for yes. It was a society that lived behind walls, hiding its wealth from public view. The plainest Damascene exterior of stucco and cement could contain a hidden palace decorated in gold and silver. Syria lived by the code of *taqiyya*—the permissible lie. Its Moslem population was ruled by a sect, the Alawites, who rejected the Prophet Mohammed. Its nominally socialist political leaders were among the most rapacious capitalists in the Middle East. Indeed, the Syrians seemed sincere about only one thing: their hatred of Israel.

Levi stayed overnight in Damascus, in a businessman's hotel downtown called the New Omayed. It was clean and relatively comfortable. He checked to make sure that the two packets were secure in the false bottom of his briefcase. The case had been beautifully designed. Anyone searching it would have to destroy it to find the false bottom. And any forced entry into this secret compartment would release a vial of acid that would destroy whatever documents had been hidden there.

Levi was hungry. He walked to the diplomatic quarter and dined in an excellent French restaurant called Le Chevalier. He feasted on crevettes, grilled in garlic butter. He drank most of a bottle of wine. He felt relaxed, which made him tense. As he walked home, he could sense the inquisitive eyes watching the foreigner, slightly tipsy, as he walked down the street at midnight.

Levi serviced the first Damascus drop the next morning. He went to the agricultural exhibit at the Damascus trade fair. The agent, he had been told, was a Sunni professor of agronomy at the University of Damascus whose father had been killed by the Alawites. His chosen revenge was to provide documents about Syrian efforts to monitor Israeli communications.

Levi chatted casually with a member of the staff at the agricultural exhibit. On the exhibit table, right where it should be, was a prospectus on new techniques in chicken farming. He picked it up and turned the pages slowly until he felt a small envelope. When he was confident that nobody was looking, Levi slipped the envelope in his pocket. It was so easy, so simple.

The final pick-up was scheduled for the next morning. Levi spent the rest of the day touring the city. Perhaps he would make it back home after all.

When Levi returned to his hotel that night, he had a fright.

Someone had gone through his things. Not just the maid, but a professional. He had left the briefcase closed on the bureau. Someone had opened it and gone through the commercial documents. The signs were obvious: the papers weren't aligned the same way he had left them, and the piece of hair he had left on the top page of the agricultural contract was gone. Levi's heart was pounding. His forehead was sweating. He went into the bathroom and looked at his face in the mirror. What he saw was fear.

So what, he told himself. So they have looked at my papers. So much the better. They confirm that I am in the import-export business and have travelled to Syria to sign a contract. They will call the tomato farmer who gave me lunch, and he will confirm my alibi. They will call the hotel in Aleppo and they will confirm my alibi. So why am I worried? They haven't found the false bottom of the briefcase and there is no other evidence—none—that I am anything other than a French businessman.

Levi picked up the phone and heard a hollow sound, as if something was drawing just a bit of power off the line. They are watching me, Levi told himself. Somehow, they know. I am a dead man.

The last drop was in the Damascus souk. Levi didn't want to get out of bed the next morning. He wanted to stay, to hide under the covers, to call in sick. But he got up, motivated as much by hatred of his work and a desire to be done with it as by anything else. He dressed and went to the souk. It was natural, he told himself. The last day in Damascus, any visitor would go to the souk. He didn't notice any surveillance on the way, but he didn't find that reassuring. They have put their best team on me, he thought.

The souk was a vast stockyard of merchandise. Hundreds of merchants did their business in rows of steel-roofed sheds, selling a profusion of wares and trinkets. There were men selling fine linen for ladies, checkered kaffiyehs for the men, hammered brass, exotic birds, ill-fitting suits from Czechoslovakia, cheap shoes from Egypt that proclaimed on the insole: "All Lether," house plants, garden plants, tiles, fake papyrus documents, real papyrus documents, mirrors with the name of Allah written in script on the glass, prayer rugs with a compass built into the rug so that the pilgrim would never be confused about the direction of Mecca. Levi had studied the hand-drawn maps of the souk so many times before he left Beirut that he felt he knew the location of every bric-a-brac merchant in this vast square mile of commerce.

His instructions were to go to a particular stall in a particular shed, where there was a merchant who sold fine wooden boxes, inlaid with mother-of-pearl. He shouldn't go directly there, but browse, amble, watch his tail. When he reached the particular stall, he should admire the merchant's work and ask to see his finer boxes, which were usually kept inside the shop. Levi should browse until he found a particular box, with a design on the top in the shape of an elephant. A very unusual box and design. There could not be another one like it in the souk. He should buy the box, take it back to his hotel, and remove the intelligence that was hidden inside.

The merchant himself would know nothing about Levi, who he was, what he was doing. So far as the merchant knew, Levi was just another customer. A foreigner, which meant that he would probably pay double what anything was worth. The merchant was the uncle of Levi's agent. And the agent, Levi understood, was very good indeed. He was a Palestinian who worked with one of the radical factions that were headquartered in Damascus. He was worth the trouble.

Levi approached the stall. The merchant, dressed in dark trousers and pajama tops, gave him a toothless smile.

"Good price, very good price," said the merchant.

Levi nodded. He picked up some of the cheaper boxes and returned them to the rack.

"Les grandes boîtes?" he asked in French. Then he tried English. "Where are the big ones?"

The merchant smiled. Here was a discerning customer. He escorted Levi inside. Levi glanced at the passageway to see if anyone was watching. Several other merchants were glowering at him, but he assumed that was simple avarice and envy. He entered the tiny room, illuminated by a naked bulb. Arrayed against the wall was a profusion of inlaid wooden boxes, perhaps one hundred of them. Levi began his browsing, checking each box for the mark. He saw a tiger, several horses, and a numbing sample of stars, squares, and circles. But no elephant.

Where was it? Levi was starting to sweat. The merchant was nodding and rubbing his hands, waiting for Levi to buy something. Levi looked again quickly through the inventory. He was sure now. The elephant wasn't there. He looked out the window of the shop. Who was that man in the baggy brown suit? Had he seen him before? Had he been sitting at another exhibit table at the trade fair yesterday? No. Maybe. Levi couldn't be sure. His head was spinning. He turned apologetically to the merchant.

"Rien. Rien du tout," said Levi.

The merchant, not understanding French, nodded and smiled.

"Good price, very good price," said the merchant.

By that time Levi was out the door.

The agony came when Levi was finally out of the souk, sitting in a café, with time to consider what had happened. The box hadn't been there. The agent hadn't been able to deliver it. Why not? Had he been caught? Was he being followed? Or was he just late delivering it? Or had he forgotten the day? Levi felt sick. He tried to eat a sandwich but couldn't. All he wanted to do was smoke cigarettes. And get caught, and have it done with, rather than continue the cheap drama that was eating his stomach out.

The instructions were very clear about what Levi should do if he missed the drop on the appointed day. He should wait a day and try again.

For Levi, it was the additional waiting that was excruciating. We can all be brave when we have no other choice. In those brief moments when heroism is required in extreme circumstances, it is usually present. When a soldier is actually under fire, his nerves become calm. He follows orders. The agony is in the waiting. Thinking, dreading, fraying the nerves to the point that they are too thin to bear the load.

Maybe we can do it once, the thing that scares us. Perhaps we can summon enough courage to do one time the thing that terrifies us, gritting our teeth, closing our eyes. But twice is impossible. To go back a second time, after we have stretched our nerves so taut we fear they will snap, that is beyond all but the fearless, whose nerves are dead.

And yet there was Levi the next morning, rising hollow-eyed after a sleepless night, going back to do it a second time.

Praying now that it would end soon. Holding his cyanide tablet in his clenched palm like a sacrament.

Everyone seemed to be looking at Levi curiously the next morning. He told the man at the front desk he would be staying another day. More shopping. The man arched his eyebrows. Nobody stays in Syria an extra day unless they have to, the look seemed to say. What a fine souk you have here in Damascus, Levi told the desk clerk. I think I'll go back.

Build a legend, Levi told himself. An explanation for everything except the final act. But the man at the desk gave him that look again. The doorman's eyes followed him into the street. The taxi driver asked him twice where he was going. Am I going mad? Levi asked himself. Or am I a doomed man?

He took a different route through the souk this time. Past the rug dealers who shouted out at him as he passed. Boukhara. Qom. Tajik. Like a verbal atlas of the Middle East. At least they wanted his business. Past the brass merchants selling pots and pans and ashtrays. Past the gold souk with its tiny stalls, each miserly merchant carrying his fortune with him like a snail wrapped in his shell.

He arrived in the precinct of the box merchant. His heart was pounding and he could feel the beat of his pulse against his watchband. I can't do it, he said to himself. There is still time to turn around, go back to the hotel, drive the car to the border and freedom. But of course he kept walking.

When the merchant saw Levi, he did a two-step jig. Of course he was happy: A foreigner who browses once and comes back the next day will pay *four* times what something is worth.

"Je retourne," said Levi.

"Special price!" said the merchant, licking his gums with his tongue.

"Yes," said Levi. "Very good." He looked around. The souk was almost deserted, even though it was mid-morning. Had they closed it off to prevent people from seeing the arrest? That was silly. They didn't operate that way. But who was the man in the gray suit selling trinkets across the way? Had he been there the day before? It didn't matter. It was too late.

"Very special price," said the merchant, tugging at Levi's sleeve. He escorted Levi inside and left him to browse, rubbing his hands.

Levi looked at the boxes slowly and deliberately. No mistakes this time. There was the tiger. There was the horse. He turned each one over this time, thinking that perhaps the design might be on the bottom. No, no. His heart was sinking. No, no, no, no. He had spent nearly ten minutes studying the boxes. The merchant was getting impatient. He had come to the end without finding what he was looking for.

There was a man outside, browsing. Shit!

Levi looked at the merchant. The man was expecting a sale. He would have to buy something. An idea came to him almost as an afterthought.

"More boxes?" he asked quietly. "Don't you have any more boxes?"

"More?" said the merchant.

"Yes," hissed Levi. Yes, you scrofulous, lice-ridden old bastard. Go get the other fucking boxes.

The merchant disappeared into a closet at the back of the one-room shop. He emerged carrying four boxes decorated with inlaid mother-of-pearl. One showed the Great Mosque at Mecca and the Kaaba stone; a special box for Saudi customers. One showed a naked houri. Big tits and a flabby stomach. One showed the flag of Palestine, which made it subversive.

And one showed an elephant.

Levi feigned interest in the box with the naked woman. He looked at it closely. Then at the one of the elephant. Then at the naked woman. Then he took the elephant in his hands.

"How much?" said Levi.

The merchant looked at him through very narrow eyes. What did he know? That a foreigner wanted to buy one box out of a hundred. That he insisted on this box, which had only arrived yesterday and did not even have a price tag yet?

"As you like," said the merchant. It was the time-honored beginning of negotiations with a foreigner. Make him start the bidding, for in his nervousness, he will almost certainly offer too much.

Levi thought a moment. He wanted to make a reasonable offer, but he had no idea what the box was actually worth.

"Fifty," said Levi. "Fifty pounds."

The merchant clucked his tongue and gave Levi a look of reproach. He reached for the box, shaking his head.

"How much?" asked Levi again.

The merchant took out a piece of paper. He wrote out the number 500.

"What?" asked Levi in genuine astonishment. "Five hundred Syrian pounds?"

The merchant nodded.

"Impossible," said Levi. He took the piece of paper and wrote out 100. The merchant shook his head.

"No, no. Four hundred."

"Two hundred," offered Levi. I don't believe this, he said to himself. This is the worst moment of my life. I'm nearly paralyzed with fear. And I'm standing here haggling with an asshole merchant about the price of a wooden box.

"Three hundred," said the merchant.

You sick, demented bastard, thought Levi. But another voice told him, Play the game.

"Two hundred and fifty."

The merchant looked Levi in the eye, measuring the limits of extortion. He could see the fear and the need, without knowing why.

"Three hundred."

"Okay," said Levi. Who gives a shit? This is insane.

The merchant wrapped the box carefully in tissue paper, then in brown paper, which he tied with a neat string.

"Fatura?" said the merchant, using the Arabic word for receipt.

"Yes," said Levi. Why not?

"How much?" asked the merchant with a corrupt smile that was all gums and saliva.

You crooked Arab camel jockey, son of a whore, are you really asking whether to falsify the receipt? Is that what you think this is all about? Taking a cheap little wooden box through customs with a phony receipt?

"Three hundred," said Levi. He could not help but laugh as he said it. As the sound of laughter came out of his parched throat, he felt something snap inside him.

"As you like," said the merchant.

* * *

Levi walked out of the shop clutching his parcel. He lit a cigarette. It was the best taste of his life. He saw a soldier, strolling down the arcade, gun in hand. He should have been scared, but he wasn't anymore. The absurdity of the encounter in the shop had cleansed him, momentarily, of fear. He walked slowly through the souk, stopping in one stall to buy some pistachios for the trip home. As he bought them, he realized: I am going to make it. That is why I have bought the nuts. They aren't a cover for anything. I'm going to eat them on the way home.

He had one more bad moment, at the Syrian border. That was always the worst time, leaving any country. The security forces know that is their last shot, so they play games. They invent reasons to ask questions and make you squirm.

In Levi's case, it was the way he said the word *marhaba*—hello—to the border guard. He rolled the "r" slightly. Which would be fine, normally. Except that the one thing that every Arab policeman knows about native Hebrew speakers is that they roll their "r's" making a sound in the back of their throat. But then, so do many Frenchmen from Marseilles.

The border guard studied Levi's passport. He checked in his book. He took it back to show his superior, a fat colonel. The colonel came out and asked Levi questions. What had he been doing in Syria? Where had he been? Who had he seen?

Levi answered the questions serenely. He knew why. His nerves were finally broken. There was nothing left to feel scared with. The colonel finally sent him on his way. Levi drove across the border into Lebanon, eating pistachios.

Levi didn't see the fruit of his labor until many months later. It was sent to Tel Aviv, where a Mossad officer decoded the message that had been hidden in the box with the mother-of-pearl elephant. It proved to be an extraordinary piece of intelligence.

The message from the Palestinian agent in Damascus said that the leadership of the Popular Front for the Liberation of Palestine had concluded that there was an American agent inside Fatah. The reason they were so sure, the agent reported, was that the Old Man had boasted to the PFLP leaders a few months ago that he had a secret channel to the White House. When the radicals called him a liar, the Old Man said that he had obtained the secret text of an American peace plan more than a year ago.

The agent in Damascus didn't know the identity of the American contact in Fatah. But he reported the guesses made by the PFLP leadership. The American agent had to be someone high up in the Fatah intelligence network. Only an intelligence man would be given the job of intermediary, the radicals said. The most likely suspect, concluded the agent's report, was the young man who had risen so quickly in the Rasd—the Old Man's pet, Jamal Ramlawi.

PART VII

Spring 1971 – May 1972

31

Beirut; Spring 1971

Mohammed Nasir Makawi, known as Abu Nasir, was a dark, intense man with a thin face and a thick mustache. He was Fatah's chief of intelligence and he looked the part. His eyes were deeply set and so ringed with circles that they seemed to be perpetually in shadow. Like many of the best Arab intelligence officers, he had a deadpan, expressionless face that gave nothing away.

Abu Nasir lived in Beirut, on the sixth floor of a building on the Rue Verdun, a busy street that sloped southward from the center of West Beirut toward Corniche Mazraa and the sea. He worried about the security and planned to install a blast-proof metal door at the entrance to the apartment. He wasn't sure what to do about electronic surveillance. One of his Russian friends had advised him that the only way to be certain you weren't bugged was to build new walls, ceiling, and floorboards on top of the old ones—covering over any hidden microphones. That seemed like too much work. So Abu Nasir played the radio.

The apartment was sparsely furnished. A brown couch with too much stuffing, an easy chair covered in the same fabric, a large television set that dominated the living room, a small wooden table, and a cheap, machine-made tapestry that spelled out the name of Allah in elaborate Arabic script. The only real decoration was a large nargilleh pipe, which stood next to the easy chair. The blinds were drawn tight, which added to the dark and desolation of the room.

Abu Nasir sat on his brown couch, watching a banal Egyptian soap opera on Lebanese television. He was waiting for his young deputy, Jamal Ramlawi.

Jamal was late. He is romancing some young woman, Abu Nasir thought to himself. That is his weakness. He had called Jamal that morning at the apartment where he was staying in Fakhani. Come by this evening for a talk, Abu Nasir had said. Just you and me. I will explain to you what we are planning. As he made the invitation, Abu Nasir had heard the voice of a woman in background, singing in Italian.

The bell rang. One long and two short. Abu Nasir opened the door and embraced Jamal. The young man was dressed more neatly than usual, in gray trousers and a blue shirt rather than his usual jeans and leather jacket. His hair was slicked back against his head. The younger man kissed his host twice, and then a third time. Abu Nasir looked almost frail in the embrace of his young protégé.

Abu Nasir excused himself to fix coffee. That was part of life in the shadows: You learned to mend your own trousers, sew your own buttons, make your own coffee. He filled the pot half-full with coffee that had been ground to a fine powder, added four tablespoons of sugar, poured in a little water, and let the rich mixture come to a boil three times. The result was a thick black sludge, sweet and syrupy on the tongue.

When the coffee was done, Abu Nasir carried the pot and two small cups into the living room and poured one cup for Jamal. He poured another for himself, settled down in the easy chair, and lit up the water pipe. He sucked on the wooden mouthpiece until the room was thick with smoke. The gaunt man old man seemed oblivious to anything but his own concerns. Sucking on his pipe, blowing out the smoke. Measured, calculating.

"Have I ever told you about my village in Palestine?" asked Abu Nasir eventually, putting aside the pipe and lighting a cigarette.

"No, Uncle," said Jamal.

"Perhaps I should tell you the story," said Abu Nasir, as if he had not quite made up his mind.

"You would do me an honor."

"It is quite a long story, I am afraid."

"I would like to hear it, Uncle."

The older man nodded.

Abu Nasir liked to tell stories: long, meandering tales whose meaning or relevance often wasn't evident until the last chapter. But there was always a lesson—precise and perfectly fashioned—that would come into view slowly like the outline of a castle emerging from a thick fog. Nobody ever interrupted Abu Nasir. As he talked, he would fix his gaze on his listener. Clouds of cigarette smoke would billow around his face and blow gently away with the rise and fall of his voice.

"Do you remember the old Jaffa Road in Palestine that ran from Jerusalem to the sea?" Abu Nasir began.

"No, Uncle, I don't."

"Of course you don't. You were too young, so I'll tell you about it. The road climbed from the coast up through the hills surrounding Jerusalem. Just before it reached the city, on the last steep hillside, if you looked to the left you could see a fine Arab village, with an arc of stone houses arrayed against the hillside.

"That was the village of Lifta, and it was the home of my family for many generations.

"Lifta," said Abu Nasir again, repeating the word quietly, as if the very sound was a remnant of his lost village. "I feel as if I can remember every detail of it, though I left more than twenty years ago. The cool of the stone house in the summer; the smell of bread baking on hot rocks in the courtyard; sleeping on the roof in the summer with my father; the taste of water from the well that I thought must be bottomless.

"I watched Lifta change. Jerusalem kept pushing west toward us in the 1930s. Jews coming from Europe settled along the Jaffa Road, in a suburb called Romema. We didn't think too much about it. Jews had lived in that area since anyone could remember. And besides, some of our villagers were making money selling land to the Jews."

"You sold land to the Jews?" asked Jamal.

"We were naive. And we were greedy. Liftawis owned so much land—nearly to the walls of the Old City—that we didn't mind losing just a little bit of it. And a bit more. What did we care? We were getting rich. People said that Lifta was becoming the richest village in Palestine, which made us all feel happy and proud.

"My father was one of the richest. He made money and he built himself a grand house up on the hilltop, away from the old village of Lifta and near the Jews. That was a mark of how successful he was. It was the biggest house in the area and people from Romema would come and stare at it. My father was a very modern man. He believed in progress and sent me to high school. I would walk along the Jaffa Road to school, past the shops and markets and coffeehouses, and think how lucky we were. We took no precautions in those days. We never thought about it! The Jews were all around us. We were their landlords. What could possibly happen to us?

"As I got older, I noticed that Romema was getting bigger and Lifta was getting smaller. You couldn't even tell where Lifta was anymore, except for the stone houses of the old village on the hillside. It was all suburbs. But nobody worried. We were building and expanding and making money. There were a few young boys from the village who skirmished from time to time with the Jews along the Jaffa Road and tried to convince us that disaster was coming. But nobody in Lifta paid very much attention to them. We were so trusting and naive that we were lulled almost to sleep."

"You were fools," said Jamal.

Abu Nasir didn't answer. He looked at Jamal with the expression of bemused tolerance that older men have for impetuous young men who imagine that they have invented bravery and cunning.

"The world of Lifta was destroyed in one night," continued Abu Nasir. "I remember the date. It was December 29, 1947. The village elders had gone to a coffeehouse along the Jaffa Road to drink coffee and smoke the nargilleh. It was a room like this! Full of smoke and talk and dreams.

"The Jews kicked in the door of the coffeehouse and began shooting. Six of the old men were killed, including the moukhtar. I was asleep but I heard the shooting that night, and the wailing of the women. I thought the world was coming to an end. It was as if the entire village had been awakened suddenly from a dead sleep and we were terrified. Everyone thought the Jews would be coming next to their house! No one slept for the rest of the night.

"The next morning people began packing their bags. Nobody could explain exactly why. But the reason was obvious.

They were terrified. The world of Lifta had been built on illusions, and when the illusions were destroyed, everything else collapsed. People took small suitcases and told each other they wouldn't be gone long. They went nearby, to East Jerusalem or Ramallah or El Bireh. They would be back in two weeks—a month at most—when the situation calmed down and the fighting stopped. But the fighting didn't stop. It got worse and worse, and by the next winter the war for Palestine was over. We had lost our village."

"Or given it away," said Jamal.

"You are right, my fine young man. We gave our village away. But that wasn't the worst thing that happened that night in December 1947."

"What could be worse than that?"

"The worst thing was that we lost our self-respect. The men of Lifta panicked and fled like women, and most of them are still running. Even now, many of them can't bear to admit what happened. They have invented a myth about why they left, which they tell their children and grandchildren."

"A myth?"

"A myth of terror. They claim that they left Lifta only after Begin and the Irgun had destroyed Deir Yassin! Every Palestinian knows about Deir Yassin. It is the incarnation of evil, and it is everyone's excuse for defeat. And to this day, our elders tell themselves that they left Lifta only after the slaughter of the 250 poor villagers of Deir Yassin.

"But, Jamal, I will tell you something. It is a lie! The people of Lifta fled four months *before* Deir Yassin! They are cowards, even now. Scattered, homeless, landless. They have lost everything. And still they cannot face the truth."

"They are pathetic," said Jamal.

"Perhaps. But their emotions are human and timeless. And that is why I am telling you this sad story of my village. Because it is our story today. Do you doubt me? Do you think that we have learned our lesson and it cannot happen again? Listen to me for a moment more.

"After the catastrophe of 1948, many of the people of Lifta went to Amman. They had lost their village and their country. But in Jordan they were at least among brother Arabs, with passports and the rights of citizenship. The Liftawis built homes and businesses. They made a little money and perhaps they bought a car, or a bigger house, or they sent their children to university. Or perhaps they moved to Kuwait or Saudi Arabia and made even more money."

"I know people like that," said Jamal.

"Of course you do," answered Abu Nasir. "They are all around you. They are the face of our people, struggling, hoping, trying to survive. The Liftawis were no better or worse than the people of any other village. They made friends with the Jordanians. They grew comfortable. They believed in the liberation of Palestine, perhaps even in the dream of returning to Lifta. They supported the fedayeen and gave us money and time. They believed they had learned the lesson that to survive in a world like this, you must be strong.

"Now I will tell you the saddest part of my story. During the fighting in Amman last September, I visited a family from my village. From Lifta. They were living in Jebel Hussein near one of the Jordanian Army positions. Do you know where that is?"

"Of course," said Jamal.

"I asked them for help. I told them that our fighters needed their house to stop the advance of the King's army. I pleaded, but they refused. They told me the fighting would be over soon and they would be safe. They didn't want to have the fedayeen so close. What harm could come to them from the Jordanians? They had done nothing wrong."

"What happened to them?" asked Jamal.

"They are all dead. The whole family was killed when an artillery shell hit their house. I cried when I heard the news, even after what had happened. Here were people who had been driven like dogs from their home in Lifta only to die like dogs in Amman!"

Jamal shook his head with a mixture of sadness and contempt.

"Now I will shock you by saying something," continued Abu Nasir. "Our people hate Menachem Begin, don't they? That is an article of faith for us, isn't it?"

"Of course it is!" answered Jamal.

"But I don't hate Begin. I admire him. His people were crushed and demoralized. They had been dragged back and forth across Europe and then gone silently to their deaths.

They had trusted in the Germans—in reason and progress and assimilation—so much that they couldn't understand what was happening to them. They died trembling, with their eyes closed, lying to themselves to the very end. But not Begin. Have you ever read his book?"

"No," said Jamal disdainfully.

"You should. In this book, Begin put the matter of survival very simply. He said: 'I fight, therefore I am.' And he was right. The Jews would survive only if they were prepared to kill their enemies. Begin put his trust in the power of Jewish guns, rather than in the goodwill of others."

Jamal nodded. He was beginning to see the castle emerging from the fog.

"Begin understood something else," continued Abu Nasir. "He understood that terrorism is the weapon of the weak. That terrorism gives power to the weak by making their enemies afraid. He understood that if you have the ability to create fear, then you have power.

"I will tell you something from my heart about terrorism, Jamal. Do you know what I feel when I read in the newspapers about Palestinian 'terrorists' who have hijacked airplanes and killed civilians? Or when I read that the Palestinians are cruel and ruthless and inhuman? Intellectually I am critical, of course, because Fatah's official line is to oppose international terrorist operations. But do you know what I feel in my heart and my stomach?"

"What do you feel?" asked Jamal, almost in a whisper.

"I feel proud! It makes me happy to know that they are afraid of us. I like to see the look of fear in people's eyes when I walk down the street. If I hear someone say behind my back, 'Be careful of him! He is a madman! He is a killer!'—I am happy for the rest of the day."

Jamal nodded. Yes, he thought. That is what I feel. That is what every Palestinian feels. We may not defeat the Jews, but at least we can make them fear for their lives.

"I would like to tell you a secret," continued Abu Nasir. "It is what the Egyptians would call a secret of state. Something that Nasser said, which I swore I would never tell anyone else. But now that Nasser is dead, God rest his soul, I will tell you. The first time Nasser met the Old Man was in 1967. At the end of the meeting, after much talk back and forth, Nasser said to him: 'Why not be our Begin?' "

"Begin?" asked Jamal.

"Yes. We didn't believe Nasser. We thought he was joking. But he was right."

"What are you saying, Uncle?"

"Our people are dying! It is happening to us again. The resistance is scattered, our morale is broken, our people are in flight. This time our enemy is an Arab leader, the King of Jordan, but that is the only difference. September 1970 is the same as December 1947. Another generation is developing the psychology of defeat. They are already inventing the lies they will tell their children about the events of Black September! We are dying as a people, vanishing into history on a tide of defeat and self-deception.

"Jamal, my friend and brother, we must break out of this cycle! To survive, we must find a way to make our enemies afraid of us. Otherwise we are finished. And that is what I wanted to tell you: That will be our task, you and me. To make our enemies feel the knife of fear."

The story ended as quietly as it had begun. By now, the room was full of smoke, so dense and thick that the face of Abu Nasir was barely visible. Jamal rose from his couch and silently kissed the older man. Tears were running down his cheeks. For Jamal, that was the night that Black September was born, a mythic organization that had no leaders, no structure, no purpose or plan other than to sustain the intoxicating and deadly specter of terror.

32

Beirut; July 1971

Through the spring and summer of 1971, Jamal was the dog that didn't bark. He slipped quietly in and out of Beirut, was rarely seen in public, avoided old friends from Fatah, and even altered the conduct of his amorous adventures. As a concession to security, he stopped bringing women home. He went instead to their apartments or hotel rooms or palaces, slept with them once, and then disappeared. He felt virtuous for this modest restraint.

Jamal travelled ceaselessly, relearning languages he had half-forgotten. His passports usually said he was Algerian. They were real Algerian passports, provided by a cooperative member of the Algerian Embassy in Beirut. This particular Algerian could be trusted, Abu Nasir had advised Jamal, because he had never been tortured by the French. That was one of Abu Nasir's peculiar rules: Never trust a man who has been tortured, regardless of whether he cracked. A victim of torture sees the very worst about the world, in himself and his torturers. He loses something.

Jamal made a plausible Algerian, with his dark black hair and continental manners. He was Chadli bin Yahiya or Omar Sahnoun or Tariq bin Jedid. The names became like new layers of skin, masks on top of masks.

Jamal's task was to solve a riddle. Abu Nasir had told him to build a solid structure that was invisible, to develop the infrastructure of an organization that would not exist, to plan operations that would appear to have no planning—operations

that could be denied plausibly by the very people who had
ordered them. It was crucial, said Abu Nasir, that Black September should have no address and leave no footprints. In the
aftermath of each bombing or assassination, there should be
only the blackness and anonymity of pure terror.

Anonymity meant cut-outs. Layers of people, witting and
unwitting, interposed between the word and the deed. It
meant establishing dead drops in the major cities of Europe
for discreet communications. A boîte postale in Paris. A fictitious company in Zurich. A string of flats in London. It meant
working with a few trusted Arab intelligence officers, all So-
viet-trained, to establish a communications network using embassy codes and the diplomatic pouch.

Building a network meant expanding the frail infrastructure
Jamal had been building for many months. It meant recruiting
sleeper agents from among the thousands of Palestinian students in Europe. The recruits were kids, most of them, full of
hatred for the Israelis and the false courage of youth. Jamal's
spotters would identify the best prospects. A recruiter would
meet them, swear them to secrecy, offer them a small stipend,
and tell them that in return the Revolution would someday ask
for a favor. Then Jamal would test the novitiates. He would
send someone to try to worm and wheedle out of them what
they had talked about with the recruiter. Those who divulged
the secret, or even hinted at it, were dropped immediately
from the list. Those who said nothing remained. There were
very few who passed the test, and even those few often
proved maddeningly indiscreet.

Jamal struggled to create a competent intelligence organization out of this uncertain band of recruits. It was an agoniz-
ing and occasionally infuriating process. Jamal would fix a
time for a covert meeting in a European capital and hear his
agent respond, "Insha' Allah"—If God wills. He would repeat
over and over the need for security only to hear one of his
men boast to a fellow Arab in a crowded café that he was
doing "secret work" for the Revolution that he could not discuss. He would ask one of his agents to bring him a detailed
diagram of, say, an Israeli-owned oil facility in Rotterdam and
receive a messy pencil sketch that might as well have been a
map of the Pyramids in Egypt!

Jamal grew sick of Arabs who were tardy, undisciplined,

imprecise, easily corrupted, and self-deceiving. That, however, was his raw material, and he was determined to create from it an organization that worked. So he hammered and pushed and prodded. If the Jews could create the powerful state of Israel from the detritus of 1945, he told himself, then it shouldn't be impossible to transform several dozen Arabs into a reasonably efficient underground network.

Jamal recruited his lieutenants in Europe from among the Palestinian intelligentsia. In Paris, he selected a balding history professor. In London, a prominent businessman. In Madrid, a distinguished professor of physics. In Rome, a long-haired musician. Like Jamal, they were all aristocrats of a sort—at once proud and ashamed of their elite status.

Long before Jamal, Lenin had understood that such people make ideal recruits for a secret organization. They think in abstractions and turn the mundane stuff of politics—land, statehood, the exercise of power—into idealized images. Soon these images become so pure and fine, so embued with romance, that the death of mere mortals seems like nothing if it advances the sacred cause. The Palestinian intellectuals were perfect recruits: hungry for secrets, motivated by the noblest ideals, capable of the most extreme acts of violence.

At safehouses across Europe, Jamal began to assemble his operational files. The schedule of an Arab League meeting planned for Cairo in November; the floor plan of a German factory that built electric motors for the Israeli defense industry; photos of the Jordanian embassies in Paris and Berne; a map showing the route travelled by the Jordanian Ambassador to London on his way to work; airplane schedules and train timetables for a dozen cities in the Middle East and Europe; stacks of false passports and piles of untraceable cash.

As far as the world could see, Fatah was in disarray, still in a period of drift and disorientation after the Jordan debacle. Fatah leaders issued conflicting statements: one day calling for the overthrow of the king, the next day urging reconciliation. There was a search for scapegoats, with the Syrians blaming the Old Man and the Old Man, in turn, blaming a grand conspiracy that included the Jordanians, Americans, and Israelis. Rather than conduct a rigorous critique of his mistakes in Jordan, the Old Man proclaimed that "unity" would solve the PLO's problems.

It was the silly season. Egypt's new president announced that 1971 would be "the year of decision"—war or peace—and then did nothing at all. In that same spirit of confusion, the PLO debated in private whether to face reality and accept the existence of Israel and then voted at a PLO congress in Cairo in February 1971 to reject any solution short of the destruction of the "Zionist Entity."

The Old Man's outward actions were so clownish and counterproductive that a sensitive analyst might have been suspicious. Was it possible that these public antics were really a sideshow? Was something happening in the shadows? There were tiny fragments of evidence. A hint of a new Fatah underground emerged in May 1971, when the Jordanian government disclosed what it said was a secret PLO plan to assassinate Jordanian officials. But nobody paid much attention. It was too easy to believe that the Old Man was as incompetent as he looked.

The first person on the CIA payroll to notice anything peculiar was Fuad. He had maintained sporadic contact with Jamal ever since the disastrous meeting with Marsh the previous summer in Rome. At one of these infrequent meetings with Jamal in mid-1971—arranged simply as a reminder that the Americans were still in the game—Fuad sensed that something had changed in Jamal. The freewheeling playboy had turned serious. The question was why.

The meeting took place in a coffeehouse in Fakhani late on a Thursday afternoon, the start of the Moslem weekend and the traditional boys' night out in the Arab world. In the old days, Fuad and Jamal had often met on Thursday evenings for coffee, then whisky, then food, then women.

Fuad arrived late, looking sleek in a pair of wraparound sunglasses. He greeted people in the coffeehouse. They smiled and called his name. Fuad was, by now, a regular in the Fatah-controlled neighborhood of Fakhani. Everyone knew him. He was a rich Lebanese leftist, a friend of the Revolution.

Jamal was already there waiting, smoking a cigarette with one hand and drumming his fingers on the table with the other. He looked tired and overworked, with deep circles under his eyes. The young Palestinian scolded Fuad for being several minutes late. He glanced frequently at his wristwatch.

"You're behaving more like an American than an Arab," said Fuad jokingly after a few minutes of desultory conversation.

"And what is wrong with that?" answered Jamal. "There is much that we could learn from the Americans."

"There is?" asked Fuad, unable to mask his surprise.

"We need help! Sometimes when I watch my Arab brothers, I think maybe we should contract the Revolution out to the Americans. Or the Germans. Or even the Swiss!"

Fuad laughed. But he wondered: What is Jamal telling me? Why is he so tense?

"Do you know what the Arab national slogan should be?" asked Jamal.

"What?"

" 'Fut aleina bukra,' " said Jamal. Stop by tomorrow! It was a favorite expression of the time-wasting Egyptians, an Arabic equivalent of *mañana*.

"What is keeping you so busy these days?" asked Fuad.

"Administrative work."

"What kind?"

"Paperwork," answered Jamal wearily. "The Old Man asked me to help with the finances. The Martyrs' Funds. Investments. Money from the Saudis and the Kuwaitis."

"A lot of money?" asked Fuad.

"Millions," said the Palestinian. "Tens of millions. The Revolution is rich. But the work isn't very intcresting. It is bank accounts and deposit slips and paperwork. I find it dull."

"Bureaucracy is the curse of the Arabs," said Fuad.

"You are wrong, my friend," answered Jamal. "The curse of the Arabs is the Arabs."

Fuad looked at him curiously.

"You said before that you need help. Do you mean it?"

"From who?"

"From my friends."

Jamal laughed. Was he thinking of Marsh and the look on his face as a briefcase of hundred-dollar bills tumbled at his feet? The Palestinian lowered his voice and spoke to Fuad.

"I don't ever want to see your American friends again. And

I warn you: If they come after me, I will kill them."

Fuad nodded. He changed the subject. What did Jamal think of the new Lebanese cabinet? It was a joke, a scandal. Everyone was for sale. Fatah probably had more Lebanese on the payroll than did the Lebanese Ministry of Interior. And the Sunni politicians in West Beirut, they no longer even pretended to be independent. They just did what Fatah instructed. Lebanon would be better off if it was run entirely by the Palestinians! They drank a friendly toast to the Revolution. A few minutes later Jamal broke off the meeting. He had a headache, he said. They would meet again in a few months.

Fuad watched Jamal walk away toward one of the anonymous apartments in Fakhani where he now stayed when he was in Beirut. It was useless to try to follow. Worse than useless. It was suicidal.

The next day Fuad sent a message to Rogers. He left it in the drop at the Souk Tawile.

Fuad's message was simple but inconclusive: Our old friend is up to something. He is telling transparent lies about his activities, but that is to be expected. What is strange is the way he looks. He is tired and tense. His eyes say that something is different. He is angry. He talks of killing Americans, but I don't believe it. Watch him if you can, because I think he is going underground.

But there was nobody to do the watching. The Beirut station had lost two diplomatic cover slots and 10 percent of its budget. The Middle East was on the back burner again. The war in Indochina was taking up more and more of the agency's resources. There was no time or money to mount a new surveillance operation against a Palestinian intelligence officer simply because a Lebanese contact agent thought that he looked tired and tense.

Rogers received a peculiar call in midsummer from Father Maroun Lubanani. Peculiar, Rogers thought, because they had not seen each other in months.

The Maronite priest invited Rogers to join him for a walk in the hills above Kaslik. It would be a chance to talk, he said. Rogers, dressed in tennis shoes and blue jeans, arrived at the gate of the University of the Holy Ghost at the appointed hour. He was surprised to see Father Maroun waiting at the

gate, dressed in a full Alpinist's uniform of lederhosen, kneesocks, and a Tyrolean hat. The priest was sitting unsteadily on
the silver perch of his walking stick.

Rogers tried to think of something to say about this out-
landish costume that wouldn't sound insulting. Nothing occurred to him, so he kept his mouth shut.

Father Maroun greeted him stiffly in French.

The American intelligence officer and the Lebanese priest
set off in tandem up the steep slopes of Kesrouan. The priest,
though bulky as ever, was surprisingly agile. He seemed to
enjoy clambering up the trail at high speed and then pausing
to wait for the American to catch up. They climbed for nearly
an hour. Father Maroun led Rogers across a mountain stream,
along a narrow ledge, through a dense stand of pine trees, and
then into a clearing that was completely hidden from below. It
was a high meadow, covered with the softest, greenest grass.
Below was the university, the seacoast, and the blue Mediterranean.

Father Maroun stopped and flipped open his walking stick.
Rogers sat down on the grass and lit a Marlboro. The priest,
to Rogers's surprise, took a pack of Camels from his leather
shorts.

"I didn't know you smoked, Father," said Rogers.

"All Lebanese smoke," said the priest.

They sat there, the priest on his walking stick and Rogers
on his haunches, smoking their cigarettes and gazing at the
matchless beauty of the Lebanese mountains in midsummer.

"This is magnificent," said Rogers.

The priest looked at him and nodded solemnly.

"You must remember this," Father Maroun said, "when
you are wondering to yourself someday: What are those crazy
Lebanese fighting about?"

Rogers nodded. He wondered whether he was in for another recitation of the torment and triumph of the Maronite
Church.

"When you called me, Father, you said that you had something you wanted to discuss."

"Oh yes," said the priest. "I do indeed. Most definitely."

He waited for the priest to begin. When he didn't, he prodded him.

"Well, what was it?"

"What?"

"What you wanted to ask me."

"Ah yes, of course," said the priest. "What I wanted to ask you was, what do you think about the leadership of the Palestinian guerrilla group, Al-Fatah?"

That's an odd question for a Maronite priest to be asking me, thought Rogers.

"That depends on who you are talking about," he replied. "Some of the Fatah men strike me as dishonest braggarts. Others strike me as sincere. Some are intelligent and others are fools. From what I can gather, most of them are corrupt."

"Yes, to be sure," said Father Maroun. The answer apparently was not exactly what he had wanted. The priest had taken off his Tyrolean hat, and Rogers could see that his brow was covered with sweat.

The Lebanese priest lit another cigarette, swallowed hard, and continued.

"What do you think of Jamal Ramlawi?"

Rogers didn't miss a beat. There wasn't a twitch of the nostrils or a movement of the eyes out of the ordinary.

"My impression is that Ramlawi is bright and capable, but I don't know much about him," he answered evenly. "What's your impression?"

"Me?" asked the priest. "Oh my goodness. I don't really know. I don't know too much about him myself."

"Then why do you ask?" queried Rogers.

The priest was looking more and more uncomfortable. Looking at Father Maroun, sweating in his leather pants and kneesocks, Rogers had an odd thought: Is it possible that the padre is wearing a wire?

"I was just wondering," said the priest, "whether this man Ramlawi is perhaps someone we could, I mean, possibly in the future, quietly of course, with complete discretion on our side, perhaps . . ."

"What?" asked Rogers.

"Talk to," said the priest. "About the situation in Lebanon."

"I have no idea," said Rogers. "Why don't you ask him yourself?"

"That is so awkward. You know how Lebanon is. We cannot talk with other Lebanese, let alone with Palestinians. We need a mediator. An interlocutor."

"Sorry, Father, but we can't help on that one. We only know one side in the transaction. Which is you."

"I see," said Father Maroun.

"Perhaps," said Rogers, feeling slightly peeved and malicious, "your Israeli friends can help."

The priest looked for a moment as if he might fall off his walking stick.

"I beg your pardon?"

"Just a thought," said Rogers. "If you ever meet any Israelis, you might pose the question to them. I gather they have awfully good contacts with some of the Palestinians."

"They *do?*" asked Father Maroun, his eyes widening.

"I believe so," said Rogers. "Perhaps they can help you."

"Jesus, Mary, and Joseph!" The priest shook his head. He had the look of a man who has heard, for the first time, a suggestion that his sweetheart may be two-timing him. He looked pale. His expression had gone from the nervousness of a few minutes ago to one of shock.

Rogers felt sorry for him. But not sorry enough to do anything about it.

"Perhaps we should be heading back," he suggested.

"Yes," said the priest with relief. "Let us go back at once."

They walked down the rocky slope in silence. Rogers turned the strange conversation over in his mind. If the Israelis had sent Father Maroun on this fishing expedition, it was an unusually sloppy operation. Perhaps it was simply their way of putting the agency on notice, firing a warning shot at the Beirut station. Or perhaps, thought Rogers, it was not an Israeli gambit at all. Perhaps Father Maroun was completely genuine. He was a religious man, who cared deeply about his country. Perhaps he truly wanted to establish a quiet channel of contact between the Maronite Church and the fedayeen. If so, Jamal Ramlawi was an obvious candidate. Sophisticated, close to the Old Man. Perhaps Father Maroun's nervousness was simply the discomfort that any outsider would feel wandering into the secret world without knowing the rules. Perhaps his naivete was the clearest sign that his intentions were pure.

Either way, Rogers concluded, it was probably best to assume that the Israelis would hear about the conversation. He would let Hoffman, who was edgy about anything involving liaison with Mossad, file the cable back to Langley about the unlikely overture from the Maronite cleric.

When Rogers returned to the office that day, he had another odd communication. There was a note waiting for him from Solange Jezzine. It was written on cream-colored stationery, so firm and heavy that it seemed to have been starched, and it smelled faintly of perfume. A red ribbon was tied in a bow at the top of the notepaper, like a red garter atop a pair of silk stockings.

The note itself was as provocative as the package. Solange invited Rogers to come pay a visit, alone.

Rogers sighed and shook his head. What an extraordinary woman! He penned a brief note saying no, thank you. I'm awfully busy just now. The worst thing about work, Rogers wrote, was that it left too little time for play. Perhaps another time. When he walked out of his office that afternoon, Rogers thought he saw his secretary, who had brought the Jezzine letter up from the front desk, smiling at him as if they shared a secret.

The Fatah campaign of terror began in Cairo on November 28, 1971, when a team of four Palestinians murdered the Jordanian prime minister. They shot him in broad daylight, in front of a crowd of other dignitaries, as he was entering the lobby of the Cairo Sheraton. Witnesses said that one of the gunmen kneeled over the body of the dying Jordanian official and licked his blood. The assassins were immediately captured by Egyptian police. They said they were members of a previously unknown organization called Black September, which took its name from the expulsion of the PLO from Jordan in September 1970.

The next target was the Jordanian Ambassador to London. As the Jordanian official neared his office one day in December, a gunman standing on a traffic island shot at his Daimler limousine with a submachine gun. The ambassador survived. The gunman, an Algerian, escaped. The Jordanians attributed the operation to the same network that had murdered their prime minister. Fatah spokesmen denied responsibility and blamed Black September. Investigators rushed to gather evidence about this new terrorist faction, but they came up with nothing but rumors. The group was frighteningly discreet. It was like an animal that left no tracks.

A few months later, the bombs began to explode in Beirut. They weren't large devices; often they were little more than sticks of dynamite, meant to confuse and demoralize the Lebanese. Beirutis blamed their favorite villain—Palestinian, Syrian, or Israeli—depending on their political perspective. The painful truth was that nobody really knew who was responsible. It was the year of the bombs.

Black September soon struck again in Europe. This time they attacked targets linked to Israel. Israeli-owned oil facilities in Rotterdam and Hamburg. An electronics plant in West Germany that did extensive business with Israel. They also executed five suspected members of the Jordanian Moukhabarat. The terrorists were becoming heroes in the Arab world, spawning a series of copycat operations. There was jealousy within Fatah, as various lieutenants tried to develop their own terrorist networks.

The Israelis soon escalated their attacks against Fatah. After a fedayeen raid inside Israel, the Israeli Army invaded South Lebanon. The Israelis stayed for four days. Officials in Jerusalem claimed they had struck a decisive blow at the guerrillas. The Israeli operation exacerbated the Lebanese political crisis, as poor refugees from South Lebanon—mostly Shiite Moslems—streamed into the slums outside Beirut. The Lebanese pleaded for decisive action, which their corrupt and paralyzed government couldn't provide.

Black September continued its campaign of revenge. The group attacked a Jordanian airlines office in Rome, a Jordanian airplane in Cairo, the Jordanian Embassy in Berne, the Jordanian Embassy in Cairo. The group also staged a spectacular but ultimately disastrous operation against Israel. Members of Black September hijacked a Sabena Airlines flight to Tel Aviv and held the passengers hostage at Lod Airport. Israeli commandos, disguised as mechanics, stormed the plane and killed two of the four hijackers.

The Israelis attacked Lebanon again, this time with air strikes against Hasbayah, Marjayoun, and other towns and villages in South Lebanon that had become guerrilla bases.

The Israeli raids produced heavy casualties among Lebanese civilians. The Lebanese government briefly considered buying antiaircraft missiles from France to protect its territory. The deal collapsed when Lebanese fixers began demanding huge payoffs for certain interested Lebanese government officials.

The new wave of Palestinian terror became the favorite spectator sport of the Western world. The Fatah leaders, who had nearly disappeared from public view, suddenly found journalists arriving by the score from Europe and America, clamoring for interviews. The Palestinians had become, once again, figures of horror and fascination. The Old Man appeared on magazine covers in his dark glasses and stubbly beard. While his acolytes in the West urged him to shave and dress respectably, the Old Man stuck to his guerrilla garb. He understood that the whole point of the exercise was to look like an outlaw, a blackguard, a despicable and terrifying symbol of violence. Jamal understood it, too. As he made his rounds in Europe and read the extravagant accounts of Black September's terrorist exploits that were appearing in the newspapers, he could only laugh. Abu Nasir had been right. The ability to create fear is a powerful weapon.

33

Rome; April 1972

Omar Mumtazz was arrested on April 7 at Rome's Fiumicino Airport. A plainclothes customs official noticed him nervously chain-smoking while waiting for his baggage on a flight arriving from Beirut.

When the nervous-looking Arab grabbed his luggage and headed toward the green "Nothing to Declare" exit, the customs officer stopped him and pointed him toward one of the uniformed officers in the red line. Omar Mumtazz still might have made it if he had kept cool. But when the Italian customs official asked to see his passport, Mumtazz slipped a hundred-dollar bill inside the document. This is a Mediterranean country, he told himself. This is how we do business in the Mediterranean.

The customs official opened the passport and watched the green bill float gently to the floor. He gave a thin smile and called to his captain. A few moments later Mumtazz was taken by three armed men to a cramped office, where he watched with mounting apprehension as a customs official cut through the false bottom of his suitcase. Out of the opening tumbled four fat packets of heroin.

Mumtazz made a terrible row. Though he had only an ordinary Libyan passport, he claimed that he was an intelligence officer who had done work for the Italians. He had powerful friends! He demanded to see someone—immediately!—from the Servizio Informazione Difesa.

The Carabinieri thought he was just another two-bit Arab

hoodlum in a fancy suit. But he made such a racket, even after he was punched several times in the stomach, that a Carabinieri officer finally placed a telephone call. An hour later a bedraggled major from the SID arrived and the Libyan began to lay out his story.

"I know something that is very important," he said. The major dully nodded his head.

"I know someone who is planning the worst crimes! The very worst! A Palestinian!"

"Dica. Dica," said the bored major.

"I will tell the information to a senior officer. To him only!"

One of the Carabinieri kicked the Libyan in the shins. He screamed and looked around the room desperately.

"The president!" he shouted. "They are planning to kill the President of the United States."

The SID major took Mumtazz to a basement cell at the Ministry of Defense on Via Venti Settembre. There, the Libyan told his story to a captain who listened intently and took careful notes.

The Libyan claimed he had information about a new Palestinian terrorist organization that was planning a string of spectacular operations culminating in the assassination of the American president. He said he had met the group's chief of operations—a man who called himself Nabil—in Rome a few months earlier. He had provided Nabil with women, introducing him to several German girls he knew in Rome, and later with guns and explosives. As he narrated the tale, Mumtazz watched the Italian captain to gauge his interest and see if he was taking notes.

Mumtazz gave a brief physical description of Nabil. He was tall and strikingly handsome, with thick black hair and a clean-shaven face. He spoke several languages, including English and some Italian. He was aloof, secretive about his work, and highly intelligent. He liked to drink and smoke and seemed to have an inexhaustible appetite for European women.

When Mumtazz got to the Palestinian's sex habits, he noticed that the Italian officer was looking at him dubiously.

"Every word is true!" protested the Libyan. "If you don't

believe me, ask one of your own men in the Italian Embassy in Tripoli. Giuseppe Rosso! He knows me! He will vouch for me!"

The captain wrote down the name. But as he did so, he arched his eyebrows high on his forehead.

"I have tapes!" said the Libyan, leaning forward as if sharing a great secret.

"Tapes?" asked the Italian captain.

"Yes!" said the Libyan triumphantly. "Tapes! Of Nabil talking to me on the telephone about his plans. In code!"

The SID man put aside his notebook and picked up the telephone to call a colonel.

"Immunity! I give you nothing without immunity!" shouted the Libyan as the captain dialed the number.

"No immunity, no tapes!"

Mumtazz told his story again, for the third time that day, to the SID colonel. The more senior his interrogator, the more details he provided. The colonel listened and then telephoned another colonel in a different department of the intelligence service. There were consultations. Mumtazz was asked to remain overnight and provided with hot food and a soft bed.

The next morning, when files had been checked and cables received from the Italian Embassy in Tripoli, the SID men met again for further consultations. Yes, said one of the colonels, the service did in fact have a tenuous relationship with a Libyan named Omar Mumtazz. He was from one of the wealthy old Libyan families that had collaborated with the Italians during the colonial period and prospered later under King Idriss. According to the SID man in Tripoli, Omar Mumtazz was a young dilettante, half-ideologue, half-pimp. He travelled in unusual Arab circles—the criminal underworld and the radical political fringe—and had provided occasional tidbits of information about Libyans, Syrians, Palestinians.

The Italian officials agreed that Mumtazz should be asked to confirm his story. If he could indeed furnish tape recordings of Nabil, then the SID would recommend to the Italian Ministry of Interior that the drug-smuggling charges against him be dropped.

The offer was conveyed orally to the Libyan. Feeling cocky, Omar Mumtazz asked for it in writing. Whereupon one of the SID colonels slapped him twice on the face and walked out of the room.

Mumtazz dropped his request. The tapes were in a safe deposit box at a branch of the Banca Commerciale Italiana, he said. He was taken there by two soldiers dressed in plainclothes. To their surprise, the Libyan emerged from the bank vault after several minutes smiling and clutching a reel of tape. The colonels back at headquarters were even more surprised when they played the tape and heard on it the voice of an Arab man, talking in English in what sounded like a private code. He said he needed four suits and ten pairs of shoes and would pick them up at eight o'clock.

Mumtazz explained that in the code he had worked out with Nabil, the message meant that the Palestinian wanted four pistols with silencers and 100 kilos of plastic explosive, and would pick up the shipment at four the following day.

There were several other items on the tape. One was a conversation between Mumtazz and the Arab man about arrangements for a party; the other sounded like a man and woman making love. The panting and moaning went on for more than twenty minutes, and when the woman began praising the man's sexual prowess in fluent Italian, one of the colonels turned off the tape.

Eventually they referred the case to General Armani. It seemed to be a potentially delicate matter. Something the Americans should know. Or perhaps, something the Americans shouldn't know. The colonels weren't sure. The general would know. He was everything an Italian general should be: tall and trim, silver-gray hair, suave and cunning. Even when he made mistakes, they seemed to younger colleagues to be the *right* mistakes. The general listened to the tape and then talked to Mumtazz.

"What evidence do you have about the plot to kill the American president?" demanded General Armani. "That is the most important thing you have told us, but there is nothing on the tape about assassination. I think you must be a liar."

"Of course there is nothing on the tape!" said the Libyan. "Would the Palestinian be so stupid as to talk about such a matter on the telephone?"

They had discussed the plan to kill the president during a meeting in a café in Rome, Mumtazz explained. At the meeting, Nabil had asked him to obtain a sharpshooter's rifle for the job. The plan was to shoot the American president during one of his foreign trips. The Palestinian didn't say when or where.

General Armani nodded wearily, with a look that said: I believe nothing. In fact, he was unsure about the assassination plot. It was plausible. But then, it was also implausible. The general was certain of only one thing: he had something that would be of profound interest to the American Embassy. The Americans were obsessed about assassination plots. The one sure way to get their attention was to provide intelligence reports that someone was planning to take a potshot at the president. General Armani smiled.

"Basta!" said the general to Mumtazz. Enough.

"Excellency, please," whined the Libyan. But the general was gone and the guards were taking Omar Mumtazz back to his cell.

General Armani made two copies of the tape. He took one with him to the American Embassy on the Via Veneto. He gave it to the American military attaché along with transcripts of the interviews with Mumtazz that detailed the assassination plot. The attaché said he was profoundly grateful to General Armani for his help and was certain that his fine work would be appreciated in the highest councils of NATO.

Spare me, thought the general.

The military attaché was the senior representative in Italy of the Defense Intelligence Agency. He sent a flash cable to the DIA operations center and forwarded the tape itself by overnight pouch. His cable included the stunning allegation— "a Palestinian plot to assassinate the president"—that started bells ringing and lights flashing all over Washington. There was much commotion within the national security bureaucracy, rousing the Secret Service, the FBI, the NSC—and, not least, the DIA's crosstown rival, the Central Intelligence Agency.

General Armani put the second copy of the tape in his briefcase. He called his wife Anna and told her that he would be home late for dinner. When he left the office, he walked briskly down the Via Venti Settembre to Via Delle Quatro Fontane, where he ducked into a café and made a quick telephone call.

The general reached his Israeli contact at home. They met an hour later in a quiet café off the Via del Corso.

"We ran across something of interest this week," said the general.

"And what is that, my friend?" said the Israeli. He was smiling and squinting at the general.

"We grabbed a cheap Arab smuggler at the airport. To save himself, the man told us an interesting tale. It involves a Palestinian who seems to be acquiring a small arsenal here in Europe."

"Who told you these things?" asked the Israeli as if he had not quite heard the name.

"I cannot tell you who. It doesn't matter, anyway. He is just a cheap hoodlum. I have something better for you."

"And what is that, my friend?" asked the Israeli, still smiling and squinting.

"The Palestinian. On tape," said General Armani. He nodded to the newspaper he had placed on the table when he entered the café. Inside it was a cassette tape of the Palestinian.

The Israeli nodded. Otherwise, his expression didn't change. Still the squint. It was the very ordinariness of Israeli intelligence officers that made them trustworthy, the Italian general had concluded long ago. Their bad teeth, bald heads, squinting eyes, poor posture. They were too ordinary to play the self-deceiving games that led most intelligence services to disaster.

General Armani explained the meaning of the code used by the Palestinian. The suits and shoes, and how they really referred to pistols and plastic explosive. The only thing he left out, other than Mumtazz's name, was the plot to kill the

American president. Let the Italians get sole credit for that one.

General Armani left the tape in the folded newspaper when he got up from the table. The Israeli sent the cassette that night to Tel Aviv, where it was added to a growing Mossad file on the activities of Fatah's intelligence service.

34

Washington/Beirut; May 1972

The CIA attacked the problem systematically. They compiled
a list of known Palestinian operatives who might fit the profile
of "Nabil"; next they prepared an audio analysis of the tape
recording, so that the voice could be matched with others on
file as neatly as if it were a fingerprint. Then, with help from
the NSA, they compared the voice of Nabil to tape recordings
of various Palestinian suspects.

In less than a week, it was obvious to agency officials that
the CIA had an embarrassing problem on its hands. The voice
matched identically with that of someone who was well
known to the agency. A Palestinian whose conversations had
been recorded at various CIA safehouses for more than two
years, and who had nearly been recruited by the agency a year
earlier. The files showed that the Palestinian had even been
assigned a cryptonym: PECOCK.

Edward Stone interrupted a spring yachting weekend to
deal with the "Nabil" crisis. The situation was a nightmare, as
far as Stone was concerned. He arrived at his office on a
Sunday dressed in white flannel trousers, well-worn Top-
siders, and a frayed sweater. The Middle East Division chief
pulled the files, read and reread them, and turned the possibilities over in his mind. Was the Palestinian seeking revenge
because of the humiliating incident with Marsh? Was Fatah
striking back at the United States because of American com-
plicity in the destruction of the fedayeen in Jordan? Were the

commandos simply lashing out blindly at the ultimate symbol of American power? The questions went on and on. A threat to assassinate the president was a serious problem in itself. But when the assassin was a former CIA asset—a man who had spurned a recruitment effort—then it was positively a disaster.

Stone saw the Director first thing Monday morning. The Director was in his private dining room, eating his breakfast, when Stone arrived. He was picking the soft doughy bread out of the middle of a hard roll. That was one of the Director's eccentricities, the taste for soft bread from inside hard rolls. Like many well-bred men, he had invented his own version of table manners.

Stone summarized the intelligence reports. The man on the tape was unquestionably Jamal Ramlawi. There was no reason to doubt the Libyan's statement that he had provided weapons and explosives to the Palestinian. It was a case that contained the most worrying possibilities, Stone said.

"What in the hell is going on?" grumbled the Director. "This fellow is our man in Fatah, isn't he?"

"Yes and no," said Stone. "We tried to recruit him but failed."

"So he has a motive."

"It would appear so."

"Oh shit," said the Director. He stood up from the table and walked to the window. Stone noticed that the legs of his gray pinstripe trousers were covered with tiny flakes of bread crust.

"What connection does this business have with Black September?" asked the Director.

"I don't know," said Stone. "Perhaps none."

"Well, find out. Because if we're walking into a terrorist war between Black September and the United States of America, I would like to know about it. To be more precise, I would like to avoid it. Understood?"

"Yes, Director."

"You must solve this problem. Immediately. We will not have Palestinians out there shooting at the president. Or at any other American, for that matter. This is an election year. We don't need terrorists killing American citizens anywhere. And certainly not this year. Right?"

"Yes, sir."

"Solve it!" repeated the Director.

Stone nodded.

"There is the question of the Italians and the other liaison services. What should they be told?"

"Don't tell anybody anything," answered the Director emphatically. He added that he didn't, for the moment, plan to share information about the identity of Nabil with the White House, let alone foreign governments.

The Director sent Stone packing for Beirut that same Monday. A military jet was placed at his disposal.

During the long plane ride to Beirut, Stone struggled to think through a plan of action that would put out this fire, and perhaps prevent the next one from igniting, as well.

Stone was exhausted when he arrived in Beirut. He had arranged a brief stopover in Europe, for several hours, but not long enough to sleep. When he landed in Lebanon, he went immediately into a meeting with Hoffman and Rogers.

The meeting was held in the bubble, the soundproof room deep inside the embassy that the CIA used for its most sensitive meetings. It was all white and lined with so much acoustic-damping material that words seemed to die in the air as soon as they were spoken.

Stone outlined the intelligence from Rome and the subsequent process of investigation that had convinced the CIA—beyond any doubt—that the Nabil who was allegedly plotting to kill the President of the United States was the same person as PECOCK, whose case was already well known to the Beirut station.

"What do you gentlemen think?" asked Stone, when he had finished with his briefing.

"I think that somebody's dicking us around," said Hoffman gruffly.

"And who might that be, Frank?"

"I'm not sure who yet, but somebody is. I mean, why would a Palestinian commando whose main interest in life is fucking white girls suddenly decide to kill the President of the United States? It doesn't make sense. Golda Meir, maybe. The King of Jordan, maybe. But not the President of the

United States, for Christ's sake. Even Palestinians aren't that dumb."

Stone looked away from Hoffman. His face was impassive.

"Tom?" asked Stone, nodding toward Rogers.

"I don't know," said Rogers. "PECOCK has a motive for going after us. He certainly felt betrayed after the Rome meeting. But not to the point that he would do something stupid. I agree with Frank. The assassination plot sounds a little farfetched."

"That makes it unanimous," said Stone.

"I have another thought," said Rogers. He was thinking, at that moment, about a message he had received several months ago from Fuad, noting the changed personality of Jamal Ramlawi.

"Please," said Stone. He was rubbing his eyeballs.

"It's simple, really. If we can believe what 'Nabil' said on the tape about obtaining guns and explosives, then it follows that he is building a network in Europe. Otherwise, he would just buy the stuff here in Beirut, which would be much easier. He's buying it in Europe because he intends to use it in Europe. For terrorist attacks against Fatah's enemies."

"Which means?"

"Which means that perhaps we have blundered into the fringes of Black September. And that our Palestinian friend is one of its leaders."

"That thought has unfortunately also occurred to the Director," said Stone. "It makes this case rather awkward."

"Awkward, my ass," said Hoffman. "It makes this case fucked up. Let's not mince words. What happened in this case was that a certain Mr. John Marsh made an inept attempt to buy a Palestinian, who got pissed off and became a major league terrorist, and is now turning his guns on us. That sounds like a fuck-up to me."

"It isn't helpful to personalize this, Frank," said Stone.

"Isn't it?" said Hoffman. "Because it seems to me that if the geniuses back at headquarters had listened to Rogers a year ago and not put the screws on this Palestinian kid, maybe we wouldn't be in this mess."

Stone was rubbing his eyeballs again.

"Do you know what this reminds me of, Frank?"

Hoffman grunted a no.

"It reminds me of the old days in Germany after the war, when we were running our crew of Abwehr agents. Do you recall, for example, the unfortunate Czech agent from Prague? The one I was so enthusiastic about, whom you correctly pegged as a stinker."

"I remember."

"Tom, did I ever tell you the story?"

"Yes, sir," said Rogers, remembering Stone's account that night at the Athenian Club and the moral: If your intuition tells you an agent is unreliable, dump him.

"Doesn't this case remind you a bit of the man from Prague?" asked Stone again.

"Slightly," said Hoffman. "But it reminds me even more of the agent from Budapest. Willy, I think his name was. Do you remember Willy?"

"Who's Willy?" interjected Rogers.

"Ask Mr. Stone to tell you about Willy some time," said Hoffman.

Stone looked even more tired than before.

"Poor dumb Willy," continued Hoffman. "He learned one of the little secrets of the spy business, which is that sometimes we burn our agents. The people who have trusted us with their lives. We may not like it, but we do it. Isn't that right, Mr. Stone?"

"I'm going to get some sleep," said Stone, rising from his chair abruptly. The three men exited the surveillance-proof conference room in silence.

When the meeting broke, Rogers sent an urgent message to Fuad. He ignored the usual security rules and delivered the message orally, by telephone. The message was simple: Find our old Palestinian friend, no matter where he is. Tell him we need to meet him as soon as possible, within forty-eight hours at the very latest. Warn him that if he refuses the meeting, he faces the most serious consequences. Rogers spoke loudly throughout the conversation and by the time he finished, he was almost shouting. His tone left no doubt that this was a crisis.

* * *

The Americans were lucky. The Palestinian was in Beirut that week. He had arrived from Europe two days earlier and was leaving again the next Monday. Fuad found him in Fakhani, walking near the Arab University campus toward one of the Fatah offices. He hailed him like a long-lost brother and embraced him on the street. As he kissed the Palestinian on the cheek, Fuad whispered in his ear: "I must see you urgently."

Jamal said he was busy.

"It can't wait!" said the Lebanese. His voice was sharp and clipped. Fuad steered the Palestinian toward a large open area on the way to the new stadium, where they wouldn't be overheard.

"The Americans say they must see you within forty-eight hours on a matter of the highest importance," Fuad said. "They make threats about what will happen if you do not meet with them."

Jamal clucked his tongue. He muttered an Arabic expression that means: So what?

Fuad took Jamal by the elbow and tried to talk to him as a friend.

"This is serious," he said. "Do you remember the first American that you met? The one who called himself Reilly? I have never heard him so upset. He is always the calm one. You must come to the meeting. The Americans don't make threats unless they are serious."

"I will think about it," said Jamal.

"No," pressed Fuad. "They need an answer now."

"Impossible. I need to talk to someone."

"I will wait here in Fakhani for the answer," said Fuad.

"Go back to Hamra."

"I will wait here."

The Palestinian gave up. He left Fuad standing near a lamppost on the road outside the stadium.

If the decision had been left to Jamal, he would not have attended the meeting with the Americans. Rome had soured him on dealing with the United States. But the decision, in the end, wasn't his to make. It was the Old Man's. Jamal sent a message to the Old Man's personal secretary requesting a quick audience. It was granted late that afternoon. The Fatah leader refused his young protégé nothing.

Jamal explained that the Americans had made an urgent request. He quoted Fuad. A matter of the highest importance. A threat of retaliation.

The Old Man smiled as he listened to Jamal. An odd smile of satisfaction.

"I don't want to meet with them," said Jamal. "The Americans are not trustworthy. It is too sensitive a moment. My work is too delicate right now, too dangerous."

The Old Man was still smiling.

Jamal explained his reluctance with various circumlocutions. He was vulnerable. He knew sensitive information. There were operations that could be compromised. He didn't say what he really meant: that he was one of a tiny handful of people who knew the secret of Black September; that the Americans might try to force him to divulge the secret. But he said none of that. The rules of the game required that no one even mention the words "Black September" in the presence of the Old Man. Jamal noticed, as he talked, that the Old Man wasn't really listening. His eyes were wide with what appeared to be—how could it be?—a look of hope.

"I think we have won," said the Old Man, when Jamal had finally finished.

"What, Father?" asked Jamal.

"We have won! The Americans are frightened. They have come to talk peace. That is why they want to see you. They understand that they need our help. You must see them."

"I think you are wrong, Father," said Jamal.

"I am right!" said the Old Man, beaming with the optimism that coursed through his veins like water through a rushing river. "We have won. Thanks be to Allah! You will see the Americans. That is an order."

Jamal rejoined Fuad that evening. Yes, he would see the Americans. Fuad was overjoyed. He outlined the details. They would all meet in Fuad's apartment in Ras Beirut the next afternoon. That was as close as they could come to neutral ground. Fuad pledged on his honor as an Arab and a Moslem that no harm would come to Jamal.

"If the Americans try any tricks, I will shoot them myself," said Fuad. He patted a bulging object under his jacket. It was the first time Jamal had ever seen Fuad carrying a gun.

Fuad's apartment was on a side street off Hamra. The street teemed with life. Sidewalk vendors noisily advertised lottery tickets and bootlegged cassette tapes. The neighborhood butcher hacked away at a carcass of beef hanging in his doorway. And a Turkish restaurant filled the air with smoke and the smell of charcoal and spices.

Stone, Hoffman, and Rogers made their way through this commotion and were waiting in Fuad's apartment when Jamal arrived. The Palestinian was dressed in his usual defiant outfit: leather jacket, silk shirt open at the neck, and black leather boots.

Rogers met Jamal at the door.

"No guns," said Rogers.

Jamal removed an automatic pistol from a shoulder holster.

"Sorry, but I'll also have to frisk you." He did so quickly and found nothing. He then escorted Jamal into the living room.

Rogers made the introductions, calling Stone "Mr. Green" and Hoffman "Mr. Brown." Jamal regarded the three Americans warily. None of them had the self-importance of the man he had met in Rome. "Mr. Green" looked like an Englishman. As for "Mr. Brown," he was overweight, his shirt was sticking out of his trousers, and he had a soup stain on his tie.

Stone took charge of the meeting. He had a military man's way of asserting command naturally and spontaneously, through simple changes in his voice and posture.

"I have come urgently from Washington because of a matter of the highest importance to the United States government," Stone began.

Jamal nodded. He pushed his hair back off his forehead.

"I would like you to listen to something," said the American, turning to a large reel-to-reel tape recorder on the table next to him. Jamal nodded again.

Stone flipped the switch on the tape recorder. The division chief watched Jamal's face carefully as the recorder played the conversation between him and Omar Mumtazz. Throughout the conversation, even during the exchange about suits and shoes, Jamal's face was impassive.

"We have absolutely no doubt that this is your voice," said Stone, after turning off the machine. "I won't trouble you with an explanation of the technical methods of analysis that allow us to be so confident that it is you. We also understand the meaning of the coded message. It is a request by you for guns and explosives."

Jamal blinked. He took out a Marlboro cigarette. Stone continued.

"There is only one thing that concerns me. We have been told that you are planning to kill the President of the United States. If this is true, I must warn that you have embarked on a most dangerous course. One that will have ruinous consequences for you and your organization."

Stone bowed his head gently, like a priest who has just given a condemned man the last rites.

"Is there anything you would like to say?" asked Stone.

"Yes," said Jamal, his eyes flashing with anger. "The Libyan is a liar. If you believe him you are a fool."

"The Libyan?" asked Stone blankly.

"Yes, of course, the Libyan! The Libyan named Omar Mumtazz, who smuggles guns and drugs. The Libyan who knows me as Nabil. The Libyan who has taped my phone calls. The Libyan who has made up a tale about me killing the president."

"Ah yes," said Stone.

Jamal relaxed slightly.

"Without of course confirming that this fellow—Omar, did you say?—was the source of our information, let me ask you a question. Why would someone invent a tale like that about an assassination plot?"

"To make himself important," answered Jamal. "To give himself something to bargain with. I don't know why. You tell me. Why do people sell false information to intelligence services? It happens every day."

"Well, you're quite right there," said Stone. "Yes indeed. People do peddle false information. Quite right."

"Of course they do," said Jamal.

"But let me ask you another question. Why would you want to purchase this little arsenal of equipment? I believe the list included four pistols with silencers, one hundred kilos of high-velocity explosives. Why would you want to acquire these items?"

"That isn't any concern of the United States!" said Jamal.

Hoffman, who had been listening in silence, leaned forward in his chair toward the Palestinian.

"Bullshit," he said. "It's our business now."

Stone smiled genially at Hoffman and then turned back to Jamal.

"Perhaps you would like to tell us why this isn't any concern of the United States."

"Fatah is a military organization," answered Jamal. "We are in a state of war with Israel. That is not a secret. We say it in every statement, every speech, with every breath we take. Also, it is not a secret that we are engaged in a struggle with other Arab regimes that want to destroy the Palestinian Revolution. Every military organization needs weapons. I won't discuss the issue further. It is not your concern."

"Young man!" said Stone sharply. "You needn't lecture me. I am not entirely unfamiliar with the logistical requirements of military combat. But I fail to see what that has to do with a cache of weapons and explosives in Rome, and a plot to kill the President of the United States."

"There is no plot to kill the President of the United States," said Jamal again.

"Yes, of course." Stone smiled solicitously. He had the look of a bridge player, watching the cards fall just as they should, each one dropping to the table despite the best efforts of the other side to resist.

"Mr. Ramlawi," said Stone, using Jamal's real name for the first time. "There are many questions that I could ask you. I could ask you about the organization called Black September and your own connection to it. I could ask you about the role that Fatah intelligence has had in establishing this organization. I could ask you where you were several months ago when an oil depot blew up in Rotterdam. Or where you were when an electronics plant in Hamburg was attacked. And I am quite sure that I would, in time, obtain the answers to such questions."

Jamal was looking at the door, at the windows, obviously wondering whether he could escape.

"Don't even think about it, asshole," said Hoffman. "One move from that chair and you're a dead man."

The Palestinian settled back uneasily in his chair.

"The point I wanted to make," continued Stone, "is that I could ask you those—shall we say, awkward—questions. But I will not, for the moment."

"Good," said Jamal. "It's none of your business."

"Let us assume, for the moment, that you are right. The military operations of Fatah are no business of the United States. None whatsoever. Let us go further and assume, for the moment, that the organization that calls itself Black September is none of our business, either. Now, you are a clever young man. Perhaps you can tell me what would allow me to make such assumptions, that Fatah and Black September are of no concern to the United States?"

"I don't know," said Jamal.

"The answer is quite obvious, really. What would allow us to make such assumptions is the certain knowledge that the United States and its citizens are in no way threatened by Fatah and Black September. Do you follow me?"

Jamal cocked his head and looked at Stone curiously.

"I know nothing of Black September," said Jamal.

"Of course not," said Stone.

"But I can tell you," said Jamal, "that Americans are not targets of Fatah."

"You don't say," said Stone. "Ah, how I wish I could simply take your word. But the problem, you see, is that there is no bond of trust between us. We have no reason whatsoever to believe your assurances. None. Now, how can we remedy that? I see only one way, and that is for you to make a gesture to demonstrate that you are telling me the truth. A gesture of good faith. Shall I proceed?"

"Yes," said Jamal.

"The question is, what sort of a gesture would be appropriate? Do you have any ideas?"

"No."

"Then I will make a suggestion. I would like you to order your men in Rome to dispose of the equipment obtained from the Libyan—the guns and explosives—in a place where we can monitor the disposal and confirm that it has taken place. Your people needn't know why you are taking this action. You can tell them that the equipment is defective, if you like."

Jamal studied the American.

"What difference would it make if we did throw away the guns and explosives?" he asked. "We could always get more weapons from some other source."

"Yes, of course," said Stone. "Quite right. As I say, this is simply a gesture of good faith."

"What if I refuse?"

"Then we will go and get the weapons ourselves."

"Is that your proposal? That we turn over the guns and explosives in Italy?"

"Well, no," said Stone. "Not entirely. There is one other thing I have in mind. It's the most important part, really. It would be a sort of agreement between us as gentlemen, summarizing the outcome of our conversation today."

"What do you mean?" asked the Palestinian.

"It is what we in America would call an 'understanding.'"

Jamal leaned forward, wanting to be sure that he heard every word.

"I would like your assurance that neither you nor your organization will conduct terrorist attacks against American citizens or facilities. Not today, not tomorrow, not next week, not next year. As you can see from my presence here in Beirut, we take such matters very seriously."

Jamal nodded. The Old Man was right, he thought to himself. They are scared.

"In return," continued Stone, "I give you my assurance that my organization will regard your conflict with Israel as a state of war in which the United States is not a combatant. We will not interfere with your operations, so long as they don't jeopardize American property, citizens, or interest. We will not interfere with the Israelis, either. We will leave them free to do whatever they can to destroy you. We may even applaud some of their actions. But we will not become involved directly. It is not our fight."

Stone paused and smiled. "Can we reach such an understanding?"

"I cannot give you an answer," said Jamal. "These are very important questions. I am not the one to decide them."

"Of course not," said Stone. "I quite understand. But perhaps you can relay our message to the appropriate person."

"Perhaps I can do that," said Jamal. His head was spinning. He was remembering what the Old Man had said more than two years ago, when he had first authorized contact with the Americans. We need a door to the West. Now that door seemed to be opening at last.

"What should I tell the one who makes decisions?" asked Jamal.

"Exactly what I have told you."

"That the Americans are proposing a non-aggression pact?"

"Nothing quite so grand as that," responded Stone. "We are simply saying that the United States is not a belligerent in the Arab-Israeli conflict. That is, and has traditionally been, the basic premise of our policy in the Middle East. We are asking you, in recognition of that fact, to avoid targeting Americans."

"When do you need an answer?" asked Jamal.

"Tonight," said Stone. "By midnight."

"What if that is not possible?"

"Then we have a very serious problem on our hands."

"I will do my best," said Jamal.

"Good," said the division chief. "We'll be here waiting for you."

Stone rose and shook the young Palestinian's hand. Rogers returned his automatic pistol and escorted him to the door.

They spent the late afternoon and early evening playing poker. Hoffman won $400. His luck was uncanny.

Hoffman, exhilarated by his winnings, offered to make dinner. He sent Fuad out to buy food and two six-packs of beer. When Fuad returned with the groceries, Hoffman made a makeshift apron out of a bath towel, entered the kitchen, and prepared a dinner of spaghetti with meat sauce, garlic bread, and ice cream with hot fudge sauce. The meal was excellent. The hot fudge sauce was especially good, made from melted squares of bittersweet chocolate. After dinner, Hoffman suggested more poker. There were no takers, so Hoffman played solitaire.

* * *

Jamal returned just before midnight. He was red-faced and out of breath. Rogers put him through the same drill as before, collecting his pistol and frisking him. The room smelled of garlic and chocolate.

Jamal sat down in a chair. He had tidied up his clothes since the earlier visit and was now wearing a business suit. It was almost as if he felt he were present at an historic occasion, like the signing of a treaty that ended a war.

"I have an answer," said Jamal.

"Very good," said Stone.

Jamal was still puffing slightly. He seemed to have trouble actually saying the words.

"So what is it?" demanded Hoffman. "What's the answer?"

"Yes," said Jamal. "The answer is yes. I bring you that word from the highest authority of Fatah."

"And what is it that Fatah is saying yes to?" asked Stone.

"Fatah will not attack American citizens or property, on the understanding that the United States will take no side in our conflict with Israel. And we will dispose of the weapons in Italy."

"One small point," said Stone. "It goes without saying that I cannot speak for Congress, or for our various politicians. I speak only for my agency."

"What is more powerful than the CIA?" asked Jamal.

"What indeed?" answered Stone. "Do we have an understanding, then?"

"Yes," said the Palestinian.

"Excellent!" Stone turned to Rogers.

"You work out the details with Tom here. I trust that the two of you can meet from time to time to compare notes on the matters we have discussed. That won't pose any problem for you, I hope."

"We have met before," said Jamal. "We can meet again."

Stone put his hand on Jamal's elbow and walked with him slowly to the door of the apartment.

"I am *so* pleased to have met you," said the American. He said it like a headmaster bidding farewell to a guest at a tea dance.

Rogers was still savoring the evening's events several hours later over drinks in a bar on Hamra Street. Hoffman had suggested the Black Cat, but Rogers had talked him out of it. Somehow, that didn't seem like the right place for Stone, so they went to the St. Georges instead.

Rogers was awed by Stone's performance and told him so. The division chief had manipulated the Palestinian as gently and precisely as if he had controlled him with invisible wires. He had led the Fatah man through a maze of options and decisions, convinced him that what served the agency's interests equally served his own, and allowed him, in effect, to recruit himself. And he had worked this miracle with a man suspected of planning to kill the President of the United States!

"There is one thing that I should tell you in all candor," said Stone, downing his second martini.

"What's that?" asked Rogers.

"I don't believe I mentioned to you earlier that on my way here from Washington, I stopped off in Rome for several hours. I had one of the boys from the Office of Security give this Libyan fellow—Mr. Mumtazz—a polygraph test."

"What happened?"

"Generally, he did fine. But on that absurd business about the assassination plot, he flunked."

Hoffman raised his glass in a toast.

"You did a swell job," said Hoffman. "No bullshit. It's a pleasure to watch a real pro at work. But I gotta tell you, my friends, that the fun in this case is just beginning."

The glasses clinked. There was an interlude of silence as they drank and reflected on the extraordinary events of the past few days. Rogers remembered something Hoffman had said the previous day.

"Tell me about Willy, the agent from Budapest," said Rogers.

"Naw, you don't want me to tell that old story now," said Hoffman. "Not when we're celebrating."

"Yes I do," said Rogers.

Hoffman looked at Stone. The division chief nodded yes. Tell him the story.

"Okay, but it doesn't have a very happy ending."

"Just tell me the damn story," said Rogers, who was slightly drunk.

"All right. We were running a string of agents in Eastern Europe after the war. A lot of them had worked for the Germans. They were tough little men. They hated the Russians and were eager to work for Uncle Sam. But they were also scared shitless that we would sell them out."

"Why?"

"Because they weren't stupid. You said you wanted to hear the story, so shut up."

"Sorry," said Rogers.

"Willy was the one I liked the best," continued Hoffman. "He was a Hungarian, about forty years old. His whole family had been killed in the war. Blown to smithereens. At first I thought he was trying to atone, or get revenge, or something. Later on it occurred to me that he was probably just trying to make some money. Who knows? Anyway, we were running him in Hungary and he was doing jim-dandy work for us. He had a friend in the Hungarian security service who let him photograph documents. It was a nice little operation."

"What went wrong?"

"One day the Brits approached us. They said they had evidence that our little man was a crook. Supposedly he was smuggling American cigarettes into Budapest to make a little extra dough. It was stupid of him and made him a security risk. So we were pissed. We called in our man for a crash meeting. We did it in an insecure way. Sent him a letter at his home address. Nobody gave a shit. We thought the guy had screwed us. In any event, this poor little fucker came to the meeting with me and Stone shaking like a leaf. He was a mess. He didn't have good answers to any of our questions.

"I still kind of liked him. Felt sorry for him. I don't know why. But the Brits said he was bad news. Mr. Stone agreed, and I agreed. Everybody agreed. So we told him sayonara."

"Did you ever corroborate what the Brits said?" asked Rogers.

"No," said Hoffman. "I told you. Nobody gave a shit."

"What happened to Willy?"

"He was dead within six months," said Hoffman. "Served him right, in a way."

"Why?" asked Rogers.

"Because he was a fool, to have trusted us."

Stone stopped by Rogers's office the next morning on his way to the airport. The older man looked fit and pink-cheeked. He was dressed in what, for him, were casual clothes: a bow tie, tweed jacket, gray trousers, and ancient but well-shined brown Oxfords. Stone closed the door behind him, looked for the couch, and when he realized there wasn't one, sat down in a chair beside the desk.

"You are couchless," observed Stone.

"Yes, sir," said Rogers.

"What rank are you these days?"

"I'm an R-6," said Rogers.

"And when will you receive your leather couch and cherry-wood credenza?"

"R-3."

"Ah well, that's something to look forward to, isn't it?" said Stone sardonically. "Sometimes I marvel at the pettiness of the United States government. Do they really imagine that people are motivated by the desire to obtain additional office furnishings?"

"Some people probably are," said Rogers.

"Would you like a couch?" queried Stone. "I'll get you one."

"I don't really care, to be honest."

"No, of course you don't."

Stone adjusted his bow tie so that the two ends were precisely even and then got down to business.

"I want to discuss details," said Stone.

"About handling the Palestinian?"

"Precisely," said Stone. "God is in the details."

Rogers nodded. Where is the Devil? he wondered.

"Now then," said Stone. "I think that you should meet with PECOCK every few months, you or one of your agents. Keep him on a long leash. Don't inquire too much about what he does. You're not his nursemaid."

"What do we do about the Israelis?" asked Rogers.

"Nothing."

"But won't they try to do something about Jamal?"

"I have no idea," said Stone. "I can't predict what anyone will do. Not the Israelis. Not us. Not our Palestinian friend."

"What is he, exactly?" asked Rogers.

"I beg your pardon?"

"I mean, is PECOCK an agent? An asset? A contact? What sort of relationship do we have with him?"

"Ah, yes," said Stone. "Sticky wicket. What *is* this all about? Strictly for bookkeeping purposes, we will treat what took place yesterday as a recruitment, even though it wasn't one in the usual sense. We will enroll this fellow immediately as an active agent, assuming that he follows through in Rome. The fact that he doesn't consider himself an agent is fine."

"That doesn't pose any problem?" asked Rogers, remembering all the consternation this same question had provoked two years earlier in the discussions with Marsh and Stone.

"No problem whatsoever," replied Stone serenely.

"Forgive me for asking, but does that mean the Palestinian won the argument?"

"Nobody won," said Stone. "It simply means that we have learned our lesson and will not insist on control. In essence, we are accepting his definition of the relationship. If he asks, you should encourage him to believe that we have embarked on a sort of 'liaison' with him as a senior inteligence officer of Fatah. We have such arrangements with all sorts of disagreeable people. As I say, it isn't a problem."

"Yes, sir," said Rogers.

"Good," said Stone, rising from his chair.

"Can I ask one more question?"

"Of course."

"Do you think that the Palestinian is involved in Black September?"

"Possibly." said Stone. "Quite probably."

"Does that bother you?"

"What do you mean?"

"Does it bother you that we are working with a terrorist?"

"Oh," said Stone.

He turned and gazed out the window.

"Let me answer your question frankly, and you will forget that I ever said these words. Morality in the abstract is too large a problem for me to get my arms around. I leave it to moral philosophers. What I do understand is the practical matter of protecting the lives of American citizens. I have no doubt—none whatsoever—that the relationship we are embarking on will serve that goal. The rest is too complicated."

PART VIII

June–November 1972

35

Tel Aviv; June 1972

Yakov Levi's desk at Mossad headquarters looked out on the disorderly urban landscape of Tel Aviv. The building was in the center of Tel Aviv, near the old Haifa railway station, in the midst of the noise and commotion of the city. Levi was settling into his new job as the desk officer handling intelligence about the Palestinian guerrillas. He was still savoring his transformation. He was a hero. He had an office. He was home.

Levi gloried in the ordinariness of his new life. In Beirut he had gone to the office each day trussed in a silk tie and a business suit. Here he wore an open-neck shirt, loose-fitting gabardine slacks, and, in summer, a pair of sandals. Levi's body seemed to relax as well. His hair lost the tight, wiry curl of Beirut and became softer and looser. The knot in his stomach also seemed to loosen and he stopped chewing antacid pills. He spoke Hebrew all day and night and revelled in it. When newly arrived immigrants approached him on the street speaking English or French, he would feign incomprehension.

Levi liked taking long walks at lunchtime. He would leave the Mossad headquarters building and walk down Arlosoroff Street toward the sea. He would pass Dizengoff Street, where many of the fine shops and stores were located, then continue past Ben Yehuda Street until he reached the beach and the Mediterranean. How different the sea looked here than it had in Beirut. So much calmer and cleaner, breaking on the soft sand of Israel rather than the rocky coast of Lebanon.

What Levi couldn't quite fathom as he took these walks through the city was that all of the people around him were Jews! The people watching the movie in the theater on Ben Yehuda; the women in the department stores, the sales ladies and the customers, too; and the beautiful girls on the beach with golden brown skin, and the men playing paddle ball who were trying so hard to impress them. They were all Jews. That was the miracle of it. There was no one else to impress, to seduce or be seduced by.

The first few months he was back in Israel, Levi sometimes acted a little crazy. He went one day to a kiosk on Dizengoff Street that sold hand-lettered T-shirts. Levi asked the shirt man to make one that said in Hebrew: "The Arabs can go to Hell!" He wore it back to the office where a colleague told him gently to take it off.

Israel in 1972 was a country that, like Levi, was trying to learn how to relax. The great battles to establish the state had been fought and won. The problems now were of less heroic dimensions, like those of most other countries. The effort to fill the land with people had brought a huge migration of poor Sephardic Jews from Morocco. As a result, there were now rich and poor Jews in the land of Israel. The rich ones were white and from Europe and the poor ones were black and from North Africa. And there were the problems that result from being powerful: The 1967 war had annexed vast amounts of land, far larger than the nation itself, which had to be policed and administered. It was a new sensation for Israelis, to act as an occupying army and see the looks of fear and hatred on the faces of their defeated enemies. Why do they hate us so? the Israelis wondered. We are only fighting for our right to exist.

A new word came into general use during the early 1970s to explain what the Israelis were fighting against. It wasn't the Egyptians or the Syrians, who had already been trounced. It certainly wasn't the Palestinians, whose name most Israelis preferred not to pronounce. It was the "terrorists." They were the enemy of Israel, and of the whole world.

Israel in 1972 revelled in its ordinariness, but also feared it. The country was pulled in two directions at once: inward, toward the particular and unique identity of the Jewish people, which Judaism has celebrated throughout history; and outward, toward universal values and emotions.

Levi wondered whether that was the paradox of modern Israel: If the Jews were now like everyone else, with a state and army of their own, how then were they still special and different from everyone else? Had they been chosen by God to be, after 5,000 years of suffering, a people with the ordinary problems of combating terrorism, maintaining defensible borders, and administering occupied lands?

Levi threw himself into his new job. He had arrived home just as the trauma of Black September was beginning, so there was plenty of work in his department. He spent the day collating information, analyzing it, struggling to see the pattern in the lengthening string of terrorist operations in Europe. He combed the files looking for the names, dates, and places that would help solve the riddle of Black September.

It was slow going. Some days he spent so much time looking at the pictures of Palestinian suspects, reading the transcripts of intercepted Arabic communications, and analyzing the Lebanese press that he wondered whether he had really left Beirut after all.

Levi worked in a section with ten other officers. He wasn't the most senior man but, thanks to his recent tour in Beirut, he was the most experienced analyst of the fedayeen organizations, and the other officers deferred to him. Levi gradually realized, too, that the Old Guard of Mossad regarded him as one of their own. Levi wasn't sure why—perhaps it was his European background—but he was pleased. Things like that mattered a great deal in the Mossad. There was no private club in the world that had a more elaborate status hierarchy than the Israeli security service.

The members of the Old Guard had nearly all been born outside of Israel. Many of them had been intelligence officers for the Haganah or Lehi or Irgun at the time of the war of independence in 1948. They had arrived in Palestine from every corner of the globe. Refugees all, they had fled Europe in the 1930s for China, Russia, India, America—and travelled from there to Eretz Israel. They seemed to speak every language in the world. Was there an operation in Ethiopia?

There was sure to be a Mossad man who spoke fluent Amharic. Was there an operation in the Far East? There were speakers of the Mandarin and Cantonese dialects of Chinese, speakers of Japanese, Korean, Thai, all of whom had suffered through the war years and made their way to the Jewish homeland. The Old Guard had been trained in the cruelest school the world has ever known, and they didn't let the younger men forget it.

The younger Mossad officers were a different breed. They had come into the security service not from the desperate exile world of the 1930s and 1940s, but from the Israeli Army, from the proud and self-reliant military arm of the new Jewish state. They had joined Mossad after proving themselves in the special operations units of the army and navy. They were, in their own way, just as tough as the refugee generation.

When Levi looked at his younger colleagues, he saw hard, muscular bodies and dark faces. Many of them were Oriental Jews, whose families had lived in Baghdad or Casablanca or Cairo. They might have difficulty speaking English and German. But they spoke perfect Arabic. And that, Levi suspected, was exactly what the state of Israel needed in the 1970s.

The glory days of the Mossad were over. Eichmann and the other Nazi war criminals had been caught. The Jewish networks in the Soviet Union, which had allowed Mossad to obtain Khrushchev's secret speech to the 1956 Party Congress, had mostly been broken. There wasn't much need, any more, to send terrified couriers through Russia and Eastern Europe gathering the tidbits of intelligence that Mossad had used to trade with the Western intelligence services. The Israelis didn't need to beg and barter just to stay alive any more. That much had been assured.

Now the tasks were different. The problem was manipulating the environment around Israel. Rewarding friends and punishing enemies in the Middle East. The young men around Levi had earned their reputations not in Moscow or Rome but parachuting into Kurdistan to help the Shah of Iran make trouble for Iraq; or parachuting into southern Sudan to help foment a civil war. Or travelling secretly to Morocco to help teach the Moroccan Army how to defeat the Polisario guerrillas. Those were the new challenges, and they involved what the new breed of Mossad liked best: Playing games with the Arabs, driving the Arabs crazy.

The security establishment prospered because everyone accepted the rules. Every able-bodied Israeli male served in the military—every journalist, politician, avant-garde intellectual—and they all accepted the basic imperatives of military discipline. The interests of national security came first: the journalist agreed to be censored; the politician agreed not to question the government about certain sensitive matters; everyone agreed to protect the security agencies—Mossad; Shin Beth, the Israeli FBI; Aman, or military intelligence; Unit 8200 of Aman, which collected signals intelligence; Unit 269 of the army general staff, which conducted secret operations; and the Scientific Research Bureau, or "Lekem." And of all these elite units, the most elite was Mossad—the Institute. If the security of Israel was the nation's secular religion, the officers of the Mossad were its high priests.

Levi submerged himself in the world of Black September. He became the daily watch officer for that account, the person who sifted through each day's harvest of agents' reports and communications intercepts for information that might help the Israelis to prevent the next attack. Levi found that easy. He was a well-organized man. He liked to make lists, read through old files, pull bits of information from his memory and match them with current intelligence.

Levi worried that he was always a few steps behind the people he was tracking. His gut told him that Black September was a ruse, that its operations were really the work of Fatah. But that wasn't enough. He needed proof: the names of the people who planned the operations, who provided the weapons, who serviced the drops, who paid the gunmen. He needed to peel away the cover and see the machine at work, to see how each piece fit together in the covert organization.

As an exercise, Levi gathered every fact he could find about two Black September operations: the bombing of an electronics plant in Hamburg and the sabotage of an oil terminal at Rotterdam. He began to see a pattern, a distinctive signature that identified these operations and others as the work of a particular individual. The operations had several obvious common characteristics:

—They were meticulously planned. The bombs exploded where they were supposed to, when they were supposed to. They did the damage that was intended, no less and no more. Warnings were delivered when appropriate. Credit was taken in a distant capital, usually just a few minutes after the attack.

—They were clean. There were no obvious clues. Frightened Arabs weren't caught running from the scene. Fingerprints weren't found. Guns with traceable serial numbers weren't captured.

—They were professional. Levi suspected that the planner must be a trained intelligence officer, who knew how to cover his trail. Checks of the Arab underworld in Europe, and of agents who operated on the fringe of the guerrilla movement, failed to turn up any clues. Inquiries with arms dealers who might have supplied weapons and explosives also produced nothing. Whoever was planning the operations was skillful enough to keep several layers of cut-outs between himself and his handiwork.

—They were the work of someone who spoke German. Though Black September operated across Europe, it seemed to strike in West Germany with unusual regularity. Whoever was planning the operations felt comfortable there, spoke the language, understood the culture.

The German-speaking requirement triggered something in Levi's memory. There was a Palestinian operative in Beirut who had been renowned for his continental charm, and his ability to bed down women from every province of Europe. What Levi remembered now was the voice of that Palestinian, recorded by a surveillance tap placed by a Mossad agent, declaring his love in German to a beautiful Fraülein. Levi began then to focus his research on this particular Palestinian. When he imagined the face of Black September, he saw not an anonymous figure in the shadows, but a smooth-shaven young man in a black leather jacket.

Levi had another hunch, one that he had begun to formulate long ago in Lebanon. The Americans are not stupid, Levi reasoned. They must have tried to penetrate Fatah, just as we have. In recruiting an agent, where would the CIA turn? To the intelligence service of Fatah, of course! That's what spies do. They recruit other spies. Otherwise, what was the point?

So Levi opened a second, parallel investigation. He asked the registry for the files that Mossad had compiled on American penetration of the Fatah leadership. The librarian was apologetic. There wasn't one particular file on that subject. Mossad officers had gathered information on the topic, of course, but it was scattered among various files. So Levi began reading.

He came across a crucial bit of evidence almost by accident. He was sitting one morning in the registry, a dark and windowless room in the center of the Mossad headquarters building, trying to decide what files to request that day. He had already combed the registry on Fatah, on the Old Man, on Jamal Ramlawi and a dozen other Palestinians.

On a hunch, he requested the files on the Popular Front for the Liberation of Palestine. Perhaps the PFLP had explored the possibility that Fatah had been penetrated by the Americans. Levi spent the morning reading reports from agents and case officers. He worked through lunch. Late that afternoon, as he was opening what seemed like the hundredth manila folder of the day, out fell something that looked eerily familiar. It was the coded message that had been hidden inside the elephant box in the diabolical maze of the Damascus souk. Attached to it was a decoded version in Hebrew, which he had never read before.

Levi could scarcely believe what he was reading. The PFLP intelligence report seemed to confirm that Levi's two investigations were focusing on the same subject. The operations chief of Black September and the American penetration agent in Fatah appeared to be the same person!

Levi reported his initial findings to his division chief.

"Go slow," said the chief. "It's too speculative."

"Speculative?" asked Levi, feeling a knot in the stomach he remembered too well from the old days.

"And too dangerous if you're wrong. Look some more."

So Levi went back to his files. He read them once again. He found more details. Then in early June there was a startling development in the case. A piece of intelligence arrived from Europe—from a friendly official in Rome—that was so

unmistakably clear and so obvious that it forced Levi's supe-
riors to pay attention to what he was saying.

Levi delivered his briefing on Jamal Ramlawi to the intelligence chiefs in late June 1972. They met away from the
downtown offices, in a more modern compound on a hill
overlooking the Haifa Road, just before the turn for Herzliya.
The sign out front said: "Ministry of Defense, Bureau of Research."

The group was called in Hebrew the *Rashai*. The Chiefs.
That was enough.

Levi waited in the hall outside the meeting room for the
Chiefs to finish another piece of business. He was nervous.
Not the fear in his gut he had known when he was an officer
conducting operations in enemy territory. It was more like
shyness. In Beirut, his only true emotion had been fear, and
that had necessarily been mute. Now Levi had to speak for
himself.

A uniformed aide opened the door and motioned for him to
come in. He was surprised by how bright it was, bright with
the sunlight of Israel in midsummer.

The men at the conference table were dressed as Levi was,
in open-neck, short-sleeve shirts. Most of them were smoking. Many of them were bald. It might have been a philoso-
phy seminar at the Hebrew University. The faces and the room
would have looked almost the same.

Levi's eye focused on an older man sitting at the far end of
the table. He was a short man with bushy eyebrows, and he
was smoking a pipe. Levi imagined that he must be the chief
of the Mossad. In truth, Levi had never met the chief and
wasn't even sure of his real name.

"So?" said the little man with the bushy eyebrows. It
was a brief rhetorical question, which he answered for himself. "So this young man is Mr. Levi, and he has come to
us today to tell us about his research into Black September.
Is that right?"

"Yes," said Levi. His voice sounded like a frog croaking.

"So?"

"My briefing concerns a Palestinian named Jamal Ramlawi," began Levi. "First, I will tell you what we know about
him. Then I will tell you what we suspect."

"Yes, yes," said the short man with bushy eyebrows. "Don't keep us waiting."

"Yes, chief," said Levi.

"Don't call me chief," said the little man.

"Yes, sir," said Levi. He must be the head of the service, Levi thought. That is the way the head of Mossad should look. Like everyone's uncle.

"First, what we know," said Levi. "We know that Jamal Ramlawi is a leader of Black September. Until two weeks ago, that was a near-certainty. Now it is a certainty, thanks to a piece of intelligence that we obtained from Rome. I believe that most of you have heard the tape recording of Jamal Ramlawi. Yes? I have brought along a tape recorder and can play it now if anyone would like to hear it."

"We've heard it," said the man with the bushy eyebrows.

"The Rome tape proves what we have suspected for many months," said Levi.

"What is that?" asked the little man skeptically, puffing on his pipe.

"It proves that Jamal Ramlawi, a senior Fatah intelligence officer, is the chief logistician of Black September. It proves that he obtained weapons and explosives for Black September in Italy, and probably in other countries of Europe, too. The tape is evidence of what we have been trying to tell the world. Black September *is* Fatah."

Another man spoke up. One that Levi had missed in looking around the room. He didn't look like an Israeli; he looked like an American. A professor at the Harvard Law School, maybe. He was tall and thin, so fit that his body seemed almost stringy. He was dressed in loose khaki slacks and a white button-down Oxford-cloth shirt. He wore a pair of clear plastic glasses, which gave him a slightly boyish look. He spoke with a quick, sharp tone of voice that was at once intelligent and impatient.

"The tape doesn't prove that," said the button-down professor. "What you said may be true. I personally have no doubt that it is true. But the tape does not prove it. The tape proves only that Ramlawi made arrangements to obtain four automatic pistols and one hundred kilos of explosive in Rome. It doesn't even prove that, actually, but we will take that on faith."

Levi's throat felt dry. He took a drink of water and continued his briefing.

"The tape is only the final piece of information. We have collateral evidence of Ramlawi's role in Black September. We have photographs of him meeting with a man who was arrested in Cairo last year after the Black September attack on the Jordanian prime minister."

"Soooo?" said another voice from around the table. He was a fat man wearing a knitted yarmulke. "So what do photos prove? Proximity. Contact. And what is that, my friend? Nothing!"

"We have transcripts of the Egyptian interrogation of the Black September terrorists in which they say they received training from a man who fits the description of Ramlawi."

"Oh very nice!" said a tall, thin man sitting by the window. "So now we're depending on the Egyptians for our intelligence? God forbid! How do they know anything? What are they all of a sudden, geniuses?"

Everyone laughed.

Levi realized then that he was getting razzed. That this group liked nothing better in the world than giving young officers a hard time. He set his feet more squarely under him and continued the briefing.

"We have other collateral evidence about Ramlawi's involvement in Black September, but I won't bore you with it. Take my word for it. I have analyzed the evidence carefully, and I tell you on my honor that it is accurate. The man is involved in Black September operations. Period. Take my word for it or find another analyst."

"Not so loud, please," said the man with bushy eyebrows. He relit his pipe. He was happy now. He didn't want facts. For all Levi knew, the Chiefs had all spent more time with the files than he had. They wanted analysis.

"Now I will turn to the interesting part," said Levi. "Here we are not dealing with hard facts, but with speculations—guesses—that are based on the available evidence."

"What is your speculation?" said the little man. "Just tell us. Don't make a big production of it, please."

"The speculation is that Jamal Ramlawi is an American agent."

There was a momentary silence in the room, broken by the

sound of chairs moving, cigarettes being lit, pipes being puffed.

"That's crazy," said the little man with bushy eyebrows. "Completely crazy. Why would our friends the Americans do this? Tell us the evidence for this crazy theory."

"The evidence is complicated," said Levi.

"Soooo?" said the fat man with the knitted yarmulke. "Do we look stupid?"

"First, we know that Ramlawi is impulsive. We know that in Beirut he led a wild life. Chasing women. Dozens of women. We think that he even had an affair with the wife of a French diplomat."

"Very nice," said the tall, thin man by the window. "They deserve each other."

"We know Ramlawi is a pet of the Fatah leadership," continued Levi. "We know that he was one of the Fatah men who was sent to Egypt for a special training course in intelligence. We know that he speaks many languages, including English, French, Italian, and German. We know that he has travelled extensively."

"Sooooo?" queried the fat man. "What does this have to do with the CIA?"

"I'm coming to that," said Levi. "In Beirut, we collected the travel histories of everyone flying in and out of Beirut International Airport."

"We know. We know," said the man with the bushy eyebrows. "Whose idea do you think that was? Eh?"

"I'm coming to the important part," said Levi testily. "In analyzing the travel records, we find two instances in which Jamal Ramlawi was out of Lebanon in 1970 at the same time as a CIA case officer working under diplomatic cover at the American Embassy in Beirut."

The law school professor rapped his pen against his glass.

"Mr. Levi," said the law school professor quietly. "What is the name of this CIA officer?"

"Rogers. Thomas Rogers."

"And where did they go, the terrorist and the CIA man?"

"To Kuwait in March 1970, and to Egypt in May 1970. We cannot confirm that they actually met. But we are sure that they went to those countries at the same time."

"It could be a coincidence, of course," said the button-down professor. "Even twice in one year. But it is interesting, I must admit."

"Yes," said the little man with the bushy eyebrows.

"Yes," said the fat man in the yarmulke.

"Continue," said the professor.

"The second important piece of evidence is an agent report in the files about a visit to Rome in July 1970 by an American intelligence officer. I wouldn't have found it at all, since it never went into the Fatah file. I noticed it when I was researching the background of the Italian general in Rome who provided us with the tape."

"Go on, go on," said the little man. "Spare us the details."

"According to this agent in Rome, the American intelligence man had flown in specially to meet with an Arab agent, a Palestinian perhaps. The Italians never figured out who he was supposed to meet. Neither did we. But last week I had one of our friends do a travel check to see if anyone interesting had travelled from Beirut to Rome in July 1970. And guess who popped out from one of the MEA passenger lists, travelling with a phony Algerian passport that he has used several times since then?"

"Ramlawi," said several voices around the table.

"Correct," said Levi, beaming.

"And who was this American who came to Rome?" asked the button-down professor.

"Marsh. John Marsh."

"And why did Mr. Marsh come, and not Mr. Rogers?"

Levi thought for a moment.

"I don't know," he said eventually.

"Good," said the professor. "If you had answered that question, I would have suspected that you were making everything up. Sometimes the correct answer is that we don't know what the correct answer is."

Heads around the table nodded sagely. Levi nodded too.

"Go on!" barked the little man with bushy eyebrows. "What are you waiting for?"

"After Rome, everything gets a little fuzzy," said Levi. "We have a report from an agent in Lebanon. I know a little about him, since I used to collect his reports from dead drops. He is a priest, and something of an amateur detective in his spare time. This may be a little hard to understand, so bear with me. The priest had received from his Mossad case officer in Europe a list of people in whom we had some intelligence interest. One of them was Jamal Ramlawi. So he took it upon himself to put a question to Rogers, the CIA man, about Ramlawi."

"He did what?" asked the fat man with the knitted yarmulke.

"He asked Rogers, the CIA man, for information about Ramlawi."

"What an idiot!" said the fat man. "And what did Rogers say?"

"He told the priest to ask the Israelis."

"Ach!" said the fat man. "What an idiot we have for an agent."

"What else?" asked the professor.

"One last thing. An agent's report that I carried out of Syria myself. I didn't realize it at the time, but it was a report from a Palestinian inside the Popular Front for the Liberation of Palestine."

"Yes, yes. We know the name of the group," said the little man with bushy eyebrows. "What did the report say?"

"It said that the leadership of the PFLP was convinced that there was an American agent inside Fatah. The PFLP leadership wasn't sure about the identity of the agent, but they suspected that it was Ramlawi."

"Well, well, well," said the little man. As he talked, he inserted a pipe cleaner in the stem of his pipe and withdrew a wad of wet brown goo. "So, now we are getting our intelligence from the lunatics in the PLO, is that what you are telling me?"

"We take it wherever we can get it," said Levi.

"Correct," said the law school professor with the clear plastic glasses. "And since you understand that fact of life so well, perhaps you can answer the big question."

"What is that?" said Levi.

"The big question is what should we do about all of this?"

"You want my recommendation?"

"Why not?"

"Let me think."

"Not too long," said the professor. "If you think too

long, you will become like the rest of us. Don't think. Just
say."

"We could try to use Ramlawi ourselves. Threaten to expose his contacts with the Americans if he doesn't agree to
work with us."

"Wrong," said the professor. "Interesting, but wrong. The
Palestinian would just assume that the Americans had told
everything to their Israeli friends. Trying to blackmail him
would accomplish nothing. It would only cut off the American connection. Any more ideas?"

"We could make an approach to Rogers, the CIA officer.
Or to Marsh, the one who was in Rome."

"Wrong again. Too risky. We do not want to start recruiting
CIA officers. We don't need the aggravation. Do you want to
know the correct answer?"

"Of course," said Levi.

"Don't do *anything*. At first, that is always the best thing
to do. Nothing. Just watch and wait. Don't make the water
muddy by stirring it up. Be patient."

"Yes, sir," said Levi.

That was it. People began rising from their seats. Levi felt
deflated, somehow, to have travelled this far, assembled all
this material, only to be told to do nothing. Perhaps it
showed, because as the group was filing out of the room, the
button-down professor and the diminutive man with the bushy
eyebrows both walked over to Levi.

Levi watched them approach and wondered, which one is
the boss? Which one is the true face of Mossad? The wily
little man with the sardonic sense of humor or the clipped,
carefully controlled analyst? The man in the button-down shirt
approached Levi first and shook his hand.

"My name is Natan Porat," said the man in the clear
glasses. "I am the chief of the service. You did a fine job
today. Keep up the good work."

He motioned to the short man with bushy eyebrows.

"This is my deputy, Avraham Cohen," said Porat.

"You give a nice briefing, Mr. Levi," said Cohen.

Porat took Levi aside. He seemed even more American
up close. He didn't sweat. His hair was trim. His voice was
clipped. He didn't gesture when he talked. He seemed to
Levi almost bloodless. Porat looked with his clear eyes

through his clear glasses. He spoke the language of the "A" students who run the modern-day security services around the world.

"We will do something about the Ramlawi problem, I assure you," said Porat. "But you must understand that it is delicate. It is a little awkward to learn that an American agent is directing the operations of the leading terrorist group in the world."

36

Tel Aviv; September 1972

Levi was at his desk when the first reports began to come in
from Munich. Eight Palestinian terrorists had infiltrated the
Olympic Village at dawn on the morning of September 5 and
were holding eleven Israeli athletes hostage.

Like the rest of Israel, Levi spent that day listening to the
radio. You couldn't escape the news. Levi had a radio in his
cramped office. There was one in the cafeteria. There was
even a radio in the usually noiseless stacks of the registry. It
was much the same in every office building and house in
Israel. People stopped what they were doing and stared at the
radio, listening to the awful news from Germany.

The bulletins came every hour from Munich. There were
not eleven hostages, said the radio, but nine. The terrorists
had killed two of the Israeli boys when they seized the building. All the hostages would be killed, reported the radio, unless Israel released 236 Palestinian prisoners. The terrorists set
a deadline of noon, then 1:00 P.M., then 5:00 P.M., then 10:00
P.M. They asked for three planes to fly them and their hostages to an Arab country. The Germans agreed. The hostages
were heading to the airport.

Israel sat by the radio and listened and prayed. People went
home, had dinner, lay awake in bed listening to the news.
Levi stayed at the office. Just after 1:00 A.M. in Israel, the
announcement came. Thanks be to God! All nine Israeli athletes had been rescued. A spokesman for the German Federal
Republic announced that a rescue operation had succeeded.

The Israeli prime minister, listening to the radio like everyone else, opened a bottle of Cognac to celebrate.

Israel radio continued to carry confirmation that all the hostages were safe until it went off the air at 3:00 A.M. The late editions of the Israeli newspapers bannered the glorious news. "Hostages in Munich Rescued," said *The Jerusalem Post.* "All Safe After Germans Trap Arabs at Military Airport."

Israel woke up the next morning to the horror of what had really happened. Israel Radio went back on the air at 6:00 A.M. with a somber announcement that the earlier reports had somehow been mistaken. A German effort to storm the getaway plane had backfired. All nine Israeli athletes were dead. A massacre had taken place in Munich.

Levi was as stunned as anyone else in Israel. Perhaps more so, for he had allowed himself in the few months that he had been back home to relax. He had begun to forget in those months what he had felt every day and every minute outside Israel: the feeling of vulnerability, the feeling that you could be killed at any moment by merciless enemies, the feeling that you were hated by the world—and would always be hated—simply because you were a Jew. Those feelings returned now for Levi like a ruptured wound inside his brain.

Levi took a walk that day and saw a city of red-eyed people, who had begun the day sobbing and were still stunned with grief. In the park benches along Jabotinsky Street, some old people were sitting and crying. A crowd had gathered spontaneously at the German Embassy. Levi heard the noise from several blocks away. The crowd was singing a song in Hebrew, *"Am Yisrael Hai"*— The People of Israel Live. Someone had drawn the number 11 on the pavement, the number of victims. Someone else had brought eleven candles. People were arriving with posters. "Never Again." "Why No Olympic Solidarity for Jews?" "An Eye for an Eye." An old woman was handing out black ribbons. Levi took one and put it on his arm.

What was it that had shaken the country so? Levi wondered as he walked back to the office. It wasn't the number of people who had been killed. In the annals of terrorism against the state of Israel, eleven victims wasn't a unique tragedy but a mere moment in a nearly continuous pattern of violence. It wasn't the brutality of the killings, either. Dying in a hail of gunfire, after all, was not the worst way to die.

What was it, then, that made Levi and everyone he encountered that day feel so shattered by the events in Munich?

Perhaps it was the innocence and helplessness of the victims. They were athletes, symbols of the simplest and purest virtues of the nation. The strongest, the swiftest, the least tainted by the corruptions of life. They had come to Munich believing that twenty-seven years after the end of the Holocaust, Jews could come to Germany without fear. They had accepted an invitation to come and play with the other nations of the world. And it had ended with a pile of Jewish corpses.

Levi walked back to the office, sick at heart, wanting to talk to someone and also wanting to hide. The office was somber. Small groups of people talking quietly, secretaries staring blankly at their typewriters. I should do something, Levi thought. I shouldn't sit and grieve. He went to the files and assembled a quick profile of the leaders of Black September. It was an offering to the vengeful God of Abraham and Isaac. He took it upstairs to the floor where the Chiefs had their offices. The reception desk was empty, so Levi walked down the hall until he reached the door of the deputy director, Avraham Cohen. The door was open. Cohen was sitting at his desk with his eyes closed. His head was bobbing slightly. Cohen was saying a prayer. On his arm, Levi saw, was a black armband.

Cohen raised his head eventually. His eyes were red and surrounded by dark circles.

"What do you want?" asked Cohen. The bark was gone from his voice.

"I thought this might be useful," said Levi, handing him the file on the leaders of Black September.

"Do you know where these bastards are?"

"Some of them," said Levi.

Cohen was silent. The bushy eyebrows, usually so animated, were at rest. Cohen was studying something on his desk, Levi noticed. It was a newspaper story listing the names

of the eleven hostages—now the eleven victims—and brief
biographies of each of them.

"This is the story of our people," said Cohen.

"Yes," said Levi. "I know."

Cohen didn't seem to hear him.

"Truly," he said. "This is the story of Israel. Those boys in
Munich were a map of who we are."

"What do you mean?" asked Levi.

"Listen to me," said Cohen, picking up the list from off
his desk. "Let me tell you who these boys were. A wrestler
who arrived in Israel just three months ago from the Soviet
Union. Another wrestler from Russia. A riflery coach from
Rumania. A weightlifter from Poland. A wrestling coach
from Rumania. Can you listen to more? Eh? Do you want
to hear more?"

"Yes," said Levi.

"A weightlifter from America. A weightlifting coach from
Poland. A weightlifter from Libya. A track coach from Tel
Aviv. A fencing coach from Rumania. A wrestling coach from
Germany, whose parents survived the Holocaust only to see
their son die in Munich."

Cohen put the list back on his desk. He put his head in his
hands for a moment and then turned back to Levi.

"They are all from somewhere else, did you notice that?
Eh? They came here to Israel to be safe and we let them
down. You and I, the Institute. They trusted in us to keep
them safe and we let them die like helpless Jews in Germany."

"Yes."

"And do you know what we should do about it?" asked
Cohen, his voice rising, his eyebrows taking flight.

"No," said Levi.

"We should kill the bastards! Every one of them."

The next several days brought a flood of intelligence
about the Munich incident. Much of it came across Levi's
desk. There were stacks of telephone and wireless intercepts, cables from every Israeli embassy in Europe, reports
from agents and tipsters around the world about the Munich
operation. The sheer volume of the material overwhelmed
Levi. Somewhere in the mountain of paper there might be a

message saying that the massacre had been planned by the president of Egypt himself, but it would take days to find it. The problem, Levi decided, wasn't collecting intelligence. In the modern era of communications intercepts, that was easy. The problem was analyzing it in time to make a difference.

Much of what came in during those first few days was predictable and not very helpful. Black September had issued a four-page mimeographed statement in Cairo during the first few hours of the operation, declaring that the Israeli athletes were "under armed arrest" and explaining the conditions under which they would be freed. The Fatah leadership in Beirut issued a statement denying any responsibility for the Munich operation. Arab press reports generally condoned the massacre and said it was really Israel's fault for oppressing the Palestinian people.

What struck Levi, as he began to sift through the intelligence, was how cleverly Black September had planned the operation. They had known exactly where to go in the Olympic Village to reach the Israeli quarters, how to penetrate the supposedly tight security, when to stage the attack for maximum surprise. They had managed to smuggle a small arsenal of weapons into West Germany undetected. They had been able to deliver precise demands in Cairo, several thousand miles away, shortly after the attack began. And they had, in the final moments at the airport, seen through the West German ruse and exacted a bloody price by killing all the hostages. Clearly, these were not amateurs.

The West German police provided the first good clue. They combed the employment records of all the companies and contractors that had worked on the Olympic Village, looking for the "inside man" who might have helped Black September. They soon discovered that one of the architects who had worked on the Olympic Village was a well-educated Palestinian. Levi ran his name and passport number through the computer and found that Mossad maintained a small file on him. He was a Fatah sympathizer, born in Haifa and educated in Europe. He had attracted Mossad attention because of a report that he had attended a meeting in 1971 with a Fatah intelligence officer. A man named Jamal Ramlawi.

Communications intercepts added more clues. The analysts in Unit 8200 noted unusually heavy wireless traffic between the Fatah headquarters in Beirut and a transmitter in East Berlin on the day of the Munich operation. The analysts were still trying to break the code and decipher the communications. But they already had a working hypothesis: East Berlin was the Fatah command post for the operation. Someone there had been running the show.

The Israelis asked the West Germans for permission to review the names of all Arab passport holders who had entered East Berlin from the West during the previous month. The list duly arrived on Levi's desk. Among the hundreds of names and numbers, one caught Levi's eye like a bright red flag. It was an Algerian passport, issued to someone named Chadli bin Yehiya. A quick check in the files confirmed that the same name and passport number had been used once before by Jamal Ramlawi.

Levi fed his intelligence reports to the Chiefs, who were holding daily meetings to plan their response to Munich. They gathered now, not in a sunny conference room on the way to Herzliya, but in a dark command bunker under the streets of Tel Aviv. In the dark, they were preparing to fight a war in the shadows.

Rosh Hashana, the Jewish new year, was celebrated three days after the Munich massacre. It was the end of the 5,732nd year of the Jewish people. "Who will live and who will die?" asked the traditional Rosh Hashana prayer. "Who by fire, who by sword?" The president of Israel issued a new year's message to mark the beginning of year 5733. He spoke of the tragedy in Munich. "To the conscience of the world, we cry: 'Let there be no rest till this evil arm is cut off!' To the bereaved—parents and wives and children, friends and colleagues—we say: 'The wounded hearts of all the nation feel with you. How shall we comfort you?'"

The Knesset delivered a simple answer when it met a week after Munich. Revenge.

The Israeli parliament passed a resolution declaring the terrorists "enemies of humanity" and vowing to "act with perseverance against the terrorist organizations, their bases and those who aid them, until an end is put to this criminal activity." The meaning of that opaque language was hinted at in a dispatch by the military correspondent of *The Jerusalem Post*, who wrote: "Israel is expected to meet the terrorists on their own terrain in order to combat the rising wave of terror, using tactics which will be both unconventional and damaging."

Israel, in other words, was embracing the weapons of its enemies in the war against terror.

37

Tel Aviv; October 1972

The Director of Central Intelligence travelled to the Middle East in October, a month after Munich. The trip had been planned long ago, but the terrorism problem gave it a sharper focus. So did a White House announcement in mid-September that the president had decided on a tough new anti-terrorism program. The Director wasn't sure what that was all about. He wasn't aware that there actually *was* any new presidential policy on terrorism, or indeed any policy at all. Nevertheless, he sensibly delivered to the president, Eyes Only, a copy of his itinerary with the notation: "Hope to gather support for our new anti-terrorism program during the trip."

The trip marked the first visit ever by a sitting DCI to Israel. A stopover in Tel Aviv had never before seemed advisable, given the sensitivities, not to say paranoia, of the Arab intelligence services. The Director had decided, to hell with Arab sensitivities, and scheduled a trip that would include stops in Jordan, Israel and Lebanon. That seemed safe enough. All three countries were regarded in the Arab world as wholly-owned subsidiaries of the CIA anyway.

The Director travelled in style. He brought his wife, his tennis racket, his tuxedo, his smoking jacket, his golf clubs, and a sun reflector for poolside. He also brought several secretaries, code clerks, bodyguards, and, to help with the locals, the chief of the Near East Division of the clandestine service, Mr. Edward Stone.

They all piled into a comfortable Air Force 707, one of the

fleet of planes that is available for top government officials when they travel abroad. This particular plane was known as "the Tube" because it had no windows, and for that reason it was shunned by most of the big shots. But it was the Director's favorite. He thought it cozy. The plane was laid out inside like a small apartment, with a bed, a sitting room, a kitchen, a lounge, and, in the forward section, an elaborate, state-of-the-art communications system.

The Israelis were delighted that the Director was coming and seemed eager to use the trip to taunt the Arabs. The Israeli air traffic control tower near Tel Aviv took the bold step of communicating directly with the Director's plane while it was still on the ground at Amman and suggesting a flight plan that would take the plane due west, across the Jordan River. The Jordanians were outraged by this violation of their airwaves and sent up several fighters as a gesture of protest. The Jordanian fighters circled the Amman airport for a few minutes and then returned meekly to the ground when the Israelis scrambled a squadron of F-4 Phantoms.

The pilot of the Director's 707 rejected the Israeli flight plan, on the ground that Palestinian guerrillas on either side of the river might try to shoot the plane down. He opted for a slightly longer, and considerably safer, route that passed over Syria and Lebanon, headed out toward Cyprus, and then circled back over the Mediterranean to Israel.

The Mossad chief, Natan Porat, met the Director's plane when it landed at a military airport near Tel Aviv. So did the CIA station chief from the embassy. There was a brief confusion over whose car the Director would ride in: one provided by the Mossad or one provided by the station. The Israelis had brought a shiny new Mercedes, the CIA a somewhat dilapidated Lincoln Continental. The Director reluctantly opted for the Lincoln.

The Director checked into the Tel Aviv Sheraton on the beach, sent his wife off shopping with the ambassador's wife, trounced Stone in a set of tennis, showered and shaved, and headed off to a formal meeting with the Israelis. He was dressed in his usual gray pinstripe suit, which in Tel Aviv made him stand out like a visitor from another planet.

* * *

"It is a pleasure to welcome our friends into our midst," said Natan Porat.

He was seated in a small conference room in the Mossad headquarters building near the railroad station. With him were the Director, Stone, and the deputy chief of the Mossad, Avraham Cohen.

Porat looked, in his way, even more American than the Director. He was dressed in a blue suit, a striped tie, black shoes. He might have been a high-class undertaker, except for the clear plastic glasses. Porat was the new Israel. Born in America, he had emigrated to Palestine as a teenager in 1946 and fought in the war of independence. He had entered the Israeli security service before he was twenty.

Porat, sharp as a razor, had brought along the perfect foil in Avraham Cohen: short, genial, avuncular, reassuring.

"Welcome to our friends," said Cohen, echoing Porat. "That is what we call the CIA. 'The Friends.' Did you know that?"

"I did not," said the Director.

"It's true. The British call you 'the Cousins.' But we think of you as 'the Friends.' "

"Well then," said the Director, looking for something to toast with and, finding nothing, putting his hand over his heart. "It's good to be among friends."

"I hope that we can talk as friends, about the problems that we must face together," said Porat.

The Director nodded.

"We don't always agree, as you know, about events in the Middle East. We compete at times for attention and support. Some of your Arab acquaintances, such as Jordan, are our enemies. But for all that, we are friends."

"Undoubtedly," said the Director. "We don't always agree. But we want the same things in the long run, I'm sure."

There was a pause. The meeting was off to a proper, if somewhat stilted, beginning.

"Say," spoke up Cohen. The tendrils of his eyebrows reached nearly to his hairline. He had a merry look on his face that was quite at odds with the somber tone of the gathering.

"Speaking of competition reminds me of the story about the two Hassidic Jews who wanted to be as rich as Rockefeller. Have you heard that story?"

"I don't believe so," said the Director. He looked toward Porat dubiously.

"Ah good," said Cohen. "Two Hassidic Jews are talking one day. One of them says, 'Imagine what it would be like if you could be as rich as Rockefeller.'

"'Let me tell you something,' says the second one. 'If I was as rich as Rockefeller, then I'd be *richer* than Rockefeller.'

"'How can you be richer than Rockefeller?' says the first.

"'Because even if I was as rich as Rockefeller, I'd still teach a little Talmud on the side.'"

The Director laughed vigorously. Porat looked at him with a bemused expression that seemed to say: Can it be that this man has never heard a Yiddish dialect joke before? Are we the first Jews he has ever met?

"We have prepared quite a program for you," said Porat. "Tomorrow we'd like to give you some briefings on how we look at the Middle East, and explain how our service operates. But before your official program begins, I hoped that we could talk informally here about some matters of mutual interest."

"Delighted," said the Director. "What can we do for you?"

"Actually," said Porat, "it is *we* who would like to do something for *you*."

The Mossad chief picked up a brown envelope from the table next to his chair and handed it to the Director. Inside were three documents in Russian, along with several dozen photographs and technical drawings.

"Your Soviet analysts may find these useful," said Porat. "They explain some recent changes in Soviet design requirements for missile guidance systems. Our specialists tell me they're quite interesting."

"I thought the Soviet had rolled up all your networks," said the Director.

"That's what the Soviets think, too," replied Porat with a wink.

The Director, who had learned a little Russian years ago, leafed through the collection and nodded appreciatively.

"Coin of the realm. Any more where this came from?"

"We'll see," said Porat.

The Mossad chief withdrew another brown envelope from the table and handed it to the Director.

"More goodies?" said the Director, opening the second envelope. This one contained the names, photographs, and passport numbers of a dozen Arabs.

"These gentlemen are Palestinian terrorists," said Porat. "Most of them are members of the PFLP, although some also maintain contact with Fatah. Several are connected with Black September. We have reason to believe that they are planning attacks against American targets over the next six to twelve months. We thought you would be interested."

"Indeed we are," said the Director. He handed the packet to Stone, who began leafing casually through the dozen photographs. Porat watched Stone intently as he thumbed through the packet. Stone paused for an instant when he saw the face of Jamal Ramlawi.

"We like to help our friends," said Porat crisply. "And we hope that our friends will help us."

"What can we do for you?" asked the Director once again.

"Israel has a terrorism problem. That is no secret to you. What you may not realize is that we have decided to take the most aggressive measures to deal with the problem."

"What does that mean?" asked the Director. As he spoke, he was picking pieces of lint off the legs of his gray pinstripe trousers.

"I will tell you exactly what it means," said Porat. "We are going to war with Black September. We intend to eliminate its leaders—every one of them—before they kill any more of our people. And we will punish those who planned the Munich massacre in the only way that is appropriate."

"I don't think I need any more details, thank you," said the Director.

"Good."

"I have a question, Nathan . . ."

"Natan," said Porat, correcting him.

"What I'm not clear about, Natan, is what you want us to do?"

"Let us talk frankly," said Porat. "When we ask for your help in fighting terrorism, we have in mind something quite specific. We assume that the United States tries, just as we do, to develop contacts within the terrorist organizations."

"No comment," said the Director.

"Of course not. But you asked me what we want and so I am telling you. We don't know what contacts you may or may not have. That is none of our business. But we do want your help, whatever it might be, in destroying the Fatah terrorist arm that calls itself Black September. We will destroy this organization—and its leadership—whether you help us or not. But we would prefer to do it with your help."

The Director cocked his head and looked at Porat out of one eye. "But you haven't told me yet how you want us to help you," said the Director.

"This is the Middle East," said Porat, smiling. "A merchant does not name his price. So let us leave the question of how you might help us to the imagination."

"Very well," said the Director. "Let us leave it to the imagination. We'll get back to you."

There was another pause.

"Say, Director," said Cohen. "Listening to you talk about agreeing with Natan reminds me of the story about the rabbi and the two suitors. Have you heard that one?"

"I suspect not," said the Director.

"Okay. There was this rabbi from Lublin who tried to resolve a quarrel between two men who both wanted to marry the same woman. Are you sure you haven't heard this one?"

"Quite sure," said the Director.

"Okay. The rabbi asks the first suitor to come and make his case, and the young man says he should get the girl because he has money, a good job, a handsome face. When he finishes, the rabbi says, 'You're right, I agree with you.'

"Then the second suitor arrives and argues his case. And he also has a long list of reasons why the woman should marry him. Fame, fortune, eternal bliss. The rabbi hears him out and says: 'You're right. I agree with you.'

"Now the rabbi's wife, who has been listening to all this, goes over to the poor rabbi from Lublin and says he is crazy to be telling both of the suitors he agrees with them. She tells him he has to make up his mind and choose.

"'You're right,' says the rabbi. 'I agree with you.'

This time everyone laughed.

The Director repeated the punch line to himself several times.

The meeting turned from serious business to ceremony. Glasses of vodka were poured, Polish-style, and toasts were drunk to friendship and cooperation. Stone took Cohen aside as they were leaving and said that it might be a week or so before the Director would have a response to Porat's request for American help in dealing with Black September.

"What are they up to?" the Director asked Stone several hours later.

They were walking along the beach. The Director didn't dare discuss sensitive business with Stone in his hotel room, or even in the American Embassy. That was asking for trouble, given Israeli surveillance technology. Even on the beach, Stone was carrying a small portable radio to mask the conversation from the ears of any long-range antennae.

"It's a squeeze play," said Stone.

"Explain what that means for an old friend who never played baseball."

"The Israelis want us to give up Ramlawi," said Stone. "It couldn't be more obvious. They know we won't admit openly that we're running him as an agent, but they evidently suspect it. Putting his picture in with the other Palestinian mug shots was a clear tip-off."

"Obviously," said the Director. "But of what?"

"That he's on their hit list," answered Stone. "They probably mean what they said. They seem convinced that he's part of Black September. Apparently they also suspect he was behind the Munich operation. And they probably do suspect that Ramlawi is planning to attack Americans. Maybe they've even heard about 'Nabil's' supposed plot to kill the president. But that's not really the message, the simple fact that they regard Ramlawi as dangerous to American and Israeli interests."

"Then what is the message?"

"The message is that they are onto us. They know that we have contact with Ramlawi. And they are planning to kill him."

"And?"

"And they want our help, either by passing on the intelligence take from Ramlawi, or in finding him."

"And killing him."

"Yes."

They were walking toward a more crowded area of the beach. Several girls were out frolicking in the late afternoon sun. They were dressed in tiny bikinis, little more than string and loose triangles of fabric. The Director, still dressed in his gray pinstripe suit, looked appreciatively at one of the girls. Though only a teenager, she had the largest breasts the Director could ever remember seeing. They were so firm that they barely seemed to move, even when she was running. The girl smiled back flirtatiously. Apparently men in pinstripe suits were exotic on the beach at Tel Aviv.

"I rather like this place," said the Director.

The Director waved at the girl and walked on. He and Stone looked decidedly odd. Two men in business suits walking on the beach, one of them carrying a portable radio.

"Edward," said the Director, resuming the conversation. "Is there any reason to doubt that they're right?"

"About what?"

"About Ramlawi being involved in Black September and Munich and all that?"

"No," said Stone. "Probably not."

"Well, then, why not burn him?" said the Director. "He's expendable, isn't he?"

"Excuse me," said Stone. "I didn't get that."

"Burn him! Dump him. Give the Israelis what they want."

"Betray Ramlawi?"

"Absolutely," said the Director. "Why not? He sounds like a bloody bastard."

"Perhaps," said Stone. "But he's our bastard."

"What has he done for us?"

"Not much, yet. But we're only beginning."

"He's a big boy," said the Director. "Let him fend for himself. Need I remind you that this is an election year?"

The Director was looking at a young Israeli maiden emerging, dripping wet, from the sea.

"I would add," said Stone, "that the Palestinian has placed his trust in us. He's our man."

"Not any more," said the Director.

"Director," said Stone gently. "I suspect that the Beirut station may have some reservations about this course of action. They have developed a relationship with Ramlawi. Perhaps we should discuss this with them before throwing him overboard."

"Sure," said the Director. "I am quite happy to talk to anybody. But I'm not likely to change my mind."

Ahead on the beach, another stunning, dark-haired woman in a tiny bikini was approaching. The Director tipped an imaginary hat. The woman smiled.

"Time for a swim," said the Director.

The Director made the grand tour of Israel. He visited the Wailing Wall and put a cardboard yarmulke on his head. He toured the Israeli nuclear facility at Dimona. He visited the Holocaust Memorial at Yad Vashem. He sat by the pool in Tel Aviv with his sun reflector, looking at pretty girls.

Porat was the perfect host. Helpful, congenial, undemanding. He and his wife Naomi, a psychiatrist, gave a charming dinner party for the Director and his wife. Somehow, despite the presence of many Israeli officials, the party had the feel of an evening at home with the family, including several loud family quarrels.

Nothing more was said about the Israeli request for help in the war against terrorism. Nothing more needed to be said. The Americans were on notice.

38

Beirut; October 1972

"I hate babysitting," said Hoffman to the members of the Beirut station. "But when the baby in question is your boss, what can you do?" Hoffman was holding a morning staff meeting, making final plans for the arrival of the Director in Beirut that afternoon. He looked harried.

As Hoffman talked, he was munching on a jelly donut. Hoffman was very fond of jelly donuts, especially a particular overstuffed version made by a company in New Jersey called Tast-EEE-Kreme. He had considered it a major coup several months ago when he found an old Air America contact who was willing to drop off a case of donuts in Beirut every month on his way to Oman. Hoffman was holding the jelly donut in his right hand, unaware that when he gesticulated to make a point, jelly was oozing out of the half-eaten donut onto the conference table.

"If they had asked me," Hoffman continued, "I would have told the Director that the trip was a waste of time. But they did not ask me, so here we are." A code clerk discreetly rose from her chair and scooped up the jelly with a napkin, before Hoffman could put his elbow in it.

"Seriously," said Hoffman to no one in particular. "It's one thing to entertain some asshole congressman from Illinois who wants to tell you how to solve the problems of the Middle East. That I can handle. The conversation is about my speed. Yes sir. No sir. My goodness, that's an interesting idea. No, indeed, we hadn't thought of that one.

"But the Director is different, boys and girls. When he shows up, it's time to turn off the bubble machine. If he asks you a question, you better answer it honestly. Anybody who tries to bullshit the Director should look for another job, starting tomorrow."

Hoffman's administrative deputy took over a discussion of the logistical arrangements, while Hoffman went to his office, unlocked the safe, and retrieved another jelly donut.

Hoffman, for all his grumbling, had done all the right things to prepare for the Director's arrival. He had repainted the rooms of the CIA station a pleasant off-white. He had arranged a dog-and-pony show with the new head of the Deuxième Bureau. He had asked Ambassador and Mrs. Wigg to host a small dinner party for the Director that evening. And, prodded by the Wiggs, he had scheduled a day trip to the mountains, stopping for lunch at the birthplace of Khalil Gibran.

Hoffman, responding to an urgent cable received the previous day from Stone, had also set aside several hours that afternoon for a private meeting with the Director in the bug-proof conference room at the embassy. Hoffman didn't know who was supposed to attend the meeting or what it was about. Details would follow, Stone's cable said.

The Director's plane arrived at the Lebanese Air Force base in Rayak, in the Bekaa Valley, rather than at Beirut Airport. Security worries. The experts from Langley thought it was too dangerous to fly the 707 in over the Palestinian refugee camps at Sabra and Shatilla that adjoined the northern edge of the airport. The experts seemed to imagine that Palestinian camp dwellers were in the habit of firing surface-to-air missiles, willy-nilly, at passing airplanes.

Hoffman went to the airport to meet the VIPs. He was dressed in his best gray suit, which unfortunately was fifteen years old and no longer fit very well. He buttoned the trousers below his stomach, leaving an abundant expanse of white shirt that was not quite covered by his suit jacket. To make matters worse, the collar button of Hoffman's white shirt popped as he was trying to close it just before the plane touched down.

The Director stood at the top of the stairs and looked out at the massed limousines, the bus for lower-ranking aides, the official greeters with pasted-on smiles, and the crocodillic faces of the American ambassador and his wife, poised in a welcoming tableau.

"Frank, come on up here," bellowed the Director to Hoffman. Hoffman loyally bounded up the ramp to his boss.

"No more tours!" said the Director.

"What?" said Hoffman.

"*No more tours,* God-damn it!" said the Director. "I've had enough sightseeing this week to last a lifetime. If I see another Roman ruin I'm going to call in artillery and close air support. Understand? My wife is even sicker of touring than I am, aren't you, dear?" The Director's wife nodded.

"Okay," said Hoffman. "But would you mind telling that to the ambassador yourself?"

"Yes, I would mind," said the Director. "You do it. That's part of your job. Tell him whatever you like. But *no more tours!*"

Hoffman led the Director and his wife down the stairs and over to the Wiggs, who were waiting stiffly, smiles affixed. There was the usual round of handshakes and pleasantries. How was the trip? Isn't the weather lovely? As the Director and his wife prepared to head for their car, the ambassador spoke up again. He seemed to want to discuss the schedule.

"We are *so* looking forward to the round of visits we have planned for you, Director," said Ambassador Wigg.

"And we're *so* eager to show you our Lebanon," said Mrs. Wigg, clasping the Director's wife gently on the arm. "This is quite a country, you know. Skiing in the morning and swimming in the afternoon. And the nightlife is magnificent. They call it 'The Paris of the Orient.' Did you know that? It will be such fun."

The Director coughed, not very convincingly.

"The Director is feeling a little, uh, sick," said Hoffman.

"What a nuisance," said Mrs. Wigg. "I hope that won't spoil our plans."

"Uh, actually, the Director's wife is also feeling a little under the weather. Quite sick, actually."

The Director's wife coughed on cue.

"Afraid so," said the Director. "We're feeling a bit of a chill right now. If you'll excuse us."

The Director took his wife by the arm and together they

followed Stone and a bodyguard toward a waiting limousine.

"What a shame!" said the ambassador to Hoffman. He sounded crestfallen. Mrs. Wigg was fuming, too angry for the moment to protest.

"I hope it isn't serious," said Ambassador Wigg. "What sort of illness do they have, exactly?"

"We'll get back to you on that," called out Hoffman as he opened the door of the limousine and prepared to depart.

"Gun it!" said Hoffman to the driver, and off they roared, leaving behind the befuddled ambassador and his wife, the motorcycle outriders, and the secretaries, code clerks, and hangers-on.

"So what's the big deal?" asked Hoffman later that day when the Director and Stone arrived in the bubble, the bug-proof room within a room where the station held its most secret discussions. Rogers was also there, at Stone's request.

"Just the usual skulduggery," said the Director. "Before we start, Frank, I wonder if I could have a Tab?"

"What's a Tab?" asked Hoffman.

"It's a soft drink," said the Director. "A dietetic soft drink."

"I'm afraid we don't have any of those in Lebanon, sir," said Hoffman. "I can check, but I kind of doubt that we can find any."

"Don't bother," said the Director. "How about a Sprite?"

Hoffman looked at Rogers quizzically. Evidently he didn't know what a Sprite was, either.

"Tom," said Hoffman. "See if you can find a Sprite for the Director."

Rogers left the room. He returned a few moments later with a bottle of Seven-Up and a straw.

"That's just fine," said the Director. "Thank you, Tom."

"So what's up?" asked Hoffman.

"I think we have an opportunity to do a favor for our Israeli friends," said the Director.

"Oh yeah?" said Hoffman, already slightly on guard. "What's that?"

"I understand you're running a Palestinian agent who is a member of Black September. Is that right?"

"What our boys do on their own time is up to them," said Hoffman.

The Director didn't laugh.

"Is he a member of Black September?"

"Beats me," said Hoffman. "Tom?"

"Yes, probably he is," said Rogers.

"Why don't you ask Mr. Stone?" said Hoffman. "He knows this case as well as we do. He was in the room when the little pecker agreed to work with us. Isn't that right, Mr. Stone? In fact, if memory serves, Mr. Stone was not entirely uninvolved in the recruitment."

"I'm quite aware of Edward's involvement, Frank, and I don't question what anyone has done up to this point."

"You don't?" asked Hoffman warily.

"No," said the Director.

"Good," said Hoffman. "Because we haven't done anything wrong. Least of all Tom Rogers, who has done a first-rate job on this case from the beginning."

"Of course. The point is that now we have an opportunity to do something useful with the leverage we have acquired through our contacts with this fellow."

"Such as?"

"Edward," said the Director, turning to Stone. "Why don't you explain the interesting discussion we had in Tel Aviv?"

"Yes, Director," said Stone. He looked embarrassed.

"The Israelis seem to have stumbled onto the fact that we have a relationship with Ramlawi."

"So what?" said Hoffman. "Who we talk to is none of their fucking business."

"Perhaps, but in this case, they believe that we're dealing with someone who is planning terrorist operations against Israel. They even seem to think that Ramlawi was behind the Munich hostage incident."

"Tough shit," said Hoffman.

Stone shot a glance at Hoffman, as if to say: Calm down, boy. But it did little good. Hoffman was angry. Rogers watched the conversation unfold with a sense of dread. Another station chief might have tried to duck the issue, say what was politically sensible, cover his ass. But not Hoffman.

The Director spoke up.

"The Israelis have asked for our help in dealing with Black

September. They have implied, but not said directly, that they would like us to do one of two things: either provide them with some of the intelligence we're getting from Ramlawi, or help them find him."

"And suppose we tell them to fuck off?" said Hoffman.

"They have made it clear that they intend to kill the leaders of Black September, including Ramlawi."

"What did you tell them, Director, if you don't mind my asking?"

"I told them that we would get back to them."

"I trust, sir, that you didn't in any way confirm their speculation that we have been in contact with Ramlawi?"

"Of course not," said the Director. "That would be unprofessional."

"You're God-damned right it would be, sir," said Hoffman.

The Director narrowed his eyes. He was a man who prided himself on his composure. He displayed emotion rarely, and only when he was very angry.

"Easy, Frank," said Stone gently.

"I apologize, Director. But this whole conversation makes me very uneasy, to be honest."

"And why is that?" asked the Director.

"Because what the Israelis are proposing is totally outrageous. We should be telling them to take a walk, instead of driving ourselves crazy like this. Ramlawi may be the biggest shit who ever lived. But he met with us in good faith. We shouldn't throw him to the wolves now, just because it may be expedient. When we decide to work with someone, we make an implicit promise that we're not going to shop him to the next guy that comes along."

"Oh come now," said the Director. "Let's grow up. We shop people every day. That's part of our business."

That remark seemed to touch an especially raw nerve in Hoffman. He grew red in the face.

"I don't need any lectures about the real world, Director. I may not have gone to Yale, it's true. But that doesn't mean I don't understand the way the world works. I've been running agents for nearly thirty years. In that time, I have screwed enough people simply because someone from Yale told me to. I don't want to do it again."

"Don't press your luck, Mr. Hoffman," said the Director.

Hoffman ignored the warning.

"We used to have a saying in the FBI," he said. "It was very simple: 'Protect your sources.' Even the dumbest FBI agent understands that. He knows that when someone trusts you, you don't knife him in the back. But I guess we're too smart for that in the agency."

The Director, who had regained his own composure, affected a weary look.

"Frank, we needn't turn this into group therapy. It's very simple. The Israelis have asked for our help. I have decided that we should respond positively. The only question you need to think about is how to carry it out."

"Carry what out?"

"Provide the Israelis the information they want about Ramlawi."

"So they can kill our agent?"

"I have no idea what they will do with the information." That's their problem."

"Let them get their own fucking information."

"Frank," said the Director. "This isn't a debating topic. It is an order."

Hoffman stood up from the conference table. His tie was hanging loose in his collar because of the popped shirt button, and his belly had pushed out even farther over the tops of his trousers. He looked exhausted. He strolled to the translucent wall of the bubble, deep in thought, while Rogers, Stone, and the Director watched in silence. All of them were dreading what they knew was coming next.

"I'm sorry to sound like a troublemaker, Director," said Hoffman slowly. "But what you're proposing to me just doesn't sound right. I wish I could just tell you what you want to hear. But just this morning I was telling my staff that anyone who lies to the Director ought to be fired, on the spot. So I have to tell you the truth, which is that I don't feel comfortable about shopping Ramlawi to the Israelis. Even if it is an order."

Rogers took a deep breath. He felt as if he had just heard someone dictate his resignation letter.

"What about you, Tom?" said the Director to Rogers. "You're Ramlawi's case officer. Do you feel the same way as Frank?"

"Can't we keep the kid out of it?" asked Hoffman.

"I'd like to answer the question," said Rogers.

"Don't," said Hoffman. "You have a good career. Don't screw it up."

Rogers ignored Hoffman's advice and turned to the Director. His voice was calm and even.

"I agree with Frank," said Rogers. "I don't think we should betray Ramlawi. I think the Israelis will understand. They don't betray their agents, even to help their friends. And we shouldn't either."

Stone, who had watched the confrontation develop during the last few minutes and move nearer and nearer to an irrevocable break, decided at this point to intervene.

"Perhaps we should take a breather for a few moments," he suggested. "Cool off a bit."

"Very well," said the Director.

"With your permission," said Stone quietly to the Director, "I would like to have a few words with you privately."

The Director nodded. Hoffman and Rogers left the room.

"What in heaven's name is wrong with Frank Hoffman?" asked the Director when he and Stone were alone. "That was virtual insubordination a few moments ago."

"Yes, sir," said Stone. "I know."

"Well, what are we going to do about it?"

"Director," said Stone gently, "we are on the verge of losing two very fine men. Before we get to that point, I think you ought to listen to what they're saying. Frank gets a little emotional sometimes, but he means well. And Rogers is one of our best young officers."

"So everyone keeps telling me. I was inclined to agree until about five minutes ago."

"Maybe Rogers has a point."

"What?"

"Maybe he has a point. The Israelis certainly don't tell us who their agents are. They might lose respect for us if we betray one of ours."

"Lose respect?" said the Director. "I doubt that very much. People don't lose respect when you help them. They're grateful."

"Not always. Not if you're doing something questionable."

"Edward," said the Director sharply. "Aren't you losing sight of the fact that we are running an agent who may be the world's leading terrorist? Doesn't that make you a little squeamish?"

"A little," said Stone. "But that's water over the dam."

"Not over my dam."

"We made the decision to deal with him, on the assumption that it would help save American lives. Already he has given us some useful information, and we stand to get far more. Whether the decision to work with him was right or wrong, we made it. And I'm not sure that we should go back on it."

"The rebellion in the ranks appears to be growing," said the Director.

"Let's look at the practical side of this."

"Yes, let's."

"If you order Hoffman to turn over intelligence on Ramlawi, he'll quit."

"Evidently. Fine old fellow. Gone to seed a bit in Beirut. Sorry to see him go. Next."

"If you order Rogers to turn over intelligence on Ramlawi, I suspect that he will also quit."

"Pity. A fine career ahead of him. He would be foolish to do so. But I can't stop him. So that's the end of it."

Stone swallowed hard. He had hoped the discussion would not reach this point. He thought, momentarily, about his pension, his friends, his career ambitions, and then plunged ahead. There was no stopping now.

"There is one final item, Director."

"What is that?"

"If you order me to turn over the intelligence on Ramlawi, I will also quit. With great sadness and reluctance. But I will not carry out an order that I think you will have cause to regret later."

The Director was dumbstruck.

"You can't be serious," he said after a moment's reflection.

"I am."

"But I don't *want* you to leave. I trust your judgment. I depend on you."

"Then listen to me."

"Very well," said the Director.

"I think I can suggest a sensible compromise."

The Director's demeanor changed at the mention of the word "compromise." His face perked up, and you could almost see him adjusting and refiguring his mental calculus of the Ramlawi problem.

"I'm listening," said the Director.

"The compromise is very simple. We won't help the Israelis kill Ramlawi. But we won't help Ramlawi stay alive, either. We will do our best to stay neutral in this war."

"What do we tell the Israelis?"

"We tell them that of course we'll help them. They are our friends and allies. And then we give them something that has nothing to do with Ramlawi. COMINT. Or satellite photos. They're always asking for satellite photos."

"And if they ask specifically about Ramlawi?"

"Tell them you don't know what they're talking about. We never met the man."

The Director looked at his nails, examining them for dirt.

"That is not unreasonable," he said eventually.

There was a knock at the door.

"Let them in," said the Director.

"Stone and I have come up with a plan," said the Director. "Something that will be responsive to our Israeli friends without offending the delicate sensibilities of the Beirut station. Edward, why don't you explain what we intend to do?"

Stone gave a brief explanation of his plan. The only thing that was clear when he had finished was that the crisis of a few minutes ago was over. Rogers relaxed and smiled with relief. But Hoffman looked more taciturn, and spent much of the rest of the meeting staring at the walls.

39

Beirut; October–November 1972

The dinner party that night for the Director and his wife went
ahead according to schedule. It was hosted by Ambassador
and Mrs. Wigg, who swallowed their pride and decided to
ignore the rebuke at the airport. There was a lenghty guest
list: Frank and Gladys Hoffman; Tom and Jane Rogers; Youssef Majnoun, the head of the Lebanese Deuxième Bureau, and
his wife Brigitte; the recently appointed deputy chief of the
Deuxième Bureau, Samir Fares, and his wife Hoda; Edward
Stone, who was accompanying the Director; and as an extra
woman to make the table come out right, Solange Jezzine, the
estranged wife of the former head of the Deuxième Bureau.

It was a pleasant enough evening. The American men
seemed a bit tired, especially Frank Hoffman. The chief of the
Deuxième Bureau, Majnoun, was so intent on impressing the
Director that he made a nuisance of himself. Samir Fares and
his wife were clever and witty and made a favorable impression on everyone, most of all the American intelligence officers at the table, who had been paying Fares a generous
stipend the last several years.

What the Director himself seemed to enjoy most was his
conversation in the drawing room after dinner with the charming extra woman, Madame Jezzine. She was radiant: dressed
in a stunning low-cut gown that showed off her figure, and
wearing her hair up off her shoulders in a way that highlighted
her long neck and cheekbones. She looked, the Director remarked to Mrs. Wigg, like an Arab princess.

Solange flirted elegantly with the Director, asking him about his athletic interests, expressing astonishment about his age. Jane Rogers, deep in conversation with Edward Stone about life in Beirut, couldn't help overhearing the conversation and admiring the wiles and beauty of her friend Solange. The Director himself seemed ready enough to spend the rest of the evening with the Lebanese beauty. So he was dismayed when, after twenty minutes of conversation, Solange Jezzine excused herself and strolled out toward the garden, where Tom Rogers was talking to Samir Fares.

"Am I interrupting anything?" asked Madame Jezzine.

"Oh no," said Fares. "I was just telling Mr. Rogers about the village where I was born. He must be very bored hearing about Lebanese villages. Why don't you rescue him?"

"Happily," said Solange.

"Would you like another drink, Tom?" asked Fares.

"No thanks," said Rogers. "We have to be leaving soon."

Fares walked inside, leaving the two of them alone in the garden.

"Why have you been avoiding me?" asked Solange. She asked the question like a spoiled little girl, her lips pouting.

"I haven't," said Rogers.

"Yes you have, and you shouldn't!" said Solange. She had slipped her arm through Rogers's and was walking him slowly down a gravel path in the garden, away from the house and the light.

Rogers felt his heart beating. He felt dreamy and light-headed. It was pleasant, for once, to be in the power of someone else's personality. Solange leaned her head a little closer to his as they walked along the path. He could smell the perfume behind her ear.

Solange stopped. She turned her head up toward Rogers and spoke in a whisper.

"I'm on fire," she said.

She kissed him on the mouth. Or he kissed her. It was impossible to know which. As they kissed, Solange put her arm around Rogers's neck and gently stroked the hair at the nape of his neck. Rogers felt himself becoming aroused, which embarrassed him. Solange pressed tighter against him for a moment, as if to say, Yes, I feel it. I want it. Then she pulled away, smiling coyly and regally.

"You must visit me," she said. She kissed him gently on the cheek and walked alone back toward the house.

Rogers composed himself. When he returned to the drawing room, the party was breaking up. The Director, deprived of Madame Jezzine's company, had suddenly become tired and was saying his goodbyes to the Wiggs.

Jane Rogers was still rapt in conversation with Stone. It turned out that Stone had known Jane's father, the Colonel, in London during the war. Jane was explaining, in a low voice, the volunteer work she had been doing with Palestinian women at the Makassed Hospital, which Stone heartily approved. The two of them were hoisting a second glass of brandy when Rogers walked over and mentioned that it was getting late. Jane gave Stone a kiss, said goodnight, and went upstairs to get her coat.

"Marvellous woman," said Stone to Rogers. "I knew her father in the war."

What a wonderful evening it was, said Jane as they were driving home. What a fine man Mr. Stone was.

"He saved my job today, I think," said Rogers. Jane waited for him to explain, and when he didn't she assumed that it was one of those things that her husband would tell her, if he could.

A week after the Director's visit, Hoffman left on a trip to Saudi Arabia. The trip had come up suddenly, he said. He would be back in a few days. Rogers felt uneasy. Hoffman had kept to himself since the meeting with the Director and Stone, and whenever Rogers had tried to draw him out, Hoffman had made a crude joke or otherwise evaded Rogers's queries.

Hoffman looked ebullient when he returned. He stopped by Rogers's office on his way back from the airport and Rogers thought at first that it was a practical joke. Hoffman was wearing a well-cut silk suit and smoking a fat Cuban cigar.

"How do I look?" asked Hoffman. "Like a million dollars, right?"

"You look great," said Rogers. "What happened in Riyadh? Did you hit the daily double at the camel races?"

"Better than that," said Hoffman. "Much better than that."

"What's better than money?" asked Rogers.

"Even more money!" said Hoffman. "And that's what you're looking at!"

"Maybe you should explain what's going on," said Rogers.

"Gladly," said Hoffman. And with a flourish, he withdrew a business card from his coat pocket and handed it to Rogers.

"Arab-American Security Consultants, Inc.," read the card. "Frank Hoffman, President."

"Oh shit!" said Rogers.

"You don't like the name?" said Hoffman. "I was going to call it 'AA-Arab-American Security Consultants,' so it would be first in the telephone book. But then I realized that the Arabs don't have telephone books, so what would be the use?"

"I'm not talking about the card," said Rogers. "I'm talking about the fact that you're quitting the agency. I can't believe it."

"Oh that," said Hoffman. "You'll get used to it."

"No I won't," said Rogers.

"Have it your way," said Hoffman. He was relighting his cigar.

"What happened? When did you do it? I thought everything had been settled between you and the Director."

"Let's face it," said Hoffman. "I had to quit. I mean, really, how could I stay after what happened? I had no business talking to the Director like that. In an outfit like ours, you obey orders or you quit. It's that simple. The Director should have fired me for insubordination. I decided to save him the trouble."

"Wait a minute," said Rogers. "Aren't you being a little easy on the Director?"

"Maybe," said Hoffman. "But I'll tell you the truth. The Director may have been out of line the other day. But it isn't really his fault. The truth is that this is a rotten business. You do terrible things and usually you don't think about it. And then one day, you just get sick of it. You decide you just don't want to eat another bite of the shit sandwich."

"So what are you going to do?"

"Security! Didn't you read the card?"

"Yeah. But what does it mean?"

"For starters," said Hoffman, "it means taking very large amounts of money from Saudi princes who are terrified that their Arab brethren are going to cut their throats. I intend to sell these gutless bastards the latest in security technology. Whatever will help them continue whoring and drinking in reasonable safety. Bodyguards, bullet-proof limousines, alarm systems. How the fuck should I know? I've only been in this business a few days."

"So that's why you went to Saudi Arabia."

"We call it client development, in my new line of work," said Hoffman. "And I'll tell you, the Saudis are ready to be developed. The way I figure things, the richer they get, the more scared they'll get, which means more money for yours truly. After just one trip, I have already lined up contracts worth nearly a million bucks. How does that grab you, junior?"

"Frank, there is nobody in the world I would rather see get rich than you."

"Don't suppose you'd like to join me in this raid on the Saudi treasury? I could use a partner."

"I don't think so," said Rogers. "I'm not quite ready to pack it in here."

"Go fuck yourself then."

"Have you told the front office yet?"

"Of course I have," said Hoffman indignantly. "Just because I've become a businessman doesn't mean I've become dishonest. I told the Director and Stone ten days ago, just before they left Beirut."

"They certainly kept it to themselves," said Rogers.

"They're that way, if you hadn't noticed. They don't tell the troops any more than they have to."

Rogers looked at Hoffman, resplendent in his new suit, a silk handkerchief in his pocket, a pair of expensive alligator shoes on his feet. Rogers shook his head. There was something he didn't quite understand.

"You know, Frank, somehow I never imagined you as a businessman. In fact, it never really occured to me that you were all that interested in making money."

"Life is full of surprises, kid," said Hoffman. "Sometimes we do things for no reason other than the simple fact that we fucking well feel like it. And do you know what? It feels good."

With that, Hoffman headed off to his own office, a bou-

quet of flowers in his hand to give to his secretary, Miss Pugh.
Rogers looked at the card in his hand, bearing the imprint of
Arab-American Security Consultants, and laughed from deep
in his gut, for what seemed like the first time in a very long
while.

Several days after Hoffman's announcement that he was
quitting, Rogers travelled to the mountains east of Beirut to
meet with Samir Fares of the Deuxième Bureau. It was a
routine meeting, intended partly to reassure Fares and his colleagues in the Lebanese intelligence service that Hoffman's
departure didn't imply any change in agency policy toward
Lebanon or the Middle East.

On his way back, Rogers did something that, for him, was
very unusual. He acted on impulse.

He was driving along the road looking at the scenery when
it occurred to him that he was near the village where the Jezzines lived. And he decided, without really thinking about it
very much, without considering the consequences for his marriage or his life or anything else, to stop and pay a visit to
Solange Jezzine. He had dreamed often enough about having
an affair with her, in a casual sort of way. But his idle fanta-
sizing had very little to do with the deliberate, impulsive decision that day to turn the wheel of the car hard to the right,
head down a different road in the Lebanese mountains, and
step on the gas pedal. It had less to do, at that moment, with
sexual desire than with curiosity, an impulse to do something
different, whose outcome wasn't predictable or even under his
control.

As Rogers drove the car up the cedar-lined drive toward
the Jezzines' house, he felt his heart racing. Gone were the
tough-looking young men with automatic weapons who used
to police the grounds in the old days, when General Jezzine
ran the Deuxième Bureau. Manning the front gate instead was
an older man who looked like a gardener.

Rogers gave his name to the gatekeeper, who phoned to the
big house on an intercom and then waved Rogers through.
Rogers parked his car in front of the great stone mansion.
There was no sign of the general, or of anyone else, for that
matter. As Rogers stepped out of the car, he saw a woman's
face peering down at him from an upstairs window.

He rang the bell. A maid answered the door and escorted him to the living room, where she asked him to wait. There was a great stack of European fashion magazines on the coffee table. Rogers admired the pictures. Many of the women, he thought, had the same radiant and exotic look as Solange. He turned the pages. His palms were moist. The maid returned after five minutes carrying a vellum envelope on a silver tray. It was like the letter she had sent Rogers many months ago. Crisp and creamy and tied with a red ribbon. Inside the envelope was a note: "My darling. You have come to me at last. In a few minutes, I am yours."

The seduction began as Rogers sat there on the couch, the vellum notepaper in his hand, imagining Solange. He could see her body. The long curves of her legs, the gentle slope of her thighs, the fullness of her breasts, the radiance of her face. The scent of her body, not just the perfume bought in Paris, but the fragrance of olive and jasmine on her skin. The look of her eyes, so deep and dark, inviting pleasure and seduction.

There was a sound on the stairs. Rogers turned and saw her walking toward him, dressed in a silk robe, even more beautiful than he had imagined. Her lips were open in the shape of a kiss. She walked toward Rogers silently, took his hand in hers, and led him to a room that had once been the library, but had now been made over into a kind of harem chamber. There were no couches, only large pillows on the floor. A broad shaft of light streamed through the filmy curtains that covered the windows, and there was a slight breeze blowing.

Solange closed the door and locked it. Rogers moved toward her hungrily, but she held up a finger, bidding him to stop. I will take you, her eyes said. She took his hand and led him to one of the large pillows and bade him sit down. She took his shoes off, one by one. Then his socks. She unbuttoned his shirt, one button at a time, then gently unfastened his trousers. She was a courtesan now, kneeling gracefully on the floor before Rogers. As she leaned toward him, Rogers glimpsed through her silk robe the curve of her breasts. She was all softness.

When Rogers was naked, Solange rose from the floor and stood silently before him. She slid the silk robe off her shoulders so that it clung briefly to her breasts and then fell gently to the floor. She was perfectly naked except for a gold chain around her waist, hanging low on the curve of her belly.

Rogers thought momentarily of the consequences of this act of pleasure and disorder. But only a moment.

"Come to me," said Solange Jezzine as she arranged herself on one of the fat pillows on the floor. And Rogers did. He surrendered himself entirely to the woman, her beauty, her eroticism. He closed his eyes and felt a wave of pleasure. It was a heady feeling, like falling from a great height in a dream.

PART IX

June 1978 –
January 1979

40

Washington; June 1978

"The most competent intelligence service in the world today is the Mossad," proclaimed John Marsh from the podium of a small conference hall in Arlington, Virginia. "It pains me to say that after all these years, but it's true."

There was a burst of applause from the audience of conservative intellectuals, Republican congressional aides, trusted diplomats, and former intelligence officers who had gathered for a conference hosted by the Center for the Study of Responsive Intelligence. The Center was a sort of organized cheerleading section for the old-boy network of the Central Intelligence Agency. It seemed to exist chiefly for the purpose of holding conferences to excoriate the current CIA management, especially the new Director, Charles "Chuck" Hinkle.

The topic of this particular gathering was "Rebuilding the CIA: How and Why." John Marsh—recently retired from the agency—was the featured speaker. Dressed in a blue pinstripe suit, his hair slicked back against his head, Marsh looked slightly like a gangster. He wagged a finger at his audience as he continued with his lecture.

"You all know what has happened to CIA," Marsh admonished them. "The agency has been raked over the coals by its critics. Its secrets have been exposed for all the world to see. It is the laughing stock of the other Western intelligence agencies. It is a sad, sad story.

"Certainly there were misdeeds in the past. Certainly there were some overzealous officers and unwise operations. And certainly there are things that need to be corrected. Nobody questions that. There is always room for improvement. But can't we all agree that there are limits to responsible criticism? Shouldn't our critics in Congress and the press remember that without a strong intelligence agency, they wouldn't have the freedom to be so critical?"

There was more applause from the audience. A twenty-five-year-old congressional aide, dressed in a green Dartmouth blazer, shouted "Hear! Hear!" Marsh realized that he was rather enjoying his new life as a public speaker.

"I would like to share a little secret of my own with this group," said Marsh. "Nothing classified, of course. I wouldn't do that, not even for a gathering of friends. But I would like to tell you, in my own words, why I left the CIA several months ago after nearly twenty years with the agency.

"As many of you know, I spent most of the 1970s working on congressional liaison for the agency. Our office tried to keep Congress from opening Pandora's box, and I must admit to you that we failed. They asked for our dirty linen and, despite the efforts of some of us, the agency gave it to them. Do you know what bothered me most? The fact that we lacked political leadership—in Congress, in the White House, and yes, even at the CIA—that was willing to say no."

There was more applause.

"So after watching this process of self-flagellation, I decided that enough was enough, and I got out."

More applause. Marsh nodded his head in gratitude.

What Marsh said was not precisely true, at least not the part about leaving the agency. It was true that he had spent the 1970s in the backwater of congressional liaison after he was dumped as operations chief of the Near East Division. But he had done poorly even at that modest job. His colleagues complained that he was successful only in dealing with the most conservative members of the House and Senate—preaching, as it were, to the converted. So Marsh was removed from congressional liaison, brought back to Langley in a dead-end desk job in the Office of Security. And finally, when he neared the twenty-year mark, Marsh was offered early retirement with a generous pension, and took it.

"What we see at the CIA is just another example of our national disorder," continued Marsh. "We see it in every area

of our national life. There is a lack of discipline in our
schools, on college campuses, in the news media. There is a
lack of control. A feeling of drift and uncertainty. A feeling
that we're being pushed around at home and abroad."

Marsh was nearing the end of his speech. He put his hands
on either side of the lectern, like a sea captain holding the
wheel steady in rough seas. Though his audience didn't know
it, he—John Marsh—knew what he was talking about when
he spoke of the anarchy of the times. His own family was in
chaos. His daughter had dropped out of college to join a com-
mune. His son had been expelled from private school because
he was caught using drugs.

But John Marsh wasn't talking about his own problems
that day, he was talking about America's.

"We need to stand firm," said Marsh. "We need to stop the
decay. And the place to begin is with our intelligence agencies, which are the sword and shield that protect our free-
doms."

There was loud and sustained applause, followed by many
congratulatory remarks from people who gathered around the
podium. A conservative newspaper columnist asked Marsh for
a copy of the speech. The director of the Center for the Study
of Responsive Intelligence suggested the possibility of Marsh
joining his staff. A professor approached Marsh and asked for
his help with a book he was writing about Soviet intelligence
operations.

The scene testified to one truth about Washington in the
late 1970s. The conservatives had learned the arts of leaking
and self-promotion. And in the process, some of the old discipline had gone. The conservative intelligence officers who
had spent their careers protecting the nation's secrets were
now, in retirement, spending their days taking journalists to
lunch, issuing learned reports on intelligence matters for
friendly think tanks, writing position papers for political can-
didates. Something had come unstuck.

As the meeting began to disperse, a short, balding man
approached Marsh. He had a face that was slightly reddish
and freckled, and eyes as sharp as a hawk's.

"What an interesting speech," said the man in a voice that
had a trace of a European accent. "But I think maybe you
flatter us Israelis too much."

He handed Marsh a card.

"My name is Shuval," said the man. "I work at the Israeli Embassy."

Marsh shook his hand.

"Perhaps we could have lunch sometime," said Shuval. Marsh, basking in the attention, accepted the offer, and he was pleased when several days later, Shuval called and suggested a time and place.

Ze'ev Shuval was the chief of the Mossad station in Washington. In contacting Marsh, he had a particular purpose in mind, one assigned to him by the terrorism adviser to the new Israeli prime minister. The task was to reopen a matter that had lain dormant for the last few years—the question of American penetration of the PLO—and find out as much as he could about a particular suspected agent.

The new Israeli government was considering reviving an old plan, the terrorism adviser had explained to Shuval. They wanted to finish the job that had been started six years ago—of punishing those who were responsible for the Munich massacre. There was one man still alive—the man who had planned the operation, in fact—and that was deeply troubling to the new Israeli government.

"We need to know whether this man is still under CIA control," the adviser told Shuval. "We aren't afraid of offending the Americans if we have to. But we want to give them a chance to say no. And maybe it is not so bad for us if this contact between the Americans and the PLO is broken."

The terrorism adviser gave Shuval a list of people who might know details of the case. At the top of the list was the name of John Marsh.

They met at an out-of-the-way Chinese restaurant off Wisconsin Avenue, in Bethesda. Only one other table was filled.

"We admired your work very much," said Shuval quietly when they had been seated. "Especially when you were handling the Near East. We were shocked when you changed jobs."

Marsh was flattered. It had been many years since another intelligence officer had praised his work.

"I tried to do what I thought was right. But others disagreed with my views."

"So I gather," said Shuval. He didn't push the point. He didn't push anything.

The waiter arrived and took their orders. Marsh deliberated between Szechuan beef and Hunan beef and then decided to have duck with orange sauce. Shuval ordered egg foo yung.

"I don't suppose that you would be interested in doing some consulting work?" asked Shuval.

"I'm afraid not," said Marsh. "Thanks for the offer, but I don't think that would be appropriate."

"Of course. I simply wanted to ask you the question."

"Just so we understand each other," said Marsh. "You ask and I answer. That's the way I like things. Straightforward, on the table, yes or no. I think we get into trouble in our business when we forget the basics."

"We look at things the same way," replied Shuval. "That is what frightens us about our dealings with America. Often, they are not businesslike. We never know exactly where we stand."

Marsh nodded earnestly. He felt that he had found a soulmate. This is why the Israelis are the best, he told himself. Because they understand that intelligence is a business, a business in which control is paramount.

"We worry," continued Shuval, "that in the end the United States will betray us. They will keep assuring us until the last moment that they will never abandon us to make a deal with the Arabs. And then they will abandon us and make the deal."

"Not if your friends have anything to say about it."

"You are kind," said Shuval. "But I will give you an example of what worries us." He leaned forward over the table.

"We think that in the end you will make a deal with the Palestinians. You will get tired of terrorism and the threat of an oil embargo and so you will make a deal with the PLO. We see signs of it already."

"What signs?"

"I will give you one example," said Shuval matter-of-factly. "We have assumed for some years now that you have an agent at the top of Fatah named Jamal Ramlawi."

"No comment," said Marsh.

"It makes us very nervous, this relationship."

"No comment," repeated Marsh.

"You know that we tried to kill this fellow Ramlawi more than once? Not because he was working for you, but because he was a terrorist."

"I am aware that you tried to kill him, yes."

"And we may try again. But we have a question that troubles us. Is this man actually an American agent? And if he is, why can't you control him? Why does he seem able to do as he likes?"

"Control him?" asked Marsh. "Did you say, control him?"

"Yes. Control."

"That's the problem," said Marsh, almost inaudibly. "We never had control."

"I see," said Shuval. He closed his eyes and thought for a moment, then opened them and smiled.

"You understand of course that I am not at liberty to discuss the case," said Marsh.

"Of course I understand," said Shuval. "And I wouldn't ask you to."

"Good," said Marsh. He was relieved. Relieved to have hinted to someone, at last, what had gone so wrong that day in Rome long ago. And relieved that he had not "said anything."

They finished the meal in pleasant conversation and agreed to meet again.

"It is a pleasure to deal with a professional," said Shuval, knowing precisely the right button to push with John Marsh.

Shuval filed a cable for the prime minister's office that afternoon. The cable advised that a CIA source with first-hand knowledge of the Ramlawi operation had suggested that Ramlawi was not a controlled American agent, after all, but something different. The implication of that was obvious: Go ahead. Do it! Kill him! The prime minister's terrorism adviser certainly took that view. But the chief of Mossad, Natan Porat, was more cautious. He wanted to take another pass at the Americans. In particular, one specific American.

41

London; September 1978

Levi checked into a small hotel in Sussex Gardens, just north of Hyde Park. It wasn't even a hotel, really, more like a bed and breakfast. The administration department at the Institute in Tel Aviv had booked the room. They said it was more secure than a real hotel, but that was nonsense. It was cheaper. Levi didn't complain. In those days of the plummeting Israeli shekel, a trip to London under any circumstances was a treat.

The Israeli intelligence officer unpacked his bag and, when he was done, looked at himself in the mirror. He had put on a few pounds in the last several years, so that his body no longer looked as if it had been wracked on a torture machine. And he was losing his hair. He stood before the mirror and combed several long strands of hair carefully across the top of his head.

He decided to take a walk. His route took him down Sussex Gardens, past the rows of tourist buses from Holland and France, to the Bayswater Road. Sidewalk artists were lined up against the wrought-iron fence bordering Hyde Park, hawking their wares to gullible passers-by. The art works were hideous: tangled constructions of metal that resembled air-conditioner parts more than sculpture; stylized paintings of waves pounding the seashore at sunset; the inevitable portraits of winsome, malnourished children and fluffy cats playing with balls of string.

Levi entered Hyde Park and ambled toward the body of

water known as the Serpentine. He was thinking about Rogers, trying to imagine where he was, what he was thinking. It was an old game for Levi, one he had been playing for nearly ten years. He liked to put himself in Rogers's place, holding the same cards that Rogers did, trying to imagine how he would play the hand. If Levi had the American network of agents in the Middle East, how would he run them? Would he encourage them to work for peace with Israel? Or would he advise them to be militantly anti-Israel, to protect their cover?

And if one of his agents proved to be a terrorist, what would he do about it? Probably nothing, Levi decided. There was always a good argument for doing nothing.

Levi walked along the bank of the Serpentine. Ducks were paddling in the muddy water. Other ducks were waddling off to join their mates asleep on the grass.

The question at hand, Levi reminded himself, was not what he would do if he ran the American networks in the Middle East, but what Rogers would do. What would the great Rogers do, for example, if an officer of the Israeli security service approached him out of the blue in London and hinted that the Israelis were reviving an old plan to kill the CIA's man in the PLO? What would he say? What emotions would he betray?

Levi headed back toward his hotel, crossing the dirt path that circles Hyde Park. A group of girls on horseback were trotting by, led by a riding master with a prim face and tall black boots. The horses never broke into a canter, let alone a gallop. That was forbidden in Hyde Park. Just a slow, steady trot.

The Rogers game was of more than academic interest for Levi that day. After nearly ten years of imagining his American counterpart, Levi was finally going to meet him. They were both scheduled to attend an anti-terrorism conference hosted by the British Foreign Office. Levi felt nervous, like a voyeur who has watched and imagined someone in secret a thousand times, and is finally about to shake his hand.

The Arabs were everywhere in London that September. In the fancy shops on Knightsbridge buying suits and shoes; in the less fancy shops on Oxford Street buying television sets; even in Marks & Spencer's buying underwear. They were the perfect parvenus: incalculably rich and desperately insecure at the same time. They were a merchant's dream. The jewelers near the Park Lane hotels had learned to expect Arabs walking in off the street with their mistresses and buying, on the spot, diamond necklaces worth $50,000. There seemed to be no upper limit on what the Arabs would pay for something they wanted. The more expensive it was, the more they seemed to like it. Perhaps they realized—better than anyone else—that with the oil boom of the 1970s, the world had gone off balance. Values were askew. The Arabs had a proverb that summed things up well: "When the monkey reigns, dance before him."

At hotels around the city, other security officials were gathering for the terrorism conference. Several Frenchmen from the SDECE, looking tough and cagey as roustabouts at a circus; a small group of West Germans, exceedingly competent but wary of demonstrating it in front of their NATO allies, lest they bring back bad memories; the Italians, led by an elegant, white-haired general named Armani, who had survived so many purges and reorganizations of the Italian security service that he was now regarded as indispensable, even by his enemies. All the conferees, except Levi, had splendid hotel rooms, cars at their disposal, generous expense accounts. Counterterrorism, like oil, was a booming business that year.

Across the Park from Levi, Rogers was checking into a grand hotel on Park Lane. The hotel was embarrassingly opulent. A queue of Rolls-Royces stood waiting out front. The hotel doorman looked disdainfully at any tip smaller than a fiver. Through the lobby marched a series of overdressed blondes, many of them on the arms of men twice or three times their age. Professionals, thought Rogers. One of the women, a blonde in a slit skirt, smiled seductively at Rogers. He looked the other way.

Rogers hadn't really wanted to stay at such a fancy place, but Hoffman had insisted. One of his Saudi clients now owned the hotel, he explained. Why shouldn't they accept his hospitality? If the world was crazy enough to dump all this money in the laps of the Arabs, reasoned Hoffman, the least the Americans could do was enjoy the spillover. Rogers said he would think about it and then booked a room at a more modest hotel, nearer the American Embassy. But when Hoffman asked again—and said that he was flying in himself from Riyadh just to meet Rogers for dinner—Rogers had relented. How could he say no to Hoffman?

The bellman carried his suitcase to the elevator, making conversation about the weather. Rogers was still in a daze from his flight, unshaven, half-asleep, and slightly hung-over.

As the bellman pushed the button for the fifth floor, a stunning woman walked into the elevator. She was most remarkable, with olive skin and dark hair, wearing an elegant Parisian dress and made up in the china-doll way of a Lebanese princess.

It can't be, thought Rogers.

He studied the woman from the side: the curve of her body, the black mascara ringing her eyes, the expensive perfume.

It couldn't be, Rogers thought again.

The elevator doors were closing when a foot, shod in a pair of Bally loafers, kicked them open again. A swarthy man walked in and stood beside the woman. He nuzzled her cheek and whispered in her ear. Rogers strained to hear. The man was talking in Italian and the woman was answering, in Italian. Rogers took a deep breath and exhaled slowly. It was not Solange, after all.

The elevator door opened at the third floor and the couple disappeared down the hall. Rogers felt relieved. That particular wound had taken a long time to heal.

Rogers said the name to himself. Solange Jezzine. What he hadn't reckoned on, the day he plunged from the heights with Solange in his arms, was the loss of self-esteem. It was like breaking a mirror. It destroyed an image of himself. He hadn't paid a price with Jane, at least not directly. That was what Rogers had found so disorienting. He had expected the predictable scene: the jealous wife discovers her husband's infidelity and is shattered by it; the husband confesses his misdeeds and eventually is absolved. But it didn't happen that way. Rogers was instead left alone with his guilty conscience. Jane knew that something was wrong but didn't know what it was. She assumed it had to do with work and didn't press the point. The thought that her husband was sleeping with another woman simply never occurred to her.

That loyalty was at once Rogers's curse and his salvation. Jane had an image of her husband that did not encompass the possibility of infidelity. She regarded him as virtuous and assumed, therefore, that his conduct would be virtuous. It was that simple. Jane's noble image of her husband survived in her mind, but not in Rogers's. And that was the trouble. Rogers found it increasingly painful, as the weeks and months passed, to see this gap between what his wife imagined him to be and what he was. So eventually he confessed. Not to his wife, or to a priest. But to the Near East Division chief, Edward Stone. And he was absolved.

Hoffman greeted Rogers with a loud hello and a bearhug when they met at the entrance to the hotel's Grill Room. This boisterous greeting perturbed some of the other guests waiting to be seated, but Hoffman didn't seem to care. The headwaiter addressed him as "Monsieur Hoffman" and escorted him to a table in the corner, facing the door. Next to them sat an Arab gentleman and a pneumatic blonde in a tight black dress and spike heels.

"I love the bimbos in this hotel," said Hoffman as he sat down.

Rogers laughed. He hadn't seen Hoffman in years, and had missed his raunchy talk and irreverence. Hoffman looked the same, except more so. His girth had increased slightly, but he had a better tailor now, so it was less obvious. He was smoking a gold-tipped cigarette.

"My friend, we live in the age of excess!" said Hoffman.

"Thanks be to Allah," said Rogers in Arabic.

"I will give you one example of very recent vintage— about two hours ago, to be precise—that suggests the depths to which our brethren in the land of Allah have sunk. A tale of greed and depravity. Does that have any interest for a prominent government official such as yourself?"

"Does it involve sex?"

"Of course!" said Hoffman. "And it is personal! This morning I get on the British Airways flight in Dhahran to come see my old friend, Tom Rogers. I take my seat in the first-class compartment intending to get a little shut-eye when a worthy Oriental gentleman sits down beside me. He introduces himself. He's a Saudi. Some sort of prince. Uh-oh, I think. There goes my nap.

"As soon as the plane is airborne, Abdul orders a drink. It's only eight-thirty in the morning, but he wants a whisky sour. An hour later he's smashed and telling me his life's story. What can I do? I figure maybe this will be good for business. So I listen to his bullshit, have a few drinks with him, tell him a few stories. By the time we're over the English Channel, I'm his closest friend in the world. He can't do enough for me.

"'Mr. Frank,' he says to me. 'When we land in London, do you know what I have waiting for me at my hotel?'

"'No, Abdul,' I say. 'I do not.'

"'Mr. Frank, waiting for me at my hotel are two beautiful French whores. And because you and I are such close friends, Mr. Frank, when we get to the airport, I will make a phone call to the hotel.'

"Great, I think. He's going to give one of the girls to me. But, noooo. That's not what he has in mind.

"'Mr. Frank,' he says. 'When we get to London, I will call my friends and get two French whores for *you,* too.'"

"Two?" said Rogers.

"These people are insane!" answered Hoffman. "What's wrong with just *one* fucking French whore, for Christ's sake? Honestly, the Arabs are completely nuts. As I was saying, we live in an age of excess."

The waiter arrived to take their drink orders.

"I'll have a whisky sour," said Hoffman.

Rogers, who didn't actually like whisky sours very much, decided it was futile to resist. It was, as Hoffman said, the age of excess.

"Me too," said Rogers. "A double."

The dining room was filling up with guests. Two men with very long hair arrived. They looked like rock stars.

"Faggots," said Hoffman not very quietly as the two walked past the table.

"How's business at Arab-American Security Consultants?" asked Rogers.

"Great," said Hoffman. "Except we had to change the name to Al-Saud Security Consultants."

"Why?" asked Rogers.

"My Saudi partner decided he liked the other name. What could I do? Everybody down there has a Saudi partner. He's not a bad guy. Spends most of his time in Monte Carlo."

"I gather his name is Al-Saud," said Rogers.

"You got it."

"And you're making money?"

"Tons of it. It's embarrassing, actually. I have never seen suckers like these guys. Guess what our hottest selling item is?"

"Tell me."

"A $10,000 machine that can tell you, when your phone rings, who's calling. So you can decide whether to answer or not."

"That sounds great," said Rogers.

"That's what the Saudis all say when I show it to them. But they're so fucking stupid they don't realize it only works if you pre-program the machine to recognize the telephone numbers of everyone who could possibly call you. And do you know what? They never complain. Sometimes I wonder if they even plug it in. Maybe they just put it on the coffee table as a conversation piece."

"The perfect market."

"It is," said Hoffman. "Although to be honest, I've had a few bombs, too."

"Like what?"

"I had a scheme to import donuts into Saudi Arabia from New Jersey. Fresh, delicious donuts. I had the perfect guy to handle the air freight. We formed a company, Arab-American Aeropastries. I put a lot of money into it. But it was a bust."

"Why?"

"The fucking Saudis don't like donuts, that's why."

The waiter returned with the drinks.

"Do you have any bagels?" asked Hoffman.

"What are bagels, Monsieur Hoffman?" asked the waiter.

"Forget it," said Hoffman.

He took a big swig of his whisky sour.

"How's about you?" asked Hoffman. "I gather through the grapevine that you are a bigshot now."

Rogers looked around him. The Arab at the next table was feeling up his girlfriend under the table and looked entirely preoccupied. There was nobody else close by. Even so, Rogers lowered his voice.

"The grapevine has it wrong," said Rogers. "I am a mere special assistant to the new Director."

"Hinkle?"

"Correct. Chuck Hinkle. Which means I am close to power but have very little of it myself."

"Who is this guy Hinkle, anyway?" asked Hoffman.

"He's a friend of the president. He ran his campaign in California. Years ago he was briefly with the agency under commercial cover, posing as an overseas rep for one of the airlines, so he thinks he knows everything about the business. He's not a bad guy. A little skittish sometimes. Spends too much time lecturing us about management by objectives and other gems of wisdom from the corporate world. But he's learning."

"So what's his game?"

"Technology," said Rogers. "That's everybody's game these days. People are sick of running agents. It's too much work, and if you're not careful you end up in trouble with Congress. People nowadays figure why take the risks. Machines are so nice and clean. They listen in on conversations. They look inside buildings. They take pictures from the sky and then study them and tell you if anything has changed on the ground since the last time they made a pass. You don't have to recruit them, run them, hold their hands when they get nervous. You just turn them on. That's what I spend most of my time on, actually. Technical collection."

"What a waste," said Hoffman, "if you don't mind my saying so."

"I still keep my hand in," said Rogers. "I get to Beirut every year or so for a walk-on with some of our old friends. But I'm basically out of it."

"How's old donkey dick?" asked Hoffman.

"Who?"

"The Palestinian."

"Oh. He's fine. In fact, he has been invaluable to us the last few years."

"Is he still getting as much pussy?" asked Hoffman.

"He's married now," said Rogers.

"So?"

"Seriously," said Rogers. "The guy has been a lifesaver for us since the Lebanese civil war began. We had a bad spell before that. Black September killed two of our diplomats in Khartoum in 1973, and to this day nobody is sure whether our man knew what was going on. But these days he's a hero. You remember the evacuation of the Beirut embassy in 1976? Well, he managed the security for it. He's everybody's buddy now. Even the Christians like dealing with him."

"Yeah, yeah," said Hoffman. "But is he still banging the German girl with the big bazoooms?"

"His secret," continued Rogers, ignoring his former boss, "is that he has built Fatah intelligence up into an outfit that has something to trade."

"You're kidding me. Those guys couldn't pour piss from a boot if the directions were written on the heel."

"Times have changed," said Rogers. "In the last five years, Fatah intelligence has helped save the lives of the leaders of Egypt, Morocco, and Jordan. They trade information with everybody in the Arab world now, and they know everything. They feed it all to our man, and he tells us. It's a gold mine. When he gets information about a plot against one of our diplomats now, do you know what he does with it?"

"What?"

"He sends his own people to arrest the terrorists for violating Fatah policy."

"Bullshit," said Hoffman.

"It's true," said Rogers. "The guy is a hero back at Langley. The Director even invited him to come to Washington in 1976, after the civil war ended. It was in December, right after the election. Our boy met with the outgoing DCI and the incoming Secretary of State. Some very heavy hitters."

"How did he do?"

"Smooth as silk," said Rogers. "Mr. Reasonable. He made a lot of friends."

"Are you sure we're talking about the same guy?" said Hoffman. "The person I remember was a wild-ass kid who had trouble keeping his pecker in his pants. The guy you're talking about sounds like he graduated from Yale."

"Same guy," said Rogers. "Something happened to him after you left. He grew up."

"I'll tell you what happened to him. The Israelis scared the shit out of him. That son of a bitch is lucky to be alive. If he's become such a sweetheart these days, maybe it's because he thinks that snuggling up to Uncle Sam will keep him alive."

"That's ancient history," said Rogers. "The Israelis aren't still after him."

"Don't be so sure," said Hoffman. "The Israelis have very long memories, my friend."

The waiter was hovering near the table, waiting for Monsieur Hoffman and his guest to place their orders.

"I'll have the filet of sole," said Hoffman. "And a steak."

The waiter's eyeballs expanded as he wrote the order on his pad, but he said nothing.

"Just the steak for me," said Rogers. "And a salad."

"Do you have any chocolate sauce?" asked Hoffman.

"Of course," said the waiter.

"I'll have that for dessert," said Hoffman. "No ice cream. Just chocolate sauce. Hot, please."

The waiter smiled. He evidently regarded Hoffman as a culinary idiot savant.

Rogers had been mulling over a question during this interlude, and when the waiter left, he spoke up.

"There is one thing that confuses me," he said.

"What's that, my boy?" said Hoffman.

"I wonder sometimes whether the Israelis really did try to kill our man."

"They say they did. They brag about it! How they killed twelve of the leaders of Black September. How they nailed Abu Nasir in his apartment. How they tried to kill our boy in Scandinavia and blew it. Just read *Time* magazine."

"Then why did they fail?" said Rogers. "If they tried so hard to kill our man after Munich, why didn't they succeed?"

"Maybe they're not quite as brilliant as you think they are," said Hoffman.

"Or maybe they're even smarter."

"Bullshit," said Hoffman. "If you want my opinion, they're overrated. They're hot dogs. That's what I tell my Saudi clients. They love to hear that."

"Do you believe it?"

"Actually, no," said Hoffman. "The Israelis run a nice little service. But they make mistakes. Everybody makes mistakes."

The first course arrived. The waiter deftly fileted the fish while Hoffman looked on approvingly.

"What about us?" asked Rogers when the waiter had left. "How do we look to you now that you're out?"

"You really want to know the truth?"

"Yes."

"Pathetic."

"Why?"

"Let's face it," said Hoffman. "The United States, strictly speaking, doesn't have an intelligence service any more. Once the Senate Intelligence Committee and the House Intelligence Committee and this committee and that committee are finished pulling on the yarn, there isn't much sweater left. Honestly, now, would you entrust your life to an intelligence service that turned its secrets over to a bunch of fucking congressmen? These people must be insane."

"So what are we, if we aren't an intelligence service?"

"As near as I can tell, the agency today is a collection of lawyers, accountants, lobbyists, and bureaucrats. With a bunch of fancy hardware up in the sky. But when it comes to making things happen on the ground, there's nothing left. It's amateur hour. In my humble opinion."

"That's great," said Rogers. "A real morale booster. Is that what your Saudi friends think?"

"They can't understand what's going on. They're so mesmerized by America that they can't believe we're as incompetent as we look. Every time we fuck something up, they invent a new conspiracy theory to explain how it's really a devious new American plot against the Arabs. Want to hear the latest conspiracy theory?"

"Definitely," said Rogers. "Maybe it will cheer me up."

"The Saudis think we're behind the rise of Khomeini in Iran."

"But that's silly," said Rogers. "Why would we threaten our own client?"

"Think about it. Maybe it's not so crazy."

"Frank," said Rogers. "You've been out in the desert too long. You're beginning to think like them."

"Maybe so," said Hoffman. "Maybe so. But I'll tell you one thing. I'm very glad I am *not*, in fact, one of them. Yessiree. I thank my lucky stars every night that I am not a reasonable, pro-Western Arab trying to keep it together. And do you know why?"

"Why?"

"Because if I was, I'd have to depend on the United States for help. And that, my friend, is a losing proposition these days."

42

London; September 1978

Levi scanned the group of several dozen men gathered in a corridor in Whitehall, looking for Rogers. He had a recollection of him from Beirut: tall and thin, dressed in a corduroy suit, looking sensible and self-possessed, peering over the top of his glasses. But that was nearly ten years ago, and that general description seemed to fit half the men in the corridor.

There were no name tags, of course. It wasn't that sort of group. Indeed, the very fact of the conference was a secret. They were meeting under the nominal auspices of the British Foreign Office, in a secure conference room in the interior of a great gray pile of a building along Whitehall. The arrangements for the meeting, the speakers list, and the guest list had all been drawn up by officers of the British Secret Intelligence Service, MI6.

A British junior official was serving coffee from a silver urn as Levi approached.

"White or black?" said the official.

"White," said Levi. When he saw the vast amount of milk poured into the coffee, he wished he had said black. His hand jiggled as he took the coffee, and a small white wave lapped over the top of the cup and into the saucer.

Levi was nervous. Not in the way that he used to be, when he was collecting intelligence from dead drops in Kiev and Aleppo and the sweat dripped down his sleeve in a trickle of fear. This was different. It was a fear of failure. Levi, in all his career, had done very little recruiting. How would he establish rapport with Rogers? What would he say to him after so many years of watching him from the shadows? It was the anxiety of a blind date.

The talk in the corridor, as best Levi could hear from the buzz of conversations in various languages, was about two recent developments in the Middle East: the Camp David peace agreements between Egypt and Israel, which had been signed two weeks earlier; and the rapidly deteriorating situation in Iran. A German was praising the bold diplomacy of the American president. A Frenchman was complaining about the weakness of the Shah. It was like hearing two sides of the same argument. The competent and incompetent faces of American foreign policy, walking side by side.

The British junior officer had moved away from the coffee urn and was ringing a small brass bell, signalling that the morning session was about to begin. There was still no sign of Rogers. Levi joined the line heading into the conference room. He took his place at the table, marked with a small Israeli flag rather than a name card.

A tall man in a blue suit entered the room just then and took the seat marked by an American flag. There were traces of gray in his hair, but otherwise he was as Levi remembered. Levi tried not to stare. The American was smiling, shaking hands, studying the program, scribbling some notes. Then, Levi noticed, he stared off into space for a moment, looking at nothing in particular, lost in a cloud of thought.

The first presentation was from the Spanish Ministry of the Interior about its success in dealing with Basque terrorism. What success? Levi wanted to ask. But he didn't. It was much too gentlemanly a gathering for that. The Spanish official was very calm and earnest. He didn't ask the French representative seated across from him the awkward question: Why do you allow these Basque bastards to cross the border along the Pyrenees? Of course not. That would be impolite.

After an hour of Basquing, the delegates took a coffee break. The same junior official returned to the same silver urn. Despite the lack of name tags, most of the delegates already seemed to know each other. It was an old boys' reunion. Find Rogers, Levi told himself. He looked for the American and, to his relief, saw him standing alone in the corridor, regarding the other delegates dubiously.

Levi approached carefully, not wanting to scare Rogers off.

"What's next on the program?" asked Levi offhandedly.

"Let me see," said Rogers looking at a program. "A presentation by the Dutch on South Moluccan terrorism."

"Perhaps that will be interesting," said Levi.

"Perhaps," said Rogers.

There was a pause. Go ahead, Levi told himself. Do it.

"Aren't you Tom Rogers?" asked Levi.

"That's right," said Rogers. "How did you know?"

Levi smiled.

"My name is Yakov Levi," he said, extending his hand. "I am from Mossad."

"Pleasure," said Rogers.

"I have heard a great deal about you. I have looked forward to meeting you for many years."

"Is that right?" said Rogers, eyeing Levi. "Should I know you?"

"Maybe so. Maybe by a different name."

"Maybe," said Rogers, though he couldn't place the face.

There was silence. Rogers looked at his watch.

"What are you doing here?" said Levi, trying to make conversation.

"The same thing as you," answered Rogers.

Levi stared at his shoes and then spoke up again.

"I served in Lebanon once, actually. At the same time you were there. That's why I know about you."

"Is that right?" said Rogers, with a flicker of genuine interest. "So you were in the Mossad station in Beirut? We always assumed there must be one, but we never knew where it was."

"We are better at keeping secrets than you," said Levi.

"Where was it, if you don't mind my asking?"

"West Beirut."

"But where?"

"Sorry," said Levi. "That's a secret."

The British host was ringing his little bell again.

"I don't suppose you feel like sitting this next session out?" asked Levi. "We could go and take a walk."

"Afraid not," said Rogers. "I'd like to hear the Dutch presentation. They had a hostage rescue operation last year that was first-rate. Israeli quality."

"I know," said Levi. "We trained them."

They walked back toward the meeting room together.

"Perhaps we can meet later," said Levi.

Rogers thought a minute. Why not? He was curious about this inquisitive Israeli intelligence officer who claimed to know so much about him.

"Sure," said Rogers. "Let's meet outside after this panel breaks up. At the entrance to the building on Whitehall."

Levi nodded.

The mysteries of Dutch anti-terrorism policy were duly explained, and an hour later Rogers and Levi were strolling up Whitehall toward Trafalgar Square. It was a brisk British fall day, cold and crisp, with clear skies. Rogers noticed that Levi walked much faster than he did: with short, quick steps that outdistanced Rogers's slower, ambling gait.

The conversation proceeded by indirection, each man feeling and probing, neither quite sure what the other was up to. It was a game of cat and mouse, except that they were both cats.

"When were you in Lebanon?" asked Rogers.

"Late 1960s, early 1970s," answered Levi.

"Before the deluge."

"Yes," said Levi. "Before the first deluge."

"There will be another?"

"Of course," said Levi. "In Lebanon, there will always be another deluge."

There was a pause. A double-decker bus full of tourists rumbled by. What is he telling me? Rogers wondered. What is he getting at?

"It's your show now," said Rogers over the rumble of the bus.

"What?" asked Levi.

"Lebanon. It's yours. We're out of it. Israel has all the players."

"We have some," said Levi. "We have the Christians."

"You're welcome to them," said Rogers, thinking of some of his old contacts.

"But you have some players, too," said Levi.

"Such as?"

"The Palestinians."

"I'm not sure I follow you," said Rogers, narrowing his eyes.

"Nothing," replied Levi.

They walked in silence, each man trying to understand what the other had meant by each maddening fragment of conversation. It was like trying to start a game of chess with only pawns on the board.

"What do you handle in the Mossad, exactly?" asked Rogers. "If you don't mind my asking."

"A little of this, a little of that," said Levi. "But mostly I deal with the Palestinians."

"I know a little about the Palestinians."

"I'm well aware of that, Mr. Rogers."

"You must be busy these days."

"With what?" asked Levi.

"With Camp David."

"Not so busy as you might imagine," said Levi. "In my opinion, there is less there than meets the eye."

"How so?" asked Rogers.

"Do not misunderstand me. We are very pleased to have a peace treaty with Egypt. But the rest, about the Palestinians, is meaningless. I must tell you honestly, our new government has no intention of giving the Palestinians a homeland in Judea and Sumaria. But I'm sure you understand that, don't you? You understand very well the hostility of our new government toward the Palestinians."

"What are you telling me?"

"Simply that the new government is prepared to take the most extreme measures."

What did that mean? Rogers let it drop. He was waiting to see a pattern in Levi's questions, but so far all he saw was that he was the target for something. The Israeli wanted to send him a message, but what was it?

They reached Trafalgar Square. There was the usual squadron of pigeons gathered on the statuary, and the usual throng of tourists competing with them for the available space. Rogers looked for a place to sit down, but every available space was covered with bird shit. He took out a pack of cigarettes and offered Levi one. The Israeli accepted. Rogers lit a match, and cupped it against the wind. He lit Levi's cigarette and then his own. They continued strolling up St. Martin's Lane.

"Mr. Rogers," said Levi. "I would like to mention something." He cleared his throat.

Okay, thought Rogers. Here we go.

"There is one Palestinian in whom we have a special interest."

Roger's brow furrowed slightly. "Oh really? Who's that?"

"His name is Jamal Ramlawi. He is the head of Fatah intelligence."

"I know who he is," said Rogers. "What about him?"

"You know that we hold him responsible for the Munich massacre, don't you?"

"Yes," said Rogers. "But that was six years ago. I thought that whole business was over."

"Not for us."

"What do you mean?"

"Jamal Ramlawi is still on the top of our list."

Rogers looked at him curiously? Why do they want to get him? Why now? And why are they asking me for permission? We've been through this once already, and they know the answer. The answer is silence. What do they expect me to say? 'No! Don't kill him! He's ours!' That was the very thing that Rogers, by the rules of the game, could not say.

Rogers smiled an impenetrable smile.

"Is that right?" he answered blandly. "Still on the top of your list, eh?"

"Yes."

"What sort of list might that be?"

"You know what I am saying, Mr. Rogers. You know what kind of list."

"Let me get this straight," said Rogers. "You are telling me that the new Israeli government is planning to kill Jamal Ramlawi?"

Levi said nothing. His face was turning red. He gave a slight nod.

"And why are you telling me this?"

"Because I thought it might be of interest to you."

Levi looked at Rogers, so deliberate in this conversation, dragging out every word. He wanted to shake him: Say it. Say it! Say no. Say we can't kill him because he works for you.

Say you want him alive. Just say it. Tell us. That's all we ask.

But Rogers said nothing. He walked in silence for what seemed like a minute, his face utterly still, his head lost in thought. At length, he spoke again.

"I don't know what you're talking about," he said. "Please tell that to your colleagues back in Tel Aviv. Tell them that Tom Rogers doesn't know what they're talking about."

"Very well," said Levi. He looked crestfallen. He had failed.

"It's time we got back," said Rogers. "We've got the Canadians on Quebec separatism."

They crossed Trafalgar Square again and walked in silence back down Whitehall. Rogers lit another cigarette. This time he didn't offer one to the Israeli. When they neared the Foreign Office, Rogers excused himself and sat down on a bench in Parliament Square. He had an unsettled feeling in his gut, like what you feel when you remember a promise made long ago that you had almost forgotten. Rogers mentally reviewed his schedule over the next few weeks and decided that he could spare a few days to see some old friends in Beirut.

43

Beirut; October 1978

Fuad sat in his hotel room, waiting for Rogers. He said a prayer silently, not on the floor facing Mecca but in his T-shirt, facing the mirror. Fuad missed his old apartment, but what could he do? It was gone, the victim of a stray artillery shell from Christian East Beirut.

Rogers was coming! It was a great event. They hadn't told Fuad why Rogers was coming, but they never did these days. They just said that Rogers was coming to Beirut on a brief mission, and that he wanted to see Fuad as soon as he arrived. What could that mean? Fuad hoped it didn't have anything to do with Camp David, which had already become a curse word in West Beirut.

A few minutes after 8:00 A.M., Fuad saw a familiar figure in the distance. It was Rogers, unmistakably. Tall and slim, his hair blowing slightly in the wind, his face intent and detached at the same time. Rogers neared the hotel. He was dressed in a gray flannel suit, a blue striped shirt open at the collar, and a pair of cowboy boots. To Fuad, he looked ageless and rumpled in the relaxed way of the Americans. There was a half-smile on his face and an absent expression. He disappeared from Fuad's view as he entered the hotel.

Fuad listened for Roger's footsteps. He knew the sound by heart from a hundred meetings in safehouses and hotel rooms. Rogers would take the stairs, not the elevator, to make sure that no one saw which floor he stopped at. There would be the sound of his shoes reaching the top stair, a pause as he looked around, a slow amble for a few steps, then a quicker pace. Then a soft knock and the code words.

There was a knock.

"Am I early?" said the voice outside the door.

"No, you are right on time."

The American entered the room, closed the door firmly, and then opened it a crack to make sure that he hadn't been followed. The hall was empty. The two men, case officer and agent, embraced each other, exchanged pleasantries in Arabic, and offered each other cigarettes.

"You have come back!" said Fuad.

"There isn't much left to come back to," said Rogers. He walked to the window and pulled back the drapes a few inches to survey the ruined city. It had all changed. The American gazed out toward the kidney-shaped swimming pool of the hotel, now filled with debris, and to the skyline beyond, which became increasingly pockmocked with shellholes as it moved toward the Green Line that divided the Moslem and Christian halves of the city. There had been considerable new damage in the last few months, caused by artillery duels between the Christians in East Beirut and the Palestinians and Syrians in the West.

Rogers cursed under his breath.

"I am glad that you have come back," said Fuad. "I knew that you would! It is part of your nature."

"No it isn't," answered Rogers. "It's part of my job."

He gestured toward the window. "This country has gone mad."

"Yes, it is your nature," said Fuad, continuing as if he hadn't heard. "It is inescapable."

Fuad pointed to a Koran on the coffee table and recited something in Arabic. It was a sura from the Koran: God is the light of Heaven and Earth. His light may be compared to a niche which contains a lamp, the lamp within glass, and the glass shining as if it were a star of pearl.

"You are becoming more religious, Fuad," said Rogers. "That's sensible."

"We are all prisoners of fate."

"Have it your way," said Rogers. "But I should warn you that I'm not staying for very long."

They sat down on the couch and reminisced. As they

talked, Rogers was struck by the passage of time and the changes it brings. Even in someone like Fuad, who had seemed impervious to time. Rogers could remember the eager young Lebanese agent of 1969, in love with America and everything it stood for, eager to discard his Arab identity like an unwanted skin, ready to help America liberate the Arab world from its torpor and backwardness. The Fuad of 1969 would no more have quoted the Koran than jumped out the window. But times had changed.

"I need your help on something," said Rogers.

"I am at your service," replied Fuad.

"I need to see Jamal Ramlawi in a hurry. This week. In the next few days if possible."

"Why not? I think he is in town. I will see what can be arranged."

"Don't ask him," said Rogers. "Tell him!"

While Rogers waited for Fuad to arrange the meeting, he paid a call on Samir Fares. Fares had been named head of the Lebanese Deuxième Bureau two months earlier. When Rogers had heard the news back in Washington, he had been delighted. But it had reminded him of a promise he had made to Fares long ago.

Fares suggested that Rogers pick him up at his new office, in the Presidential Palace in Baabda, in the hills above East Beirut. The Beirut station provided a car and a driver, a tough little Christian named Youssef. The trip gave Rogers a quick and depressing tour of the city. It was like visiting a person who is dying.

The journey began in the shopping district of Hamra, once the elegant meeting place of East and West, now as faded as the cosmopolitan ideal it represented. They drove past the shop where Rogers had bought birthday gifts for his wife, and past another shop where he had once bought, in a reckless moment, a string of pearls for Solange Jezzine. Both stores were now shuttered and closed.

They drove on past blocks of bombed-out buildings, a no-man's-land inhabited now only by snipers and Kurdish refugees, which signalled the approach of the Green Line. Rogers lit a cigarette. So did the driver. In Lebanon, Rogers remembered, smoking was a kind of ritualized sacrament, administered several dozen times a day.

Rogers had crossed the Green Line before, but he still found it unsettling. Rogers hated snipers. They were a symbol of the sickness that had seized the country: bored teenagers, hiding behind sandbags on either side of the line, gobbling speed to stay awake, earning $100 a month plus a chance to swagger around town with automatic weapons, shooting at people without knowing who they were. The only consolation, Rogers thought, was that their aim wasn't very good. In that regard they were Lebanese. Better at the show of things than at the substance.

They were near the line. Rogers heard the sound of gunfire a block or so away. He slouched down low in his seat as the Lebanese driver put the accelerator to the floor, and held his breath until the car was safely across to the other side.

Across the Green Line lay the Christian strongholds of East Beirut and the mountains beyond. Here there was more evidence than in West Beirut of orderly government and prosperity: the municipal parking lots and trash dumps organized by the Phalange Party, the bumper-to-bumper traffic of BMWs, Jaguars, and Mercedes-Benzs. But it was still thug-land.

As they climbed the hills toward the Presidential Palace in Baabda, Rogers could see the city spread out below like a ragged quilt. He could see the layers of destruction that had been inflicted over the past four years, marking the recent history of Lebanon as precisely as layers of sediment.

The damage began at the core of the city and radiated outward like a hail of machine-gun fire. The first casualties had been the grand facades of the old business district, where buildings had been shelled from both East and West during the worst days of the civil war. Now the fine buildings were crumbling ruins, covered with ferns and moss, and weeds grew in the streets.

Next came the battered walls of the residential neighborhoods near the Green Line—Sioufi in East Beirut and Ain el-Mreisseh in West Beirut—which had been shelled heavily in the recent renewal of the Christian-Moslem bloodletting. Then to the southwest, the Palestinian refugee camps of Sabra and Shatilla. Shelled by the Christians, bombed occasionally by the Israelis, yet still the boisterous capital-in-exile of the Palestinians. And finally in the distant southern suburbs, the seemingly random destruction of the Shiite-Moslem slums—deprived, brooding, ready to explode.

Rogers surveyed the devastation with a sense of resignation and disgust. He remembered a phrase that one of the Christian militias had popularized a few years earliers. "Al Arab Jarab" —The Arabs are leprosy.

The Presidential Palace, modern and gleaming white, seemed to Rogers almost a parody of Lebanon's condition: grand but empty. It was a place of soundless, marble-clad halls; of vast desks at which the few Lebanese government officials in evidence pretended to work; of suites of offices that, on inspection, housed only people to make tea and coffee for the pasha down the hall.

Rogers disliked visiting the palace and was relieved when he saw Fares waiting at the entrance. The Lebanese intelligence chief was dressed much as before, in a tweed jacket and bow tie, looking like a fugitive from an Ivy League faculty lounge. He looked healthy but overworked.

Rogers suggested that they take a drive, alone. He dropped the embassy driver at a café near the entrance to the palace, and took the wheel.

"Mabruk!" said Rogers, using the Lebanese word for congratulations. "You've done it!"

Fares smiled graciously and put his hand over his heart.

"I am grateful to my friends," said Fares.

"We had nothing to do with it. Don't kid yourself."

"It is a dubious honor, actually," said Fares. "I am the head of an intelligence service that doesn't have a country. We are like a brain with no body."

Rogers told him he was being too modest. They made small talk for a few minutes, asked about each other's wives, traded gossip about old friends. Eventually Rogers got around to the point.

"I wanted to see you for a reason," he said.

"Knowing you, I did not expect that it was just a courtesy call," said the Lebanese.

"Years ago I made you a promise. Do you remember what it was?"

"Of course I do."

"I promised you," said Rogers in a slow cadence, as if he was reciting a catechism, "that if you ever became head of your service, we would release you from the arrangement you had made with us and allow you to serve your country with a clear conscience."

"Yes," said Fares. "That is what you said."

"I want to keep that promise."

"I'm touched," said Fares. "But it is not that simple, is it?"

"Why not?"

Fares looked at Rogers curiously.

"Let us be honest. You can tell me that I am free, that I am no longer under your control. But what will happen when you find yourselves in extreme difficulty, when you need a favor? You will come to me, at least I hope you will come to me, and you will ask me to help. You will tell me that I am free to say no, but we will both know better."

"A promise is a promise," said Rogers.

"That is just the problem, Tom," replied Fares with a sad smile. "A promise is a promise. And no more."

Rogers looked stung. He had come a very long way to try to settle accounts with people he cared about, and his first check was bouncing. Fares saw that he was upset and tried to patch the conversation back together.

"You are worrying too much about this," said Fares. "You are acting like it is the kiss of death to work with the Americans in the Middle East. But it isn't. It is very valuable. I am the proof! Everyone in Lebanon knows that I am friendly with the Americans. They do not know the precise details, but it is no secret that I am well connected with the American Embassy. And do you know what? It helps me! The Syrians take me more seriously. The Egyptians take me more seriously. Because they suspect that I work for the CIA."

"Baloney," said Rogers. "Nobody trusts a spy. Not even in Lebanon."

"You are wrong," said Fares. "In Lebanon, we do not take someone seriously until we know that someone in the West is prepared to buy him."

Rogers had a look of exasperation. He wanted to resolve the problem.

"I have a proposal," he said. "I have cleared it with the Director. The deal is this: You are terminated, as of now. The annuity for your wife and children remains in effect. But you don't owe us anything anymore. We will assume that our relationship is finished."

"Fine," said Fares. "And I will assume that our relationship continues."

"I give up," said Rogers.

They reached Ashrafiyeh in East Beirut and headed up the coast road toward Jounie, toward the apartment along the beach where they had once met with a frightened young Lebanese Christian boy named Amin Shartouni, who had talked of something called *la puissance occulte*—and had eventually been killed by it.

Rogers was lost in thought. Fares was glancing at his watch.

"I'm afraid I have a meeting back at the palace," said Fares apologetically. Rogers changed direction and headed back toward Baabda.

"By the way," said Rogers, "whatever happened to the Palestinian Christian who trained Amin Shartouni? The man we called the Bombmaker."

"We see his bombs, but not the man himself. He has gone deeper underground in the last few years. They all have. It's much harder now to find out what's going on. When you pick up a rock now, you don't see the bugs underneath. You just find dirt."

"The Bombmaker is still alive?" asked Rogers in a tone of disappointment.

"Most certainly. From what little we pick up, he is busier than ever. All of the groups use car bombs now, and he is the master."

"You would think someone would kill him," said Rogers.

Fares laughed.

"Who would kill him, Tom? Everyone deals with him a little when they need him. What purpose is there in killing him? He doesn't know anything, except how to make bombs. And even if he died, his students are everywhere, in all the groups. There are many, many people in Lebanon now who know how to make bombs."

Rogers shook his head. They drove back to Baabda mostly in silence. As they neared the gate to the Presidential Palace, Fares spoke up.

"Do you remember a woman named Solange Jezzine?" he asked. "The wife of my predecessor?"

"Of course I do," said Rogers. "She is not a woman that you forget."

"You knew her a bit, didn't you?" asked Fares. He spoke matter-of-factly, as if he knew the whole story.

"A bit," said Rogers. He thought of her sharp eyes and soft body. "Whatever happened to her?"

"She's remarried," said Fares.

"Oh really?" said Rogers. "To who?"

"To a very rich young man. He is an arms dealer, the agent of the Saudi minister of defense. It is a very lucrative job, as you can imagine. He's very active in Lebanon, too. Sells guns to both sides."

"Does she still live in Lebanon?"

"No. She mostly lives in Paris now. And Marbella. Would you like her address? I am sure they can find it back in the office."

Rogers paused to think. Did he want the address, the passion, the exhilarating plunge from a high place, and the long convalescense?

"No," said Rogers eventually. "I don't think so."

They reached the entrance to the palace. Rogers stopped the car. Fares sat in his seat for a moment, trying to think of what he wanted to say.

"We have a saying in Lebanon," said Fares. "Like so many other things, it is something that we borrowed from the French."

"What is it?" asked Rogers.

"'Seule le provisoire dure,'" answered Fares. "'Only the temporary lasts.' Goodbye, my friend."

As Fares watched Rogers's car leave the palace grounds, it occurred to him that Rogers was an unlikely spy. He was a man who yearned for permanency in a business where that was impossible. He seemed to want relationships that were built on trust, honesty, a sense of mutual responsibility. Fares suspected that it was this quality of idealism that made Rogers seem so American—and perhaps also dangerous to those who worked with him. Rogers had a will to believe things that were not always true.

44

Beirut; October 1978

Rogers waited for Jamal in a safehouse in the West Beirut neighborhood of Ramlet el-Baida. When he entered the apartment, he had an eerie feeling that he had been there before. There were the same flowers, the same bottle of whisky on the sideboard, the same packs of cigarettes on the table. The same tape recorder in the wall, no doubt.

Rogers looked at his watch. Jamal was late. As he waited, Rogers thought back eight years to another meeting with Jamal, in another safehouse on the beach in Kuwait. And how, in closing his recruitment pitch, he had made Jamal a promise. We don't make mistakes, Rogers had said. We will keep the fact of our relationship with you secret. And how he had added: "I haven't lost an agent in ten years."

There was a sharp knock at the door, followed by the exchange of code words. In walked Jamal. Rogers didn't bother to ask him if he was carrying a weapon. West Beirut was Fatah's town now. They had the guns.

"Ahlan, Reilly-Bey," said Jamal.

"Hello, Jamal," answered Rogers.

Jamal looked older. Still fit, still handsome, but with signs of age and stress. The wild black hair was now combed neatly in place. The face had the doughy look of clay that has been kneaded and packed and massaged into place one too many times. The black leather jacket was gone, replaced by a brown one. Rogers noticed something else. For the first time he could remember, he saw a look of sadness in Jamal's eyes.

"You have a lot of nerve coming to see me now," said Jamal.

"What do you mean?"

"After Camp David! The Old Man is furious. He says you have betrayed him. After all our fine talk in secret about solving the Palestinian problem, after our conversations in 1976 when I went to Washington to meet the great Director of Central Intelligence. After all that, what do you do? You let the Israelis and the Egyptians sign a separate peace treaty that leaves us in the cold."

"It wasn't my doing. Talk to the president."

"We would like to do that very much," said Jamal. "But we can't."

Jamal's manner was aggressive and insistent. That much hadn't changed. He spoke earnestly, like a former student who wants to convince his old professor how well he has done in life. Who wants to show that he is a serious person now and not someone to be trifled with.

"Camp David is not the end of the story," said Rogers. "There is more to come."

"You have been saying that for eight years. We are getting tired of hearing it."

This was not the conversation Rogers wanted to have. Not at all. He changed gears.

"I bring you greetings from the new Director, Mr. Hinkle," said Rogers. "He sends you his personal thanks for your help in protecting our diplomats and citizens. He says that the American people owe you a debt of gratitude that can only be expressed, for now, in secret."

Jamal touched his heart. Was it the politeness of the Arabs, or an example of the inexplicable, mesmerizing power held by whoever happened to hold the position of Director of Central Intelligence?

"That is kind of the Director," said Jamal. "Please give him my regards. Tell him that whatever our differences on the political level, we will continue to abide by our promise to protect American citizens."

"He will be pleased," said Rogers.

Jamal nodded. He took out a cigarette and lit it.

"Jamal," said Rogers. "I have something that I want to tell you." But Jamal wasn't listening. The mention of the Director and security cooperation had sent him off on a new tangent.

"I have a spy story for you," said Jamal. "You can tell the new Director when you get home."

"I'm not sure that he likes spy stories. And there is something important I have to tell you."

"He will like this one," said Jamal. "Do you remember the man they called the Snake?"

"The man from the PFLP?" said Rogers. "The super-terrorist."

"Yes. You read that he died, didn't you?"

"Yes," said Rogers. "Of leukemia. In a hospital in East Germany."

"That is not how he died," said Jamal with a thin smile.

"It isn't?"

"No. He was murdered."

"How?"

"He was radiated to death."

"What in the hell are you talking about? Where was he radiated to death?"

"In Baghdad."

"How?"

"Aha. Now you are interested. I will explain. The Snake was working then for the Iraqi Moukhabarat. Whenever he went to see the chief of the Moukhabarat, he would be received in a special waiting room, which had been constructed just for him and shielded with lead."

"Lead?"

"Yes, lead. The Iraqi would make the Snake sit there in that waiting room for thirty minutes, maybe an hour. The Snake thought nothing of it. You know how the Arabs are. They always keep you waiting. But all the time he was in that room, they were pointing an X-ray machine at him, beaming it through a hole in the wall."

"What happened to him?"

"He got sicker and sicker. Just as all the newspaper stories said at the time. But he didn't know why. He went to Algeria for treatment. And then finally to East Germany."

"Where the diagnosis was leukemia."

"Yes," said Jamal. "But when he died finally in East Germany, they made an autopsy. And that East German autopsy report was very interesting. It spoke of 'unnatural complications' in the case. We have a copy of the autopsy report, if you are interested."

"Of course I am interested," said Rogers.

"Would you like to know what the payoff was for the Iraqis?"

Rogers nodded.

"Look at the oil production totals for the OPEC countries in the months before and after the Snake's death. You will notice a large increase in Iraqi production and a roughly equal decrease in production by Saudi Arabia."

"That's the damnedest story I've ever heard," said Rogers. "Why don't we know about this?"

"Because you are slipping," said Jamal with a wicked smile. There was silence.

"Jamal," said Rogers again, more insistently. "I asked for this meeting because there is something I have to tell you."

"Very well," said the Palestinian. "What is it?"

"I want you to be very careful," said Rogers slowly. "Your life is in danger."

The Palestinian laughed.

"You came all the way to Beirut to tell me that? That is hardly news to me, my dear Mr. Reilly."

"Your life is in danger," Rogers repeated, "from the Israelis."

"The Israelis have given up on me! They know that I am invulnerable."

"Don't be so sure that they have given up," said Rogers. "Remember that there is a new Israeli government, and there are old plans that can be dusted off."

"What of it? Our fates are all in the hands of Allah."

"Let's cut the crap," said Rogers. "I am trying to save your life. So listen to me."

"I am listening."

"I want to tell the Israelis that you have been working for us. That you are off limits."

"No."

"Why not? I think they suspect as much already."

"No," repeated Jamal.

"But why not?"

"Because what you said is false. I don't work for you. I work for my people."

"Yes, of course. But you're in danger . . ."

Jamal cut him off.

"My answer is no. I will not depend on the charity of the Israelis. I would rather be dead."

Rogers realized that he was getting nowhere.

"I have another proposal," said the American.

"What is it?"

"I want you to leave Beirut."

"Maybe you did not hear me before," said Jamal, his voice rising. "I am not yours to command. You don't tell me where to go."

"I know. I understand. I'm only suggesting that perhaps now, for a little while, you might think about going somewhere safer than Beirut."

"For me, there is nowhere safer."

"You are impossible!"

Jamal smiled for the first time.

"Yes," he said. "I am."

"Look," said Rogers. "If you won't listen to reason, there isn't much we can do for you. But there are a few things. What kind of car are you driving?"

"Chevrolet," said Jamal.

"Bullet-proof?"

"Yes."

"We can get you a better one."

"All right," said the Palestinian. "I accept."

"What kind of radios do your bodyguards use?"

"East German."

"They're junk," said Rogers. "The Israelis can easily intercept the signals. We'll get you new radios. Fuad will bring them to you."

"Fine," said the Palestinian.

"What else?"

"That is enough," said Jamal.

"No, it isn't," said Rogers. "What else, God-damn it!"

"Mr. Reilly," said Jamal, putting his hand on Rogers's shoulder. "If the United States cannot keep its friends in the Middle East alive, then it is the United States that has serious problems, not me. So I will trust in your good offices."

"I told you once in Kuwait that I had never lost an agent," said Rogers. "And I don't intend to start now."

"Yes," answered Jamal. "You did tell me that. And do you remember what I answered? I told you that I was not your agent."

They talked for a few minutes more and then Jamal excused himself. He had a meeting with a visiting intelligence officer from Japan. It was getting to be an industry, Jamal said, this business of security cooperation.

After Jamal left, Rogers sat for a while in the apartment, thinking of what Jamal had said. "I am not your agent." Rogers had to admit that he wasn't sure what Jamal was. He wasn't a CIA agent. He certainly wasn't an ally of the United States. He was something awkward, in between. The American relationship with him was, in that sense, out of control.

45

Beirut; January 1979

The Israeli special-operations team entered Lebanon mostly through the Beirut International Airport. They came one by one, as businessmen travelling on various European passports. They were well trained and intensely motivated. Among them was the cousin of one of the Israeli athletes who had been killed at Munich.

Their mission was to finish once and for all a job that had been started years ago—and to make no mistakes. But even professionals make mistakes.

There were little hints, tipoffs, bits of evidence. The first came from the Mossad officer in East Beirut who was responsible for liaison with the Lebanese Christian militia. He paid a visit to the Christian militia's chief of intelligence one day in early January and said that he would be away for several weeks. He added that it would be wise to stay out of West Beirut for a while. When the Lebanese Christian pressed for details, the Mossad man just winked.

What the Israeli didn't say was that most of the Mossad station was quietly slipping out of Beirut. There was no sense in leaving them there, vulnerable and without good alibis, while the special-operations team did its work.

The incident seemed odd to the Christian militiaman. So he sent his own agents to check the logs of Beirut hotels and car-rental agencies and the records of arriving airline passengers to see if there were any unusual developments. It took him a week to gather all the information, and most of it was useless. But he did eventually notice one peculiar detail. Three cars had been rented by foreign passport holders from a particular car-rental agency in East Beirut that week. That seemed strange. Foreign visitors didn't usually rent cars in Lebanon. They took taxis. Stranger still was the fact that all three cars had been reserved by the same travel agent in Paris. When the militiaman called the number of the Parisian travel agency, it had been disconnected.

The Christian intelligence man wasn't sure what to do with the information, so he did what intelligence officers usually do. He traded it. As it happened, he owed a favor to the head of Lebanese military intelligence, Samir Fares, who had recently helped his men obtain some American-made electronic-surveillance equipment. So he simply passed along to Fares his scanty evidence that the Israelis might be up to something.

Fares was busy that month with an escalating war in the streets of West Beirut between Syrian, Iraqi, and Libyan agents. So he didn't pay any real attention to the militiaman's tip until he got another piece of information—this time from an agent in a small and very secret Christian underground group called Al-Jabha, which was said to have close ties to the Israelis.

Someone was trying to monopolize the group's bombmaking business, the agent complained. Al-Jabha's workshop in the mountains had been commandeered by one member who was especially close to the Israelis. The man had brought special welding equipment to the garage, along with sheets of heavy steel plate. That was state-of-the-art for car bombs, the agent explained. The sheets of steel were welded under the car, around three sides of the bomb, so that the force of the explosion would blow out in a particular direction.

It wasn't fair, the agent said. Lebanon was a country of entrepreneurs. Nobody should try to monopolize the bombmaking business.

The intelligence reports made Fares nervous. Somebody—apparently connected with the Israelis—was planning to hit an important target in West Beirut. But Fares had no idea who or why. He made a mental list of the possible targets: the Sunni prime minister, the Shiite speaker of parliament, several Druse members of the cabinet. The security of these Lebanese officials was Fares's responsibility. He called in the officers who were responsible for protecting them and issued an alert: The Lebanese Moslem officials should alter their normal travel routines until further notice—and stay off the streets of West Beirut.

Fares thought of other possible targets. There were various Druse, Sunni, and Shiite religious and political leaders, of course. But the most likely targets were among the Palestinians. The Old Man was planning to travel that week to Damascus, along with many of the other Fatah leaders. But Jamal Ramlawi, the Fatah chief of intelligence, was still in town. Fares wondered whether he should send Ramlawi a warning.

Fares did one other thing. He sent a brief report to the new station chief at the American Embassy, a man named Bert Jorgenson who had recently arrived from Kuwait, with a request that a copy be sent to Tom Rogers in Washington.

None of these tips and hints would have come to Rogers's attention if Father Maroun Lubnani hadn't panicked.

The Maronite priest had gone off to meet with his Israeli case officer, as he did once a month. The Israelis were meeting much more openly with their agents in Christian East Beirut now, ever since the civil war and the partition of Beirut. Why not? The Israelis were in open alliance with the Christians. They were the new kings of East Beirut!

Father Maroun had gone, as usual, to an apartment building on the beach south of Jounie. He had dressed in his bathing costume, as he did each month, and sat by the indoor pool waiting for the Israeli to meet him there. He had waited and waited. But his Israeli contact hadn't arrived. So he had followed orders. He had come back to the beach apartments the next day, at the same time, and sat by the pool again, feeling increasingly embarrassed as he watched the nubile Christian girls in their bikinis parade past him.

The Israelis never made mistakes, Father Maroun told himself. But the hours passed that second day, and the Israeli contact still didn't arrive. Finally, after waiting too long by poolside in an ill-fitting swim suit, Father Maroun panicked.

Father Maroun's case officer had made a simple and forgivable mistake. In his haste to get out of Beirut, the Mossad officer had forgotten to notify his contact in the Maronite clergy that their meeting that month would be postponed.

Father Maroun was worried. The Israeli officer would not miss a meeting unless something was very, very wrong! So he did what he had been told to do in an emergency. He called the Israeli Embassy in Paris and asked for his special emergency contact there by name.

A voice came on the line.

"What is happening?" said Father Maroun, his voice trembling. "I went to meet my friend, but he has disappeared!"

"Calm down," said the voice. "Your friend is busy. Something important has come up that requires him to miss his meeting. Everything is fine. Your friend will contact you in several weeks in the normal way."

"Very well," said Father Maroun, much relieved.

"Please do not call this number again," said the voice. The line went dead.

A brief intelligence report on the conversation came across Rogers's desk two days later, in the midst of a thick pile of other reports from around the world, with a note from the watch officer: "FYI." After his visit to London and Beirut the previous September, Rogers had asked to see as much of the raw intelligence from Lebanon as he could.

The call had, in fact, been monitored by American intelligence, which tapped all calls going in and out of the Israeli Embassy in Paris, as well as much of the telephone traffic in and out of Lebanon. The intelligence report noted the basic details: the caller was a Maronite priest named Maroun Lubnani. The person he called was a Mossad officer in Paris who, it was thought, handled some Lebanese accounts.

What caught Rogers's eye was the name of Maroun Lubnani, which brought to mind the figure of a stout Lebanese cleric dressed in lederhosen. But as he read the intelligence report, he found it intriguing. Why the panic? What were the Israelis up to? Why were they breaking off meetings with agents?

Rogers felt his stomach churning. He pulled from a file another recent SIGINT report from Lebanon that had come across his desk several days earlier. The signals people had captured a transmission from Lebanon by a high-speed transmitter, which sent coded communications in rapid bursts. It was state-of-the-art equipment and only used for sensitive jobs. Rogers had assumed, when he first saw the report, that the Soviets were up to something.

Now he suspected that it was the Israelis. And he thought he knew what they were doing.

It was late. Nearly 5:00 P.M. in Washington. First, Rogers sent a cable to Jorgenson, the new station chief in Beirut. Jorgenson wasn't a genius, but he would have to do. "Request your help urgently on a sensitive matter," the cable said. Jorgenson called back from his home on an unsecure line. That was a bad sign.

"Can't help you, my friend," said Jorgenson. "We're mighty tight this week. Big project going."

"I have a feeling this may be more important," said Rogers. Jorgenson's last big project had been a conference on Arab folk art.

"Maybe it is, and maybe it isn't," said Jorgenson. "But if you're talking about something sensitive, then I'm going to need some paperwork. A finding. A memo from the general counsel. A note saying you've briefed the appropriate committees."

"But we don't have time for that, Bert. Somebody could be dead by then."

"Sorry, Tom. But rules are rules. The days of the rogue elephant are over!"

"For Christ's sake!" said Rogers. He was almost shouting.

"Sorry, pal," said Jorgenson amiably. "Can't help. Maybe you can scare up a little local talent. Some of your old pals. We don't see much of them any more. Be my guest."

Rogers cursed. Jorgenson rang off.

Rogers's next call was to Fares. It was past midnight in Beirut when he reached him.

Rogers apologized for waking the Lebanese chief of intelligence. He wouldn't have called at all, Rogers said, except that he had a tip that somebody might be planning a major operation in Lebanon.

"Didn't you get my message?" asked Fares sleepily.

"What message?"

"I sent a message to the embassy nearly a week ago passing along some interesting information that had come our way. I asked the embassy to forward it to you. Didn't you get it?"

"No," said Rogers. He was fuming. Calm down, he told himself.

Rogers thought for a moment. He was in trouble. His options were all bad. There wasn't time for him to go to Beirut. The CIA station there wouldn't help. Time was running out. There was only one alternative.

"Samir," said Rogers. "A few months ago I promised I wouldn't ask for your help again. But I need a favor. Will you do something for me?"

"Of course," said Fares. "Tell me what it is."

"Can you send someone you trust to an address I will give you. When your man gets there, a friend of mine named Fuad will be waiting for him. Could you have your man tell Fuad the information that you sent to me via the embassy."

"I will go myself," said Fares.

Rogers gave him Fuad's address and room number in West Beirut and thanked him, haltingly.

"It is nothing," said Fares. "We are friends."

Finally Rogers called Fuad. He talked carefully.

"Marhaba," said Fuad groggily in Arabic when he picked up the phone.

"This is your old friend," said Rogers. "The man who first met you on the beach."

"Yes," said Fuad. "I know who you are."

"I think that someone is trying to make trouble for another friend of ours."

"Who?"

"The man I met in Amman."

"The man in black?"

"Yes," said Rogers.

"Bad trouble?"

"The worst."

"When will it happen?"

"I don't know. Maybe soon."

"What should I do?"

"I'm sending someone to visit you tonight. He'll tell you what he knows. You can trust him. He is discreet. But don't tell him who we are trying to protect. That's none of his business. That's nobody's business but ours."

"Okay," said Fuad. "Should I ask the people at your old office for help?"

"No," said Rogers. "They're useless."

Fuad was silent.

"Good luck," said Rogers. He put the phone down.

"Goodbye, Effendi," said Fuad.

Fares arrived at Fuad's hotel just before dawn. When Fuad opened the door of his room there was a look of surprise and recognition on each man's face. Each one knew the other by reputation, but neither knew until that moment that they both shared a link with Rogers.

Fares described the intelligence reports. A Christian militia leader had been warned by an Israeli to stay out of West Beirut. Another Christian had complained that someone new was in the car-bomb business. A rental-car agency in East Beirut had received reservations from a nonexistent travel agency in Paris. Somebody, said Fares, was being set up for a hit, and he wanted to know who.

"Are they trying to kill one of Rogers's people?" demanded Fares.

"I cannot tell you that, General," said Fuad.

Rogers is protecting an agent, thought Fares. A Moslem agent in West Beirut.

"I am ordering you to tell me," said Fares.

"I still cannot tell you."

"I can have you arrested."

"I hope you will not do that," said Fuad coolly.

Fares decided that he liked Fuad. He was a worthy agent for Rogers.

"No. Of course I won't arrest you," replied Fares. He relit his pipe. He thought about who the target might be, surveyed a mental list of the people the Israelis would want to kill and the Americans would want to protect. And suddenly it was obvious to him who the agent was. And just as obvious why Fuad was on orders not to give his name to the head of a Lebanese intelligence service that was thoroughly penetrated by the Israelis.

"How can I help you?" asked Fares.

"Do you have the license numbers of the cars that were rented by the travel agency in Paris?"

"Yes," said Fares. He gave Fuad a piece of paper with the numbers written on it. There were three cars—a Ford, a Volkswagen, and a Mercedes—each with a license number.

"We must find these cars," said Fuad. "If we find the car with the bomb, then we don't have to worry about the target."

"I will send out a team of men this morning," said Fares.

Fuad said he would join in the search.

"How soon are the Israelis likely to move?" asked Fuad.

"I got this information a week ago," answered Fares. "It could be very soon."

When Fares had left, Fuad called Jamal's apartment. His wife answered. Jamal wasn't there, she said. He hadn't come home the previous night. He must be working. Then Fuad called Jamal's office. A bodyguard answered. No, Jamal wasn't there. No, he didn't know where he was. Fuad tried the health club where Jamal sometimes went in the morning. No, he hadn't been in. He called two women who he thought might know Jamal's whereabouts. When he asked if Jamal was there, one of them hung up. The other one laughed.

It was already nine-thirty. It was getting late. Fuad left his hotel, looking for a needle in the haystack of Beirut.

Fuad tried to put himself in the mind of an Israeli intelligence officer. If I was trying to kill Jamal Ramlawi with a car bomb, Fuad asked himself, where would I put it? Not near his office. That area was too heavily guarded by the fedayeen. The chance of getting caught was too great.

No, thought Fuad. If I was trying to kill Jamal, I would put the bomb near the Palestinian's apartment. Or on the route between his apartment and his office. Or on the route between his apartment and his health club. Or on the route between the health club and his office.

Fuad took a taxi to the area where Jamal lived, in a district of West Beirut known as Verdun. The area was packed with cars, some parked, some honking their horns and pushing their way slowly through the morning traffic. They were going nowhere. There were thousands of cars to check and Fuad was stopped in a traffic jam. He decided it was better to leave the cab and explore the area on foot. In the crush of West Beirut, he would be able to move more quickly that way.

Fuad searched first along Rue Verdun, between Jamal's apartment and his office. He grasped the piece of paper with the license numbers on it, by now ragged and dirty with sweat. It didn't matter. A Ford, a Volkswagen, and a Mercedes. The license numbers of each were engraved on his brain after a few minutes. He moved as quickly as he could along Rue Verdun, checking every Ford, Volkswagen, and Mercedes he could find. Though it was January, he was sweating profusely. The check of Verdun Street took him an hour. He found nothing. None of the tags matched the ones on his list.

He ducked into a small appliance store on Rue Verdun and called Jamal's office again. Yes, he had finally arrived, but he had left again. No, he didn't say where he was going. Perhaps to his apartment. Perhaps to the health club.

Fuad took a taxi back to Jamal's apartment and checked that area once again for cars. New cars had arrived, dozens of them. Especially Mercedes. He glared at them, hating them— every car an enemy, every one a potential killer. There were too many cars to check. He had already checked Verdun once. What about the health club?

Fuad was feeling increasingly desperate. He made his way along Rue Abdallah al-Sabbah, toward the health club. He passed the cars in a run so that they seemed almost a blur. Pedestrians stopped to look at him. People do not run in the streets in Beirut unless something is wrong. A policeman stopped him and asked to see his papers. Fuad had to give him 20 Lebanese pounds and invoke the name of the head of the Sûreté before the policeman let him go. He was losing time. The clock was ticking. There was nothing on Rue Abdallah either.

Where, then?

Shit, thought Fuad. What does Jamal do in the morning, on days when he has been out the previous night? He goes first to the office, to inquire about business, then to his apartment to sleep, to change clothes, to see his wife. My God! It must be Rue Verdun!

Fuad looked for a taxi. He waited. No taxis. Where were they all? Finally one appeared. It already had a passenger, but he flagged it down anyway. The driver said he was going to Corniche Mazraa. Verdun! shouted Fuad. The driver said he would let him off at the bottom of the street.

"Y'allah!" said Fuad. Let's go.

When they got to Verdun, the driver wanted to haggle over the fare. Fuad threw a ten-pound note at him and began running up Rue Verdun, looking at more newly arrived Mercedes, Fords, and Volkswagens. His head was spinning. He passed Rue Bechir Qassar, Rue Anis Nsouli, Rue Hassan Kamel. Shit! Where is the car? Where is the car? The road curved right, past Rue Habib Srour, past Rue Nobel. He was nearing Jamal's apartment. It was a quarter-mile away. He was running along the sidewalk, head down, looking at license plates, when he heard a loud honking noise. He ignored it at first and turned his head finally just as the car was passing at high speed, trailed by a Land-Rover full of armed men.

It was Jamal's Chevrolet, honking other cars out of the way, racing up the street toward his apartment. Fuad heard the roar of the engine and the din of the horn. He screamed as loud as he could but the car was gone.

Fuad stopped dead in his tracks and held his breath. He counted ten seconds. Then fifteen.

Then he heard the explosion, several blocks away. A crack and then a rumble like thunder in his ears, echoing through the crowded streets. Then the screaming of so many people and the wailing of sirens.

Fuad sat down in the street and sobbed.

It was a large and well-designed bomb, detonated by remote control, containing the equivalent of 50 kilos of TNT. The explosion was very powerful, even by Beirut standards. It killed twelve people and injured seventeen.

Fuad eventually got up off the street and went back to his hotel. He could not bear to pass near the scene of the bombing. The Verdun area was swarming with people now. Fatah security men, policemen, Lebanese security men, journalists, curious thrillseekers. Fuad wanted to be anywhere else. He stayed in his room and closed the curtains so that it was dark at midday.

When the radio announced several hours later that Jamal Ramlawi had died on his way to the hospital, Fuad slashed his wrist. He watched it bleed for ten minutes and then applied a tourniquet. Even his grief was useless.

PART X

Epilogue
London; 1984

London; 1984

Fuad survived the anguish of that first car bombing. But Rogers's death in the embassy bombing four years later broke his spirit. Fuad decided then that he had seen enough of Lebanon—and enough of the Americans—and moved to London. The agency offered him a handsome settlement, asked him to sign a contract pledging eternal silence about his intelligence activities, and then wished him well. It was easy enough to let Fuad go. Other than Rogers, no one had ever really known him.

Fuad bought himself a flat in London, in a modern building north of Hyde Park called the Pentangle. It was an odd neighborhood, once the home of the prostitutes who serviced the gentlemen who lived south of the Park. Now it was composed almost entirely of foreigners. Saudis, Nigerians, Iranians, Lebanese, Kuwaitis, Venezuelans. A modern class of whores. People who had made money abroad and, for whatever reason, had found it prudent to settle down in London. Fuad loved the neighborhood. It was the perfect place to hide.

Fuad bought himself a dog, an enthusiastic Yorkshire terrier, which he liked to take on walks in the park. And as he took these walks, out in the open spaces of London, he turned over in his mind the events he had witnessed in Lebanon, the deaths of Jamal and Rogers and so many thousands more.

The news from Lebanon seemed to get worse, week by week. In October 1983, a truck bomb exploded outside the Marine barracks at the Beirut Airport, killing 241 people. The

United States reacted like a wounded Cyclops, bellowing, flailing about, making a loud noise but doing little damage. A World War II battleship lobbed shells the size of Volkswagens at Druse militiamen in the Lebanese mountains. Navy planes dropped iron bombs on Syrian gun positions. This display of firepower did not impress the local warlords. The foreign minister of Syria summed up the local sentiment when he remarked that the Americans seemed "short of breath." In February 1984, to the surprise of no one, the Americans pulled up their tents and fled from Lebanon, leaving a situation far messier—and infinitely greater in human misery—than when they had first begun to play the role of benevolent proconsul several decades before.

One day, when Fuad had been in London nearly a year, he walked into an electronics shop on the Edgware Road and bought himself a tape recorder. He took it back to his apartment and began dictating a message for the one American to whom he felt he owed an explanation—Frank Hoffman, the man who had first spotted him, recruited him, and introduced him to Tom Rogers. He recorded many different versions of the message, and finally settled on one that said most of what he felt. He sent it to Hoffman in Saudi Arabia.

When Hoffman received the tape, he listened to it once, had his secretary transcribe it, and then destroyed it. It did no one any good. He sent the transcript to Edward Stone in Washington. The transcript read as follows:

"Effendi:

"I have been trying for a very long time to understand what went wrong for my friends the Americans in Lebanon. Now I see a part of the story, and I think I should tell you. It is hard for Arabs to talk plainly and honestly. Usually we do the opposite. But I will try.

"I will begin by telling you a proverb that I told my friend Tom Rogers the morning before he died, when we had breakfast together. It is a *hadith,* a saying of the Prophet Mohammed, and it is as follows:

"A simple Bedouin in the desert asks the Prophet: 'Should I let my camel loose and trust in God?'

"'No,' says the Prophet. 'Tie down your camel and trust in God.'

"That *hadith* expresses what we Arabs understand and you do not. Promises and good intentions are less than nothing. This is a land of liars. Do you perhaps understand the meaning of this proverb, Mr. Hoffman? I want to think that Rogers did, but I am not sure. With Rogers, I always thought he understood everything, until later, when I began to think back, I was not so sure. When I told him the *hadith* about tying down the camel that morning in Beirut, he said, 'Trust us.' But I think that was the problem. Look what happened. He is dead.

"What I think I have learned, Mr. Hoffman, is something about the United States. At first, after Rogers was killed, I thought that all of you were incompetent. But now I realize that it is more complicated than that.

"I will try to explain. When you first met me, I was in love with America. I was only twenty. America is an easy country to fall in love with at that age. When we are twenty, we think that anything is possible, and we don't worry about failing because we will always have a second chance. That was what seemed so liberating about America—that sense of possibility—but perhaps I was just in love with being young.

"Was there ever anyone easier to recruit than me, Mr. Hoffman? I recruited myself. And I have never regretted working for you. Not even for one day. I know that many Arabs criticize you now, but I am not one of them. The agency was the part of America that I liked the best, the part that understood the way the world is. It is easy to have the ideals of a twenty-year-old, but you need the cunning of a fifty-year-old to achieve them. When I met you and Mr. Rogers, I thought, Maybe there is a chance. Maybe these Americans have the toughness. I thought: These men are cynical enough to do good. And that was when I began to think that America truly could liberate the Arab world.

"I was wrong. Americans are not hard men. Even the CIA has a soft heart. You want so much to achieve good and make the world better, but you do not have the stomach for it. And you do not know your limitations. You are innocence itself. You are the agents of innocence. That is why you make so much mischief. You come into a place like Lebanon as if you were missionaries. You convince people to put aside their old customs and allegiances and to break the bonds that hold the country together. With your money and your schools and your cigarettes and music, you convince us that we can be like you. But we can't. And when the real trouble begins, you are gone. And you leave your friends, the ones who trusted you most, to die.

"I will tell you what it is. You urge us to open up the windows of heaven. But you do not realize that the downpour will come rushing through and drown us all.

"I have been thinking about why Jamal died, and why Rogers died. And I finally realized: They are linked. They are the same story.

"Jamal died because of what I was just saying about America. You seduce us to work with you, but you are not strong enough to protect us. Jamal said something to me once, which I will always remember. It haunts me now. We were having an argument about working for the Americans. He told me that I shouldn't trust the Americans, because they would never truly love the Arabs. I told him he was wrong. Rogers and the agency were sincere, I said.

"Jamal answered me: 'You are right. America loves us. But it is the love of a man for his mistress. We are fun for a night. Maybe for a whole month. But do not ever forget that this man America is married to someone else, and he will always go back to his wife in the end.' And who is this wife? I said. But I knew the answer. The wife is Israel. And that is what killed Jamal. The wife got jealous and killed the mistress.

"We really are such fools, we Arabs. We really deserve what we get from you. That is why I cannot complain too much. It is our own fault.

"I thought that Mr. Rogers would live forever. I loved him as if he was my own brother, and when he died, the part of me that had hope also died. I could not work for anyone else. So I tried to understand what killed him.

"One answer is easy. He was killed by the thing that he was trying to stop. There was a disease of terrorism that began to infect this country about the time he came to Lebanon. He saw it. He understood how dangerous it was. He told me so many times. He knew that people were learning how to make little bombs, then big bombs, then car bombs. I would not even be surprised if he had once known, somewhere, the very man who made the bomb that killed him. Lebanon is a small country, and Mr. Rogers knew everyone. The people who paid for the bomb were probably Iranians. But they had caught the disease from Lebanon. That is where it began. Even the Iranians come to Lebanon to fight their wars.

"So maybe what killed Rogers was that he was unlucky. He saw the debris falling all around him and he forgot to get out of the way.

"But the more I thought about what happened, I decided that something else killed Mr. Rogers. It had to do with Jamal. Perhaps it was a kind of curse.

"You may think that Rogers's mistake was to lie down with the Devil. I understand what you are thinking. You say that he had a pact with a man who was a terrorist, and that this pact opened the door that let in the wind that blew down the house. If you make a deal with a man whose hands are covered with blood, some of it sticks to you. And if the Americans had not helped Jamal, maybe Lebanon would have survived the disease. Maybe the civil war would not have come and destroyed the country, setting loose all the madmen. I know what you are saying, but you are wrong.

"The truth is very simple, Mr. Hoffman. So simple that it took me many months to see it. It is this: The only man on earth who could have saved Tom Rogers that day at the embassy was Jamal Ramlawi. He was the only person the Americans had ever known in Lebanon who could have penetrated the terrorist cell, learned of the plot, and stopped the car with the bomb before it reached the embassy. But Jamal Ramlawi was dead, and there was no one else to save Tom Rogers.

"Now you know what I know.

"Effendi:

"Do you know what I just heard on the radio? It is a report from Lebanon. The radio says that the Lebanese Christians have decided that they need an ally against the Syrians. So they are allowing the Palestinian fighters to come back into Lebanon, to fight against the Syrians. Can you imagine this? We fought a war for ten years, Christians and Moslems—we killed 100,000 people—because the Christians believed that it was necessary to push the Palestinian fighters out of Lebanon forever. And now they want them to come back!

"So now we know what this war was about, Mr. Hoffman. It was about nothing."

Educated at Harvard and Cambridge universities, DAVID IGNATIUS is an award-winning journalist and Associate Editor of the *Washington Post*. From 1980 to 1983, he covered the Middle East for the *Wall Street Journal*. It was there that he first heard the intriguing rumor that was to provide the basis of AGENTS OF INNOCENCE.

TOP-SPEED THRILLERS WITH UNFORGETTABLE IMPACT FROM AVON BOOKS